3

THE
WINDSOR FACTION

THE
WINDSOR FACTION

D. J. TAYLOR

PEGASUS BOOKS
NEW YORK LONDON

THE WINDSOR FACTION

Pegasus Books LLC
80 Broad Street, 5th Floor
New York, NY 10004

Copyright © 2013 by D. J. Taylor

First Pegasus Books cloth edition September 2013

Interior design by Maria Fernandez

Library of Congress Cataloging-in-Publication Data is available.

ISBN: 978-1-60598-478-0

10 9 8 7 6 5 4 3 2 1

Printed in the United States of America
Distributed by W. W. Norton & Company

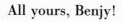

All yours, Benjy!

The object of life, after all, is not to understand things, but to maintain one's defences and equilibrium and live as well as one can; it is not only maiden aunts who are placed like this.

—William Empson,
Seven Types of Ambiguity

Always the following wind of history
Of others' wisdom makes a buoyant air
Till we come suddenly on pockets where
Is nothing loud but us.

—W. H. Auden,
'Paid on Both Sides'

CONTENTS

Prologue

December 1936

There was supposed to be a troop of marines attending, in full regimental dress, but with the coming of the rain they had all drifted away. Instead, the gravel path to the church was guarded by a couple of police constables. They were big men, made bigger by the triangular oilskin capes they wore against the drizzle, and one or two of the more nervous mourners had settled for an alternative route that ran across the field and the stile-gate at its corner. The policemen stood together, heads bowed as if conferring, but said nothing. Sometimes they walked a little way down the drive and then, reluctantly, as if thinking better of this, toiled back again.

Beyond the church, squat, Romanesque, and unwelcoming, the land rose dramatically to a landscape of low hills and arsenical-looking grass. Despite the rain it was unusually hot for the time of year and there was mist stealing up from the fields, which made them seem ominous and sub-tropical. An explorer in khaki shorts and a pith helmet appearing suddenly from the back of the thorn hedge would not have seemed out of place. One of the fields had been set aside for use as a car park and the slamming of the car doors was keeping the flock of rooks that lurked there on their mettle.

The members of the press corps were gathered by a low wall on the church's nearer side. The policemen had not spoken to them, but indicated by gestures that they could come no closer. They were about a dozen strong, and included a handful of photographers, although nobody worth photographing had yet arrived.

'Why are you wearing a black arm-band? Nobody said anything about black arm-bands.'

'My editor said it was *de rigueur*. He said it was the sort of occasion where a man would be judged by his turn-out.'

'I see.'

The volume of traffic was beginning to increase: Rolls-Royces, Daimlers, an antique shooting brake that almost went over into the ditch. The chauffeurs hung about in groups and smoked cigarettes. It was nothing to do with them. Sometimes, when a particularly auspicious-looking vehicle hove into view, the pressmen would break off their conversation and set off in pursuit, until a glance from one of the police constables sent them back.

'Who's that man there? Over by the rhododendrons?'

'Oh, he's from the American Embassy, I think.'

'Is Kennedy here?'

'I don't think they'd let him come, do you?'

Several of the embassies had sent representatives. Their pennants drooped on the bonnets of the ambassadorial limousines: blue and white; red, gold, and azure; scarlet and black. A farm labourer walked past the outer edge of the car park, head down and incurious, wheeling a bicycle. The rain was coming down heavier now, and the mist had begun to recede. From the church tower, muffled at first, then with increasing resonance, a bell began to toll.

'Depressing noise, that bell. Just the sort of thing that makes you want to go and cut your throat.'

'Well, what did you expect? A line of chorus girls and a chap in an evening suit singing "Dapper Dan Was a Very Handy Man"?'

The men of the press corps were civil to each other. They had been following this story for nearly a year. Its premature conclusion had shocked them. They needed all the information they could gather.

'Terrible thing to have happened.'

'Terrible.'

'My editor said it was a well-known fact she was suffering from tertiary syphilis.'

'My editor said that when they opened her up for the operation they found she was three months pregnant.'

'My editor said she had a death wish. Had all her pugs put down the day before she died, and then spent £2,000 of His Majesty's money at Cartier.'

'Our man in Washington said a chap at the FBI said she'd been bumped off by MI6.'

On a pond a quarter of a mile away, a pair of swans settling themselves on the surface of the water like pieces of origami; jingling along the tarmacked road from the village, a landau pulled by grey horses; some scraps of confetti, left over from a wedding, staring up incongruously from the grass. One or two genuine celebrities began to arrive: a famous Bond Street couturier; Lady Furness, magnanimous in black; Major Metcalfe, inscrutable in a top-hat. The press corps looked on with respectful interest.

'Wasn't she the one who started it all in the first place? Asking her to look after him while she was away on holiday?'

'I heard there was money changed hands. Pimping for the heir to the throne, you might say.'

'That's pitching it a bit strong, surely?'

'Not as strong as my editor wanted to pitch it. Only he thought he'd have trouble with the Archbishop of Canterbury.'

'Either of the ex-husbands here?'

'Haven't seen them. You'd have thought Mr S. would be here. Perhaps they smuggled him in through the vestry with the choirboys.'

Lady Colefax. Lady Cunard. A continental royal or two whose names no one could remember. The Cinque Port Warden . . .

'A fellow told me they were burying her at Frogmore.'

'Frogmore! Heaven knows how they got permission for that.'

'Well, he's the King, isn't he? He doesn't need permission.'

'Even so, Frogmore.'

. . . The Deputy Governor of the Bank of England, *vice* the Governor, indisposed. The Leader of the Labour Party. Mr Chamberlain and his flaxen-haired son. And finally, making a great deal of noise on the gravel, preceded by a motorcycle outrider, a funereal pennant flying on its prow, the hearse . . .

'Will you look at that—a coronet of lilies. There's a piece of cheek.'

'Would they be Baltimore lilies, do you suppose?'

'Ask Schenectady over there. He's an American. He'll know.'

They were Welsh lilies, sent up that morning from Pembrokeshire. The rain continued to drip over the reporters' notebooks, obstructing their attempts at shorthand. It was nearly twenty-five past two. The noise of the bell had ceased. Inside the church, organ music had begun to sound. Somehow, there was a sense that a vital part of the jigsaw had yet to be fitted into place, that church, mourners, coffin, cameramen were as nothing in its absence. Then at last, so haltingly that its passage along the asphalt lane might have been a slow-motion shot from a cinema film, another car came gradually into view.

'So he's come, then.'

'He could hardly have stayed away in the circumstances.'

'Even so.'

'Even so.'

The bell had begun to clang again. Three fields away the rooks stirred uneasily. The policemen, no longer conferring but straight-backed and attentive, saluted wildly.

The car looked as though it might be going to proceed all the way to the church door and then thought better of it, rocked a little on its chassis, and came to a halt.

And so they buried Wallis Warfield of Baltimore, lately of Claridge's Hotel, formerly the wife of Lieutenant Earl Winfield Spencer, and subsequently of Mr Ernest Simpson, after whose death, like a vast medieval siege engine grinding into gear, slowly yet inexorably a great many things happened that would almost certainly not have taken place had she lived.

❖

MRS SIMPSON'S DEATH

By whatever yardstick one chooses to evaluate it, Mrs Simpson's death can only be regarded as a tragedy of the first order. To her circle of intimate friends, it is an unmitigated hurt. To the much larger collection of persons who knew her in society, it will be a source of unaffected sorrow. To the King who hoped to make her his wife, it is an appalling blow. We cannot pretend to have liked Mrs Simpson, or thought her influence anything other than injurious, but the fact remains that her passing encourages a substantial number of people to reflect on the transience of human affairs and the undoubted truth that a star which at one moment burns brightly in the evening sky may at the very next second plunge dramatically to earth. To them we offer our heart-felt commiserations.

The doctor called to Mrs Simpson's suite at Claridge's on the evening of 13 December diagnosed acute appendicitis, and an ambulance was immediately summoned to take her to the Middlesex Hospital. Whether the apparent delay between her admission and the decision to operate has any significance, we are not at liberty to say. But it is a fact that she died not of peritonitis, nor of surgical complications, but of heart failure on the operating table, and that no blame can be imputed to her medical attendants either during the surgical procedure or in the days leading up to it.

It would be wrong of us, at this solemn moment, not to recall her many admirable qualities. She was, by all accounts, a staunch, though occasionally capricious, friend, a witty conversationalist, and an accomplished hostess. Whatever her failings, a woman who had brought a King and Emperor to such a pitch of infatuation that he was prepared to forsake his throne for her should never be underestimated. At the same time it would be equally wrong to ignore the fact that her passing is highly convenient. Here, not to put too fine a point on the matter, was a monarch prepared to abandon every responsibility brought to him since his boyhood in pursuit of an alliance which the vast majority of his subjects would have deplored. It is neither disloyal, nor merely callous, to suggest that if Mrs Simpson's unlooked-for passing has not saved a nation from disaster, then it has at any rate saved His Majesty from himself.

Mrs Simpson is barely a week in her grave. This is a time for grief and sober reflection, not fanciful prognosis. Let us not forget, amid these constant references to a King's sorrow, that there were two other men united with her in the sight of God, with their own misfortunes to bear. But in tragedy there very often stirs resolve. We live at a time of grave social and political difficulty, where the ghosts of an old Europe gibber and fret as a new continent begins to take shape around them, in which it is essential that the compact forged between a monarch and his people should not be put asunder. Mrs Simpson was a good friend to the King, and the value of her friendship to him should not be belittled. But now he needs a better one.

Spectator, 22 December 1936

4 January 1937

On the way down to the fort, bumping into each other's hips on the Daimler's shiny leather seats, they played the poetry game.

'Now here's one,' he said. '*Oh, to be in England/Now that April's there/ And whoever wakes in England/Sees, some morning, unaware . . .*'

'Tennyson?'

'Certainly not.'

'Coventry Patmore?'

'Now you're being silly. It's Robert Browning. Y-your turn.'

'All right: *Whither, O splendid ship, thy white sails crowding/Leaning across the bosom of the urgent West/That fearest not sea rising, nor sky clouding/Whither away, fair rover, and what thy quest?*'

'That's easy. Bridges.'

'I can see I'm going to have to keep that copy of Palgrave locked up if I want to win this.'

Later, when the gravity of the situation occurred to them, they stopped playing the poetry game and stared unhappily out of the window at the passing countryside. Here in Virginia Water the winter had raised its head suddenly and bitten hard. The verges were white with frost, and on the village greens they came upon people breaking up the ice on the ponds. They passed a road sign with the fort's name on it, and the realisation that their quarry was in plain view encouraged them to talk again.

'Where on earth did he go at Christmas?'

'I don't know. Nobody knows.'

'Did he see Mamma?'

'You know very well he didn't. Mamma would have said.'

'I suppose he went off somewhere with that dreadful Major Metcalfe.'

'I don't think he went off anywhere. I think he just *broods*.'

'I wonder what Mamma makes of it.'

'She told me she thought it was for the best. One of the ladies-in-waiting said she'd told her that Wallis . . . dying like that was an act of *providence*.'

They were in sight of the fort now. The Duke thought, as he always thought at these times, that there was something absurd about its crenellations, its high turret, the expanse of wild garden that unfolded behind it, here in anodyne Surrey. Gingerly, for the ice still lay on the rutted gravel, they got out of the car and stood looking around them, a little disappointed in the end to discover that everything was exactly the same as they remembered it.

'I never understood why your father ever let him have this place.'

'I never understood either. I remember him saying at the time that it would only be used for i-immoral purposes.'

'Oh, I don't know. He made rather a good job of clearing up the garden.'

'There was something f-*fanatical* about that. Don't you remember that time the Stamfordhams came here for dinner and he was scything away the bracken and wouldn't see them, and had the servants bring him a cup of tea and an orange?'

For some reason the air seemed to grow colder the nearer they approached the house. There was no one much about. The footman who opened the door seemed new to the work. Unrecognised and unannounced, they made their way along the dark hall and into the drawing room, where a small fire burned in the grate and the day's *Times* lay rustling its pages on an occasional table. The breeze that disturbed it was coming from the drawing-room windows, which were half open and urged them out onto the terrace.

Ten yards away, a slight figure in a brown overcoat, hair flying away from the side of his head as the wind lifted, was inspecting a rusty saw, staring at it in a way that suggested it was Excalibur, newly plucked from the stone. Not for the first time, the Duchess was reminded of a small boy, rather frightened and uncertain, half-drowned in secret grief.

'David, my dear fellow . . .'

'Bertie . . . Elizabeth . . .' He brandished the saw for a moment, rather as if only courtesy forbade him from cutting the pair of them in half on the spot, and then put it down on the corner of a stone settle. It descended onto the terrace with an almighty clatter. 'What on earth are you doing here?'

It was difficult to know how to answer this. The Duchess took the measure of her brother-in-law who, she decided, looked thinner, older, and more tired, but by no means as dishevelled and detached as people had maintained. The saw was still quivering on the flagstones like a living thing.

'Oh, David,' she said, half-humorously, 'you are dreadful. Really you are. You go to ground like an old badger in its sett and don't see anyone. And such a terrible thing to have happened, too. We felt we simply had to come down and see you.' At the back of the Duchess's mind was the memory of a letter she had written him two months before, when the crisis was at its height, which her brother-in-law was supposed to have torn up and thrown away in disgust. 'Anyway,' she went on brightly, 'we thought you might like to see us. Mamma especially asked us to come.'

It was about three o'clock now, and the light was already beginning to fade over the garden. This gave the icy grass a sinister fairy-tale look, as if the Queen of the Snows might suddenly emerge from the undergrowth, grasp the King by the hand, and drag him off into some penumbral cavern far underground.

'I had a letter from Mamma,' he said. The peevishness had gone, to be replaced by an immense old-world courteousness. 'Do you know what she wrote? She told me—no, she begged me—those were her exact words—to do my duty.'

'Did she?'

'Yes. Wasn't that odd of her? Do you know what I said when I wrote in reply? I told her that I hoped she would do hers.'

'David,' she said. 'It's simply freezing. You can't stay out here. At least give us tea or something. And you mustn't be annoyed with Mamma. She minds it just as much as everyone does.'

They went back into the drawing room, where the footman who had opened the door was lurking vaguely. 'These are their Royal Highnesses the Duke and Duchess of York,' the King said, clearly feeling that some kind of explanation was needed. 'You'd better fetch us some tea.'

The Duchess found herself measuring him up again, this time against the portrait that Sickert had painted of him the previous year, and making generous allowances as she did so. The youthful bloom had gone; there was no question about that. But she was a good brave girl, and determined that the things she had come to say should be said.

'David,' she said again, 'we don't mean to pry, really we don't, but what do you do while you're here?'

'What do I *do*?' The King seemed to think that this was an astonishing question, not so much impertinent as thoroughly bewildering. 'What does anyone do? There are the gardens to keep up. And I read my letters. You would be surprised how many people have written. Mr Roosevelt has written. Herr Hitler has written.'

There was no answer to this, to Mr Roosevelt and Herr Hitler. The tea came in a kind of Russian samovar with curious Cyrillic inscriptions on the lid (Perhaps Marshal Stalin had written? Who knew?) and as it was being set down the Duchess noticed the portrait staring out incongruously from a clump of foreign royalty and a picture of the last Tsar and Tsarina doing the sword dance.

'You must miss her very much,' she said loyally.

'She was very kind to me,' the King said. 'I don't think Mamma ever understood.' The implications of this remark, and the possibility that other people might not have understood either, were so awful as to be instantly put aside. The tea, which turned out to be dreadful, was no help at all.

'The girls sent their best love.'

There was no knowing how long this might go on. At one point the footman returned with a telegram on a silver tray, which the King placed in the pocket of his jacket unread. Outside it began to rain, and the room seemed to have an air of such inexpressible melancholy that it was all the Duchess could do to prevent herself from running out into the twilight. Finally, the Duke spoke:

'David, you mustn't mind us asking. But what are you going to *do*?'

'What am I going to do?' The King gave a little cracked smile, not quite bitter, but rueful, gestured with his hand at the portrait of Mrs Simpson, who looked more Giaconda-like than ever, and then at *The Times*, as if the two were somehow connected and a bridge might be built between them that would solve the world's problems forthwith. 'Why, do you know, I am going to follow Mamma's advice. I am going to do my duty.'

The vague footman had disappeared and they had to let themselves out. The chauffeur, well wrapped up in his coat with the engine running, had fallen asleep over a Thermos flask. In the car, speeding back to Piccadilly with its warm nursery and its corn-haired children, they played the poetry game again (*Eternal spirit of the chainless Mind!/Brightest in dungeons, Liberty!/Thou art—*) but the events of the past half-hour had badly unsettled them and so they stopped.

The Drift to War

. . . One notable feature of the last few days of peace was the personal involvement of the King. At the Privy Council meeting of 24 August, to which news of President Roosevelt's urging of a peace conference was brought as the Councillors convened, he is reliably reported to have begged the Prime Minister, Mr Chamberlain, to leave no avenue unexplored. The final German proposals of 26 August—the cession of Danzig, a 'corridor' and a plebiscite on the Saar principle—were conveyed to him by the

Foreign Secretary, Lord Halifax, shortly before they were taken to the Cabinet table.

The claim, made by a London evening newspaper, that His Majesty had volunteered to fly to Berlin with the aim of brokering some last-minute agreement in the presence of Herr Hitler and President Moscicki of Poland was later denied, but he is believed to have despatched a private telegram to the German Chancellor on 28 August—this as German troops were taking up their final positions—reminding him of the ancestral ties that united their two countries and regretting the inflammatory language of recent communiqués.

The difficulties experienced by both British and French nationals in leaving the principal Polish cities awakened in him the keenest interest. Nothing, as Mr Chamberlain later remarked, could have exceeded His Majesty's determination that the descent into armed hostilities might somehow be prevented, his desire to play a part in bringing the opposing sides together, or his despair when, on the morning of 1 September, these efforts were shown to have been in vain . . .

The Annual Register, 1939

In another sign of the increasingly uncertain international situation, shipping companies operating in the Far East have reported an unprecedented rise in applications for tickets to western destinations. A representative of the Peninsular & Oriental Company confirmed that passages from Colombo, Rangoon, Singapore, and Penang could not be obtained for the next six weeks, and that tickets were privately changing hands for several times their original value.

Speaking to the annual meeting of the Imperial Business-men's Federation, held yesterday at the Cordwainers' Hall, Mr E. C. Devereux of the Colonial Office deplored this tendency:

'While the Government appreciates the pressure to which expatriate citizens are subject, there is a grave danger that our commercial interests may be compromised. We appeal to business people to remain where they are.'

The Times, 27 June 1939

PART ONE

CHAPTER 1

The Monkey at the Temple Door

In the week after they went south from Kandy to the white-stone villa behind the government building at Colombo, a change came over Mrs Kirkpatrick. The few words of Sinhala which she had thought suitable for use in the hill country were quietly put aside; the copies of the *Island News*, with their rousing stories of cobras found lurking in lavatory cisterns, gave way to ancient volumes of *Blackwood's*; the King's portrait—rabbity, put-upon, and quite unlike the man Mrs Kirkpatrick had once shaken hands with on the Sovereign's Lawn at Cowes—was taken out and fixed to the dining-room wall to watch them while they ate.

The rain fell against the villa's angular, sea-green windows and wreaked havoc among the frail terrace grass, but it could not wash these illusions away. They were as fixed and incontestable as title deeds, church bells, the view over the fields beyond Henley—all those things that Mrs Kirkpatrick imagined she had brought with her from England and was sometimes startled to discover that she had left behind.

Like many people who live by the will, Mrs Kirkpatrick's intransigence was uniquely her own: specialised and thoroughgoing. She was a tall, ungainly woman who thought her height an advantage and had never noticed the ungainliness, and had a curious, extravagant, sea-horse face which people would have made jokes about had Mrs Kirkpatrick been the kind of person about whom jokes are made.

Just now, accompanied by the butler, she was making a tour of the villa's reception-rooms. There were ransacked cabin-trunks all over the red-tile floor, and a giant cauldron that none of the servants could account for was lying in the drawing-room fireplace. Mrs Kirkpatrick had not liked openly to blame the Harrisons, their predecessors, for the cauldron, but as she went about her inspection she meditated a little note that could be sent with it up-country to Trincomalee. Outside, the late-afternoon sun was burning over the lawns, and the dwarf conifers had not stirred for twenty minutes.

Mrs Kirkpatrick had spent her life inventorying houses and knew exactly what to do. Greenly purposeful and studiously intent, she looked like a large, eager bird racketing through corn. The rooms fell away from her as she marched towards them; their ornaments dwindled into insignificance. It was only she who was real.

Alone among the servants, the butler had grasped the force of her personality. He brought a chair for her to sit on as she examined worn chintzes, shook his head over an elephant's-foot waste-paper basket that had begun to rot at the base, picked up the forgotten handkerchiefs that Mrs Kirkpatrick routed out from under chairs or beneath sun-blanched linen-cupboards. These, too, would be sent up-country to Trincomalee.

The villa had been built in the 1870s and was showing its age, but the Governor General had sent up a box of ice, and the cook spoke English, and Mrs Kirkpatrick thought she had got the best of the bargain.

Twenty feet above her, from the vantage point of a cane chair set at right angles to the open window, Cynthia sat looking out over the garden. She liked gardens, finding them restful and invigorating but also full of interest: the moral equivalent of a painting by Claude Lorrain she had once seen in the National Gallery. From below, her mother's voice could be heard saying something about a defective curtain-rail, but by an effort of will she managed to banish it from her mind.

The garden, which had not perhaps been very well designed, was divided into four quarters: a silent, hoopoe-haunted lawn, a variegated clump of rhododendron bushes leading to a series of ornamental ponds, and the line of miniature fir trees. At first she had thought it empty, but now, looking closely at the rhododendron bank, she saw a native servant with a watering-can moving stiffly through the jungle of flowers. From below, the voices of her mother and the butler broke urgently out of the silence again, like static from a radio, and then fell away.

She was a tall, thin, pale-faced girl of twenty-one who, although she had been spoiled since birth, frequently told herself that she had not had much of a life. Sometimes she thought she would like to mannequin in one of the big department stores in Oxford Street, and at other times she thought she would like to be an undergraduate at Cambridge and bicycle to lectures in a black stuff gown, but as neither of these things seemed likely to happen she was forced to find solace in scenery.

The gardener had disappeared into the flower-jungle, and she thought about the sea at Bentota, the warm scent of the Indian Ocean and waves that were one moment green and the next blue, and the next some odd compound that words could not express. Then, quite unexpectedly, they were swept away by other things: autumn bonfires burning in the Oxford college gardens; the bright red buses cruising down Regent Street; smoke in a pale sky; and she wondered how lost that old England was to her and what might be the effect of seeing it again.

Twenty minutes later, on her way downstairs, she met her father coming up: linen-jacketed, white-trousered, and with a copy of *Plays Pleasant and Unpleasant* wedged under his arm. He was quite intellectual for a tea-planter and had once taken out a subscription to the *New Statesman*. A lizard, no bigger than a sardine, went scampering over the stair-rods and they watched it run.

'The Bannisters are at the Caradon, your mother says,' he told her. He meant to be kind, but he had a rather startled way of looking at her, as if she had been born into tragedy, spirited away from them at birth, and only recently coaxed back.

'I didn't think they were arriving so soon,' she said. The lizard's tail had not quite disappeared into the hole beside the air-vent. 'Do they *like* it at the Caradon?'

Mr Kirkpatrick tapped the copy of *Plays Pleasant and Unpleasant* with his forefinger. Perhaps Shaw had the answer. 'Your mother said the food was worse than ever, and one of the beds had betel-nut stains in it. At any rate, they're coming to dinner tomorrow.'

'Nobody ever has a good time at the Caradon,' Cynthia suggested, adding the news of the Bannisters coming to dinner to other contingencies that would need dealing with: the copy of *The Constant Nymph* that had turned up again in the Government House library, and the letter she had been meaning to write to her cousin Harriet in Perthshire. The implications of the Bannisters' visit she ignored. They could be addressed later.

'They say Bannister's selling that estate of his,' Mr Kirkpatrick said. He looked even more startled, as if he had been struck by lightning. 'I can't say I blame him, in the circumstances.'

Ceylon was not all it had been to Mr Kirkpatrick.

They tried one or two other exchanges of this kind, but their hearts were not really in it. After a bit she left him on the stairs, with their odd protrusions of light and shade, and the sun burning through the bottle-green windows, and went on down into the body of the house.

The worst thing about living in the East, she thought, was that everyone always spoke as if they were in a play by Noël Coward. There was no getting away from this. Even the lowliest colonial official acted up to his part, and a request to send the bearer with a chit was uttered as if it needed a round of applause. Meanwhile the copy of *The Constant Nymph* had reappeared in the Government House library and the Bannisters were coming to dinner.

In the kitchen, low-ceilinged and shadowy, with fly-papers tacked to every available surface, Mrs Kirkpatrick was working herself up into belligerence. This was part of her myth. There were times when Cynthia wanted to explore the source of her mother's considerable grudge against the world and most of the people in it, but this was not one of them. Instead she waited until Mrs Kirkpatrick had stamped on a phantom cockroach and examined a piece of fish that lay under muslin on the chopping board.

Here, in the aquamarine light of the late afternoon, the kitchen was a depressing place. The copper pans and the roasting spits that hung on the far wall might have been implements of war, and Mrs Kirkpatrick's face and torso looked more sea-horse-like than ever, quite green and erect, aggressively balanced on her shiny, silk-covered legs. In the end she said, 'I really don't think you should wear that dress, Cynthia.'

'Why on earth not, Mother?'

This, it went without saying, was not the way to deal with Mrs Kirkpatrick. She required obliquity, or even outright dissimulation. Mr Kirkpatrick had once defused quite a serious argument about the decor of the Nuwara Eliya Club by claiming to have seen a mongoose asleep in the waste-paper basket.

Mrs Kirkpatrick could be quite subtle when she tried. 'Well, I don't think it's the sort of thing Henry would like to see you in.'

It was quite a good dress, bought in Maddox Street and brought with them on the boat the previous year.

'As if Henry cared what kind of dress anyone wore.'

'Well, of course I can't order you to wear anything,' Mrs Kirkpatrick said, with an attempt at mildness that fooled neither of them, and Cynthia, staring at her through the shadows, very nearly threw herself on her shoulder and told her that the dress would be cut into fragments that night. But Mrs Kirkpatrick was not the sort of woman on whose shoulder you could throw yourself.

After dinner a rather gruesome couple named Atherton, ancient cronies of Mr Kirkpatrick's, arrived to play bridge, and she sat on the least uncomfortable of the six cane chairs and ate mangosteens out of a paper bag without caring where the juice went.

Twenty feet away the four grey heads bobbed gamely through the shadows. The conversation, it occurred to Cynthia, was orchestral: stray themes taken up here and there, abandoned and renewed, sometimes erupting into crescendo; like listening to some very bad musicians play an even worse symphony. When she could bear it no longer she went out into the dense, blue garden and thought about the Bannisters, and Henry, and their implications for her emotional well-being, and the possibility that a rule she had followed as a young girl about trying to keep the things that really mattered to you at one remove might now have to be broken.

A few pale lights from the army camp had sprung up in the distance, and the remoter parts of the garden seethed with vagrant nocturnal life. When she went inside her face seemed paler than ever and Mrs Kirkpatrick looked up from the bridge table and said, 'Gracious, Cynthia. Have you been crying?'

'No, Mother, I haven't.'

'Well'—triumphantly—'you've spilled mangosteen juice down the front of your dress.'

'Have I? Oh, bother.'

'You'd better let me tell them to get some hot water and lemon.'

Long months later, whenever anyone asked her what it had been like in Ceylon, she would always say: *Oh, it was quite fun, in a way, only it was terribly hot, you know, and the grass seeds got inside your stockings and you were always ruining dresses.* But this was not said with any conviction.

The Athertons left at ten, whereupon the household went to bed in a frenzy of groaning teak-boards that took an hour to subside, and she found herself sitting up late under the oil lamp, while the scarab beetles blundered into the grille-mesh of the window frames, writing the letter to Harriet.

So you can see, given how Mummy usually feels about men—you remember how rude she was to Johnnie Allardyce after we came back late from that dance?—that it's rather odd when she starts pimping *for Henry Bannister.* If Harriet didn't know what 'pimping' meant, she could look it up in the dictionary. The wax Victorian dolls, with their crinolines and bustles and stagnant blue eyes, simpered at her from the dressing-table as she wrote.

There was not a great deal to do at the villa during daylight hours. In fact, there was not a great deal to do at any time. The garden, which had been cool and mysterious by night, turned hot and noisy, and the bougainvillea burned so bright in the sunshine that it might have been overlaid with poster-paint. Mr Kirkpatrick went off to see his broker at Galle Face Green. Mrs Kirkpatrick had herself driven to Madame Bandaraike's salon in Barnes Place, where the assistants had names like Evangeline and Margot and spoke in passable imitations of Home Counties accents. There were times when the mock-familiarity of the East was agreeable. All too soon, though, these dusty approximations of the real thing began to grate.

Cynthia found she could dispel the thought of the Bannisters, which would otherwise have oppressed her, by concentrating on the routines of the day. In this spirit she played three sets of tennis on the cinder court at the back of Government House with a son of one of the attachés who was waiting to go out to Burma to join the Imperial Police, and—rather wilfully, for she knew her mother would have disapproved—went to the Pettah for a brace of pineapples, and it was only as she turned into the villa's driveway at six o'clock, with the gravel rasping under her sandals, and her fingers leaving four whorled, indelible marks on the cover of *The Constant Nymph*, which she had borrowed from the library, that the enormity of what her mind had been keeping from her struck home.

But there was no getting away from it. There was the Bannisters' car—it was an antique Armstrong Siddeley with the top taken down—and there, though currently invisible, were the Bannisters. The uneasiness that had been with her in the early part of the day came barrelling back, and she remembered a film she had once seen that the villa's frontage seemed perfectly to reproduce—the car sending up black, elongated shadows, the native servant attending to the dust-piles on the step.

A more resourceful girl, she thought, would have snapped her fingers and made the scene disappear, discovered some more authentic life in the heat that sprang from its ashes. But she was not that girl, and so she stepped indoors, left the bag containing the pineapples on the trestle table in the hall, went upstairs to change into a print frock that made her look like a schoolgirl, and by degrees descended to the drawing-room where her parents and the Bannisters sat in conclave.

'I believe I heard that Ronald Reagan was staying at the Galle Face,' Mrs Bannister pronounced, with a certain amount of sarcasm, as she came into the room. 'Now, who would he be?'

'A film chap, isn't he?' Mr Bannister offered, looking keenly at his hostess. 'That's who he is. A film chap.' But there was no point in appealing to Mrs Kirkpatrick. Disdain of popular culture was a central tenet of her myth.

'And here's Cynthia,' Mrs Bannister said, with an indescribable attempt at archness, and a slight air of surprise, as if Cynthia had arrived wearing a Pierrot costume. 'My dear, you're looking frightfully well.' There was a faint suggestion that Ronald Reagan had been rather too easily given up and might have to be returned to later. 'Isn't she looking frightfully well, Gavin?'

'Frightfully well,' Mr Bannister confirmed, with what appeared to be no interest at all.

The Bannisters' amiability, their conversational brightness, their feigned unworldliness—Mrs Bannister knew all about Ronald Reagan— was deceptive, Cynthia thought, for they were, at heart, sinister people. Brought together in the Kirkpatricks' drawing-room, they might have been a triptych of Egyptian deities—Horeb, say, and a couple of his satellites—zealously guarding the entrance to the underworld.

Mrs Bannister was a gaunt, stringy, curry-complexioned woman, the highlight of whose life had been to give birth to her elder daughter in a *dak* bungalow seventy miles short of Rangoon, attended by a Chittagongian midwife who spoke no English. Mr Bannister, who sat in Parliament for one of the Sussex constituencies, said less but arguably had to be watched more. Henry had come to ground a little away from the others, with his legs crossed so awkwardly at the knee that they might have been tied together with string, inspecting the garden with the air of one who would do some pretty serious things with its arrangement if given the chance.

Now that she had reached the centre of the room and been disposed of by his parents, he looked up and caught her eye. In the circles in which she moved, Henry was regarded as 'rather an awful man.' On the other hand, the concept of awfulness was not easily gone into. Why exactly was Henry awful? He was about twenty-three or twenty-four, had read Greats at Oxford, which Mrs Kirkpatrick said was a sure sign of intellectual capacity, and was supposed to have political leanings. The superciliousness that went with this was only skin-deep, although he had a rather frightening way of attending to you when you spoke, which upset the more timid of his listeners. But Cynthia, in her print dress, tired after her exertions on the tennis court and among the Pettah fruit-stalls, thought that whatever happened in the course of the evening, she would not be intimidated by him.

'Cynthia dear,' her mother said, in what even for her was an absurdly loud voice, 'do come and have something to drink.'

They were drinking gin-and-Italian, which in itself was a mark of the esteem in which the Bannisters were held by their hosts, Mrs Kirkpatrick wisely regarding vermouth as the resort of foreigners and degenerates. She helped herself from the tray—the silver one, she noticed, which had been presented to Mr Kirkpatrick by the planters' association and presumably routed out of the strongbox—and, arranging the dress to conceal as much of her legs as possible, sat down on a mahogany foot-stool equidistant from her father and Henry and sufficiently remote from either of them to discourage conversation. The gin-and-Italian went to her head and she began to take a more benign view of the world.

Over dinner an explanation of the Bannisters' presence in Colombo was eventually vouchsafed, not by anything so banal as a straight answer to any of the questions occasionally put to them by Mr and Mrs Kirkpatrick, but in a series of hints which it was possible to thread together, like the clues in an acrostic. It turned out that Mr Bannister had been flown to Delhi, at Lord Beaverbrook's expense, as part of a delegation agitating for Empire Free Trade, with Henry in the role of aide-de-camp. There was also talk of the Bannisters' elder daughter, the one born in the *dak* bungalow, now married to what by all accounts was an exceptionally dreary man in the Foreign Office, and their elder son, who had a rather mouldy-sounding hunt-secretary's job somewhere in Leicestershire.

'Such a *pity* the King can't be persuaded to *hunt* anymore,' Mrs Bannister declared, in a blizzard of ghostly italics, as if she had several times gone on her knees in pursuit of this object.

'Oh, I don't think he can be persuaded to do anything these days,' Mr Bannister chimed in. 'They say the Palace simply despairs.'

They had dinner in the big dining room with the green, distempered walls, with the fans winnowing the dense air above their heads and crumpling the overseas edition of the *Daily Telegraph* from which Mr Bannister tried to corroborate a cricket score. The white sauce that the fish came in tasted of cornflour, and the gravy smothering the guinea fowl tasted of nothing at all. Henry, she noticed, kept his head down over his plate, but his face had that rapt, calculating look that she disliked so much, knowing it meant trouble. It was as if they were all rehearsing a play in which she, alone, had not been given a script. Worse, as if the whole meal were a kind of conspiracy designed to test her loyalty to a cause whose principles no one had yet bothered to explain.

And she was right about Henry. They had barely reached the drawing room again, and Mrs Kirkpatrick had only just begun to tell Mrs Bannister, with whom she had adopted a comradely, daughters-of-the-regiment air, about the Davenports' cauldron, when he said, as if the thought had only just occurred to him: 'I say, why don't I take Cynthia out for a drive?'

She looked back and forth, from head to head, but the cues had all been handed out.

'What a splendid idea,' Mrs Kirkpatrick said.

'Still plenty of light,' Mr Bannister volunteered in the same bright tone he had mentioned Ronald Reagan. 'Won't be dark for another hour yet.'

'Of course,' Mrs Kirkpatrick said, 'I never really like to say anything about it, but one of the difficulties of being out here is that Cynthia so rarely gets to see any young men.'

In any other conversation, and with anyone other than the Bannisters, this would have been thought a step too far. Even Mr Kirkpatrick blinked at it. Like the gin-and-Italian, it was an example of Mrs Kirkpatrick's myth at its most flexibly remorseless. But as Cynthia knew, such demonstrations of the will could not be gainsaid, and so a minute or two later she found herself outside on the villa forecourt, in the elongated shadow of the Armstrong Siddeley, while Henry did something with a hub-cap, brushed some dirt off one of the running-boards, and finally stepped back and let his hand fall on the nearside door.

'She's not a bad old bus,' he said. 'We'll have some fun.'

A grass seed had got into the heel of her stocking again, and even now the light was so bright that she wanted to shade her eyes, and the zeal with which Mrs Kirkpatrick had abandoned her to the company of Henry Bannister made her feel acutely vulnerable. Another mother, she thought, would not have done this. Or rather—a vital qualification—another mother might have noticed that the situation had more psychological complexity than was first apparent. 'If it comes to that,' she said crossly, 'nobody asked me if I wanted to come.'

'Didn't they? I don't suppose they did. Of course, we don't have to go anywhere if you don't want to.'

She thought about the bright confederacy of the drawing room which, even now, would be sitting down to discuss the iniquities of the National Congress, or examining the photographs that Mr Kirkpatrick had taken of Sigiriya Rock when he first went there in 1907.

'No, it's all right. I'll come. I haven't been out in a car for ages.'

In the passenger seat, with the grass seed worked down under her toes and less painful, and with the hat she had remembered to bring with her to shade her eyes, she softened a little.

'That's a rather awful pair of shoes you're wearing.'

They were cream-and-brown co-respondent's brogues that would have been laughed at on a golf course.

'Yes, they are rather dreadful, aren't they? I got them at Smart & Mookerdum's in Rangoon. The sales-wallah said they were frightfully fashionable.'

The car was bowling on past hedges of antirrhinums and high laurels so tightly packed that they seemed to constrict the asphalt that ran between them and somehow increase the momentum of the car, like toothpaste being squeezed out of a tube. The made-up road went south for a couple of miles and then degenerated. Occasionally they passed a village where chickens went swarming up against the palm trees and small children with gleaming teeth looked vacantly out of doorways, and she thought of all the men she had been driven in cars by: pink-faced stockbrokers with hair cut so short that you could see the tendons on the backs of their necks like plucked fowl, land agents in shooting brakes whose gears clashed in anguish, all the flower of England's young manhood: nervous, preoccupied, and dull.

'Will your parents be taking you home soon?' he wondered, after they had nearly taken the head off a pariah dog that had strayed too close to the road. He meant England, of course.

'Early next year, Father says. Or perhaps in the winter. There are business things he needs to settle.'

'It's not a bad idea,' he said, 'with the situation being what it is.'

First her father and now Henry: everyone seemed appalled by the situation. The grass seed had moved round beneath her toes to the fleshy part of her instep.

'Well, I call this jolly pleasant,' Henry said.

'Yes, I suppose it is, rather.'

The heat of the day had begun to fade now: the sun hung in the pale sky like a blood orange. In the far distance slim black birds cruised in the thermals, like scraps of burned paper above a fire. Once, climbing Sigiriya Rock, as one did, she had had an unusual experience. Standing on the summit, with twenty miles of scrub and jungle laid out beneath her, there had come into her head the memory of a dream, vivid and prophetic, in which the terrain she now saw had floated tantalisingly before her. All this had bred a deep suspicion of the landscapes of the East, which seemed to her unreliable, prone to unexpected duplicity, not, when it came to it, safe.

Meanwhile, the car was slowing down.

'I thought we might stretch our legs,' Henry said. 'That is, if you wanted to.'

It was pretty obvious that he had decided to stretch his legs whether she wanted to or not, but she consented to step down from the car and walk a little way into the roadside clearing. Here the ground was parched and friable: the cream-and-brown brogues bought at Smart & Mookerdum's left only the faintest indentation on the path.

A part of her wondered how she had ever met Henry, and why she put up with him—Henry with his leg-stretchings, and his calculation, and the way he looked at her as she stepped down from the running-board—but another part of her was merely caught up in the immediacy of the scene, and to some extent, however much she distrusted Henry, its willing accessory. If you came out in a car with Henry Bannister and he suggested that you stretched your legs, then you stretched them. Anything else was prevarication. It was as simple as that.

In this temporising spirit she had, in the past, lingered in the rear of picnicking excursions to the Yorkshire Dales, foraged through the bracken-strewn margins of Cotswold shooting-parties. But there were no beaters here, and no pheasants. Even Henry—redder-faced now, and perspiring a little from the walk—had a curiously alien quality, as if his features were a mask that he might suddenly tear off to reveal the grinning gargoyle beneath.

Fifty yards in from the road, the jungle fell away to disclose what at first appeared to be randomly flung lumps of stone, but in fact were the last traces of a ruined temple, and they halted on the path to take stock of their surroundings. Grotesque shadows spread away beneath them over the stone floor. Far above their heads, vast numbers of bats hung, unmoving, on the upper boughs of the eucalyptus trees. Two or three monkeys slunk out of the undergrowth, stared at them for a moment or two, and then loped nervously away.

'I heard a story the other day,' Henry said, 'about a woman who was, you know, taken short in the jungle, and when she got up afterwards she found a whole tribe of monkeys was watching her. And when she went back to the people she was with, the monkeys just followed her home and simply wouldn't go away. In the end someone had to come out onto the veranda and shoot several of them with an elephant rifle to make the others leave off.'

The East abounded in stories of this kind: tuppence-coloured tales in which leopards swam across raging torrents to carry off village children left in cradles twenty feet above the ground, snakes moving in synchronised counterpoint, balanced water jars on their heads, and gangs of ape-men descended from the hills to rampage through the bazaars. Cynthia had never believed any of them for a moment.

'I don't think any of them will follow us,' she said. She had a sudden vision of Henry, who had been a prefect at Winchester, rebuking a monkey as if it had been an obstreperous small boy.

Winchester and Harrow. Lofted oars at Henley. The Hungaria River Club at Maidenhead, as portrayed by Miss Helen McKie. Where was the old world now? In the middle of the clearing it was still quite hot. Henry stood by the temple doorway—about the only part of it still standing—with the same look on his face that he had worn while inspecting the Kirkpatricks' garden, as if he was a quantity surveyor working out exactly how many tons of cement it would take to refurbish.

'I came prepared,' he announced.

'Oh, yes?' she said. She had heard this kind of thing before. Men like Henry always came prepared. If you lashed them to a ship's mast with a hawser, they would produce some Swiss Army knife with an attachment for maritime emergencies and go marauding over the side. There was no getting away from them, or the things they wanted.

He had his hand in hers now, and it was quite as disagreeably hairy as she remembered, almost to the point of furriness. If it had detached itself from its wrist and gone scurrying across the jungle floor, she would not have been surprised. Above their heads the bats hung sinister and inert.

'You're not being very kind to me,' he said five minutes later.

'I'm being perfectly kind to you. What do you want me to do?'

She had a sudden memory of him inspecting the point-to-point at Hawthorn Hill, leaning back on his shooting-stick with his bowler hat tilted over his eyes and his field-glasses three-quarters raised as they watched the horses coming over the last jump. Only two men had proposed to her so far in her life, and they had both been far worse than Henry.

'You might take off some of your things, you know.'

'Which things? Which things do you want me to take off?'

In the end she compromised and unbuttoned the front of her dress, which was presumably what he was getting at. It was no good, she thought as he ran the French letter to ground in the pocket of his jacket and began the laborious business of putting it on, she really could not go on with this. Not just Henry, but all the other things he brought with him, from the Bannisters and Hawthorn Hill to that queerly indulgent look on her mother's face. All of it had to go, but she could not for the life of her think when.

'You might just, er . . .' Henry said. He was breathing quite hard, and seemed to have come out in a surprising amount of clothing.

And so she just, er . . . which was on the whole preferable, and had the additional advantage of getting Henry's furry paw out of the front of her dress.

'Of course, Father's in the faction now,' Henry said, with maximum incongruousness.

'That's good,' she said, without having the least idea of what he meant.

And so it was done, without much pleasure, on the stone temple floor, to the great detriment of her stockings, with a shaft of late sunlight pulsing suddenly through the leaves to blind her. Halfway through, a monkey vaulted down through the ruined doorway and she saw the rictus of amusement on its evil little face before it fled back into the jungle.

Afterwards Henry threw the French letter on the floor, where it made such a squelching noise that she felt rather sick.

'That'll give someone a surprise when they come across it,' he said proudly.

It was what people like Henry did in these circumstances. They threw cigarettes out of upstairs windows and up-ended sugar-sifters over other men's heads at dances and told jokes about fishermongers' daughters who lay on the slab and said 'fillet,' and one day, she thought, she would marry one of them and be squashed into nothingness by him.

'I say,' he said, half-admiringly, as they got back into the car, 'you *are* in a stew.'

The daylight was fading away. A little further on from where the car was parked, enormous palm trees hung over the road, thirty or forty feet high. The effect was surprisingly unsettling.

'Do we go right or left here?' Henry wondered, when the trail seemed about to divide. 'I can't remember.' He seemed flustered by the twilight, not quite at ease.

Cynthia twitched her shoulder slightly to one side, not interested in these difficulties. Henry had insisted on bringing her out here. He could take her back again. Her right knee ached and she wished she had brought a jumper. The glimmer of the car's headlights illumined odd items in the roadway: half a packing case, a length of coconut matting.

'You shouldn't go at such a pace,' she said, not really concerned. She was still thinking of what Henry said about Mr Bannister being in the faction. What made her so cross, she divined, was its implication of ulterior knowledge. It occurred to her that Henry, leg-stretching, Greats-reading Henry, had confused her with another girl who presumably had this faction business, whatever it was, at her fingertips.

Not long after this Henry, who had one arm flung protectively around her shoulder, even though it was tilted away from him, and the other rather too negligently on the wheel, ran the car off the road and into a tree.

The Kirkpatricks were supposed to be good in a crisis: this was what Mrs Kirkpatrick always said. Having hit the tree, the car veered off for a dozen yards or so into the undergrowth and finally came to a halt against a second, tougher obstruction. Lying against the passenger door, where the impact had flung her, she was conscious of a dreadful pain in her side.

'Henry, I'm hurt,' she said, and then, getting no answer, only a far-off cry in the undergrowth that must have come from some animal taking flight, 'I'm hurt, Henry.'

But she saw that the driver's seat was empty. She tried to stand up, but the pain in her shoulder made her fall backwards into the car.

'Henry,' she said again, more urgently. There was some blood in her mouth, but this did not alarm her, for Mrs Kirkpatrick, who, as she sometimes said, had fallen off more horses than you would have thought possible, always maintained that, provided one was still breathing, a little blood meant nothing.

Eventually, after a longish struggle, she managed to drag herself upright. There was a dismaying stretch of time—two or three minutes at least—when his location escaped her—the blood was running all over her front now, which was another dress ruined—but then she saw what at first looked uncannily like an old sack spilling its contents over the forest path, and realised that this was Henry, leg-stretching, Greats-reading, French letter-fumbling Henry, and that was that.

As for what happened afterwards, even Mr Kirkpatrick, who never swore, allowed that it was a bloody disaster. They buried Henry in the English cemetery up on Pattayara Heights, next to a giant catafalque in green marble, put up to honour some bygone colonial vizier, that had already begun to list alarmingly to the right. A vulture sat watching from a nearby eucalyptus tree, and people tried very hard not to notice the rat-holes that ran down beneath the newly turned grass.

Oh, those funerals in the East, with the sun burning off the chaplain's bald forehead, incongruous silk hats, a smell of cinnamon, and the alien sky looming purple in the background! Cynthia had read about them in *Blackwood's*. Now she was alarmed to find them every bit as fearful as Maugham had hinted. They had let her out of hospital to attend, with her arm in a sling and the three cracked ribs bound up with surgical tape, and she fainted twice in the car. After that she felt a bit better and was able to take a tearful interest in her surroundings.

No one seemed to know whether she should be treated as the grieving widow or the silly girl who had been indirectly responsible for this horror, and one or two of the things said to her were inexpressibly painful: not because they were insincere, but because her own sincerity was so very much in question. In the end she could not bear to watch Henry's coffin— surprisingly cheaply made, she noticed, and unvarnished—being lowered into the ground, and concentrated instead on the next memorial along, which was to someone called Laurence Horatio Mainwaring, who had died at sea off Galle in 1922, and which insisted that blessed were the pure in heart. By the time she had digested this sentiment—all the gravestones had a greenish tinge, like rotting teeth, and the gilt inscriptions had begun to flake off—they were back in Government House where an Honorary Attaché with a defective palate (the Governor was up-country in Jaffna) said what a fine young man Henry was, and how his memory would live on in their hearts. The rain came on halfway through and they listened to it drumming on the roofs of the cars drawn up in the square outside.

Later on, back at the villa, she fainted again—on purpose—and had to be put to bed.

There was an etiquette, she assumed, to the predicament in which they found themselves, but nobody seemed to know what it was. They ate their meals in silence, as the rain teemed over the ragged grass, alert to the sound of footsteps or churned-up gravel in the drive. Mrs Kirkpatrick's personal myth was much in evidence: the part that dealt in stoicism, steely resolve, the cavalry charge still accomplished even if one's horse had been shot from underneath one. 'I suppose it would have been a very exhausting life,' Mrs Kirkpatrick said once, which might have been an apology.

But there were worse things than Mrs Kirkpatrick's determination to make amends. In particular, there was an excruciating interview with Mr Bannister one morning in the villa drawing room, which everyone seemed to think it was necessary to go through. This, too, was like one of the stories in *Blackwood's*. He was standing in the very centre of the room, rather impressively, with his hat in his hand and a cane wedged under his arm like a swagger-stick, and when he saw her he came forward decisively and put his hand in hers as if there were now some immortal compact between them that could never be put asunder, and she would have been prepared to concede this—the impressiveness, the hat, and the hand—had he said anything that was in the slightest degree original.

As it was he relaxed his grip, stared at her keenly—he was on the tall side, and the effect was faintly intimidating—and said, 'Cynthia, this is a terrible thing to have happened.'

'Yes, it is,' she said, wishing she could be anywhere else but here in this room, with the dreadful little pagoda-clock ticking away on the mantelpiece next to the Nuwara Eliya cricket club fixtures card. 'A terrible thing.'

'I know I shouldn't say this,' Mr Bannister said, with the brazen look of someone who is absolutely determined to say it, 'but of all my children he was the one I loved the most, you know.'

'I'm sure he was,' she said. Henry had always complained about the favours lavished on the Leicestershire hunt-secretary.

'And I need hardly say'—this, in retrospect, was the worst bit of all—'that he thought the world of you.'

'Oh, I don't know,' she said.

'I won't have us lose touch, you hear?' There was something incorrigible about Mr Bannister as he said this. 'Just because of this dreadful thing. Old friends we are and old friends we shall stay. You must come and see us *often*.'

'I should like that,' she said, thinking that whatever her mother might say, she never wanted to see Mr Bannister ever again.

There was quite a lot more of this, and she was surprised at how cross it made her. Part of her was prepared to sympathise almost indefinitely with Mr Bannister, but another part thought that he was a wicked old man saying things he did not believe in.

She was startled to find that when she thought of Henry she could remember only the unimportant things: the kink in the bridge of his nose that made him look slightly Jewish; the golfing brogues he tramped around in at home in Sussex; the way he said '*lava*-tory'; his teaching her to shoot on a moor somewhere near the Tweed and telling her that it was a valuable skill that was bound to come in useful some day. Already, a week after his death, it was as if he had barely existed, drifted away into some backwater of memory from which the most determined efforts could not drag him clear.

There was a photograph of him in an old album that had come out with them from England, a younger Henry holding a tennis racket slantwise across his chest and wearing a striped blazer, rather as if he were about to take the part of the male lead in a musical comedy, and she stared hopefully at it for quite a long while, wondering if it would disclose a second, more intelligible Henry whom she had never really known, but in the end she gave it up as a bad job. Meanwhile, the rain continued to fall, Mrs Kirkpatrick was more than usually trying, the garden mouldered under its blanket of fog, and there were times when she wished that the earth of the Government House shrubberies in which she wandered would rend itself in two and swallow her up.

Not long after this the Kirkpatricks decided to go back to England. There were three reasons given for this. The first was that Cynthia's health might benefit from the voyage. The second was that Mr Kirkpatrick had business in London. The third, it went without saying, was the international situation.

The voyage home had no charms for her. She had been here before. The flying fish in the bay at Colombo might have been sprats leaping up from their nets in Southwold Harbour for all their novelty, and the Red Sea the Round Pond at Kensington. Bereft of occupation, and without her servants to bully, Mrs Kirkpatrick went into a decline, was haughty with the stewards and stalked around the ship like a tragedy queen. Mr Kirkpatrick sat in a deck-chair making notes on the sheets of yellow legal paper that he carried round with him, went for walks around the upper deck, played quoits, and then returned to his note-making, and it was all very dull.

To revenge herself on them, Cynthia embarked on a flirtation with the ship's purser, a bald young man who said he had been to school at Tonbridge. It was not much of a romance. The bushy-haired girl in the photo frame in his cabin turned out to be his fiancée rather than his sister, and the captain disapproved so much that he forbade the purser to sit next to her at dinner. When that was all over she lay on the bed in her cabin reading the novels of E. Phillips Oppenheim, of which the ship's library possessed an inexhaustible supply, so that ever after Mediterranean scenery was associated in her mind with ticking bomb-primers and men in fedora hats skulking through the corridors of continental hotels.

At intervals along the way there came news of the wider world, and the people in the deck-chairs and rail-idlers watching the quoits games talked about Chamberlain and Halifax and Herr von Ribbentrop. The other passengers were a mixed lot—Burma policemen, with faces burned mahogany by the sun, home on furlough; chatty Eurasians with high-pitched voices travelling steerage; a university debating team coming back from a world tour—and of no interest to her. The spy novels were like a drug, softly anaesthetising the unpleasantness of the past few weeks and replacing it with expectation. England would save her, she thought, England would make her whole. When the ship reached the Channel, she stood on deck staring at the blue-grey horizon, as if it contained some vast, ineluctable secret that only she could see.

They were docking at Liverpool, which, like everything else connected with the voyage, Mrs Kirkpatrick thought inconvenient. She had already complained about the food, the familiarity of the people in the second-class berths, and the ship's doctor, who had declined to renew her stock of M & B tablets. But to Cynthia, who knew less geography, Liverpool had the edge over Tilbury or Southampton. It was all caught up in her mind—God knew how—with the Northern Lights, Lakeland rills, Romantic poetry, clipper ships racing home to port.

And so the Mersey, when they came to it on a bright forenoon in July, was a bitter disappointment. The fields on either side looked like badly painted theatrical scenery that men in white aprons might very soon come and begin to dismantle, and the smoke from the factory chimneys left smuts on the clean clothes that everyone had put on for the occasion. It was the same on the train-ride south, and possibly worse at Euston, where the sun had come out after a cloud-burst to produce fantastic Turneresque tints that were in painful contrast to the faces of the people moving below, and she thought that England had not made her whole but split her into two parts, one of them made up of cramped Midlands towns and crooked church-spires, the other composed of Chatham Street, the Grand Oriental Hotel, and the scent of jasmine.

The Kirkpatricks' London house was in Bayswater, but it had not been lived in for two years and there was a strong smell of damp. Worse, the telegram that Mr Kirkpatrick had sent to the domestic agency from Marseilles had gone astray, which meant that the beds had not been aired and there was nothing to eat. In normal circumstances this would have been the moment for a dramatic flowering of Mrs Kirkpatrick's personal myth. A year ago she would have cheerfully rustled up plates of bacon and eggs and nodded at the black beetles in the scullery cupboards without turning a hair. Now it was as if some essential part of her spirit had been quashed, and they dined off sardines and bread-and-butter bought from a grocer's shop in the debased thoroughfare around the corner.

It was the same in the days that followed. Somehow the Kirkpatricks had been subtly diminished by the month-long trip across the ocean, and though they applied themselves to their new routines their hearts were not really in it. Everything was—a word that clanged through their breakfast-table conversation like a muezzin bell—'difficult,' and the difficulty extended even to Cynthia and what ought to be done with her.

First there was a plan for her to stay with some distant relatives of Mrs Kirkpatrick's in Yorkshire, only for a letter to come explaining that the estate was being shut up and the family retiring to the dower house. Then there had been an idea that she might go shooting in Scotland—or at least stand and inspect the shooting while it took place—but nobody wanted to go north with the situation being what it was and in the end most of the parties had been cancelled. Every other day, it seemed, some bright, tree-flanked prospect would open up in front of her only for the gate that lay before it to slam resolutely shut, and the polite intimations of regret that arrived each morning in the post were her scourge.

And then there was London, which, like Ceylon, was not all it had been. It was high summer now, and most of the houses in the square had their windows open, which meant that the sound of the radio news bulletins could be heard at all hours, often in dismaying counterpoint.

The Kirkpatricks greeted the news of the Hitler–Stalin pact with stony disbelief, as something so outrageous that comment was impossible. A week later they sat in the dining-room listening to Mr Chamberlain's declaration of war.

'I never thought,' Mrs Kirkpatrick said, timorously for her, 'that it would come to this.'

'Perhaps it won't last very long,' Mr Kirkpatrick volunteered. A month in England had knocked the stuffing out of him.

'I expect it will go on forever,' Mrs Kirkpatrick said, her old stiffness instantly renewed.

The sun, flooding in unexpectedly through the high windows, drenched them in yellow-green light and sent grotesque shadows darting across the far wall. And Cynthia, staring at them as they sat in their sun-haloes, white-faced, frightened, and resentful, realised that she had no idea of the kind of people they were, or what they thought about anything, that there was a separateness about them that appalled her and in which, inevitably, she was complicit. *I am a ghost*, she thought, until the solidity of the room, the hardness of the chair in which she sat, and—a bit later—the distant whining of a siren broke the spell and drew her home.

CHAPTER 2

Duration

DURATION: A monthly review of art and letters. First issue in preparation. Annual subscription £2/10*s*. For a prospectus and all other enquiries, please contact the editor, Desmond Rafferty (author of *A Georgian Boyhood* &c.), 6 Gordon Square, London WC1.
Smith's Trade News, September 1939

There was fog hanging over the square, which meant that the houses at the northernmost end had almost disappeared. The handful that remained to view—those in whose rectangular windows lights burned, or where the wisps of vapour clung less densely to the stucco frontages—produced an oddly variegated effect, like the last remaining stumps in a mouth otherwise picked clean of teeth. Here and there, their noise hardly audible, such was the height at which she sat, a few cars crawled in and out of the murk.

The square lay in Bloomsbury's furthest quadrant, its *ultima Thule*, Desmond used to say, and was in the process of having its gardens dug up for the war effort, so that at any time of the day three or four labourers in moleskin trousers and open-necked shirts might be seen hacking away at the bushes with antique bill-hooks or making bonfires out of the swept-up branches. There was a self-conscious deliberation about the men as they went about these tasks. Like artists' models they were bent on exaggerating their picturesqueness, and the trips they made across the kerbside, pushing loaded wheelbarrows, were mostly intended to disrupt the traffic. Occasionally lorries came and took the less flammable debris away.

To the north, where the mists had begun to disperse, a barrage-balloon hung tethered over Euston Station, like one of those fat cigars you saw men smoking at taxi-ranks while they read the evening paper, only these days there seemed to be fewer cigars and fewer men to smoke them. None of this, she thought—fog, desecrated gardens, or barrage-balloons—boded well.

The magazine's offices were on the third floor of a house otherwise occupied by a doctor, a dentist, and a red-lead company: high-ceilinged and tall-windowed, but somehow never catching the light, so that even on the days when there was no fog they had a curiously sub-marine quality, as if everything in them were washing around underwater and the desks might float up to join the light-fittings unless they were weighted down. They had only been there a week, and the headed notepaper had still to arrive from the printer, which meant that letters had to be sent out with DURATION typed at the top of the page using the red ribbon.

The magazine was bound to be a success, people said, because the cinemas were closed and there was nothing else for pleasure-seekers to do in the evenings except read. Another advantage was that all Desmond's friends would be writing for it. Cynthia had one of these sheets of paper in her typewriter now, but had stopped looking at it in favour of the barrage-balloon, which seemed to her an extraordinarily sinister thing, frightful to behold but dangerous to ignore, leaving you in an endless, disagreeable limbo, frightened by the implications of what you looked at, but always conscious of its absence if you looked away. Somewhere above her head there was a stifled cry, but she was used to the noise of the dentist performing extractions and merely shook her head.

From the desk in the room's furthest corner, squeezed between a bookcase crammed with review copies and a table full of tea-making equipment, Lucy looked up from the story she was translating from the French and said, 'I say, do you know what *esculiers* are?'

'I don't think I do. Is there a hint?'

'Well, it sounds rather rude. *Avec grande excitation, il commence à caresser ses esculiers.*'

'Does it say what had happened before?'

'As far as I can make out, Jules and Ernestine are in the garden listening to the nightingales.'

There was a sound of sharp, obtrusive movement, like an animal blundering around in the dark, and the door of the second of the two inner offices that faced out into the big workroom flew open and then swung rapidly back and forth—rather, Cynthia thought, in the way that saloon doors flapped in cowboy films. Desmond loomed in the doorway. There was a coffee cup sunk into the red flesh of his fist, and he was smoking a cheroot.

'It means *buttocks*,' he said. '*With great excitation, he begins to stroke her buttocks.* Put "bottom" if you're feeling squeamish.'

'Thanks, Des,' Lucy said. 'I'm not in the least squeamish. Of all people alive, you ought to know that. Buttocks it is.'

Everyone had agreed at the outset that they would not turn a hair at anything Desmond said. This was a source of some annoyance to him, as he got most of his pleasure from the effect he had on other people. When no one rose to the bait, he grew petulant and went back into his office to sulk. He was a short, stoutish man in his late thirties, with a large, half-bald head, who had written an autobiography about how unhappy he had been at school and at university, how his first wife had never loved him, and how difficult it was to find the time to write anything. Inexplicably, this had made his reputation and now quite famous people rang up to ask him to dinner.

In his fawn-coloured jacket and his red check shirt there was also something Irish about him. He looked, Cynthia thought, as if he ought to be standing in the market square in Ennis on a Sunday morning after Mass waiting for the pubs to open. She was deeply in awe of him, as she was of Lucy, the typewriter on the desk before her, and indeed anything to do with *Duration*, but she thought that so far she had managed to hide this anxiety pretty well.

'Do you know,' Desmond said, still lingering in the doorway and dousing his cheroot in the coffee cup, 'that they painted over all the glass panes of the roof of the Wembley dog-track the other day? Apparently it cost them £300.' He was always desperate for conversation, but had never sunk quite so low as this.

'Why would they want to do that?' Lucy wondered.

'They wanted to see if they could get it to conform to the blackout regulations. But then they discovered that there wasn't to be any greyhound racing, blackout or no blackout. £300! I ask you!' Most of Desmond's utterances reverted, in the end, to money. 'What I couldn't do with that. Do you know, it's going to cost nearly twice that amount to produce every 5,000 copies of the magazine?'

'We're getting an awful lot of subscription enquiries,' Lucy said encouragingly. 'There were at least another fifty this morning.'

'Don't tell me about the kind of people who subscribe to literary magazines,' Desmond said. He had looked peevish when he dashed out of his office. Now he seemed still more ground-down, practically tragic. 'After all, I used to be one of them myself.' He waited to see if anyone would laugh, but had no luck. 'I say, though, has anyone seen Anthea? Only I need her to help me break open the petty cash tin.'

They were rather lax about time-keeping at *Duration*. Lucy and Cynthia tried to get there by ten. Desmond was sometimes delayed until as late as half-past. Mr Samways, the business and advertising manager, usually 'looked in' in the middle of the afternoon. It was now about ten past eleven.

'Isn't that her coming upstairs now?' Lucy suggested. 'Or perhaps it's Mr Wildgoose.'

It was a mark of their respective status that Desmond was known to his staff as 'Des' and the magazine's proprietor as 'Mr Wildgoose.'

While they watched to see who was coming up the staircase, Cynthia reached for her bag and pulled out the letter between the index finger and thumb of her right hand. It was the fourth time she had looked at it, without being in the least able to grasp its implications. *Dear Cynthia*, Mrs

Bannister—the Honourable Mrs Bannister, as she now remembered—had written, in her slanting, italic hand, *Although everything is very difficult at the moment, we are determined that some of the old social usages should be maintained. And so we wondered if you would like to join us on the weekend after next. No doubt Gavin will be closeted with his cronies, but there will be several young people to talk to and Hermione will be delighted to see you again.*

A shaft of sunlight burst unexpectedly through the fog and lit up the carpet in front of the desk in a way that was rather too dramatic for comfort, and the office cat—a tremendous creature that looked as if it had escaped from a Beatrix Potter book and really ought to be wearing a suit of clothes—came out from its lair behind the bookcase to bask in the glow. From the vestibule they could hear the sound of Anthea taking off her mackintosh and folding up her umbrella—something she did with extraordinary force, rather, Desmond had once said, as if she was trying to stick a pig.

Cynthia rolled the letter into a cylinder and returned it to the mouth of her bag, while the phrases it contained—the closeted cronies, the social usages that had to be maintained, Henry's younger sister Hermione being delighted—continued to roam through her head. She had no idea why the Bannisters wanted to see her. Another few seconds passed, in which the sunburst got caught up in her mind with the words in Mrs Bannister's letter, so that they hung there, gleaming and burnished like the inscriptions on a medieval scroll, and Anthea came into the room.

It was always worth being in the office when Anthea arrived. She was a tall, painfully thin girl of about twenty-four, with a chalk-white face, very pale fair hair, and an expression of absolutely unappeasable sulkiness. Usually she wore outfits that relied for their effect on maximal incongruity and the wilful jumbling of styles—chic little jackets, say, on top of dirndl skirts. On this particular occasion she was got up in a man's collarless shirt, a pair of canvas trousers, and gym shoes, while the expensive handbag she usually carried had been usurped by a kind of holdall, out of which stuck her gas mask and a copy of that morning's *Daily Worker.* On the other hand, Cynthia reflected, her earrings could not have cost less than twenty guineas.

'One of those bohemian girls, I daresay,' Mrs Kirkpatrick had offered, when news of Anthea had been brought to her.

'Hello, Anth,' Desmond said, looking at the copy of the *Daily Worker* with a kind of reluctant admiration. 'It was good of you to come and see us.' This was about as far as Desmond dared go with Anthea, who had been known to turn nasty.

'You know, Des,' Anthea said, throwing her holdall onto the spare desk and releasing a powerful scent of fish, 'that jacket doesn't suit you.'

'Doesn't it?' The cat had climbed onto the desk, the better to investigate the smell.

'No. It makes you look like a bookie at Wincanton races. Fatter, too. You ought to take it back to Aquascutum and have them change it.'

'How's Archie?' Desmond wondered. There was a faint jauntiness in his tone, but he was clearly not up to Anthea's fighting weight. 'Has he finished that story he promised me? The one about the dictator who lives in a palace made of glass waited on by midgets.'

'No. He says he won't until you pay him three guineas a page. In any case, he says Connolly's asked him to do the film reviews for *Horizon*.'

'Anthea's behaving very mysteriously these days,' Desmond announced to the room at large. 'Spends her evenings in dreadful little pubs in Soho. I can't think what she does there.'

'Well, a friend of mine said she saw you at the Dorchester the other day having lunch with Esmé Gurvitz,' Anthea said, with infinite disdain.

There was no answer to this. A silence fell over the room. The sunlight had dispersed. Its absence renewed the creeping sensation that everything—carpet, desks, the people behind them—was somehow submerged. Cynthia thought desperately about the Bannisters' house in Sussex, with its twenty-three rooms, its condescending butler and retinue of manservants, and what she might be expected to do when she got there.

They were all frozen in their attitudes, she thought—Lucy looking up from her desk, Anthea standing with her arms akimbo and her right foot wound snakily around the calf of her left leg, Desmond still loitering uncertainly in his doorway. Again the effect was somehow medieval, like the figures in a frieze. Finally the telephone rang and Anthea, answering it, began a long conversation with the caller, evidently a personal friend, in which the words 'id' and 'superego' recurred. Abruptly, the frieze disintegrated.

'If Pritchett calls about that review of the Walpole,' Desmond said with a rather despairing glance at Anthea, 'you'd better let me know.'

They said they would let him know, and he went back into his study but left the door half-open so they could see him sitting at his desk with his head in his hands.

'I don't think *esculiers* can mean "buttocks,"' Lucy said, 'because there's a sentence here about them being *malheureuses et énormes*.'

Gradually the rest of the morning passed. At intervals the telephone rang, but the callers were mostly people owed money by the previous tenants. Anthea's holdall had to be put in a cupboard to deter the cat. Lucy worked at her translation and Cynthia retyped a letter to a print-broker whose original had contained so many mistakes that even Desmond would not let it through. The twelve o'clock post brought another twenty subscription requests, a short story written in green ink and addressed to *Mr Desmond Rafferty Esq.*, and a bill for dinner for one at the Café Royal which Desmond claimed not to have eaten.

The fog had lifted now and the wind was getting up, so that the plane trees at the sides of the square moved backwards and forwards in a menacing way. The Bannisters' house was called Ashburton Grange, and she had been there now and again. She had a dim memory of hounds assembling on the lawn, iced stirrup-cup drunk out of green-patterned tumblers, and Mr Bannister looking rather ridiculous in a pink coat. Where had Henry been? But there was no place for Henry in these imaginings. Like so many things in her life, he had moved on into a place from which memory had no power to bring him back.

At a quarter to one Anthea finished the letter she had been typing with a last murderous ping of her typewriter bell. 'Hell's teeth,' she said. She had taken off her gym shoes and had been walking around the office in her bare feet. 'I'm supposed to be meeting Norman for a drink at the Ritz Bar, but I simply can't face it on my own. You'd better come with me, Cynthia. That's if you're not doing anything else.'

'Oh no,' Cynthia said, flattered to be asked. 'I'm not doing anything else.'

'You don't mind holding down the fort, do you, Lu? It would be simply angelic of you.'

There was something altogether brazen about Anthea's insincerity. It was so obviously not in the least disguised, and only an inch or so away from outright mockery. But Lucy, whose upbringing had been rather strict, always took these things very well.

When they had got their hats and coats, picked up their gas masks and, through grey, untidy streets, walked half the way to the bus stop on the Tottenham Court Road, Anthea said, rather urgently, as if it were the answer to a question she had been asked some time before: 'The thing about Desmond, you see, is that he's terribly insecure.'

'Insecurity' was not a word that had featured much in Cynthia's vocabulary before she had come to the Bloomsbury square, but she was getting used to it.

'Why is he insecure?'

Anthea's voice was, against stiff competition, perhaps the most attractive thing about her. It was unexpectedly high, lost-little-girlish and, when not being ironic, faintly earnest. 'Anthea's way of getting rich old men to propose to her,' Desmond had explained. 'She sits on their knees in the private rooms at Claridge's and coos at them.'

'Well, you see he was at school with all sorts of people who've gone on to be terribly well-known. And then he married Marietta, and thought he'd have plenty of money and be able to live in the South of France and not work for the *Listener* so much, only she turned out to be a lesbian and not to have nearly as much money as everybody thought.'

On the corner where University Street ran into the Tottenham Court Road there was a man selling newspapers whose headline ran CHAMBERLAIN TO REJECT PEACE TALKS, and Cynthia bought one and put it in her bag. Anthea stalked on ahead, hands plunged into the pockets of her mackintosh. Overhead the sky was turning grey. Somewhere a plane droned quietly. The bus, when it came, was rather full of people, but by staring crossly at a pair of middle-aged men on the upper deck, Anthea managed to procure them seats. The advertising hoardings were so close that Cynthia thought she might reach out and touch them.

'How did you come across Lucy?' Anthea asked in a bored voice.

'Actually,' Cynthia said, 'we were at school together.'

Nearer at hand now, looming at them over the tops of the houses, the barrage-balloon looked even more sinister than before.

'I'm sure that must have been fun,' Anthea said.

A little bomb of resentment that had been ticking away in Cynthia's head for several days suddenly exploded.

'Actually,' she said, 'it was, rather.'

After that they got on better.

The bus dropped them halfway along Piccadilly, next to Hatchard's book-shop, which had a wall of sandbags rising up its window. One or two men in steel helmets were wandering about. Like the gardeners in the square, they moved with an extreme self-consciousness, as if the Piccadilly shop-fronts had been expressly designed to provide a backdrop for their adventures and London was simply an expensive film-set. Cynthia tried to imagine what Hatchard's had looked like last time she had seen it, but found she could not remember. Like Ceylon, and like Henry, it was fading fast, borne on a heavy tide, drifting away into oblivion.

An impermeable membrane seemed to have slipped between the war and the great stretches of time that had preceded it. Already people talked about what they had done in the summer as if it had taken place in some far-off, mythical terrain, as if the beaches they had sat on had been ridden over by centaurs. On the lip of St James's Street there was a man in a dingy over-coat with a pedlar's pack open at his feet and a selection of domestic items spread out over the pavement. Anthea stopped and bought a pair of dusters.

'I always think,' she said, 'that when you're living with a man you should make some contribution to your upkeep.'

Grey streets; exiguous traffic; men in battle-dress; sandbagged door-ways. She was already used to these landscapes, and they no longer haunted her imagination. They went into the Ritz through the Arlington Street entrance. Here things were livelier. A couple of officers, one of them a colonel in scarlet tabs, were slapping the shoulder of a third man who looked rather sheepish about the attention he was getting. As Anthea was taking off her mackintosh, a waiter came and said something in an undertone. Anthea muttered something back, and he slunk away.

'What was that about?' Cynthia wondered.

'Oh, he said he didn't think he could let in people wearing canvas trousers, and I said that I was the Countess of Antrim and that I was waiting for my husband who was in a shareholders' meeting upstairs and he'd be frightfully cross if I wasn't admitted. Now, where's Norman, I wonder?'

They went and sat at one of the marble-topped tables, not far from the bronzed nymph perched in her grotto of artificial rocks and ferns. It took only a moment for the pink-and-green furniture and the cream-and-gold surround to work their effect, and then she was glad she had come. The place was fairly crowded: more uniformed men; people in morning coats and striped trousers; one or two girls who looked like promising imitations of Anthea without, in dress terms, having degenerated quite so far. There was no sign of Norman, whoever he was.

'I expect we shall see Des here before too long,' Anthea said. 'He's a famous frequenter of the Ritz Bar. They used to say that one of the viscounts he'd known at Oxford told him it was the only place a gentleman could be seen at, except his club, and so once he arrived in London he never went anywhere else.' There was a way in which, despite her triumph over the waiter, she seemed a little less at ease here in the cream-and-gold amphitheatre than in the street outside it, and that the joke about Desmond was intended to disguise this uncertainty.

Glancing at her face, still extraordinarily sulky beneath its halo of white-gold hair, Cynthia divined that she was looking at a superior version of herself. Somehow this thought depressed her. She would never be able to buy dusters for the men she was living with, she thought, make jokes about the viscounts Desmond had known at Oxford, or pass herself off as the Countess of Antrim. Expertise of this kind was simply beyond her: she could not imagine how you came by it, still less how you made it work to your advantage.

It was about a quarter-past one. In the house at Bayswater, Mr and Mrs Kirkpatrick would be eating warmed-up shepherd's pie and tinned peaches and listening to the lunch-time news on the radio. Somehow all this depressed her even more. Meanwhile, there was the next half-hour, or hour, or two hours—she had no idea how long Anthea would want to stay at the Ritz Bar—to be got through. There was still no sign of Norman. A man sitting at the next table, small and sharp-eyed, like a creature of the field, stared suddenly in her direction and she looked away.

Anthea stared furiously at the bronze nymph, as if she would have been happy to change places with her, given any kind of encouragement, and said, 'Well, if you're not going to tell me what you've been glooming about all morning, there really wasn't much point in bringing you here, was there?'

And so, to her surprise, Cynthia found herself telling her about what had happened on the back-road out of Colombo, the voyage home, and now the letter that had come from the Bannisters. Outside, a siren went off in the street, and three or four people at the next table said 'false alarm' at exactly the same time. Anthea listened with professional interest.

'I'm not sure I didn't come across your Henry Bannister years ago,' she said. 'Now where might it have been? Windsor Great Park? One of those boring cricket matches in aid of the Georgian Association? Rather keen on the girls, I seem to remember. So now he's dead and the parents want you to go and stay with them. Why should they feel you had to do that?'

'They're very old friends of my mother and father,' Cynthia said. 'Terribly old. In fact I think Mummy and Mrs Bannister might have come out together.'

'If I remember Mrs B rightly,' Anthea said, 'there'd have been no question of her coming out. In fact, people would have subscribed a handsome amount to keep her in. Perhaps I'm misjudging her. But as to the weekend in Sussex—and it sounds pretty grim, I'll allow—do you want to go?'

'It seems a bit of a duty, if you know what I mean.'

'Duty,' Anthea said. She was smoking a cigarette, and the smoke, partly obscuring her face, made her look like an ancient sibyl grimly pronouncing judgement in the vapour of an Attic dawn. 'That word again. Even Des has taken to using it, so you can see what an effect it's having on people. I'm not sure what I think about duty. In any case, here's Norman come at last.'

There was a tallish figure moving rather diffidently towards their table, not obviously aware of where they were, and she flung up her hand and began making wild semaphore signals.

Since the first mention of his name a good three-quarters of an hour ago, Cynthia had been wondering who Norman was. She had expected him to be young and quite probably dressed in a service uniform. In fact, inspecting him as he continued to drift—a bit more purposefully now—between the tables, she saw that he was nearer forty than thirty, and wearing only a nondescript-looking raincoat. Anthea instantly took charge of the situation.

'Norman! How nice to see you. Cynthia, this is Norman Burdett.'

Closer up, he looked even older than she had first imagined: straw-haired and not especially well shaved. As well as the raincoat, he was wearing what she recognised as a Toc H tie. One of the veins in his cheek had burst into a little spiral of pink threads. He reminded her of the kind of man she had come across once or twice in the East: vague, non-committal, humorous about odd things, guardians of some immensely private joke that they might allow you in on when they knew you better. Mr Kirkpatrick had occasionally produced people of this sort at dinner. It was not unusual for their whimsicality to disguise some bitter, private grief.

Anthea seemed not quite able to decide whether to regard Norman as a source of comic relief or as a kind of oracle who should be respectfully attended to.

'How are things in Jermyn Street, Norman?'

'Oh, they're fine. Not nearly so many pretty girls as there used to be, though.'

'Still chasing after the King's Party?'

'That's right. Still chasing after them.'

The beady-eyed man at the next table looked up at this, but Cynthia could not work out if he was staring at herself or Norman.

'And Captain Ramsay?'

Norman accepted a drink from a passing waiter. 'I will allow that Captain Ramsay has been in my thoughts.'

'Oh, he's terrible, isn't he?' Anthea said, as if they were discussing some notorious ladies' man who had given friends of hers cause for concern. 'Did you hear what he said about Mosley the other day?'

There was something faintly unreal about all this, Cynthia thought, which the ornaments of the Ritz—its long, high-backed sofas, the bronze nymph solitary in her grotto—made worse. She had been to the Ritz before, of course, in the aftermath of dances and Boat Races, but with young men who ordered champagne and looked out to see who else was there, and never with anyone remotely like Anthea or Norman Burdett.

Norman was grinning now, and looking more than ever like a variety-hall comedian about to crack a joke about his mother-in-law. 'Ladies, ladies. You don't want to hear about me. Tell me something about yourselves. How is young Mr Rafferty?'

'He's very depressed,' Anthea said. 'The first number's due in a fortnight and he says he's got nothing to put in it yet.'

'And where's he getting his paper from, I wonder?'

'That man in Chatham, I think. At least he's always talking about him. I believe that friend of Peter's at the Ministry of Supply is helping.'

The expression on Norman's face altered slightly. 'A bit of a tricky customer, that one,' he said. 'He'd better keep his eyes open.' There was some game being played with her, Cynthia thought, some odd cryptogram being solved in front of her eyes to which she had no key. Oddly, this suspicion did not upset her. She liked being in the high, cream-and-gold room, and she liked Anthea and Norman Burdett, whoever he was, and would have acceded to any reasonable request they made of her.

'I hope Des keeps his eyes open. I should mind it most dreadfully if he didn't. And who else are you interested in just at the moment?'

'Oh, the usual suspects, you know.' Norman's face had gone back to its usual vague benignity. 'Lymington. Domvile. That Bannister chap.'

Lymington, Domvile, and that Bannister chap. Cynthia shifted in her chair, curious to hear that the man who had just proffered her a weekend invitation was being suspected of something. It was past two o'clock now, and the confraternities of the Ritz Bar were breaking up. The people at the next table were clambering to their feet and shaking hands and saying they would see each other soon, and a woman with an impossibly expensive face and a Pekingese under her arm was explaining how wild horses wouldn't stop her going to Cap Ferrat even if there was a war on. Rain, falling diagonally against the high windows, enhanced this air of private fantasy, of something set at one remove from the real life going on outside.

They left Norman sitting at the marble-topped table and went out into the lobby, where the waiter who had tried to stop Anthea coming in drew himself up and gave a stiff little bow.

'Aren't we going to be awfully late?' Cynthia wondered, looking at her watch.

'I daresay,' Anthea said. One or two faint twists of colour had come back into her face, and she looked appreciably more human.

In Piccadilly there were a pair of army trucks pulled up at the kerbside and a company of lady cyclists in WVS uniforms labouring by, and they crossed over and made for the bus stop. Cynthia could not repress her curiosity about Norman. 'Is Mr Burdett in the paper trade?'

'Norman? Gracious no. He's in one of the cloak-and-dagger outfits.'

'And what is the King's Party?'

The skin of Anthea's wrist was almost translucent, so that the veins looked like traceries of blue ink. 'Well,' she said. 'You know all the people who go around saying that only the King can stop the war?'

There were two of these in the Kirkpatricks' house at Bayswater. It sounded from what Norman Burdett had said that Mr Bannister made a third. 'Of course I know about them.'

'Let's just say that the gap between wanting peace and thinking that the war becomes meaningless once you take away the aggression and the bad faith is a good deal wider than some of them imagine. And another thing,' Anthea said, rather sharply, as if the two subjects were somehow connected. 'If I were you I'd go down to Sussex for the weekend. Heaven knows, Mrs B might have learned some hostessing skills by now. And it can't possibly do any harm.'

'Do you know,' Cynthia said, noticing that the pile of sandbags outside a dress shop had been sprayed lime-green to match the window frames and puzzled by the curious note of urgency in Anthea's voice, 'I really think I might.'

Back at the *Duration* office they found Desmond sprawled in an armchair reading Burton's *The Anatomy of Melancholy*, and there was a message asking Cynthia to telephone her father. Later a truck came and removed some more heaps of foliage from the ruined garden.

Mr and Mrs Kirkpatrick had taken the war about as badly as they had ever taken anything. Becalmed in its considerable shadow, they did not feel, as they were fond of saying, themselves. Rather, their discontent had turned them into slightly faded versions of their original prototypes. None of this made them easier to live with, talk to, or even contemplate from a distance.

Mr Kirkpatrick had the proper patriot-defeatist attitude. He said: 'Nobody supports the war more than I do. It's perfectly right that we should take exception to another country that has acted belligerently. The Poles have my sympathy, just like the Czechoslovaks. But if you take away the cause of the belligerence, which in the end has very little to do with us, then what are you left with? A lot of unnecessary inconvenience. I think everyone's best interests would be served by a negotiated peace.'

Mrs Kirkpatrick, meanwhile, had joined an organisation of politically minded gentlewomen who met on Thursday afternoons in an upstairs room of the Goring Hotel where they were addressed by an Irish peer who had once worked in the diplomatic service. A plan to go back to Ceylon had been quietly jettisoned. Occasional telegrams came from Colombo.

One symptom of the Kirkpatricks' devitalised state was their attitude towards Cynthia. In the past they had tended to hover over her life, like a pair of game birds over a nest of fledglings. With demoralisation, on the other hand, came a new spirit of laissez-faire, sometimes shading into outright indifference. They were not much animated by her coming across Lucy again, and even less interested in the process of negotiation that took her to the Bloomsbury square.

In the past Mrs Kirkpatrick would have made little jokes about *Duration*, and the humour would, additionally, have canvassed a need for vigilance in the face of moral laxity. Now she merely said: 'Why it counts as war-work I can't imagine. And I suppose the people are rather highbrow.' Mr Kirkpatrick, told that Desmond had commissioned an essay by Sickert, remarked that it wasn't what he called painting and left it at that. But they cheered up no end over the invitation to Ashburton Grange. 'I think it is *very kind* of Mrs Bannister,' Mrs Kirkpatrick pronounced, 'particularly in the *current circumstances*.' The italics hung in the air like dust-motes. 'You must certainly go.'

'Of course she should go,' Mr Kirkpatrick said, who had not actually been appealed to. 'No earthly reason why not.'

The processes that had been at work on the Kirkpatricks could be observed elsewhere. London, for example, though full of people, seemed to be growing smaller and less familiar by the minute. The girls Cynthia had been to dances with three years ago had all disappeared. They were lodging with their husbands in married quarters at Canterbury and Catterick, or safely installed in dower houses beyond the Tweed. All over England everyone was battening hatches, hunkering down, storing up provisions against the gathering storm, in sharp retreat to private worlds of their own devising. There was no getting away from this. Equally there was no solace for anyone who wasn't married to a subaltern or had no dower house waiting to receive her.

None of the old consolations seemed to apply. In the past Cynthia had always been able to revive her spirits by going through the photograph albums that lay in the bottom compartment of the drawing-room sideboard. Bought over the years at Harrods, and beginning to part company with their beige-brown bindings, they were a tribute to Mrs Kirkpatrick's intent, methodical side. But there was also a kind of defiance to them, the thought of a compiler keen to tell the world that though she could, had she chosen, have been a military strategist or a translator from the Greek, she had preferred to stick pictures in Harrods albums, without the slightest lapse in commitment or intellectual attack.

Never had these photographs, in which Mr and Mrs Kirkpatrick stood diffidently in the porch of St George's, Hanover Square in their wedding finery, sauntered on the decks of ocean liners, or stared severely at the carcasses of slaughtered pheasants, failed her, and yet now there was something wrong about them. It was hard to say where the disappointment lay, but like the process of realignment that had picked up nearly everyone she knew and deposited them a little further away from her, it could not be gainsaid, and after a final, fruitless inspection of a picture showing Mr and Mrs Kirkpatrick attending the durbar in Delhi in 1923 she put the albums away. Pictures could not help her: she needed humankind.

In the end she turned up a girl called Sophie Morris, who lived in one of the adjoining squares and with whom she had once been to classes in conversational French. Sophie was a nice, friendly girl with sandy hair and rather uneven teeth who in the past had been grateful for any smiles

Cynthia had cared to bestow on her. But Sophie, Cynthia discovered, had been borne away on the same devitalising tide as Mr and Mrs Kirkpatrick. She was engaged to a young man in the Ministry of Works, had expectations of an aunt, and recoiled from any discussion of the past as if it had been an unexploded limpet-mine.

'Do you remember how cross Mademoiselle got,' Cynthia asked once, in a spirit of companionable reminiscence—they were having tea at a Lyons in the Earl's Court Road—'when Daisy Fellowes came in smoking a cigarette, with her nails painted bright blue?'

'I don't think I can have been there that day,' Sophie said. A letter had come that morning from her aunt. 'I did hear Daisy Fellowes married someone quite high up at the War Office.'

'And then there was that time she got soaking wet on the way to the Chelsea Arts Ball and said that it never rained but it Diored.'

'Simon says that some of the War Office wives are still behaving very irresponsibly. You know, having dinner parties and wondering why their husbands can't be back in time.'

'Oh, Sophie,' Cynthia said in despair. 'I know there's a war on, but you never used to be like this.'

'I don't believe you've changed *at all*,' Sophie said triumphantly.

They kept it up for a week or two. They played table tennis in the basement of the Morrises' house in Powis Square beneath the portrait of Sophie's grandfather in his Masonic apron, they went shopping for a skirt that Sophie intended to wear at the Ministry of Works' winter reception, and rejoiced in the sight of the King travelling along Piccadilly in a Daimler because it was known that he rarely went out. At the end of it Cynthia thought that she might probably have passed a competitive examination on the subject of Simon: the combinations he wore under his suit in cold weather, and the bad case of erysipelas that had kept him out of the Charterhouse fifteen in his last term.

'Sophie,' she said on one of these occasions, in a voice that she knew was borrowed from Anthea, 'I know it's awful of me to say so, but you make him sound the most boring man on earth.'

There was no going back from that, of course. The next time Cynthia rang Powis Square, Mrs Morris said her daughter was out. Two days later there came a letter saying that Sophie had joined the Red Cross Port of London Authority River Emergency Service and was busy in the evenings. So there was another friend gone west.

Against this unpromising backdrop, the visit to Ashburton Grange took on a wholly unmerited significance: a pageant, a raree show, and a *conversazione* rolled into one, with Mr and Mrs Kirkpatrick as its impresarios, its zealous sponsors, its loyal supporters denied a place at the table themselves but keen that their daughter should sample whatever sweetmeats were on offer. Mrs Kirkpatrick produced ten guineas for a new evening dress; Mr Kirkpatrick made over a little pile of half-crowns packed into a *rouleau* which he said would be useful for tipping the servants; and one of the old monogrammed suitcases that had belonged to Mrs Kirkpatrick's father and had seen service in the days of the Paris Commune was put at her disposal. Meanwhile, there was no war news worth speaking of, and nobody Cynthia spoke to seemed to find this in the least bit surprising.

CHAPTER 3

Behind the Counter

The shop was in a distant part of Maida Vale, near the Regent's Park canal. Sometimes a few cognoscenti struggled up from the Underground station. But mostly it was empty. Fifty yards away, in the square's north-western quadrant, there was a glimpse of railway lines, and every twenty or thirty minutes, in a brisk detonation of whirled pistons and black smoke, a locomotive would plunge into view. These performances, with their explosive choreography, gave the day routine: a momentary quickening of the senses; satisfaction; slow decline.

London was full of these sequestered corners, silent rookeries with the birds all gone, forgotten and despairing. He had never thought it would be like this, but it was. There was a train rushing by now, almost gone, a last carriage or two about to be swallowed up by the house-fronts, and he lit a cigarette and stared at it. The half-lit window drew out his silhouette and made him look larger than he really was, and the ash from his cigarette, which was too cheap for gestures of this sort, flaked over the knee of his suit. The pale face at the window; the cigarette smoke rising into thin air; the two or three hundred antiques drawn up behind Mr McKechnie's shop.

Mr McKechnie was out back somewhere, riffling though the piles of junk that had accumulated in the yard, but the rumour of his presence left no trace. It was only Rodney who was real. The cigarette was all smoked up now. He left the butt to smoulder on the lip of the brass ashtray next to the till. Outside the window, a small man with a chipmunk's face glanced up from the tray of books that ran beneath the ledge and he stared stonily back. Rule number one: never engage; let them come to you. The last wisps of cigarette smoke were burning out now, like a votive offering in the cleft between two ancient hills, faun and centaur standing by.

The antiques were a mixed lot. Reproductions of pictures by Winterhalter. Pewter pots. Cameo brooches that looked as if they hailed from Gainsborough films. One or two of the pieces were valuable; others a lot less so. There were no prices marked, so it was a question of knowing where to look. Chipmunk-face had his thumb on a copy of *Ayala's Angel* now. The books were sixpence each and not worth the trouble, Mr McKechnie said. On the other hand, sometimes people came in and bought them.

He was thinking about London and what he had expected to find there. Whatever it was had not surfaced, still lingered far beneath the ice. The restlessness that he had brought with him was still there, but less well hidden. Another man came into the shop, breaking into these dreams of sun-dappled thoroughfares and pigeons in flight—all that illusory balm—and began to look around. The customers annoyed him, especially the ones who knew what they were doing. They had cracked the code, and he had not. There were other codes lurking out there, but he knew he would decipher them in the end: he always did.

The man had one of the pewter pots in his gloved hand. 'How much do you want for this?' he wondered.

Not less than fifteen bob for the pewter, Mr McKechnie had said. Rodney was appalled by what seemed to him the arbitrariness of the trade. Portraits of chocolate-box blondes went for a shilling; pairs of blackened fire-irons, for which there was no conceivable use, were reserved for Croesus.

'A very good piece, sir, that,' he said. He could hear the trace of Lancashire in his own voice and shortened the 'a' so that it came out as *thet*. He had once heard Mr McKechnie telling a customer that he sounded 'quite thoroughly obsequious.' 'I couldn't take less than a guinea.'

A guinea. That showed the kind of level he was operating at these days. Cheapskates talked about pounds, shillings, and pence. He dealt in finer coin.

'It's hardly worth that,' the man said. He had a news announcer's voice, like the man who introduced *Band Waggon*. That was another thing about London to add to the dead squares and the lumbering lorries: the voices.

'Eighteen shillings, sir, would be positively the lowest I could go,' he heard himself saying, without a flattened 'a' in sight.

The man gave him seven half-crowns and a sixpenny bit. Not quite the toff his accent had proclaimed him. Rodney put the pot in a brown paper bag and handed it over, the corners of his mouth turned down. To smile was to concede: to concede, to diminish. When the man had gone, letting in a slab of freezing air from the open door, he put six of the half-crowns in the till and stowed the seventh, and the sixpenny bit, in the jacket pocket of his suit.

Outside there was another train coming—you could tell this from the distant boring noise, like a drill edging into rock—and he tensed for its appearance, the raucous swan gliding on its cast-iron lake. In the depths of his trouser pocket, his hand fell on the slip of paper with its incriminating phone number, and he took it out and stared at it. One day he would call it. But not yet.

The train had gone, the last echo of its transit disappearing among the house-fronts, but there were other noises breaking into the silence: human voices, these ones. Presently a door banged, there was a little patter of footsteps, the last vestiges of a giggle vanishing into a space where he couldn't follow it, and Mr McKechnie and his wife came in from the yard.

'Good morning, Rodney,' Mr McKechnie said, although it was the third time they had come across each other since breakfast.

'I sold one of those pewter jobs just now,' Rodney said, with burlesqued enthusiasm. 'Fifteen shillings.'

'That's good,' Mr McKechnie said. He stared thoughtfully at the pots, as if detaching one of their number had a moral implication it might be dangerous to pursue. 'Very good indeed. You'll make our fortunes.'

Mr McKechnie was fifty, and set in his ways. He liked cups of black, sugary coffee at two-hour intervals, the *News Chronicle*'s daily crossword, and not having to be disturbed by dealers. Mrs McKechnie, whose name was Loelia, was younger and less predictable. She had a habit of lurking silently in the back of the shop until everyone had forgotten her existence and then popping up with some difficult question.

'Shall I make you a cup of tea, Mrs McKechnie?' Rodney asked, with the same phantom zeal.

'No, thank you, Rodney. I'm sure you've better things to do with your time.' Like most of Mrs McKechnie's utterances, this came freighted with menace. He looked at her as she said it, but found no clue. The flapper gear had rather gone out in London, but Mrs McKechnie was still wearing it. Today she was got up in one of those cylinder dresses with a bead necklace so thickly cut that it could have been made out of old rope. She would have been about thirty-three or thirty-four, he thought, but made up for it with a line in girlish laughs.

'No, no tea, thank you, Rodney,' Mr McKechnie said. He had a sad but intermittently hopeful voice, like a Shakespearean clown, or Bud Flanagan singing 'Underneath the Arches.' 'In fact, we're just off out. There's a sale up in Camden Town that Loelia particularly wanted to see.'

'Anything good, Mr McKechnie?' Rodney wondered. He knew about the sales up in Camden Town. Deceased clergymen's libraries were pitilessly dispersed and trunks full of sepia photographs knocked down to the highest bidder.

'One or two nice little early-Victorian reproductions, it says in the catalogue,' Mr McKechnie said, one hand exploring the area at the back of his head where the black curls faded to grey. He was not quite an alcoholic, but liked to be in the pub by twelve.

'We'll be back by three,' Mrs McKechnie said, giving him one of her looks, but in such a perfunctory way that he barely stirred. 'And then you can make me that cup of tea.'

Through the shop window he watched them go out: Mr McKechnie already starting to meander; Mrs McKechnie chivvying him along; their hands clasped together as if padlocked. In their absence the shop grew larger again, less constricting to his imagination. He lit another cigarette and went along the aisles smoking it in grandiloquent puffs. Here and there the ash fell over the ersatz Winterhalters and Lord Leighton's Attic drapery. There was no doubt about it: one of the girls in the painting looked like Mrs McKechnie. And not a stitch on her, either. He smiled at the identification. And then, just as his fingers trailed over the slip of paper again, the door-bell jangled and the American came into the shop.

He never knew what to make of the American. Mr and Mrs McKechnie he could set to work to his advantage, even when they thought it was the other way around. But the American's intentions had to be guessed at. This time he took his hands out of the pockets of his overcoat and gave an infinitesimal nod.

'I thought I'd come and look you up. Seeing as how you won't use the telephone. I hope that's not inconvenient.'

'Suits me fine,' Rodney said.

'All on your lonesome?'

'That's about the strength of it.'

'That's a good way to go about things.'

'I always think so.'

This sort of banter could go on for hours; Rodney didn't mind. It was like a trial of strength: each word an extra dumb-bell. The American had started turning over the pile of brass ashtrays next to the till. He said: 'I like these. I could do with one for my office shelf. How much do you want?'

'Seven and sixpence, they are.'

As he took the ten-shilling note and delved into the till for change, the American said, 'There's a little job you might like to do for me later. Two little jobs.'

He thought of Lord Leighton's Greek girl in her olive grove. 'I don't see why not.'

The ashtray was in its brown-paper bag. He put a strip of tape over the opening to make it neat. The American said, 'You'd have to do the first one this afternoon. About four-thirty. Down at the House of Commons. You know where that is?'

'Of course I know.'

He had never been further south than Soho. But there were maps, and policemen to ask.

'Go to the main entrance and ask for Captain Ramsay. The porters will know where to find him. He'll give you a parcel, and you can bring it to me. I suppose it couldn't be simpler.'

Something struck him about these arrangements and he said, 'Why can't you go yourself?'

'Let's just say that it's easier to send someone else. Plus it creates employment. So everybody's happy. You, me, and Sir John Simon.'

'Who's Sir John Simon?'

'He's the Chancellor of the Exchequer. A fellow that has your best interests at heart, I'm sure. You can bring the parcel to the usual place.'

'What about the other job?'

'Ah, I'm not so sure about that yet. Not quite. I'll know later. Might mean you staying out.'

'It's no odds to me.'

When he had gone, Rodney looked at the ten-shilling note lying in the till and decided to leave it there. In the corner of the square there was another train coming past, but the Great Northern railway had lost its charm. It was about half-past twelve, and schoolchildren were going listlessly to their dinners. There was a trace of perfume hanging over the space near the pewter pots: Mrs McKechnie's faint but unappetising spoor. Mr McKechnie would have drunk three large gins by now and be making fanciful bids for the memoirs of General Roberts in three volumes, or ancient coal-buckets varnished over with postage stamps.

At a quarter to one he shut up the shop, in defiance of every known law, and walked the three streets to the room he inhabited in a row of identical Edwardian houses that seemed to be pressing in on each other, so that the ones in the middle looked as if they might soon be squeezed out. The room was bitterly cold and the morning's post lay on the mat: a letter from his mother, and a second letter with his name and address typewritten on the front which contained a five-pound note compressed into such a tiny square that it resembled a lump of sealing-wax. He threw the letter from his mother into the waste-paper basket without opening it and then unravelled the five-pound note, taking care not to tear the edge, and put it in a cash-box which lay on the bed. Once or twice he strained to hear sounds of movement, but the house was as quiet as the grave.

Half an hour later he walked back by a different route: along a terrace of plump, three-storey houses with steps leading down into murky areas. Here lived benign tyrants known jokily to their subjects as 'The Dad,' girls who worked as secretary-typists in estate agents' offices, and bright-blazered grammar-school boys.

Back at the shop there was trouble brewing. Manageable trouble, but trouble nonetheless, for the McKechnies had come home early. At least Mrs McKechnie was standing by the till with an unlit cigarette jammed inexpertly into her mouth, and her hat—one of those elfin bonnets with a kind of mushroom stalk on the crown—slightly askew.

'Where's Mr McKechnie?' he wondered.

'He had to go upstairs. He wasn't feeling very well,' Mrs McKechnie said. The McKechnies lived in a flat above the shop, into which unsaleable stock occasionally strayed. He thought he was going to get away without having to explain his absence, but suddenly Mrs McKechnie remembered why she was cross and said, 'Where the bloody hell have you been?'

''Fraid I had to send a telegram.' It was the best excuse of all, he had always thought. By the time you had finished explaining what it was about and to whom it was sent, nine out of ten people would have lost interest.

'It really won't do . . .' Mrs McKechnie began, but he could see that it meant nothing to her. Nothing at all. Above their heads a curious thumping noise sounded from the ceiling, like someone dropping a packing case on the floor, shifting it a few feet, and then dropping it again. 'Mr McKechnie's not at all well,' Mrs McKechnie said again, a touch absently. The smell of the perfume had gone now, to be replaced by gin. She put her hand on the till and spread out the fingers, gracefully, like a mannequin about to have her nails painted. 'I know something about you,' she said.

'What's that, then?' He didn't like people knowing things about him. 'What do you know about me?'

'I was in the back of the shop the other day, first thing in the morning, and you sold a man a cigar case for twelve shillings. The float was a pound. And then when I looked in the till while you were getting the tea, there was only thirty shillings.'

'You're forgetting the two shillings that went on the envelopes,' he said.

'There wasn't any two shillings that went on envelopes,' she said, with a kind of dreadful, pixie brightness. She giggled. 'It's all right. I shan't tell on you. Good luck to you. That's what I say.'

He shifted the angle of his shoulders, in the hope of being able to greet someone coming into the shop, but it was no good. There were never any customers in the afternoons. Above their heads came the sound of a drawn-out and calamitous descent, like a sack of potatoes being tipped slowly onto its side, and then silence. The cigarette went up and down like a lever in Mrs McKechnie's mouth when she talked.

'I don't know why I put up with this,' Mrs McKechnie said.

It was always women who did this to him, who couldn't hold themselves together, wouldn't lie down in the beds they'd made. Why was that? His mother was just the same.

Mrs McKechnie was picking up pewter pots at random, looking at them suspiciously, and then setting them down. 'I could put up with it,' she said, 'if there was anyone who understood me. But there isn't. Not anyone.'

This had happened before. It was important not to let the situation develop.

'Look,' he said, in the confidential tones of one old friend needing another to do him a favour, 'I've got to go out again. My aunt's in hospital, down at St Thomas's, and they've sent word I've to see her. Do you think you could look after the shop?'

'Oh yes,' she said. 'I could do that. After all, there's not much to do, is there? Apart from taking the money and making sure at least some of it stays in the till.' She held the four fingers of her right hand up in a kind of chevron and touched them to the side of her head in mock-salute. Still wearing her coat and the elf-bonnet, she perched on the high stool behind the till. 'I'll be a brave soldier, shall I? And if one of the dealers comes in, I can just tell him that my husband is indisposed.'

But he had lost interest in Mrs McKechnie. He wondered what would happen after he'd gone. The worst thing would be if she fell asleep at the desk or went upstairs without locking the door. It was a risk he'd have to take.

'I'm very much obliged to you,' he said. 'Truly.'

'That's all right, Rodney. What's your aunt's name?'

'Muriel,' he said, without hesitation.

'Why don't you use that two shillings and buy her a bunch of flowers?'

'Maybe I will,' he said.

When he glanced back, he could see her waiting in the window, with her hat sliding down the side of her head and one stockinged leg hauled over the other, staring out at nothing. He wondered what she and Mr McKechnie said to each other over the breakfast table, or indeed what they said to each other anywhere.

Supine under the mid-afternoon light, the square seemed suddenly wintry. In the far corner there was a file of army trucks moving slowly north. The coal-sacks piled up near the motorcycle-shop stirred in the wind like cowled monks. He went south by degrees: a bus to Marble Arch; a forced march along Oxford Street; a saunter around the garishly lit frontage of Bourne & Hollingsworth. Now and again he caught sight of himself in windows, white face glaring out of the crowd. In the Charing Cross Road he stopped at a kiosk and bought a packet of cigarettes.

It was not long until Armistice Day and there were nurses selling poppies from trays. He took one of them and pinned it to the button-hole of his coat. The light was starting to fade, and the Charing Cross Road, jumbled up with buses and lorries, was drained of colour, like some vast painting from which the pigment had been mysteriously extracted. He got on another bus and watched Trafalgar Square and the outlying stretches of Whitehall drift by. There were sandbags banked up against the foot of the column and a sentry post or two. The war was only a rumour: distant voices, ghostly knocking heard a long way off, but for a moment he imagined the bombs falling on the square: the lions split apart by thermite; the columns smashed; the bodies in the fountains. It was all the same to him. Or not quite.

On the train, two months ago, the corridors had been full of men in khaki heading south. They seemed to lack curiosity about where they were going, what might be the end of it all. Perhaps being in uniform simply inoculated you against doubts of this kind. Far above the bus the sky was smudging to grey: a line of gulls, like stitching; in the middle distance an aeroplane or two; then, towards the horizon, grotesque protrusions of concrete towers and barrage-balloons. The newspaper someone had left on the seat next to him said KING TO INTERVENE, and he wondered what the King intended to intervene in, and exactly how he went about doing it.

In Westminster Square he lost his bearings, plumped for the wrong entrance, was set right by a policeman, found himself in the end in a kind of vast holding pen talking to a man with a cockade in his hat who seemed not to think very much of him or the vestibule in which they stood. The things he had meant to say and the nonchalance he had brought with him had gone, and he waited by the gate, the man with the cockade in his hat silent and disapproving at his elbow, until a second man, tall and neatly dressed, with a brown-paper parcel under his arm, broke through the crowd around him and said, 'Are you the messenger from Mr Kent?'

'Yes, sir.' He didn't know where the 'sir' came from.

'You'd better have this, then. You know where it has to go?'

'Mr Kent gave me full instructions, sir.' That was better. What a subaltern would say to a senior officer. But it cut no ice.

'Well, make sure it gets to him as soon as possible.'

'Yes, sir,' he said again. Rodney didn't quite know what he wanted. Complicity? The hint of some other life beyond them both? He watched the man disappear into the crowd, with the light burning off the chandeliers onto the tiled floor, and then went out into the street again with the parcel under his elbow and disappointment welling up in him.

He knew that, if he wanted to, he could go and throw the parcel in the river. There was nothing anyone could do about it if he did. But there might be other parcels. He remembered the five-pound note in the cashbox, Mrs McKechnie teetering on her stool by the gunmetal till. Back in Maida Vale, Mr McKechnie would have come down from the flat by now and be mixing himself a glass of Bromo with a teaspoon the same colour as the pewter pots. Among other idiosyncrasies, Mr McKechnie wore a patent-leather truss that was attached to his spine by a complex arrangement of draw-strings. It would be quite possible that Mrs McKechnie would be tightening or loosening these attachments, like an engineer trying to calibrate the workings of a piece of machinery.

Even now, he realised, they were altogether beyond his comprehension. No doubt there were people back home who kept antique shops, who smelled alternately of sarsaparilla and gin, who had too much to drink at lunch-time and mixed themselves glasses of Bromo, who wore patent-leather trusses with black draw-strings, but they were not like the McKechnies. Perhaps this was London's signature mark, that it took mundane patterns of behaviour and made them outlandish, perverted the ordinary into unexpected shapes.

In Trafalgar Square the sky seemed emptier and less ominous, the gulls gone, and the clouds bruising into dusk. Coming up level with the first row of sandbags, he unpinned the poppy from the button-hole of his coat and ostentatiously ground it under his foot.

In the pub in Dean Street, the same pug-faced barmaid in the same floral print dress with the same strand of hair escaping the pins at the side of her head was pouring out three quart pots of stout. The bar was as garishly lit as the Bourne & Hollingsworth shop-front, so that the people sitting at it seemed pale, puny creatures dragged up from the ocean's depths, waterlogged beyond redemption. There was a plaster statuette of an imploring blind boy on the counter next to a collection box, and he put a halfpenny in it, catching a glimpse of his reflection in the silver Guinness ad that ran behind.

Five-thirty and no one much about. Two or three postmen from the sorting depot in Rathbone Street and a couple of tarts dredged out of the Meard Street culverts. He had been here three or four times and thought he was getting to know the clientele. The barmaid, giving the impression that she was engaged on something quite exceptional, that no part of her official duties called for exertions of this kind, finished with the pots of stout and gave a little pout, like an artist's model several hours before the easel, who thinks that her efforts may not have been appreciated. He ordered a half-pint of bitter and went over to the end of the bar, found a saucer full of potato chips which someone had left there and, sitting on a high stool with the parcel on his lap, began to feed them into his mouth one by one.

He had barely eaten half the chips, still with the parcel balanced proudly on his lap, when a woman came striding into the pub through the farther door, moved into the little knot of people gathered about and cut him out of them, like a sheepdog detaching an ewe from the flock. She did this quite matter-of-factly and yet also self-consciously, as if she were taking part in a scene in a film, so that the people next to them fell obediently away, in deference to this new, colonising power, while the props she needed for her performance—the spare stool, the empty space at the bar—sprang dutifully into place.

'You again,' she said. 'Rodney, isn't it? I always seem to see you in here.'

It was the third time he had talked to the woman, or the third time she had talked to him, and he wasn't in the least sure of her, what she was, what she wanted. She was tall and very fair, negligently dressed—tonight she was wearing an old mackintosh and a pair of canvas shoes—but he knew that had she knocked on the front door back home his mother would have straightaway called her 'Madam' on account of her accent.

'Oh, I don't know,' he said. 'I don't come this way so very often.' Half of him wanted the American to arrive and the other half wanted the conversation to go on for as long as the woman wanted it to.

'I expect you have all kinds of things to occupy yourself with, haven't you?' She had a way of picking up whatever he said and making something uneasy out of it. 'In all sorts of places. How are things at the shop?'

He couldn't remember telling her about the shop, but he supposed he must have done. 'Trade's not so good,' he said loftily. 'It's because of the war.'

'Well, that's good for you, isn't it?' she said. She looked extraordinarily like the girls you saw in the toothpaste advertisements or on the covers of magazines: clear-skinned, enticing, stratospherically removed from the world of buses, cindery pavements, and smoky skies that seethed around them. 'Gives you more time to go out delivering things.'

'Who said anything about delivering things?' he wondered. He was fascinated by her and scared at the same time. He had no idea why she spoke in the way she did or what form her interest in him took.

'That's what you do, isn't it?' she said. 'Deliver things. I expect you're on your way to deliver something just this moment.'

'That would be telling,' he said, thinking he could play this game too. He was proud of this conversation, proud of the woman, proud that she had singled him out, eager to be bantered with and—he half suspected—to be made fun of.

'Go on,' she said. 'I don't imagine you come in here just to amuse your-self. I expect you've got far more important things to do. I expect you're off somewhere. Buckingham Palace, is it? The Houses of Parliament? Somewhere else?'

'Don't be silly,' he said, rather sharply. She was about twenty-four or maybe a year or so older, he thought. If you'd put her in a ball gown she would have done for *Film Pictorial*, no question. 'Never been to any of them places. Don't have the inclination.'

'You're very mysterious,' she said. He wondered whether if, as a result of some miracle they were washed up on a desert island wearing loin-cloths and scrabbling for coconuts on the beach, she would still be like this. 'Not so mysterious as all that,' she said. She was sitting on her stool with her feet pointed down, like a dancer about to whirl off round the room. 'Well, it was nice talking to you again, Rodney. I hope you manage to make your delivery.'

'It's my laundry, isn't it?' he said. 'Just fetched it this afternoon.'

'That's right,' she said. 'I'm sure you did.' A moment later she was gone. He could see her in the shadowy doorway, talking to someone who might have been waiting for her.

She was probably a marchioness out slumming. He had read about this in the newspapers. The thought that he might be being trifled with made him feel suddenly exposed, less confident than he had been when he hiked up from Westminster, and he settled the parcel more comfortably on his lap. There were still some potato chips left in the saucer and he began to feed them into his mouth again.

A tall man, fattish and run to seed, came out of the Gents, pudgy fingers buttoning his fly, and rattled over to where he sat. 'Them's my chips,' he said.

Rodney looked up at him, only half interested. The last chip was a quarter-way to his mouth. 'Shouldn't have left 'em there,' he said.

'Them's my chips,' the man said again, exasperated rather than cross. 'You young—'

'Finders keepers,' Rodney said. In an ideal world, he knew, he would have found the man twopence for an extra packet, maybe even conducted the transaction himself. But he was still annoyed about the parcel. He picked up his glass and held it carefully between his fingers.

The fat man was clenching and unclenching his fists. It was nervousness, Rodney thought, not belligerence. 'There's a packet of chips owed,' he said. Some of the bluster had gone out of him now. 'It's only fair.'

'Listen, chum,' Rodney said. He knew that if the fat man came at him he'd shove the glass in the way. 'Catch me being frightened of you. If you want another packet of chips, you can bloody well pay for them.'

The fat man had picked up the empty saucer that had held the chips and was looking at it with a rather sorrowful expression, as if he half thought that by staring at it long enough he might conjure some of them back into existence.

A burly man, alerted by the barmaid, came through a side-door and said, in a placatory way, 'Now then, gents, now then.'

All this the American saw, and seemed to appreciate, as he came into the bar. Seeing instantly that it was the fat man who had to be appeased, he said in a friendly way, 'You'll have to excuse my friend here. It's his impetuous nature. It gets the better of him. What has he done now?'

'Ate my chips while I was in the lavvy,' the fat man said. His wariness suggested that he could not quite believe in the American. 'Every last one of them.'

'Is that so?' the American said. He gave a little sigh that took in the empty saucer, the abraded red skin of the fat man's face, Rodney's half-full glass, gathered them up and re-imagined them so that the bar they stood in was a different place from the one he had sauntered into five minutes before, full of glamour and intrigue. 'Well, I suppose the budget will run to a packet of potato chips.'

But whatever hopes might have been bred up in the fat man's breast were instantly extinguished, for there was no further mention of the potato chips. Instead the American sat down on the stool immediately next to Rodney, propped one of his black Oxfords experimentally against the bar, and said conversationally, 'You'll have to stop behaving like this, you know.'

'How do I have to stop behaving?' The Lancashire stuck in his voice again, like a burr.

'Let's just say you could draw a little less attention to yourself. You kick over the traces on one of my little errands and there'll be the devil to pay.'

The fat man had gone off to talk to the barmaid. Her floral print dress was grubby at the edges, Rodney noticed. He was horribly bored. Outside an air-raid siren started to go off, and then stopped even before the first person said 'False alarm.'

'I got the parcel, didn't I?'

'You surely did. Let me congratulate you on your ability to convey a small book a mile and a half through central London and not get lost in the blackout.'

He could put up with banter. Some of the other boys resented it, which led to difficulties. He said: 'What sort of a book is it?'

The American had made a little tent of his fingers, balanced on his upturned knees, and was moving his thumbs back and forth beneath it. 'Did I say it was a book?'

There were times when the American couldn't resist letting you know how clever he was. It was all the same to Rodney. Cleverness; books in parcels; pilfered potato chips: it was all the same. The bar was beginning to fill up now. A couple of businessmen in brown overcoats. A nancy-boy with a face like a cod-fish. He said: 'A book. That's what you said. Why's he giving you a book?'

'He knows I like reading.'

'Is that what it is, then?'

'Could be. And then, you see, if something ends up inside a foreign embassy it isn't easily taken out again.'

'Is that so?' Rodney was losing interest in the contents of the parcel. There were things summoning him back to Maida Vale. The nancy-boy was feeding pennies into a slot-machine with the same casual intensity Rodney had fed the potato chips into his mouth, but none of the numbers had yet come up. He said, 'Do you want me later on? For the other business?'

The American thought about this. He said, 'I don't know. It all depends. Maybe about ten. Where will you be?'

'At home, I shouldn't wonder. All tucked up.'

'Is there a telephone?'

'What do you think?'

'I'll come and find you.' He had something in the palm of his hand: parti-coloured, not much bigger than a postage stamp. 'See this?'

It was a photograph of a middle-aged man with brilliantined hair and a nose slightly out of proportion to the rest of his face. A joker's face that would have looked better staring out of motley.

'That's the chap, is it?'

'That's him. No, you can't have it. Think you could recognise him?'

'Don't see why not. Friend of yours, is he?'

'Let's just say we have interests in common.'

Rodney liked this sort of talk: ironic, archly insinuating, powdered with meaning that might not be there if you paused to gather it up.

It reminded him of cross-talk comedians on the radio. In Maida Vale the McKechnies would be trading an infinitely debased version of it as they dined off macaroni and cheese and browsed through the sales catalogues. He had once been into the room where they ate their meals: as austere and unornamented as an anchorite's cell.

When he looked up, the American was gone: his exits were rarely as impressive as his entrances. He finished his beer and went out into the street, where half-extinguished headlights glinted in the murk and there were already Christmas decorations in one or two of the shop windows. At the top of Dean Street the German pastry-cooks had a sign up that read ENTIRELY ENGLISH MANAGED AND RUN, and one or two other shops of doubtful ethnicity seemed to have changed their names.

It was about half-past six, and subdued. One lot of people had gone home and the second lot had yet to come out and replace them. Here in the blackout, London was full of wounds: the black gashes in the spaces between the house-fronts were so dark that they seemed to bleed ink. He got his bearings, lit a cigarette, and then headed north, went along Oxford Street and turned into the Edgware Road. Then, not far from Paddington, he turned left into a network of little terraces that ran parallel with Blomfield Road.

Here there was another pub with a saloon bar opening out into the pavement, empty except for a girl of about nineteen in an imitation fox-fur who sat drinking what from the smell of it was a tumblerful of peppermint cordial. When she saw him she gave him a little reproving look, too timid to register genuine annoyance but not wholly enthusiastic.

'If you hadn't come in the next ten minutes, I'd have took myself off.'

'Maybe if you had, I'd have followed you back,' he declared.

'You wouldn't have known where I'd gone,' she said, a bit hopelessly, as if she knew the futility of any kind of resistance.

'I'd have found out. You can always find out. I'd have gone to the shop on the corner and asked them. That's what I'd have done,' he said, catching the reek of peppermint again. 'You can't be drinking that. Have a gin.'

'You won't get any gin here,' she said. 'Nor whisky, neither. Beer house, this is.'

'Beer house, is it? Well, I don't mind.' He took a ten-shilling note out of his pocket and bought two half-pints of stout.

'I'm glad you came, though,' she confided. 'They don't like girls sitting on their own in there. They think they're—tarts.'

'Never you mind about that,' he said. It was an effort for him, this kind of small-talk, but he persevered. 'How'd you get on today?'

'Not as bad as last week, when all that stuff came in.' She worked in a factory that manufactured the silk canopies of parachutes. 'We had one of those pilots round to talk to us. Chap that flew a Hurricane, I think it was.'

He wasn't interested in fighter-pilots. The stout, like the small-talk, was an effort. He wondered how long he would have to stay there, and what might be said. Her hairstyle, *à la* Veronica Lake, had begun to turn in on itself, which made her look faintly crestfallen. She said, a bit suddenly, 'What do you know?'

'What do you mean, what do I know?' He was bored by all this. In the flat over the shop, the McKechnies would be listening to *It's That Man Again* or complaining that the blackout curtains were inadequate.

'Just that. What do you know? I was thinking about it this morning. You have to think of something when you're cutting out the silk, or you'd go mad. All the things I know.'

'And what did you think you knew?'

'Well, I know the English county towns. Norwich, Ipswich, Colchester and so on. Monarchs since 1066. And some French. *Où est la plume de ma tante? Directez-moi à la bibliothèque, s'il-vous plaît?*'

'School stuff,' he said disgustedly. He was thinking about the man whose picture the American had shown him, the white five-pound note in the cash-box under the bed. Two five-pound notes there would be next week, if this went through.

'Not necessarily,' she said, shaking her head in satisfaction. She looked like one of those big, flaxen-haired dolls that might say 'mama' or 'papa' if jabbed in the small of the back. 'What do you know?'

He thought about what he knew. It was not very encouraging, and mostly on the practical side.

'Listen,' he said. 'We can't sit here all night.' He knew there was no proscription at all on them sitting there all night, that lots of people—brewers, publicans—would be delighted for them to do it. 'Why don't we go back to my place? It's not far.'

He was surprised at how readily she agreed. He had not yet quite established what she would and wouldn't do. They went on quickly through the empty streets in the direction of Maida Vale. On the corner of Shelton Road she said, rather hopelessly, as if the complexities of her emotional life were beyond anyone to solve, 'My young man's in the ARP. Down at the centre in Lissom Grove.'

'He'll be freezing to death, then, on a night like this.'

'They work them very hard in the ARP,' she said vaguely. 'There's some nights he doesn't get home till four.'

'It's just this way,' he said. He didn't at all believe in the young man.

The house might have been a medieval fortress abandoned to the plague. There was no one about. In his room she became unexpectedly practical, found the kettle, filled it with water from the basin on the landing and made tea on the gas-ring. Her heels clacked on the bare floorboards next to the door. She gave a little nod at the portrait of Hedy Lamarr, razored out of *Film Fun*, that hung on the door-back: a foot-soldier watching the general pass. All this faintly disconcerted him. He had wanted her to sit on the cane chair while he managed things. It occurred to him that the room, with its dust, its tea-stains, the burnt umber paper that was coming apart from the wall, needed justifying.

'It's not much of a place,' he said.

'It's a room, isn't it?' she said, quite sharply. 'I've to share with my sister. Think about it. You could walk about here with no clothes on and nobody to see.'

'I could do that,' he conceded.

The gas-fire had begun to pulse out heat. With it came the smell that, most of all, reminded him of London: sweet, stuffy, faintly poisonous. It was there when you clambered up to the tops of buses, or in the pleasure boats cruising the Thames: warm, enticing, but calculated to put your teeth on edge. He hung his coat up on the hook behind the door.

'You got a nice landlady?' she asked.

'She's all right,' he said. 'Not the sort to interfere.'

He got the coat and her blouse off without too much difficulty. She sat back in the cane chair and looked absently at the fire, long-limbed and co-operative. Somewhere in the distance a train went by and the windows rattled. A bit later she said: 'You mustn't bite me there. It'll hurt.' There was a chocolate-coloured stain on one of her breasts the size of a threepenny bit.

He felt rather than heard the taxi arriving in the street outside, as if the silence, instead of being broken, had somehow been displaced.

'Christ!'

'What is it?' she asked, half-dreamily, as if wrenched from sleep.

'Errand I got to do.'

'It's a bit late for an errand,' she said. One of her shoulders twitched.

'No helping it, is there?'

As with the tea, she was all practicality again, taking his coat from off the hook and putting back her brassiere all in the same movement. As he made his way downstairs, the stair-rods gleaming in the half-light, he could hear the clink of tea-things.

The American had one foot on the taxi's running-board, one hand readjusting his hat. He saw Rodney's half-buttoned shirt and said, 'Guess I've interrupted you.'

'Maybe I needed interrupting.'

The cab smelled of sweat and upholstery: the second London smell, found in pub snuggeries, cheap offices, and the Warren Street car showrooms. As it moved off, the American said, 'I'll get out at Oxford Circus, but he'll take you on. There's a little club at the far end of Jermyn Street. The Julep. He'll be coming out of it about half-past the hour. That'll give you the chance to introduce yourself.' For the first time ever that Rodney had known him, his eye gave a little shiver of uncertainty, before being gathered up once again in the aura of his self-belief. 'You'll know what to do,' he said, poised halfway between statement and question.

'Sure thing,' Rodney said. He had forgotten about the girl, her breath rising and falling, the chocolate birthmark, the stair-rods' gleam. It was as if they had never existed. The road in front of the taxi was a conveyor belt with the face of the man in the photograph at its end. 'I'll know, all right.'

CHAPTER 4

Sussex by the Sea

The autumn was getting on now, and the beech leaves piled up at the track-side were a shiny copper-brown, like the warming pans you saw hanging up in the inglenooks of rural fireplaces. Thick as autumnal leaves that strow the brooks in Valhombrosa, Cynthia thought, wondering exactly where Valhombrosa was, how you got to it, and why, in the course of a notably patchy education, it had stuck in her head.

The train bored on through the Sussex Weald, past verdure so dense that it seemed faintly unreal, like scenery wheeled up from a dramatic production at some exceptionally well-funded theatre. A wood of giant oaks; a long stretch of overgrown meadow; a cutting choked with bramble bushes: all these passed in quick succession. In the distance, where the road kept disappearing from view, behind these packed embrasures, small cars skidded in and out of range.

Curiously, the sense of unreality persisted—as if, she thought, she was travelling through one of those classical paintings she liked so much, and the next clearing might bring a ruined temple and an ancient greybeard plucking a lyre to entertain a bevy of nymphs. The train, like every train these days, was rather full of people: men in bowler hats with briefcases wedged under their arms; schoolgirls in bright blue uniforms; wide-eyed women with babies on their laps. The station platforms through which they passed were always crowded: half a dozen trains, stopping simultaneously, could not have cleared the freight of humanity that lingered on them. It was a Friday afternoon, and she had got off work by pretending to go to the dentist.

At Arundel, about half the passengers disembarked, and she found herself in the vanguard of a great crowd of people scattering by degrees onto a stone forecourt where gulls tore fish-and-chip wrappers apart and the air was heavy with the smell of sea-salt. The Bannisters' Daimler was drawn up in the car park, but she did not recognise the driver.

'What happened to Eddie?' she asked, as he hauled her luggage into the boot.

'Gone off with his regiment, miss.'

The monogrammed suitcase had been a mistake, she thought. It hinted at a status to which she could never aspire.

'Volunteered, you mean?'

'That's about the strength of it.'

She waited for the second 'miss,' but it never came. That the working classes were using the war as an excuse to get above themselves was one of Mrs Kirkpatrick's most deeply felt beliefs. There would be no half-crown here.

The car bowled on through the outskirts of the town, where children on their way home from school lingered outside corner-shops and aged taxis had been dragged up onto the kerb-side, and on through side-roads fenced in by giant hedges of cow parsley, and she felt a surge of exhilaration, pure nature-worship, that even the thought of Mr and Mrs Bannister could not subdue. Unhappily, Ashburton Grange, which they came upon suddenly seven or eight miles later, seemed to have been expressly designed to quench illusions of this sort.

Looking out of the window, as the Daimler steamed up the hill, Cynthia decided that it was exactly the same: the cars drawn up on the gravel drive; the marbled Venus enthroned above a fountain whose jets had now been turned off; sun glinting in at the mullioned windows. The problem about Ashburton Grange, if you went into it architecturally, was the flamboyant redesign that someone had embarked on at the end of the nineteenth century, which had added an extra storey, topped by a medieval battlement. This gave it a slightly bogus air, as if an American actor, dressed in a hauberk and chain mail, might suddenly appear there and start directing troop movements.

Despite her resolution, she gave the chauffeur one of the half-crowns from her store, and was rewarded with a finger flicked in the direction of his peaked cap. Mrs Bannister, waiting on the top of stone steps to receive her, looked more than ever like a mad terrier. Taken out of the Eastern sun, her complexion had lost its dried-up, curry tint and grown pinker.

'My dear, it's so very good of you to come and see us.' And then, without further preamble: 'When you've taken your things upstairs, I wonder if you'd just mind coming down and stepping into the garden with me, for there's something I very much want to show you.'

What was it that Mrs Bannister wanted to show her? A nudist colony to which they had sub-let part of the grounds? A Bolton Paul Defiant in which Mr Bannister proposed to take to the skies and repel the Nazi invader? Mrs Bannister's vague, milky eyes offered no clue. They went into the house, which was as spacious as ever and clearly doing its best to ignore all thought of war's exigencies, while the chauffeur dealt with the suitcase.

'I shall give you ten minutes,' Mrs Bannister said radiantly as they stood at the foot of the main staircase, with a housemaid standing by to carry on the torch of hospitality, 'and then wait for you by the back door. Rose will show you where everything is.'

All this was very mysterious, but not quite unexpected. Her parents practised similar secrecies and evasions, withholding holiday details until the morning of departure, keeping travel plans in abeyance. These attempts to ginger up appetites that might otherwise be stricken and wither nearly always had a depressing effect. It was the same now. Sitting in her room under the eaves, which looked out over the lawns but was a ten-yard corridor and a cramped staircase away from the bathroom, Cynthia realised that she knew exactly what her hostess had up her sleeve.

Sure enough, when she came downstairs, Mrs Bannister, with a horribly glazed expression on her face, led her blithely to a spot in the garden where, beneath an elm tree, a marble tablet had been sunk into the ground. On it had been chiselled the inscription:

IN MEMORIAM
HENRY MARTINEAU BANNISTER
I MAY 1915–23 JUNE 1939
'THE MEEK SHALL INHERIT THE EARTH'

'I wanted you to see it,' Mrs Bannister said with surprising harshness, as if Cynthia had tried her hardest to stay in the house and had to be dragged out by main force.

'It looks very nice,' Cynthia said. She wondered what she thought about Henry, now four months dead and rotting, and found that she thought nothing at all. She could appreciate the idea of him—Henry the Oxford scholar, a zealous, white-flannelled Henry roaming the dewy cricket-field—but the flesh and blood reality entirely escaped her.

'Really, you know, all in all, I think he had a very happy life,' Mrs Bannister said, again rather fiercely and accusingly, as if she expected Cynthia to deny it. After that they went back indoors and the serious business of the weekend began.

In a modest way, Cynthia was used to country-house parties. She could play peggoty and bezique, and generally put up some kind of show with the other guests. These were not inspiring. There were five weather-beaten middle-aged-to-elderly men who sat with Mr Bannister on the Government back benches, but had for some reason come without their wives, a youngish man with curiously shiny hair, rather as if someone had mixed several grains of lake into a pot of black ink, and two or three girls whose business it was to be ornamental.

The guests were decently friendly—two of the old gentlemen asked to be remembered to her father—but taken as a whole there was something odd about them, the oddity being that they seemed to be in possession of some secret to which she herself had not been made party. It was difficult to put this feeling, which grew stronger during the course of the evening, into words, but there it was: a kind of unobtrusive drawing-up of ranks; a word or two spoken in unintelligible private code: a sense of people waiting for their prompts before they began to speak.

The exception to this rule was the young man with the shiny hair, who came up to her on her first appearance in the drawing room, where two of the ornamental girls were doing a jigsaw, and said: 'You must be Cynthia Kirkpatrick. They said you were coming. Isn't your father Jackie Kirkpatrick?'

She had come across Americans in the East. They had not always been reliable.

'You're very well informed,' she said. An Englishman would have taken this as a rebuke, but he gave a little smile, as if to say that knowing about the alien landscape you had fetched up in did not necessarily mean that you felt any affinity towards it.

'I work at the US Embassy,' he said. 'I suppose it pays us to know things like that. My name's Tyler Kent. Have you met Miss Chamberlain here, and Miss Mackay?'

'I can't say I have.'

She was still thinking about other Americans she had known in the East: desiccated Rotarians who sat in a collapsed state in the lobby of the Galle Face Hotel complaining about the lack of hot water; optimistic consuls ('You see, Miss, er, Kirkpatrick, President Roosevelt is a very capable man'); crapulous engineers on furlough from construction jobs up-country.

'Well, come and say hello then.' Miss Chamberlain and Miss Mackay were still bent over their jigsaw puzzle. 'You know,' he said, a shade less loudly, 'I knew Henry.'

'Did you?'

'Yes indeed. He was a hell of a fellow.'

Henry was everywhere at Ashburton Grange. His ghost came in with the pre-dinner drinks and went out last thing with the cat. There were at least seven photographs of him around the place: Henry, oar to chest, amongst a college rowing eight; in a sub-fusc suit and a scholar's gown outside the Sheldonian; with Mr Bannister on the House of Commons terrace. He looked somehow eager and expectant, as if a great prize hung in the air just a little way off, waiting to be brought down, or, alternatively, a locked door to which, only a little later, he would be given the key.

All this she found she could put up with. There was no menace in photographs and their dead, white faces. It was slightly less easy to put up with Henry's sister Hermione, who had clearly taken upon herself the task of making Cynthia feel at home at Ashburton Grange and in consequence stuck to her like a leech.

She was a plump, nervous girl with an oversized head and bobbed dark hair, of whom Cynthia had heard a certain amount in the past, with a toxic habit of blurting out semi-confidential information and then only half-seeming to regret it, who smoked cigarettes out of an amber holder and talked, rather fixatedly, about men whose relation to her was never wholly clear-cut. But still, Cynthia thought, there were worse people to be conducted around Ashburton Grange by than Hermione.

They ended up in Henry's room, untouched since his death, but not yet quite a shrine, where dust clung to the stack of dumb-bells and hockey-sticks in the corner and there were still two or three unopened letters on the desk.

'Of course,' Hermione said—she was not really *distraite*, but gave a very good impression of being so—'there wasn't any real need for him to go out East with Father. It was just that he wanted to see Ceylon again.'

And Cynthia bowed her head at the rebuke.

On the other hand, it was useful to have Hermione alongside her in the drawing room before dinner, where the press of unfamiliar faces became slightly bewildering.

'That's Lord Lymington, who edits the *Pioneer* . . . The tall old gentleman with the white hair is Mr Galloway. Someone of Father's, I don't know what he does . . . You've seen Ursula Chamberlain, I think. She was supposed to be marrying a man in the Brigade, but then somebody said he had some terrible disease and it was all off . . . The man in the doorway talking to Mr Kent is Captain Ramsay.'

Just before they went in to dinner, Tyler Kent detached himself from one of the ornamental girls and came towards her nodding his head. 'Having a good time?'

'It's not so bad,' she said, not quite seeing why she should be expected to unburden herself. 'How are you getting on with Miss Mackay?'

'Well,' he said, 'I suppose if you don't know anything about breeding gun dogs you're at a certain disadvantage. She's swell, I reckon. Works at one of the Ministries. I may run into her there sometime. What are you doing with yourself right now?'

And so she explained about the Bloomsbury square, and Desmond, and the sound of the dentist performing extractions in the room above.

'*Duration*,' he said. 'I think I've heard of that. Not quite the kind of thing we have in the States. Back home there's nothing between the *New Yorker* and the college reviews.'

He would have been about twenty-eight, she thought, and had an irritating habit of looking sideways at other people while he was talking to you.

'We ought to have a drink sometime,' he said. 'That is—if you're free.'

She was not impressed. 'It's awfully kind of you, but I'm rather busy in the evenings.'

'I'll ring you up at the office,' he said. 'Nice chance to talk to Desmond, too.'

How did he know Desmond, she wondered? The intricacies of London life were still a mystery to her: invisible cords that bound the unlikeliest of collaborators. Hermione, who had a bandeau pulled low over her spacious forehead, was smoking another cigarette through her amber holder and seemed slightly drunk. She said: 'Do you know, I was engaged to Cecil Beasant once? But we couldn't get on, we really couldn't. And they say it nearly broke his mother's heart.' After that, they went in to dinner.

No hint of war's privations had come to the Ashburton kitchen. They ate Colchester oysters, capons, a saddle of mutton, devils on horseback. The light from the chandeliers burned off the silver epergne and the butler's bald head. Outside, the garden was dim and blue in the moonlight, and she thought of the evening she had spent staring out of the window at the villa in Colombo. It seemed an eternity away. Meanwhile, there were several breezy conversations to attend to.

'. . . I mean, once you take away the fact of their invading Poland, and the bad faith, the whole thing simply becomes meaningless.'

'. . . Nobody grudges Germany *Lebensraum*, provided *Lebensraum* doesn't become the grave of another nation.'

'. . . That's right. What we need is a just colonial settlement. *Just*, mind you.'

'. . . If we're going to have a negotiated settlement, which we certainly will have to fairly soon, why can't we have it now, before any real damage has been done?'

'. . . I must say, the King's been absolutely first-rate. At least everyone knows where *he* stands.'

'. . . The mistake was to let Hitler make that alliance with the Russians. It was all Halifax's fault for going round saying the Nazis were really Bismarcks in disguise.'

There were owls outside in the garden and she could hear them swooping against the window. Tyler Kent, she saw, was looking keenly on, but with a slight smile on his face, as if he could take it or leave it.

'. . . It would be a great deal easier if everyone admitted that this is a Jew's war.'

'. . . Why is it a Jew's war, Jock old boy?'

'. . . Did you know that of the fifty-nine members of the Central Council of the Communist Party of the Soviet Union in 1935, fifty-six were Jews and the others were married to Jews? It's all in Father Fahey's book.'

'. . . Of course, Hitler must have had his reasons for what he's done.'

'. . . I've *met* Hitler. He's a reasonable man. Not at all a fanatic. Some of his speeches are strong stuff, I grant you.'

'. . . It's a shame they couldn't be got to amend the Companies Act. After all, once you know who a newspaper's shareholders are, then that's half your problem solved.'

There was something faintly conspiratorial about all this, the sense of things being said that, in other company, would have remained unspoken. It was like Jacobites toasting the health of the King across the water while outside, amid lofted torches, Protestant mobs went stamping down the street. Afterwards they went back to the drawing-room where Mr Bannister, with a dazzling lack of self-consciousness, sang in a faux-cockney accent a song called 'I'm a Man Who's Been Done Wrong by my Parents.' Outside, there were dense pockets of shadow on the lawn and the darkness welled up like ink.

Tyler Kent caught her eye and nodded.

Waking up just after dawn and standing by the window, where some unfathomable impulse had drawn her, she saw a man's figure beneath a tree, smoking a cigarette, and it occurred to her that it might be Kent, but there were streaks of mist flying in from the sea, ghostly and striated in the pale light, and within a moment or two whoever it was—Tyler, Captain Ramsay making a votive offering to the destroyer-of-all-Jews, or some other person quite unknown to her—had disappeared.

In the morning things improved. The mist blew away to the east and the sun came out. It was a hot day and Mr Bannister, in a tweed suit and hob-nailed golfing brogues that raised sparks off the concrete floor, conducted her on a tour of the stables and the outhouses where the dogs were kept. The dogs were of various kinds: an Irish wolfhound; a sickly spaniel; a pair of corgis. They were pleased to see Mr Bannister, and he them.

'Of course, the best kind of dogs have an *instinct*, don't you think?' he said. 'Why, I remember when my aunt was ill—bedridden, you know, but expected to recover—and then one morning we noticed that the corgi who'd been lying on her mattress had taken itself off to the fireplace. And would you credit it, within another half-hour she was dead?'

'Yes,' Cynthia heard herself saying. 'Yes, yes.' The sun burned against her forearms and the frock she had put on that morning seemed unaccountably heavy.

By lunch-time it was so hot that Mrs Bannister proposed an excursion. They could go down to the sea, she suggested, stay out until such time as the light lasted, and be back well before dinner. From her vantage point in the corner of the drawing room, next to a green baize table at which two of the ornamental girls sat conjuring a second jigsaw—they were indefatigable, these girls—Cynthia could not imagine that this idea would be taken seriously. But she had forgotten the exacting protocols of the country-house weekend.

Three quarters of the party said they would go. An ancient Rolls-Royce shooting brake was routed out of one of the garages, and presently a small convoy of miscellaneous vehicles set off along the pot-holed cinder track that led down, through gently descending meadows and hedges still patterned with loosestrife, towards the beach. Without in the least stage-managing the business, Cynthia found herself in the shooting brake with

Tyler Kent, Captain Ramsay, and the ornamental girls—she could not remember which was Miss Chamberlain and which Miss Mackay—and a quiet man whom she had first mistaken for somebody's valet.

Captain Ramsay, who was tall and supercilious-seeming, but at the same time not wholly correct, as if he might be about to fish a pack of cards out of his pocket and suggest a hand at nap, was still wearing his suit. On the other hand, Tyler Kent, with whom he was deep in conversation, wore a golfing jersey and a pair of highly inauthentic plus-fours with an orange check. The ornamental girls, who had clearly taken maternal advice, were swathed in jumpers and sensible shoes.

It was about three o'clock and bright for the season, so that the glow of the sunlight off the banks of fallen leaves seemed almost unhealthy, and the trunks of the elm trees had turned a sickly, disease-ridden green. Several fields away, but narrowly visible over the succession of low stone walls, a hunt was in progress, and she watched the individual chips of colour rising and falling over the impediments placed in their way so intensely that in the end they seemed to merge into a single, sinuous blur moving like a wave into the distance. This fascinated her so much that she forgot about Captain Ramsay, and Tyler Kent's plus-fours, and the two girls who had begun to discuss somebody or other's coming-out ball that had been cancelled on account of the war, and carried on staring into the space occupied by the hunt long after it had disappeared.

And so, by degrees, with the fields gradually giving way to a kind of ragged headland, strewn with marram grass, and the road barrelling down between high steps cut into the chalk, they came eventually to the sea.

The beach was so like every other beach that Cynthia had ever seen in the English southern counties that she lost interest in it from the outset. In Ceylon there would have been coconut palms, white sand, and the blue-brown froth of the Indian Ocean. Here there was twenty feet or so of gravel, some angry waves greenish at the peak and the colour of gravy below, and vast amounts of seaweed flung capriciously among the driftwood. All this was so familiar to her that she half-expected to see Mr and Mrs Kirkpatrick emerge stealthily from behind a rock and start putting up deck-chairs.

Amoeba-like when it arrived at the beach, the party now divided into half a dozen distinct and self-sufficient cells. Mr Bannister and Captain Ramsay went and established themselves on an outcrop of rock that was relatively free from sand. Tyler Kent, the light glinting so dramatically off the checks in his plus-fours that he looked rather like an abstract painting, threw stones into a tin can for the amusement of the ornamental girls. The quiet man whom she had mistaken for somebody's valet produced a copy of *Pip: A Romance of Youth*, sat down on a spar of driftwood, and began to read.

Not wanting to seem put out by her detachment from these groups, and determined to make it look as if what she was doing was her own special plan, designed to give her the maximum possible satisfaction, Cynthia stood examining the flotsam of the shore for a moment, in which, as usual, strings of onions predominated, and then went over to a spot a few yards away from Captain Ramsay and Mr Bannister, arranged her cardigan on the pebbles, and lay down on it, one hand shading her eyes from the sun.

Here at ground level it was more agreeable than she had expected. The noise of the sea was faintly soporific. The regular *plink-plunk* of Tyler Kent's pebbles against the tin can—he was a surprisingly good shot—worked in rhythmic counterpoint. She thought that, really, she was enjoying herself, while remaining darkly suspicious that the source of this enjoyment would soon be taken away.

Everything was in flux: no pattern prevailed. First she had been in the East and then, wholly unexpectedly, all that had come to an end. Then there had been the boat-ride back from one world into another. Now there was England, England and the war. There had been scarcely any military news for a week or more—a ship sunk off Norway, desultory manoeuvrings behind the Maginot Line—and everyone said that the King was urging peace. But soon, she knew, another unstoppable tide would hurtle down and smash the world into fragments. She remembered the French letter falling *slap* onto the temple floor and thought that in some ways even Henry would have been preferable to all this.

Tyler Kent had stopped throwing pebbles against the tin can now. Instead he and the girls had gone off to explore a rock pool. Their shrieks of amusement sounded horribly thin. She could have done better than that. On the other hand, she thought, why put yourself out for a man from the American Embassy who wore orange-check plus-fours? For some reason the beach still seemed haunted by the ghosts of her parents. She could see her father sitting in one of the deck-chairs with his trousers rolled up to expose his spindly calves, and she could see Mrs Kirkpatrick brewing tea on the portable Bunsen burner that someone had given her as a wedding present. Picnic baskets, supernumerary newspapers, coffee flasks, and copies of tide tables lay at their feet. Oppressed by this vision, she turned over on her side and fell three-quarters asleep.

When she woke up, from another dream about the East in which cinnamon gardens alternated with flowers gleaming in the moonlight and Henry's face reflected out of a car's windscreen, great stretches of time seemed to have passed. But a glance at her watch told her that only a quarter of an hour had gone by. If anything it was even hotter than before.

Tyler Kent and the girls had given up the rock pool and were prospecting along the beach's further end. Hermione, who had come in one of the other cars, now heaved into view thirty or forty yards away with a bulky object under her arm. This transformed into an easel and a collapsible chair, which she now erected on the sand. At a distance her head looked even more disproportionate to the rest of her body, like a pumpkin or a grotesquely enlarged horse chestnut. Nearer at hand, Mr Bannister and Captain Ramsay were still talking earnestly. For some reason the noise of the sea was quieter now and she found that she could hear what they were saying.

'I had that fellow Burdett round to see me at the House,' Captain Ramsay said.

'Burdett!' She could not tell whether Mr Bannister thought this the best joke ever coined, or the greatest piece of effrontery. 'What on earth did he want?'

'Oh, fishing, you know,' Captain Ramsay said. 'I need hardly tell you that a worse angler never existed.'

'What did you tell him?'

'I said that Halifax had the greatest confidence in what we were about.'

'Not strictly true, I'm afraid.'

'Well, perhaps not. But how is Burdett to know?'

For the first time in the conversation, Mr Bannister seemed faintly irritated. 'There'll be plenty of people in the Foreign Office to tell him.'

'Perhaps there will. And there are friends of Mr Burdett's to tell people things too. How was it that Joyce slipped off to Berlin in August?'

'I never had anything to do with Joyce, you know.'

'Neither did I. But someone who knew which way the wind was blowing told him to get out.'

'And now he's on Berlin radio three nights a week. Never mind what you said to Burdett. What did Halifax say when you saw him?'

'Well, he was affable, I'll give him that. As affable as Butler, almost. I mean, he practically said that an acceptable settlement needn't involve restoring Czechoslovakia or giving Danzig and the Corridor back to Poland.'

'Well, if that's the case why are we still committed to war? All very well to talk about official channels. What we need are a few unofficial ones.'

'Did you sound out that man in the embassy at Brussels?'

'Well, it's all very difficult. He says the Faction isn't exactly in the best of odours over there. All those memories of gallant little Belgium a quarter of a century ago, you understand.'

Much of this was horribly cryptic, like a crossword puzzle which only die-hard readers of the newspaper could be expected to solve. But without requiring any particular mental effort on her part, two links in a tiny chain of causation snapped together. Norman Burdett and the Faction. The latter, she realised, was something to do with the King's Party that people sometimes talked about.

At the same time, it was clearly something more than the King's Party, for Norman Burdett and his cloak-and-dagger show were taking an interest in it. There had been an article in one of the papers recently about the 'Tory defeatists.' And now here she was spending her weekend in a nest of them. Did that make her a Tory defeatist? Or any kind of defeatist? Abruptly, she raised her head. The voices did not stop, but she was aware that Captain Ramsay instantly gave up the topic of the embassy at Brussels for a hot speech that his wife had given to the Arbroath Businessmen's Club.

It was about four o'clock and the warmth was starting to go out of the day. There was no sign of Hermione, and as the easel lay tenantless on its stretch of sand, she decided to take a look at it. Halfway along the beach, with the green-grey water boiling about at her feet, she came across Tyler Kent walking the other way.

'Where are your friends?' she wondered.

'They went back to the car. Said it was too cold.' The sea-water had got into the bottoms of his plus-fours, she noticed, and he looked just a little less jolly. 'I say,' he went on, half-humorously, 'you never told me Miss Chamberlain was a *dook*.'

He had to say the word twice before she understood.

'What do you mean? A woman can't be a duke.'

'Well, an earl's daughter, then. All this time I've been calling her Miss Chamberlain, and it turns out she's the Lady Ursula Chamberlain.'

'I expect she was too polite to say.'

'Well, she wasn't too polite to tell me in the end.' She wondered exactly what he had said to Lady Ursula Chamberlain, and what kind of reception he had got in return. Having got this social solecism off his chest, he brightened up. 'I suppose we ought to take a look at Hermione's painting now that we're here.'

Along the horizon there were cargo ships, moving in Indian file, at least a dozen of them, remote and insubstantial, as if made out of balsa wood. Mr Bannister and Captain Ramsay were getting to their feet. Together Cynthia and Tyler Kent inspected the sheet of cartridge paper, each corner secured with an outsize clothes-peg, that Hermione had left on the easel. As might have been expected, it offered a vista of choppy waves and lowering cloud, but superimposed was a kind of vortex of wind, debris, and flailing black birds.

'Not so good, I guess,' Tyler Kent said. He sounded slightly disappointed, as if he had hoped to write an article in a weekly magazine proclaiming the discovery of a limitless new talent, only to have the cup dashed from his lips.

'No,' Cynthia agreed. She had decisive opinions about art. 'Not so good.'

'Now, Lady Ursula,' Tyler Kent said, clearly wanting to get back onto softer ground, 'designs—I guess you'd call them *boutonnières*, out of beech-nut clusters.'

This was so preposterous that Cynthia almost laughed. Instead she said: 'What do you do at the American Embassy?'

'What kind of question is that?'

She had a feeling that this was meant to be a rebuke, if not quite in the same class as the one clearly administered by Lady Ursula over her title. But she had never allowed herself to be intimidated by Americans.

'Quite an ordinary one, I should think. I thought men liked to be asked about their jobs. Most people do.'

'I guess that's so,' he said, a bit uncertainly, as if the idea had only just occurred to him. 'Well, part of the time people come and ask me questions, and part of the time I go and ask them questions.'

They could see Hermione labouring up the beach towards them. She was wearing one of her furious, dishevelled looks, and her distress seemed to grow more acute as she drew level with the easel.

'I suppose you've been looking at my awful picture,' she said bitterly.

There was a difficulty in replying to this. If Hermione was so convinced that the picture was awful, would she want anyone disagreeing with her? On the other hand, confirming her judgement might make her more miserable still. Tyler Kent seemed to have lost interest both in the picture and its creator. He said,

'It's not so bad.'

'I like the birds,' Cynthia offered. 'As if they were caught up in a tornado or something.'

Unexpectedly, this turned out to be the right thing to say. Hermione instantly brightened up. 'Yes, they're not bad, are they? Henry always used to say I could paint birds by the flock.'

So there was Henry again, bouncing up from the bracken where he had lain concealed. They wandered back to the cars, where the rest of the party had begun to assemble. It was definitely cooler now, and the light was breaking up into blood-red streaks. The rest of the sky was violet-coloured. No one had anything of any interest to report, except that one of the ornamental girls had overturned on the edge of a rock pool and grazed her knee. There was a faint smell of brine.

Staring out of the window as they trundled back—uphill, with the shooting brake's gears grinding like giants' teeth—she was startled to find the landscape completely transformed. With the light taken out of them, the trees dwindled into nothing. The fields turned grey and anonymous.

Here and there birds foraged over the stubble. Captain Ramsay, who seemed to be observing all this keenly, said, 'This reminds me of that poem of Lang's. You know the one.

> *Bring me here, Life's tired-out guest,*
> *To the blest*
> *Bed that waits the weary rover,—*
> *Here should failure be confest;*
> *Ends my quest,*
> *Where the wide-winged hawk doth hover!'*

And Cynthia thought: *So he is human after all.* The rest of the journey passed in silence.

Curiously, the rest of the weekend brought two more surprises.

The first was the discovery, outside her bedroom door, quite early the next morning, of a solitary red rose in a china pot. The rose had clearly come from the Ashburton hot-house, but there was no clue as to who had left it there. The second came when, looking through an ancient photograph album with Hermione, she discovered that a tiny figure on the edge of a tennis party, with shingled hair gathered up under a cloche hat, was her mother. For some reason she did not draw this fact to Hermione's attention, but said merely, 'How long have our parents known each other?'

'Oh, I don't know,' Hermione said. She was in a better mood, and trying to secure the edges of a photograph taken of her at a dance, which had been so over-exposed that the man she was standing next to looked as if his head had been blown off. 'Forever, I should think. Wasn't your mother brought out at the same time as mine? Just be an angel, would you, and give me that packet of corners.'

And then, all of a sudden, it was Sunday afternoon and, quite gravid with all the food she had eaten, she was standing on the front steps saying goodbye to the Bannisters and hearing them insist that she should come and see them again. That was three people who wanted to see her, she thought grimly to herself: first Tyler Kent and now Mr and Mrs Bannister.

Then, quite unexpectedly, just as the Bannisters' Daimler turned in the drive, there was a fourth, for Hermione came bouncing out of the house, caught her in a grip that was more tense than affectionate, and said, all in a rush: 'It's been so *nice* having you. Father didn't want you, you know, but I said we must. And guess what? I shall be staying in Bruton Street next month. Mother's said I can go to classes at the Tate. So we shall have to have lunch and things.'

Two minutes later the car swung out of the drive in the direction of Arundel Station. It was the same chauffeur, but this time she kept her half-crowns to herself.

When she got back to Bayswater, it was to discover that Mr Kirkpatrick had suffered a slight stroke. He had been getting out of the bath, begun to dry himself, and then found his left leg frozen to the bath mat. Mrs Kirkpatrick's discomfiture at finding him there, some minutes later, could only be imagined. She had decided not to telephone to the Bannisters on the grounds of 'not wanting Cynthia to be alarmed.'

Though appalled and disgusted by illness, Mrs Kirkpatrick was a practised comforter of the sick. She brought soup bowls of beef tea and administered it to her husband—now confined to bed but talkative—spoonful by spoonful.

CHAPTER 5

Beverley Nichols's Diary I

18 October 1939

Woke up at 6 A.M.—alone, mercifully—in one of those dreadful hotels around the back of Victoria Station. All unspeakably sordid: literally cockroaches in the bath and Levantine-looking gentlemen gossiping on the staircase. Breakfast brought in by, of all people, a coal-black Negro who looked as if he had just escaped from one of Cochran's revues. Left as soon as I decently could (why does one do these things?) and took a cab back to Hampstead, where I slunk into the house trying to avoid Gaskin's wintry eye. On these occasions Gaskin always looks exactly like the butler in the *Punch* cartoon, who, on being told by a rough-looking man that the revolution has arrived, tells him to take it round to the tradesman's entrance.

Morning papers all wondering why there is so little war news. Well, I could tell them that. It is because no one, apart from a few belligerent old men in the Cabinet, actually *wants* a war. For some reason this fact has not yet impressed itself on the newspapers.

Was just telling myself that I would never go anywhere near that hotel in Victoria again, and certainly not with *x*, when Gaskin came in, looking much less disapproving, to say that Captain Ramsay had called, and would I care to telephone him at the House. This is all a consequence of my article in the *Chronicle* last Sunday saying that our war aims should not be victory at any cost but peace at almost any price.

Ramsay not there when I telephoned, but made an appointment to see him this afternoon. Then, thinking that life must go on, even if we are engaged in a futile and unnecessary conflict, I made some notes for the India book, which Cape says he wants to bring out next year—that is, if there are any shops left to sell books, and any people left to buy them. A report in the *Telegraph* that Mosley has had dinner with the King. Don't believe this for a moment, knowing Tom, or indeed HM, but interested to see. Then, in mid-morning post, an income tax demand for £982. This is simply outrageous—it is all to pay for charabancs for ugly little children who ought to be compelled to walk to school, and I shall write and tell them so.

Later. To see Ramsay at the House. All very mysterious—great show of fastening his office door, telling clerk he must not be disturbed, &c.—but I suppose a little secrecy is necessary in the circumstances. We were interrupted several times by telephone calls which he said he simply *must* take. Ramsay a tall, courteous, rather stammering man, with that nervous look one knows so well (he was badly wounded in the war, I think). Rather a professional Old Etonian—a card from the Eton–Harrow match still on the desk, tho' the match was played three months ago, Rambler tie, &c.— but mercifully not in the way Victor Cazalet is, always going on about 'm' tutor' and the wretched Wall Game. Said he had read the *Chronicle* article, hoped there would be others like it, believed I could make myself 'very useful' if I cared to. I said, what I firmly believe, that for ten years I have been obsessed with the idea of war, and the only really unselfish work I did in my life was in the cause of peace. Now all that is shattered, and there is a temptation to think it is shattered forever.

Ramsay, who seems very well informed, knew about this. Said: 'You see, we have had you in our sights for some time, Mr Nichols.' Nice to be esteemed in this way, of course, but flatter myself that it is really only one's due. After all, one was making these points in 1930, when everyone else was dashing around in fancy dress to 'smart' parties.

As for Ramsay's scheme, it is *exactly* as I had imagined, which is to canvass sympathisers in all walks of life—parliament, the army, the civil service—and report back to Ramsay's committee, with the aim of bringing about a negotiated peace. There are apparently several hundred of them. Ramsay says he has signed up nearly a hundred Conservative MPs, and also one or two Socialists, which I rather doubt. Also that 'Ironside is with us'—impressive if true, Ironside being Chief of the Imperial General Staff. 'What about the King?' I asked, this being the one topic that everyone has been talking about for the past month. The King was a difficulty, Ramsay said. Naturally opposed to the war (apparently he sent a telegram to Berlin as late as the 24th of August!) but terrified of exceeding his constitutional powers. Would not see Ramsay, or anyone associated with him, even in private.

Much talk of 'Tom' Mosley and the Viscount Lymington—an unbalanced little man who left the Tory Party to found some obscure ginger group—which made me wonder if the whole business was simply a magnet for cranks. Ramsay seemed aware of this danger. Said he could not be held personally responsible for everything done in his name: one had to trust people's judgement. Stressed the need for absolute discretion: believes the Secret Services are listening to his telephone. Asked: would I be able to attend meetings and if necessary report on them? I said I should be delighted to do this. And undertake liaison work? I said I would do this too. He had seen the newspaper report about Mosley dining with the King. It was all lies, he said. 'The King never dines with anyone.' In fact I know two or three people the King has dined with recently, but merely smiled and nodded agreement.

Back at Hampstead I decided to cover myself by ringing up Victor and getting his opinion of Ramsay. Victor surprisingly non-committal. Said Ramsay loyal, patriotic, and unquestionably sincere. Had done nothing much in the House—a place on the Scottish Food Board the limit of his ambition—but that everyone liked him. Was almost deranged about the Jews, though, and thought that they made up most of the Soviet politburo.

Activities on behalf of the 'Faction' (Ramsay did not use this word, but apparently that is how his organisation is referred to) well known in the House, and regarded with varying degrees of suspicion/amusement/ respect.

I asked Victor point-blank: was he involved? He said no, he had no objection to Ramsay wanting peace, but had worked with him over the United Christian Front business (I dimly remember this—something to do with a free-thinkers' conference that Ramsay opposed) and didn't wish to repeat the experience. Plus there was a danger of the whole thing getting out of hand. People always say this, I notice, whenever anyone looks as if they may genuinely do something. Anyway, wrote to Ramsay saying I had the highest opinion of the work he was trying to do and placed myself unreservedly at his disposal.

Later. Dinner with Mary Ridgely Carter at 41 Portman Square. A rather tiresome American who is apparently in love with me. She had collected the Duke of Marlborough, Lady Cummings, and Mrs Spencer Elmleigh. Talk, inevitably, about the war. Lady Cummings said her son, serving in the Fleet Air Arm, reported great dissatisfaction among the men, belief that the whole thing could have been avoided, &c. This confirms my conviction that Ramsay is absolutely right in what he is doing.

Came back to find letter from *x* asking for £10 by return of post 'to be going on with,' whatever that may mean, and containing insinuations amounting to blackmail. Really! When one thinks of all one has done for him, picking him almost from the street and showering him with expensive presents, not to mention overlooking several little failings that a more fastidious man might have complained about, this kind of treatment beggars belief.

24 October 1939

Found a solitary grey hair just above my right temple. I expect it is all the worry I have been subject to recently, not least with *x*. Shocking to think that one is 41. It seems only yesterday that Willie Maugham was twitting me with being a 'coming young man.' No word from Ramsay. I expect he is 'taking soundings,' as the saying goes. In this case, I suppose, going to White's and asking the men sitting on the fender 'Do you know Beverley Nichols?'

Let us hope they say nice things!

Later. Trouble with Drawbell over my *Chronicle* article. Wanted to write a piece saying that the only honourable thing the Government can do is to call for a negotiated settlement, but Drawbell said he didn't think the readers would stand for it. Of course, he goes to stay at Chartwell so I expect that Winston has interfered, in that infuriating way of his. In the end I decided to write about Stokes, that nice Labour MP, and his Peace Aims Group, which went down well.

Somebody who knows Chamberlain says that of the 2,900 letters received by Downing Street, more than three-quarters were in favour of stopping the war. Of course, no newspaper will print this information.

Distressed to see in *The Times* a photograph of Chantleigh Hall, where I used to stay with Jimmy Chantleigh, now being requisitioned for a training camp or some other abomination. I knew those 'stately homes' and although they weren't my cup of tea I think they played a part in civilising the world, and they had their moments of beauty. And now the shutters are drawn, the music is silenced, and the lovely lawns are ploughed up to grow potatoes. It is all desperately sad.

27 October 1939

Still no word from Ramsay. I expect he has been busy in the House. There was a report in *The Times* today of his asking in Parliament whether the Home Secretary was aware that a street orator at Finsbury Park who stated that this was a capitalists' war was not arrested by the police, whereas another speaker nearby, who declared that it was a Jewish financiers' war, was taken into custody.

Talked some more to Victor about R. He said—something I did not know—that he has a son in the army, so there can be no question about his patriotism.

Everything is very quiet. The literary world quite dead, of course. I daresay that if Hugh Walpole arrived at his publishers with a new manuscript under his arm he would be turned away. All 'the writers' are scrabbling for jobs in government ministries. Well, let them scrabble! Desmond Rafferty, whom I saw in Piccadilly, has started a new magazine, to be called *Duration*. I expect it will be full of photographs of abstract painting and bad poetry.

For some reason I found myself thinking of all the time I had spent in Germany. Berlin in 1936 with Peter K., sunbathing with Hans that day at Wannsee and watching the Games from the press seats, which happened to be directly behind the Führer's box. It seems an eternity away, like medieval knights at a joust. And now when everything is blown to pieces we are still blaming other people for something which is fundamentally our fault. It is simply no use, for example, pretending that the Versailles Treaty wasn't thoroughly unfair, or that if Britain, with the resources of the Empire behind her, could not solve her problems and raise the spirits of her people in the way that Germany has, there isn't something inherently wrong with our system.

The essential problem about Hitler, surely—whatever one thinks about him privately—is that he feels he has been badly treated.

Another letter from *x* saying that, after careful consideration, he intends to 'do his bit against Fascism' and join the Merchant Navy. This was so preposterous that I forbore to reply.

29 October 1939

Ramsay writes, apologising profusely for the short notice, and asking would I care to come to a meeting in South Kensington tonight to discuss what he called 'a matter of grave national interest'? I telegraphed instantly to say that I would go—or rather sent Gaskin to do so—spent the afternoon writing my *Chronicle* article (as critical of Winston/Admiralty as I could make it) and then hurried off in a taxi to the address Ramsay had given, rather intrigued as to what I might find.

Private house in Onslow Square; butler to open the door; about 20 persons present, one or two of them rather picturesque. Admiral Domvile I recognised from his picture in the papers. Bryant, the historian, one has come across from time to time. Lady Pearson, who is, I think, the BUF candidate for Canterbury. An extraordinary woman who calls herself

'Commandant Allen'—Commandant of what, I wonder?—tiny, mannish, and dressed in a severe black uniform, of whom Ramsay spoke with the greatest respect. Ramsay's intimates, I note, refer to him as 'Jock.' Two full colonels in service dress.

Ramsay explained that the meeting's purpose was to co-ordinate activities of various groups opposed to the war which had been driven more or less underground. Some of these one had heard of—Nordic League, the Link, &c.—others deeply obscure. Air of fanaticism inevitable at such gatherings, I suppose, but struck by anti-Semitic feeling. A speech by A. K. Chesterton to the Nordic League, which proposed that using the lamp-posts was the only way to deal with the Jews, quoted several times.

All this intensely depressing. Indeed, apart from the resentment, one might have been at a meeting of a rural district council. Reassured, though, by conversation with Domvile. Small, rather supercilious little man. Says he is in constant touch with the War Cabinet (through whom, I wonder?) which is hopelessly divided—one half wanting to fight, the other ready to parley. Also that there is a definite attempt on the part of the Germans to bring forward peace proposals. This is to be done through embassy in Dublin, the offer then being conveyed to Halifax.

I suppose I must have seemed sceptical, for Domvile grinned at me—he looks exactly like Mr Punch on these occasions—and said: 'I assure you, Mr Nichols, that these negotiations are being conducted at the highest level.' It occurred to me that a meeting of this kind might very well be subject to some kind of official surveillance. Mentioned this to Domvile, who said they had two or three very reliable 'men' in Jermyn Street who kept them abreast of developments.

As ever on occasions of this kind, scarcely anything decided. I was left with a confused impression of old ladies arguing. Ramsay surprisingly tolerant of all this. Went home thinking that if I was to be of any use, it would not be by attending meetings in South Kensington. Item on the evening news saying that Expeditionary army to be reinforced by further 50,000 men. Interestingly, Domvile had told me about this. A last-ditch effort by Churchill and co. in the War Cabinet to impose their views? We shall see.

31 October 1939

Several newspapers carrying photographs of the King inspecting troops. Does *not* look well: thin, desiccated, and the rather startled boyishness that served him so well in youth now makes him seem petulant. To make matters worse, the troops he was reviewing were all Grenadiers at least six inches taller than himself. Victor said he had a blazing row with Chamberlain over the conduct of the war last week, complains that he is not kept informed, critical of at least half the War Cabinet, thinks Ironside manifestly unsuitable, &c.

Rather a shock to think that one has been reading about, I should say the King, but it is very hard to get out of the habit of calling him the Prince these past twenty years. I have a memory of him, in a tail-coat and decorations, ascending a great staircase in Mayfair and then shaking hands with Maurice Baring and Diana Cooper who came to greet him at the top. And then staying with Sir Sidney Greville at St James's Palace—this must have been in 1921—he seemed to be constantly on the telephone. Could do nothing, apparently, without consulting his comptroller. When should he wear a dinner jacket as opposed to tails? Could he be seen in an open car without a hat? Who should be placed next to whom at dinner? What he needed, of course, and never got, was a male friend he could trust and who would stand up to him. This paragon never presenting itself, he was easy prey for Lady Furness, the dreadful late Mrs S, &c.

Incidentally, Victor says he has it on good authority that Mrs S did not die of heart failure, but was poisoned—with Baldwin's connivance—by her surgeon. I must confess that when I heard this I laughed out loud. On the other hand, Mrs S's death, coming when it did, extraordinarily convenient. Victor told me that had she lived another month, he might already have abdicated, which would have put the cat truly among the constitutional pigeons.

1 November 1939

The British Expeditionary Force has apparently marched ten miles in the direction of the Maginot Line, and then turned on its tail and marched back again. I ask you!

Dinner at Catherine D'Erlanger's house in Piccadilly. All quite unchanged. The same bald-headed butler with the quivering hand. The same night light dripping wax over the exquisite Louis XV table, spoiling the veneer. Also there Peter Churchill, Barbara Back, H. G. Wells and his lady-love Baroness Budberg. Wells, who has never liked me, asked rather sneeringly what I was doing in the way of war-work. I said I was trying to keep up everyone's morale.

Talk hopelessly nostalgic: Le Touquet; Cap Ferrat; Hartnell's parties; coming back across the Atlantic on one of the ten-day boats. Remembered the conversation I had with Elsa Maxwell three months ago on the terrace at Cannes, with the lights suddenly going out, and it seeming like an omen, and Elsa's questions ('Do you remember Max Reinhardt's parties at Salzburg? Do you remember the Lido? And the parties at Constance Toulmin's palazzo on the Grand Canal?') and almost wept at the pity of it all.

At dinner put next to a youngish man from the American Embassy named Kent. Not at all the kind of American one usually meets in England: intensely gentlemanly, well-cut suit, waistcoat, and watch chain, appears to actually like wine instead of pretending to like it. I asked him what they think about the war in Grosvenor Square, and he said 'the old man' (Kennedy) is pessimistic, thinks we shall lose. Struck by the extremely large number of names of well-connected people one has met that he contrived to drop into his conversation without the least self-consciousness. Seems to have a finger in a great many pies.

Gradually it came out—I think I must have said something about the meeting in Kensington and unwittingly declared myself a sympathiser—that he knew Ramsay. The Embassy knows all about the Faction and is generally supportive. Says that Ramsay has all the members' and sympathisers' names written down in a locked ledger, and that this is occasionally given to Kent for transfer to Embassy on the grounds of diplomatic immunity, Ramsay being fearful that the Secret Services will try to abstract it. Asked whose names appeared in it (my own, for example?) but he maintains that he has never seen it unfastened. All this said quite openly while Catherine talked about Syrie Maugham not three feet away.

As I was leaving, found myself with Wells and his baroness at the door. He looked old, seedy, impossibly ground-down. Said, bitterly, did I not see that all this—he flung his arm at the row of sandbags next to Catherine's front door—represented civilisation's last gasp? I said I thought civilisation was good for a few years yet. Just as we were exchanging these valedictions, Mr Kent sidled by, dressed in a British Warm with a folded umbrella under his arm, looking every inch a stockbroker on his way to White's. Impossibly *affairé*. Like Mr Tod hatching one of his schemes against Tommy Brock.

3 November 1939

I can see that I shall have to be careful about Ramsay. This morning's *Telegraph*, for example, has an article about 'subversive' organisations.

No names are mentioned, but I have a nasty feeling that I may have met several of their representatives at the South Kensington meeting. And then he has begun to say foolish things in the House. *The Times*, I discover, carries a report of questions asked in relation to evacuee children being subject to 'moral instruction' of an unsuitable (i.e., Marxist) kind. Whereupon a Labour member asked the Minister if he was aware of the *Fascist* opinions that might be inculcated into them, and then Shinwell, when Ramsay said that 'responsible organisations' could give the Minister evidence of what he was alleging, asked whether the Minister 'had any reason to believe that the Hon. and gallant member who asked the question is associated with any responsible organisation.' All this *very* sinister.

On the other hand, Ramsay charm itself. This morning a note asking: would I go and see him at the House? Found him there with a rather sharp-faced girl called Castell, who describes herself as his aide-de-camp. Tired, but otherwise on good form. Said the Labour members exceedingly tiresome, seemed to forget he himself had a son serving in the army, &c. A certain amount of chaff about Shinwell, Ellen Wilkinson, &c. Then, when Miss Castell had been despatched on an errand, he became serious. Declared himself anxious to make use of my connections. The great thing was to secure access to the King. Did I know anyone who could help bring this off? Said I would consider, send him an answer in a day or so. Ramsay seemed pleased at this. Wondered whether to tell him I had met Kent at Catherine's and then, for some reason, thought better of it.

Later. Another row with Drawbell about my article for this Sunday's *Chronicle.* It had been agreed that I should write a piece about morale in the army, which I am perfectly competent to do, having been down to Caterham last week at considerable inconvenience, dined in the mess and absolutely prostrated myself on several adjutants' carpets in order to find out 'what the men are thinking.' (Morale, by the way, is horribly low. Nobody wants to fight, or thinks we should be in Europe at all. Several of the junior officers I spoke to openly pro-Mosley.)

Then for some reason Drawbell changed his mind and said he wanted an article on 'the national spirit.' I said, what I truly believe, that the national spirit was so depressed as to be scarcely worth writing about, also that the point of employing a columnist on one's newspaper was to allow him to ventilate his own opinions. In the end I was allowed to write a modified version of the original, but with a lot of bromides about autumn leaves falling over the barrack-room square and the proud legacy of Balaclava in place of the points I wanted to make. Really! If this goes on I shall certainly write to Lord Kemsley, who has been asking me to join the *Sunday Times* for months, and would certainly pay more money, too.

4 November 1939

Mysterious paragraph in the *Standard* saying that a man named Burdett badly injured in an assault last night in the region of St James's Square; the police seeking his assailant. Mystery lies in the hint that Burdett a Secret Service man in pursuit of 'subversive organisation' (that phrase again!) and that one of these organisations might very well be to blame. Most unusual to see anything like this in a newspaper, as cloak-and-dagger brigade usually move heaven and earth to keep reference to themselves sub rosa.

To lunch with the Margraves (Gaskin cross, as he had expected me to be home—shall have to make it up to him) and, on the way back, decided to walk through Richmond Park. Perfectly quiet and still. Deer grazing in great herds. Beech leaves in profusion. All the things one likes. For a moment it was possible to forget entirely what one fears, the awful prospect around one, only to reach Richmond High Street, with its sandbags, its officious little men in uniform, and its army lorries rumbling by, to remember every sordid detail.

Later. Reflecting on talk with Ramsay, racked my brains to think of someone who might furnish an entrée to HM. Not as easy as it sounds. Not that one hasn't 'society' eating out of one's hand, and half a dozen peers queuing up to offer one dinner invitations (there was another one came this morning from Lord Southsea—had Gaskin put it on the mantelpiece) but . . . for a start, the people who used to hang around him in the early days have all disappeared.

Metcalfe, for example, from whom he was practically inseparable, now *persona non grata* for some reason. He is supposed to be very thick with Mrs Ronnie Greville, but it is the best part of half a decade since I went to Polesden Lacey, and then there was that dreadful row about the young man who used to drive her about and in which, one ought to admit, one did not behave altogether well . . . In the end, though, came up with Ralph Straus, who certainly knew him around the time of the Mrs Simpson business, indeed used to play squash-rackets with him.

It was amusing to see how Straus would contrive to insert references to this acquaintance into his conversation. He would say: 'You know more about rates for journalism than I do. How much could I expect to get for a piece on "The Game the Prince Plays?"' 'Five or six guineas, I should think,' one would reply, rather intrigued. 'What game is it, by the way?' 'Squash-rackets,' Straus would blandly reply, as if playing squash with the heir to the throne was the most natural thing in the world. 'Is he any good?' one would wonder. 'Not bad,' Straus would reply. 'I can give him three points, but not five.'

Thought I might find Straus at the Savile, to which, for some reason, I still keep up my subscription, so looked in there the following evening. Rather a mouldy lot—decayed bill-brokers with mock-Tudor houses in Ewell Village and Sunday painters, I should say. Consoled myself with the thought that twenty years ago it seemed to me the height of glamour and *luxe*.

Sure enough, Straus ensconced before the fire. Rather gone to seed, much balder than I remembered, and showing every sign of turning into the Savile's bright particular bore. Seemed pleased when I said how nice it was to see him—there is such a thing as charm—however said there is not the faintest impediment to communicating with the King. One simply writes to Hardinge, the private secretary, and, if one is not obviously a lunatic, Hardinge or some other factotum replies. The problem, I suppose, is that so many people are lunatics.

The difficulty, Straus said—it is very entertaining when he tries to patronise one—is stirring any interest in the King, who still sees no one. Apparently each of the rooms he inhabits has a portrait of Mrs S. on the wall (how does Straus know this, I wonder?). But it had to be a very good letter, Straus said, to get past Hardinge.

Now if there is one thing I pride myself on, it is the ability to write a letter. One can think of half a dozen persons—Melba, Chaplin, Coolidge— who would not have seen one without it. And so, coming back to Hampstead—Gaskin reported that numbers of people had telephoned, but I waved him away—I sat down in the study and set to work. But how does one address a monarch? It is not as if he were the King of Greece, and grateful for any consideration he could get. In the end I merely reminded him of the occasions in the past when we had met, said that I had vital information to impart to him regarding the conduct of the war, assured him of my bona fides and 'begged for the favour of an audience'—a nice way of putting it, I thought.

Well! I daresay nothing will come of it. On the other hand, it is rather consoling to think that one has spent at least some part of the day writing to one's sovereign.

6 November 1939

Had scarcely digested the excellent breakfast cooked for me by Gaskin, in the way that only Gaskin knows how, when there came a knock at the door to say that a gentleman wished to see me on 'official business.' Wondering what this might mean, I went into the study, where the 'gentleman' had been installed, and found a man called Hegarty, dressed in raincoat and brown shoes, who asked: did I know Captain Ramsay? I replied that Ramsay had written to me in consequence of a newspaper article I had published and that I had twice visited him at the House, and wondered what business it was of his.

Hegarty very civil—has read several of my books—said that 'certain enquiries' being made into Ramsay's activities, and that it was necessary to interview various of his 'associates,' &c. He then demanded: had I been at a meeting at a house in South Kensington where Ramsay and Domvile had been present? I said that I went to so many meetings that it was sometimes difficult to recall precisely who was there, and what was talked about. 'And what was talked about at this one, sir?' Hegarty asked. Told him I really could not remember, but that naturally some discussion of war, &c.

All this lasted for nearly half an hour. Clearly Ramsay is regarded as a security risk, and the intelligence services are collecting any data on him that happens to be available. Reminded Hegarty that I had served in the First War and flattered myself that no one could regard my opinions as unpatriotic. Hegarty said, which was a relief, that this 'went without saying.' Asked: did I know Admiral Domvile? I replied, which was the truth, that I had shaken hands with him at South Kensington, but knew nothing more than I read in the newspapers. Had I ever visited an antiques shop in Maida Vale run by a man named McKechnie? This last question so bizarre that I almost laughed, but contented myself with observing that I bought my antiques in the Pimlico Road.

All rather disturbing.

Later. Thinking that I deserved a rest from Mr Hegarty, Captain Ramsay, and *haute politique*, I went down to the Criterion Bar. All horribly depressing—whisky twice the normal price, soldiers asking for cigarettes, dreadful little men reading copies of the *Racing Post*—but eventually ran into *y*, looking unexpectedly spruce. Says that war has been a godsend to people 'in his line of work.' Apparently he is making a small fortune selling black-market gin and ladies' stockings made of parachute silk.

Says that security at military installations horribly lax, officials corrupt. A fortnight ago, someone is alleged to have stolen the entire South Coast Command meat ration from a truck at Portsmouth Railway Station, most of which was subsequently sold *back* to the authorities by the people who stole it. *Y* says mess orderlies the worst of the lot. He has had six bottles of spirits from the Chelsea barracks in the last week alone.

9 November 1939

Ramsay attacked in the House again as a 'fellow traveller,' although the Speaker complained that the words were unparliamentary and had them withdrawn.

Sent (anonymously) an article from a paper called *Tribune*, denouncing me as 'an objective pro-Fascist.' Piece, by one G. Orwell, response to *Chronicle* piece I wrote a week after war was declared. How one abhors these foul little left-wing rags and their insinuation. Because a man has the courage to write what he believes, rather than following the Gadarene rush over the cliff-edge, he is to be disparaged for 'playing into the enemy's hands'!

11 November 1939

Armistice Day. Came down to breakfast to find, of all things, a letter from Hardinge thanking me for mine and announcing that the King was prepared to see me. Was so surprised that I dropped egg on my waistcoat. I am to telephone Hardinge to make an appointment. At eleven, having consumed a couple of stiff gins, I did this.

Hardinge, to whom I was eventually connected by a series of minions, very courteous. Said the King remembered me, was interested by my letter. There could be no question of an 'interview' of any kind, and nothing to appear in any newspaper. I should not be allowed to take notes or to bring any tape-recording apparatus into the Palace. I agreed to both these conditions. Said my status in speaking to His Majesty would be that of a private individual, not a representative of the press. Hardinge accepted this. Said he had terrible trouble with correspondents of foreign newspapers attaching themselves incognito to diplomatic retinues, and then harassing HM with questions he could not answer. Made an appointment to call at the Palace next Wednesday morning at 10.

Later. Pondered the absolute variety and idiosyncrasy of human experience. Here I sit in my drawing room watching Gaskin ferrying away the tea-things. Mrs De Haviland, my next-door neighbour, can be seen through the window walking her Sealyham. In the next room Grieveson, the odd-job man, is putting frames on those prints I bought at Abbot &

Holder last week. I, only a few feet away from each of them, am contemplating an audience with the King. If a writer put this in a novel, nobody would believe him—but there it is, anyway.

Made some more notes for my India book, which I really think will be rather good.

16 November 1939

Now that I have returned from the Palace I want to set down as accurate an account as possible of my visit: not only as an aide-memoire, but for the benefit of anyone else who may read this journal. After all, one has a duty to posterity as much as to oneself.

Had been rather exercised by the question of how one 'arrives' at Buckingham Palace. Does one turn up at the front gate in a taxi? Or merely accost one of the sentries on duty? Consulted Victor, who advised me to present myself at the visitors' entrance, which is apparently just around the corner in the Royal Mews. Then again, what is one supposed to wear on these occasions? In the end selected a rather nice grey suit with a very fine chalk-stripe, dispensed with cigarette case on the grounds that it would spoil the line, and bought a new bowler hat at Lock's.

Victor's advice turned out to be A1 as, having announced myself, was instantly greeted by a flunkey and sent on to 'the Grand Entrance under the arch in the inner courtyard.' Here were parked a state coach and several carriages attended by three-corner-hatted coachmen, postillions, &c., presumably having conveyed some ambassador to present Letter of Credence. Another footman (painfully spotty) to hand me over to equerry, after which Hardinge himself appeared.

Everything immensely shabby and run-down: brocade on the back of the occasional chairs peeling away; footmen's tail-coats like costumes in a pantomime. Hardinge polite, non-committal, clearly regarding me as merely another appointment in an excessively taxing day. Repeated remarks made on telephone, to which I again acceded, then took me to a room known as the '44,' so called, I believe, as it had not been decorated since 1844, where 'His Majesty,' as he rather nicely put it, 'would receive me.' The door was opened by another footman (who looked uncannily like that disreputable friend of *z*'s I met at the Blue Lantern), Hardinge said something I did not catch, and I set off across a vast expanse of shabby carpet in the direction of a desk behind which the King sat writing or, as I now think, pretending to write.

General impressions. A small, pale, nervous-looking man, seems much older than when I last saw him. A little chevron of wrinkles at the corner of his eye; pronounced air of having been hard done by. Curiously high-pitched voice. Still speaks in that drawling upper-class cockney that was so fashionable a dozen years ago: 'nothing whatever to do with it' emerging as *nudding woddever to do wiv it*, and so forth. Seemed very well informed: the morning's papers spread out on the desk with various passages marked in red ink, next to a pile of telegrams.

There are mementoes of Wallis everywhere: a portrait of her in oils on the wall; photograph of the two of them in golfing kit on the desktop, together with funereal-looking silver urn. For a moment I wondered whether this might actually contain her ashes, but turned out to be a kind of tobacco-pot. Definite air of Miss Havisham in her chamber, so that one almost expected to see ancient wedding cake sunk under cobwebs. Room could easily not have been refurbished since 1744, given general air of decay. One of the window panes absolutely cracked. Victor says that, having been castigated for his extravagance when Prince of Wales, now determined to be most frugal monarch that ever lived.

King very affable. Claimed to remember me from the 1920s. Talked about those days with great fervour: 'One always seemed to be sitting up late and never going to bed.' Enquired of various personages of those times—Hartnell, Princess Bibesco, Elsa Lanchester—some of whose subsequent careers I was fortunately acquainted with. Struck by his prodigious memory: tells me about parties he had attended as if they had happened only the other day. Something infinitely sad and self-pitying about this. Hesitant when he spoke, and made occasional notes to himself on slip of paper (about what, I wonder?).

Struck by the hold—the right word, I think—which Hardinge seems to exert over him. We were several times interrupted by Hardinge rushing in unannounced to obtain the King's signature on some document or to remind him of some trifling engagement. To this the King habitually deferred. *I* should have been much less deferential.

The war. Difficult at first to know exactly what he thinks about this, and how far a personal opinion was allowed to obtrude above the 'official line.' Said: 'You cannot know, Mr Nichols, how hard I tried to prevent it.' Thought Nazi–Soviet pact 'shocking' but understandable. Supposed that if we were to go to war with anyone it should be the Russians. Asked me what I thought of the Nazi leaders. I said I had met only von Ribbentrop, at some of the Anglo-German Fellowship meetings, and found him rather over-bearing. 'Yes, that was how he struck us,' the King said, dryly. 'And rather prone to exaggerate his influence, too. There was a time, you know, when he used to send . . .'—and here I thought he was going to mention Mrs Simpson's name, but he corrected himself—'. . . a certain lady of my acquaintance a dozen roses every morning of the week.' Said he thought Hitler had a natural respect for him, as he had for all royalty, had taken great pains to cultivate his German relations, &c.

We talked about the conduct of the war. He expressed relief that no large-scale conflict had taken place, or seemed likely to. Maintained that current situation was 'very odd. . . . Thirty years ago, if one was at war, one simply tried to defeat the other fellows as quickly as possible. That was how we all felt in 1914.' I asked about the other members of the Royal Family, what they thought, and he said: 'Oh, my brother Bertie is set on being a gentleman farmer. Doesn't come to London at all. I haven't seen my nieces since August.' So who does he see, I wonder? I asked: how did he occupy his time? Said there were always ambassadors coming to see him, people wanting him to visit. Said of all things he hated inspecting troops. Reminded him of Flanders, when a battalion's strength could be reduced by half overnight.

All this time the subject of my letter hung in the air between us. Naturally I hesitated to ask him about his dealings with the Cabinet, on the very sensible grounds that (a) it would be impertinent, and (b) he would not tell me anyway. Then he remarked, almost out of nowhere, that he considered it his responsibility to do everything he could to bring about peace while continuing to support the war effort, that there was nothing paradoxical about this, and that it was our duty to show Germany we meant business if our interests were threatened, while deprecating the whole idea of war in the first place. I said, choosing my words very carefully, that a great many people felt like this, some of them in positions of considerable influence and authority: could he not give them a lead?

The King said he gets 200 letters a week urging this step, begging him to broadcast, &c., but feels there is nothing he can do. If there are to be peace moves, they cannot be seen to come from him. 'There shall be no King's Party,' he said. 'We have been through all that before.' I replied that a King's Party already existed, in the House and, as far as one knows, in the armed forces, let alone amongst ordinary people, and it was his to command as he chose. 'I think, Mr Nichols, that the days are long past when a King of England could do anything he chose,' he said. I did not mention Ramsay's name, nor did he ask me who I represented. In fact there was a great sense of people not quite daring to commit themselves, saying less than they intended.

Just then Hardinge knocked on the door with another message, and our interview came to an end.

I got the distinct impression of an intensely shy, reserved, patriotic man whom no one will properly advise, desperate to do his duty but fearful of upsetting the apple-cart. A feeling that there was a great deal more to be said, and if the King's reluctance to say what he evidently felt could be overcome, then a great deal might be accomplished.

What Ramsay will make of this is anyone's guess.

18 November 1939

To Ramsay's house in Onslow Square, having previously sent note of conversation with HM. An extremely odd collection of persons gathered together. In dealing with R, I can never quite establish whether one has walked into a meeting of cranks, who in other circumstances would be attending flat-earth societies, or an offshoot of some immensely powerful subterranean network whose true capacity has not yet been revealed. Present: Ramsay, his wife (a rather vague and ethereal-looking woman, but given to making sharp remarks about the Jewish question), Domvile, 'Commandant' Allen, looking like an evil policewoman, a pair of Guards officers, Bannister (Tory MP), man named Gunter who says he works for the *Daily Express* but looks far more likely to be employed by the *Peckham and Deptford Advertiser.*

Naturally, everyone intensely interested in my discussion with HM. Ramsay said it confirmed what he had always believed: the King coerced by his advisers, now seeking to 'reconnect' with his people. Vital to convey to the King the strength of popular feeling, support for his point of view, &c. HM's remark about the King's Party greeted with much head-nodding.

Bannister twice asked why I had agreed to Hardinge's stipulation that none of this should appear in print. I declined to inform him that this is an inevitable consequence of one gentleman dealing with another! Ramsay said he was very encouraged. Did I think the King could ever be persuaded to speak his mind? I said I thought it was unlikely, but there was no harm in trying. Gunter several times observed in a cockney accent like a stage-burglar's, 'The King! That's what the people want. They want to 'ear from their King!' How Ramsay can have him in the house I cannot imagine.

Found out, *inter alia*, a great deal about 'The Faction' and how it operates. Halfway between a bridge club and the Freemasons, which is to say that a lot of talk about subscriptions, tea-parties, &c., alternates with more sinister intimations of quiet words in high places and back-stairs intrigues. Thus when I mentioned Hegarty's visit to Ramsay, he laughed: Hegarty's superior well known to him, not the least need to worry. Guards officers reported the mood of the troops, at any rate in London regiments, profoundly disillusioned. All 'waiting for a lead,' whatever that may mean.

20 November 1939

Important not to forget that one has a life beyond Captain Ramsay and meetings in Onslow Square. So let me state that today I lunched with Aggie, Baroness Stuhlbeck (poor woman is thinking of changing her name in the current circumstances), Lord Camrose, proprietor of the *Daily Telegraph*, and the Bishop of London. One always gets a mixed crowd at Aggie's, and this no exception.

Lord Camrose invincibly patriotic. We should drive Hitler eastwards into the arms of his friends the Russians, who would then think better of their pact and tear him to pieces. When I pointed out that we had neither the manpower nor the munitions and the aeroplanes to perform this feat, he accused me of being defeatist. Aggie, supporting me, said she wanted the war to end tomorrow and did not care how it happened—one in the eye for Lord Camrose, although he took it with good grace, 'Time would tell,' &c.

Afterwards to matinée performance of Noël's new play, about which the critics have been rather rude. Very good and well-made, audience appreciative. Wrote to Noël—he is away, I believe, but his housekeeper will send it on—saying the play a triumph and that all the critics are mad. It is fun writing letters to Noël!

23 November 1939

As I have not been getting on very well with Drawbell recently, and in addition have the beginnings of a scheme in my head which I wished to ventilate, took the opportunity of inviting him to lunch. Treated him to Roma's in Wilton Street, where I don't think he ever went before, and where the war's sumptuary privations—a rather nice phrase, which I shall have to get into an article—don't seem to apply. Potted shrimps, Colchester oysters, &c. Cost me £2 but well worth the money. Drawbell's expression throughout rather like Mr Prendergast's in Evelyn's novel who, when taken to dine at an expensive hotel and offered a grapefruit to eat, says 'My, what a big orange.'

Asked Drawbell: what would be his reaction if offered an authentic (and verifiable) statement of the King's views on the conduct of the war? Naturally, Drawbell said he would print anything I could give him. And what, I continued, if the King's views were contrary to the policy of the paper? Drawbell said that the expression of the King's opinion—provided it *was* the King's opinion—overrode all considerations of this kind. Having whetted his appetite, I then shut up shop and said merely that there was a possibility I might be able to offer him something on these lines, but early days. Drawbell so astonished that he accepted my suggestion for this week's article—our military preparedness, or lack of it—without demur.

Back home to find letter from x. He has been accepted into the Merchant Navy, but finds the other recruits 'rather a rough crowd.' Sent him a £5 note with instructions to 'enjoy himself.' I dread to think what he will spend it on.

CHAPTER 6

Lost Girls

'The one set in the women's prison is good, I grant you. But it's the one about the girls' boarding school we really ought to do.'

'What? *Miss Harrington Hunts the Hairbrush?* I should have thought that was the kind of thing that would get us prosecuted.'

'Nonsense. I've seen far worse than that in the *New English Weekly*. Far worse.'

It was raining outside in the square and the plane trees were dripping in an impossibly melancholy manner. By the left-hand corner of the gardens—quiet now, treeless, and mostly redug for potatoes—somebody had constructed a nondescript air-raid shelter, flanked by a wall of sandbags, on which Cynthia's eye unerringly fell whenever she looked out of the window. It was about eleven o'clock in the second week of November, and the rain had been tumbling down since dawn. In the distance beyond Euston, where the barrage-balloon still hung tethered like a giant cigar, the sky was quite opaque.

All this gave the light in the office, behind its moisture-streaked windows, an oddly smoky quality, as if a bonfire was smouldering quietly beyond the outer door and was about to send the place up in flames. 'Like Pissarro,' Desmond said, who had a habit of comparing most of the natural phenomena he came across to post-Impressionist painting, and had been sternly rebuked by Anthea.

'Don't be ridiculous, Des. It's nothing like Pissarro. Utrillo would be much nearer the mark.'

Desmond had accepted this dressing-down with surprising meekness. He was still rather afraid of Anthea.

'I'm not going to have everything thrown into jeopardy just because you want to run a story about a lesbian orgy,' Peter Wildgoose said, a bit tetchily but still with genuine amusement in his voice. *Thrown into jeopardy* was one of his favourite phrases, Cynthia thought, along with *found his métier at last.*

'I absolutely agree with you,' Desmond said, running his fingers through his sparse hair again so that it stood up on his head like a comb. He looked horribly out of sorts. 'Naturally, if I thought anyone was going to complain I wouldn't dream of putting it in. If it's any reassurance, I'll get it looked over by a chap I know at the MOI.'

Cynthia had stopped typing the letter she had in front of her on the grounds that the noise of the typewriter might inhibit their conversation. Now she wound the sheet of paper down a couple of notches and began another paragraph. Over at the other desk, Lucy was looking up someone's address in the *Writers' and Artists' Yearbook*. Anthea had taken off her shoes and was putting polish on her toenails. There were books everywhere, far more than there had been a week ago: new novels, sets of encyclopaedias, travel gazetteers, a history of medieval thought in four volumes. 'It's Desmond's fault,' Anthea had said unkindly. 'They think he's going to review them in exchange for all the drinks they've stood him over the last ten years.'

'Well, show it to your chap at the MOI,' Peter Wildgoose said. He was a small, cadaverous man in his late thirties, who always wore a dark-blue suit, carried a rolled umbrella under his arm and, as Lucy and Cynthia had agreed, had the most beautiful manners of anyone they had ever met. 'But I shall hold you personally responsible. In any case, we're nearly full up as it is, so I don't know where you think you're going to put it.'

'I've thought about that,' Desmond said. 'And to be perfectly honest, I don't think anyone's going to miss that piece about the Bodhisattva. But going back to Sylvester, I'm telling you, Peter, that boy will make our fortunes.'

'Well, it's a pity he couldn't start by making his own. The last time he came in here, his shoes looked as if they were being held together by pieces of string.'

This was the third conversation about Sylvester Del Mar in as many days. It was quite capable of going on all morning. Longer, even. Unexpectedly, it was brought to a close by Anthea, who, looking up from her newly painted toes, gleaming above the grey-brown fur of the carpet, said, 'Peter, you're looking awfully tired. Why don't you sit down and I'll make you a cup of tea?'

The *Duration* girls were solicitous of their patron's welfare. Desmond had several times said that when Anthea opened the door to him he always knew from the expression on her face whether Peter was in the office, as 70 per cent of her smile was reserved for him. Rather to everyone's surprise—he was a single-minded man—Peter accepted the offer of the cup of tea, lifted the cup off its saucer with the finger and thumb of his right hand, and looked as if he might be about to say something else.

'This war is becoming a terrible strain,' Desmond said hastily. 'Do you know, I was sitting in the bar of the Randolph last weekend looking at a roll of proofs I happened to have with me? There were a lot of officers camped at the next table making rather a noise, and I supposed I must have looked up once too often because one of them came over and asked to see my ID card. As it happened, I didn't have it with me—you remember how I always mislay things, and it's safer to leave it at home. My gas mask had gone as well. And do you know I couldn't convince them I was who I was? There was my name on the proofs, and on my cheque-book, but that wouldn't do at all.'

There was something rather breathless about Desmond as he said this, as if it were part of a longer confessional, long bottled up, full of discreditable secrets about himself that he burned to impart.

'What an ordeal for you to have to go through, Des,' Peter said, not wholly ironically. 'How on earth did you manage to get away?'

'Well, you'll laugh, I daresay, but in the end I told them I'd been to Eton. You'd be surprised how often that does the trick. And then one of them said that if I'd been to Eton I'd be sure to know where *Salve Divve Potens* was, so I explained, and he said I obviously had been there, and they let me go on with correcting the proofs.'

'A jolly good job they didn't look at them, Des,' Anthea suggested. 'Heaven knows what they might have found.'

'Not much chance of that,' Desmond said. 'None of them looked as if they'd know what a book was if it fell on their heads from a great height.'

Cynthia stared at him. She acknowledged to herself that she was fascinated by Desmond, while not knowing if she liked him or not. Peter she acknowledged that she did like. Peter, in fact, fulfilled practically every criterion she required of anyone, let alone a man, which was to say that he was good-looking and punctilious, drew no attention to himself unless it was by dint of not drawing that attention, and gave the impression that he regarded everything said to him as faintly amusing without quite revealing where the source of that amusement lay. She could quite easily imagine herself being married to Peter, if she could have solved the problem of how one was supposed to talk to him.

Desmond, on the other hand, she still found vaguely unreal. The self-consciousness, the gestures and declarations made for the benefit of anyone who happened to be looking on, she thought affected. The tweed suits and the bow ties, on the other hand, she found she could put up with. They were caste-marks, or rather badges of affiliation: like a tobacco jar in college colours or a prefect's tie. The Kirkpatricks had a number of professional categories for people like Desmond. Their choice in this particular case was 'highbrow'—not a category which was given much house room, but was at any rate acknowledged to exist.

While she was thinking this—a process made both more and less difficult by having the two of them a few feet away from her in the room—there came a faint scuffling noise from beyond the door and then a half-hearted rattle at the door-knob, as if the person trying to come in either lacked the strength to go any further or had serious doubts about what he or she might find on the other side.

Somehow the effect of this interruption was mesmerising. Peter put down his teacup, which Anthea returned to the shelf above the kettle. Desmond stared at the door in a kind of nervous panic, as if the physical manifestation of every nightmare he had ever had lay behind it, something that terror urged him to keep away but that duty obliged him to confront.

'Do you suppose the handle's broken?' Lucy asked innocently. 'Whoever it is seems to be taking an awfully long time.'

There was a final, decisive twist on the door-knob and a small man in a grey-brown mackintosh, apparently impelled by the force he had had to exert on the door, more or less fell into the room. To no one's very great surprise, this turned out to be Sylvester Del Mar.

'Why, Sylvester,' Desmond said, a look of inexpressible relief on his face. 'Do come in. We were just talking about you.'

'Nice things, I hope,' Sylvester said, but not as if he had any great expectation of this being the case. 'Look, I brought you those other stories you wanted to see. I was clearing out a lot of stuff in my digs and found them, so I thought I'd bring them along. It's only a step from Finsbury Park.'

There were several mysteries about Sylvester Del Mar. One was whether this was his real name, although Desmond claimed to have seen it on an official document—if not his birth certificate, then a bill of some kind. The second was how he made a living. He could not possibly have survived on the fragments of journalism that had preceded his new calling as a short-story writer. Desmond was supposed to have met him while rooting through one of the secondhand book-barrows in the Farringdon Road, and there was a suspicion that managing one of them was the real business of his life.

As well as being short and given to wearing mackintoshes, he had an oddly furtive air, as if he half-expected to be asked to turn out his pockets on the spot. 'I imagine Sylvester really thinks of me as a plain-clothes policeman,' Desmond had said once. 'Perhaps he comes and steals review copies when there's no one here. I must say, I don't much care if he does.'

'Actually, Sylvester,' Desmond said now, 'I'd be obliged if you'd just step into my office. There are one or two points about that story of yours we're putting into the first number that we need to discuss. Routine things, you understand. Nothing to worry about.'

'*I'm* not worried about them,' Sylvester said. The girls always wondered at Desmond's obsequiousness towards his authors. Sylvester, on the other hand, accepted it as his absolute and unquestionable due. 'While we're at it, you can look at this other stuff I've brought.'

Although a gleam had come into his eye at the prospect of unloading more of his work on Desmond, this came mingled with an expression of mild resentment. Being ushered into the editor's office was all very well, but it deprived him of one of the other things he liked doing, which was hanging about in the outer room talking to anyone who would listen to him and making heartfelt but sometimes startlingly ill-informed pronouncements about the war, literature, or the inconveniences of the blackout.

'Yes, why don't you go and talk to Des,' Peter said. He was watching Sylvester with a look of extraordinary fascination, as if he expected him to change shape, start reciting a poem in a foreign language, or announce that he was a German paratrooper who intended to take them all hostage.

'All right, I'll do that,' Sylvester said. His accent, in fact his whole social background, was impossible to place. He could have been a country solicitor up in London for the day, a plumber's mate who had come into money, anything. He was standing in front of Anthea's desk, staring at her typewriter as if he had never seen one before. 'And what's this young lady up to? Getting on with her work, I hope.'

Cynthia had always assumed that Sylvester would appeal to Anthea's anarchic, bohemian side. In fact she was wrong about this.

'I'm afraid I really don't have time for gossip, Mr Del Mar.'

'You know what worries me?' Sylvester said. He had given Anthea up as a bad job. 'Here you are, starting a magazine called *Duration*. Now, what happens if the war stops? What happens if there's a negotiated peace by Christmas? What do you do then, eh?'

There was a general feeling in the office that this was a good question. 'I think . . .' Desmond said, and then stopped; he always deferred to Peter in any discussion of the war. Sylvester had taken off his heavy, horn-rimmed spectacles and, extracting a brightly coloured handkerchief out of his pocket, begun to polish them with an intent, all-consuming seriousness.

'But there won't be a negotiated peace,' Peter said, a bit crossly. 'I keep hearing this all the time from Desmond's right-wing friends.' Desmond gave a tiny, guilty start. 'Hitler can keep on offering as many phoney olive-branches as he likes, and all the defeatists will carry on lulling themselves into a false sense of security. There are 12 divisions within a half-mile of the Belgian border, and in a very short while they're going to start heading west. But in answer to your initial question, Sylvester, I think *Duration* will be around for a pretty long time yet. Certainly long enough to print your story—a very good story, if I may say so—about that lesbian mistress in the girls' school and what she gets up to with her hairbrush.'

Most people would have taken this as a rebuke. But Sylvester did not look in the least upset. He had asked a question, and got an answer: that was all there was to it. Half a dozen storm-troopers breaking into the room would not have alarmed him, provided they brought an assurance that the magazine's paper supply would somehow be forthcoming. Still polishing his spectacles, as if they were a vital part of the war effort, he allowed himself to be led off into Desmond's office.

'You know something?' Peter said. Sylvester's single-mindedness about his career always amused him. 'I'm sure I've come across that chap before. Can't remember where. Ten shillings to anyone who can tell me.'

But Cynthia had lost interest in Sylvester, Desmond, and even Peter Wildgoose. She had other things to think about.

Before it had been turned into an office, the fireplace desultorily bricked up, and a row of gunmetal filing cabinets introduced into the furthermost corner, the space they sat in had once been a drawing room. Its high mantelpiece, white-painted and supported by thin, Doric columns, had been used to display invitations and sports-club fixtures. Now a line of picture postcards ran from one end to the other, offering views of the beach at Toulon, Manhattan skyscrapers, the gorge at Ronda. They were from Desmond's friends, those expatriate bohemians even now not yet returned from the far-flung nooks and crannies in which the declaration of war had found them.

Of course, if the Hun decides to come south and there isn't a boat we shall all be interned . . .

B. is here with the sweetest little German boy he picked up in Athens last summer and making the most tremendous fuss about naturalisation papers . . .

Wystan sends his love . . .

Staring at a picture of the cathedral at Lisbon, Cynthia was reminded of her parents, forgotten for a moment, but indisputably one of the things she needed to think about. Since Mr Kirkpatrick's stroke—a fortnight ago now—the two of them had begun to behave strangely. Or rather, Cynthia acknowledged, it was not that they had *begun* to behave strangely, but that, detached from the milieu in which she had been most used to observing them, their behaviour suddenly lacked context. Statements that might have made perfect sense in Colombo seemed unutterably bizarre in Bayswater. It was not that Mrs Kirkpatrick was unable to cope with the anxieties of warfare, the queues in shops, and wardens enforcing the blackout, merely that the whole thing seemed to outrage her sensibilities. She was like a philosopher set to labour on a factory production line: she could do the work, but the indignity burnt into her soul.

Mr Kirkpatrick's predicament was, in some ways, even worse. Unlike his wife, he had no personal myth to fall back on. Another man would have dramatised his situation and given it a little romance, reinvented himself as a world-weary colonial back from a lost but forever-tantalising East, a man of action now forced to be a contemplative. But Mr Kirkpatrick was not really up to this. To make matters worse, his illness had badly frightened him. There was really only one escape route open—something his wife had managed decades ago—and that was to stylise his manner.

In the fortnight that this had been going on, Cynthia had lost count of the number of times he had looked at her benignly over the top of his spectacles, fixed her with the grin of a peppery colonel staring at the Sussex pines, and remarked that the autumn was really coming on, or begun, in a purposely quavering voice, a music-hall song about being Henery the Eighth. Each of these things annoyed her, not just because they were irritating in themselves, but because they seemed to suggest that he was in sharp retreat from the person he had been, and that it would take resources she did not possess to drag him back.

Cynthia had long ago resigned herself to having lost her mother to caricature, but her father's desertion appalled her. She felt that she was losing an ally: worse, that the ally knew nothing of the process that was drawing him apart. Just now they were talking of going to Portugal, so that

Mr Kirkpatrick could recuperate. All this struck Cynthia as impractical, dangerous, and possibly illegal, but Mrs Kirkpatrick had gone into the matter, and it appeared that Portugal—neutral, navigable, and also harbouring a remote cousin of Mr Kirkpatrick's—would be prepared to have them.

The other thing that Cynthia wanted to think about was Lucy. In the past three months she had grown used to her friends—rather like the people one read about in novels—declaring themselves, sloughing off some time-honoured aspect of their character and replacing it with another, some-times using materials that already lay to hand, sometimes making use of wholly unexpected additions. And so dowdy girls remembered from the schoolroom were found to have joined glamorous branches of the women's services, while hitherto dashing young men angling for commissions in smart regiments were reincarnated as obscure civil servants.

All this was par for the course, but it was odd to find Lucy joining their ranks. They had started having lunch together—at first eating sandwiches brought from home side by side on a bench with a newspaper spread over their knees; then, when it got too cold, in Lyons or British Restaurants, which were ghastly but where the awfulness of the food at least gave you something to talk about.

'Mother told me this morning that she and Dads were thinking of shut-ting up the house,' Lucy had said on one of these occasions.

Lucy's parents lived rather modestly in North Kensington.

'Oh yes?' Cynthia said, chewing away at her sandwich. 'Where will they go?'

'Mother said they might go and stay with Uncle Mark in Flintshire. After all,' Lucy said, rather fiercely, as if replying to a question that had not been asked, 'it's not as if Dads can do anything, with his arthritis being so bad.'

The Lyons in which they were sitting was a curious place, with a cli-entele that consisted half of solicitors' clerks discussing the wiles of their trade, and half of exotic young women who sat about on stools smoking cigarettes and not appearing to eat anything.

'It's amazing how many places are being shut up,' Lucy said. 'Some-body told me the other day that half the houses in Belgrave Square are for sale.' She stopped talking for a moment and they looked at the steam rising from the urns over by the window, and the piles of rock buns lying unappetisingly on the alabaster counter. 'Actually,' she resumed, 'Dads knows a man who's letting out a flat there. We could go and look at it if you liked.'

And so, greatly daring and yet contriving to give the impression that it was the most matter-of-fact thing in the world for two people of their age, sex, and class to go apartment-hunting together, they left work early that afternoon and took a bus down to Belgrave Square.

The flat was on the top storey of a house in the north-western corner, not far from Halkin Street, and had pretty clearly been converted out of a series of attics. The four floors beneath it were occupied by a Catholic charity that exported second-hand clothing to Eastern Europe, a literary agency, the embassy of a Central American republic, and a deserted ballroom choked with dust. In the basement lurked a very old lady whose husband had fought at Inkerman. It would cost three guineas a week, which the agent, who stood politely in the doorway while they looked, said was cheap at the price.

'It would be rather exciting, wouldn't it?' Lucy said.

'Yes, it would.'

Cynthia had read a number of novels about women who shared flats together. They had titles like *The Adventures of a Bachelor Girl* and featured stockings hung up to dry in front of the gas-fire, Sunday afternoon tea parties, taxis hooting in the street outside, and liberty hall. They settled three months' rent in advance and got Lucy's father to pay a deposit against breakages.

A year ago, Mr and Mrs Kirkpatrick would have raised serious objections to a flat in Belgrave Square. Now the general feeling was that everything could have been a great deal worse. In any case, Mrs Kirkpatrick had other things on her mind. It was all a question, Cynthia now thought, of context, of finding a backdrop which confirmed the suitability of the things you wanted to do or the person you wanted to be. The people she envied were the ones who seemed able to move seamlessly from one milieu to another. Her immediate circumstances—the room in which she sat, the conversation of the past quarter-hour—were proof of this.

Desmond, she knew, would not have done for Bayswater. The particular skills he canvassed—knowingness, effrontery, irony—would have found no echo there. Peter, on the other hand, would have gone down, to use that expression of Mr Kirkpatrick's, like a dinner. As to what this ability to transcend your natural environment consisted of, what qualities in the end made Peter a sharper operator than Desmond, Cynthia confessed herself baffled.

Since Desmond had dragged Sylvester Del Mar away into his office, a silence had fallen on the room. Then, gradually, punctuated by the murmur of Desmond's voice coming through the door, the routines of the late morning began to assert themselves. A man in striped trousers and spats came selling typewriter supplies and was smartly repulsed. Somebody rang up Anthea and started a conversation in which her part consisted of repeating the words 'I think that's really out of the question' in ever more decisive tones. Peter finished what was left of someone else's tea, even though it had gone cold, and went off to forage through the bookcase of review copies to see if there was anything he could bring himself to read. Outside it began to rain again.

All this went on for about twenty minutes. Eventually, when the air of repetition became almost too great to be borne, and Cynthia almost expected the man selling typewriter supplies to walk into the room for a second time, like a character in a play, Desmond appeared suddenly in the doorway of his office, shut the door behind him, and said to Peter, 'I say, Sylvester's in rather a bad way. I don't suppose we could let him have fifteen pounds?'

'What does he want it for?'

'Well . . .' Desmond's manner was that of a headmaster whose prize pupil had unexpectedly failed to secure top marks in French. 'Apparently he's in danger of being thrown out of his digs. And I gather there's trouble with his girl.'

'What kind of trouble?'

'He didn't go into details. Those new stories he's brought in are very good, you know. Couldn't we advance him some money against publication?'

It really was raining very hard now. Peter said: 'I don't know. Perhaps we should rent him a furnished flat. Or get him a suite at Claridge's. I gather the place is virtually empty at the moment. Or, wait a minute, why doesn't he stay with you? Think of the service you would be doing literature. Never mind the companionship. I should have thought that having Sylvester complaining to you over the marmalade about how *Twentieth Century Verse* never published that poem of his, even though they said they were going to three times, would be just the thing to make breakfast go with a swing.'

This went on for some time. In the end Peter took three five-pound notes out of his wallet and handed them over. Desmond accepted this bounty with a meek little bob of his head, like a man taking the sacrament in a church. When he had gone, Peter selected a book from the shelf called *Sicilian Mornings*, picked up his umbrella, and went stiffly off through the door without saying goodbye. Lucy had disappeared somewhere, and Cynthia became aware that Anthea, her telephone conversation now over, was looking at her rather fixedly. She said, 'Peter hates giving money to Desmond's lame ducks.'

'He didn't seem to mind then. Not too much, anyway.'

'Ah, but you see Peter's such a gentleman that he has to be polite about it. But secretly he goes home and seethes. Of course he'd mind it less if Sylvester weren't such an awful little man.'

'I think he's rather nice,' Cynthia said, who could not quite quantify 'awful little man' in these circumstances.

'It will all end in tears,' Anthea said. 'Desmond's, I should think.' Over the past few days she had been at her haughtiest, gone around the office for whole afternoons without wearing her shoes, and corrected Desmond's pronunciation of *selbsthass*. There was a fountain pen in the ferrule at the end of her desk and she picked it up and stared at it as if it had mortally offended her in some way. 'How was your weekend at Ashburton Grange?'

There were a number of ways of replying to this, Cynthia thought. The safest seemed to be to say that she had had rather a nice time.

'Oh, I had rather a nice time.'

'Did Mr Bannister insist on taking to the sea in an Edwardian bathing costume? He did it once when a friend of mine was staying there. And how was Captain Ramsay?'

'How did you know Captain Ramsay was there?'

'Oh, one sees people who go to these things and they tell one about the other people who go there.'

There was something rather marked in the way that Anthea said this, Cynthia thought, as if she sat in the middle of some vast intelligence-gathering network with runners coming in daily with fresh information—things that were long centuries away from the light conversation of which her spare time usually consisted. Cynthia said: 'How's Norman Burdett?'

Anthea's face dropped. 'Actually, Norman's not very well. In fact, he's in hospital.'

'What's the matter with him?'

'If you really must know, somebody came up behind him in the blackout and hit him on the head with a half-brick.'

'Goodness gracious,' Cynthia said. She lived in a world altogether beyond physical violence.

'Goodness gracious is about right,' Anthea said. 'So anything I could tell him about Captain Ramsay at Ashburton Grange would cheer him up no end.'

Just then Mrs Kirkpatrick telephoned to say that their visas to Portugal had come through and they intended to leave the following week.

When it came to it, the Kirkpatricks were a ceremonious family. Significant anniversaries were celebrated by cocktail parties in the Bayswater drawing room. On Mr Kirkpatrick's fiftieth birthday they had dined at the Galle Face Hotel beneath the photographs of American film stars. Now, to mark the trip to Portugal, they decided to lunch that Sunday in a fish restaurant on Wilton Street.

It was not much of a lunch. By the time they got there the salmon was all gone, and the whitebait spoken for, and they had to make do with plates of mackerel in a rather nasty pink sauce. As if this wasn't enough, the restaurant was unusually crowded for a Sunday and the tables seemed to have been jammed closer together than was usually the case.

However, like most people who live by the will, Mrs Kirkpatrick was capable of imposing her personality on the situation. The prospect of the Portuguese trip had enlivened her a little, and she seemed more like the person she had previously been. In this spirit she commandeered a 'reserved' table by the window before anyone could stop her, and spoke so briskly to the waiter who came to remonstrate that he went away.

About halfway through the meal, Cynthia saw that Peter Wildgoose was in the restaurant. He was wearing a quite paralysingly well-cut suit and smiling rather sardonically to himself. There was a younger man with him, who looked as if he might have been in his early twenties, with big, saucy eyes and a startled expression. When Peter saw her he smiled again, less sardonically, and gave a little wave. Then, when she was on her way back from the Ladies', he sprang up from his chair and met her halfway across the room.

'My parents are going to Portugal,' she explained. 'We're having lunch to see them off.'

'I believe I heard something about it,' he said. Back at the table, the young man he had brought with him sat eating olives one by one off the end of a cocktail stick. 'Well, make sure you enjoy yourself.'

'You must make sure you enjoy yourself,' she insisted, with rather more skittishness than she usually allowed herself.

'Oh, I always do,' he said.

Five minutes after she had got back to her seat, a waiter came across with three glasses of champagne on a tray and said that the gentleman in the corner had ordered them to be sent. Naturally, this took some time to explain to Mrs Kirkpatrick, but when she was able to make sense of it she professed herself charmed.

'Well, I call that very civil,' she said. 'How kind of Mr Wildgoose.'

The Kirkpatricks had heard of Peter. 'Didn't his father make a packet from selling margarine in the last war?' her father wondered.

'His mother was a *Trench*,' Mrs Kirkpatrick said, which disposed of the margarine-selling forever.

After that things improved. There was something laboriously old-fashioned about the Kirkpatricks' attitude to enjoyment, but you could not question their zeal. Mrs Kirkpatrick reminisced about a famous party she had been to in the 1920s where everybody dressed up as somebody else and she had had her photograph taken for the *Bystander*. They talked about Ceylon and how it had never been the same as it was when they had first gone there, and the impossibility of ever going back, and it was as if Henry Bannister, the car's front wheel thumping into the tree-trunk, and the rat-holes leading down beneath the cemetery grass had never been.

Over at the far table Peter and his friend were eating oysters, which was odd as there had not been any when the Kirkpatricks arrived.

Finally, when they were drinking coffee and watching the taxis surge down Wilton Street, Mrs Kirkpatrick's face lost its reminiscent glaze and she began to impart some serious information. 'Of course, if you find yourself really short you must go and see Mr Cheyney at the bank . . . I'm sure Aunt Dorothy would be pleased to help if you ran into any kind of difficulty. I believe they're in Renfrewshire just at the moment . . . Perhaps your cousin Harriet would come and stay with you, if you were to ask her . . . Lucy Yeoward was always a very sensible girl, so I've no worries on that score . . . I've asked Mrs Haldane, who lives in Pont Street, if she'll keep an eye on you . . .'

Cynthia saw that all this was intended to reassure, to imply that she existed at the centre of a vast network of friends and relations, all of whom could be pressed to offer succour at a moment's notice. In fact, it had precisely the opposite effect. She had never felt so detached from the world of which she was supposed to be a part. Curiously, there was something exhilarating about this. The crowd in the restaurant was thinning out now: half the tables were empty. Standing in the doorway putting on his coat, Peter Wildgoose glanced in the Kirkpatricks' direction, raised two fingers to the side of his head and gave a mock-salute. It was a measure of Cynthia's exhilaration that she saluted back.

'What a very nice young man,' Mrs Kirkpatrick said.

The Kirkpatricks were not great ones for leave-takings. They stood on a street corner in a disconsolate and uncertain huddle while Mr and Mrs Kirkpatrick looked for a taxi. For some reason the taxis, which had been clogging the kerbside an hour before, had all disappeared.

'My dear,' Mrs Kirkpatrick said once or twice.

Mr Kirkpatrick was less oblique. 'I shall miss you, Pongo,' he said— 'Pongo' was an ancient nickname, dating from the nursery, not used for a dozen years—'and I wish you were coming with us.'

And then they were gone, off down Wilton Street in the grey November afternoon, and she stood on the pavement, lost in the world that 'Pongo' had suddenly conjured up: drinking rose-hip syrup out of a powder-blue china mug; the Hundred Acre Wood; hot summer days at Burnham Beeches.

At Belgrave Square Lucy would be rearranging furniture and positioning waste-paper baskets, but she did not want to go back there just yet. Instead she set off through Pimlico to the river. It was nearly three o'clock and there was no one much about.

A few soldiers were lugging their kitbags in the direction of Victoria Station. In the Belgrave Road a gang of Boy Scouts were picking up pieces of litter. The exhilaration was still there, fizzing about inside her, and oddly enough it had come to include Peter. She wondered what it would be like having lunch with him, and the kind of things he might talk about.

The Thames was at slack-tide and about the colour of gravy. Alone among the landmarks of her childhood, it seemed not to have been altered by the war. There was a flotilla of houseboats chained up on the Battersea side, all clanking together in the breeze, and she watched the movement of their prows against the green-grey surround. Then, without warning, a Port of London Authority barge came steaming into view from beneath Grosvenor Bridge, with a Union Jack on a pole by the foredeck and two or three dozen women with pink faces in WVS uniforms gazing excitedly over the side. A gust of wind blew down, and three or four hats went springing away into the swell. In the distance, towards the power station, there were odd little flashes of light rising above the water, like a battle being fought by unseen ships.

No, she thought, even the river had changed.

And, of course, living in Belgrave Square was not in the least like *The Adventures of a Bachelor Girl*. The flat consisted of four irregularly shaped rooms leading off a serpentine corridor, and the sitting-room windows were so large that they ran out of blackout curtains and had to make do with squares of brown paper held in place by sticking plaster.

Worse, people were always mistaking the location of the Catholic charity on the third floor and leaving parcels of old clothes on the landing which had to be taken downstairs again, and the front door-bell did not work properly, which meant that there was a difficulty about callers, several of whom had been left standing in the street.

The parts of the sitting-room windows that were not permanently blacked out looked over Grosvenor Place and beyond that the gardens of

Buckingham Palace, in which, Lucy maintained, one bright afternoon, with the aid of a pair of binoculars, she had seen the King exercising his pugs. Cynthia had not believed the story about the King, which seemed to her somehow symptomatic of the relation in which she stood with Lucy, and had something to do with a suspicion that her good nature was being presumed upon.

Meekly submissive in the Bloomsbury square, the domestic Lucy turned out to be a more exacting proposition. There was one little rota pinned to the kitchen wall about the cooking, and another little rota left next to the telephone about who was responsible for the laundry. There was also a little jar for threepenny bits to defray the telephone bill. The Beardsley prints that Cynthia had thought suitable for the sitting-room vanished overnight, to be replaced by works by Sisley and Munnings, and there were little arguments about empty biscuit-tins and stolen milk. To balance this was the odd and not always comforting sense of being beholden to absolutely no one: of being able to walk around the flat stark naked if one wanted to and dine out of a sardine-tin at four o'clock in the morning.

Later, people would insist that the early days of the war imposed a routine, at the very least a pattern, on the lives being lived out in its shadow. But this was not true. Rather, it brought a rhythm, not always heard, occasionally almost forgotten, but at all times capable of making its presence felt in unexpected ways.

The people one knew—people working in government offices, in one or other of the services, even those in reserved occupations—mysteriously came and went: summoned to distant parts of the British Isles on a whim and then, equally mysteriously, brought back again. Desmond said he knew a man who worked in the press department at Fighter Command who had been sent to Oxford, Swansea, and Inverness in the space of a fortnight. When he came back, the office in which he worked had been relocated to Slough and nobody knew who he was. All over England the tribes were in flux, reassembling themselves in new communities that broke apart almost as they were created, like a clump of iron filings endlessly responding to an unseen magnet's call.

The best times in the flat were Sunday mornings. By then one had thrown off a week's accumulated tiredness, got through the weekend's chores (with exceptions) and reached a point where one was looking out for pleasure. Sometimes this pleasure never arrived, but it was consoling to think that it might do, and it was possible to spend a very comfortable few hours with one's hair in curl-papers, reading the *Sunday Times* and waiting for the telephone to ring, and not realise, until five o'clock struck and the darkness stole over the square, that the day had been wasted.

It was on one of these days, about two weeks after they had moved in, that Cynthia, alone in the sitting room, heard the sound of footsteps coming rapidly up the stairs. This was so unusual that she opened the door of the flat and stood on the landing. Intended to be welcoming, or at any rate inquisitive, the gesture had a curiously dampening effect on the two figures she could see through the gaps in the staircase twenty or thirty feet below. Their conversation—loud, exuberant conversation—stopped, so that all that remained was the slap of shoe-leather on linoleum. The visitors were a man and a woman, and the effect of the sunlight, which came slanting in over the stairwell to create enormous prisms, was so startling that it took a moment for her to establish who they were.

'We just happened to be passing,' Tyler Kent said, as he came up level with her. 'Taking a little stroll through Belgravia, you know. So we thought we'd come and look you up.'

Somehow there was a terrific sense of purpose in the way he pronounced these very ordinary words, as if the idea of taking a Sunday morning walk, much less looking anyone up in the course of it, was a fantastically novel idea that deserved a round of applause from everybody present.

'That's very kind of you,' Cynthia said. 'How on earth did you know where I lived?'

'Oh, we have our spies,' the woman said, who turned out to be Hermione Bannister. She looked slightly less odd, although the new way in which she had had her hair done rather emphasised the size of her head, and she was badly out of breath. 'Gracious, what a lot of stairs to have to climb.'

For a moment it looked as if they might simply talk about stairs, or how they had discovered Cynthia's address. Happily Tyler Kent took control of the situation. Detached from the Bannisters' drawing-room, he looked even more watchful, and said mock-humorously: 'I believe you know Miss Bannister?'

'Don't be absurd. Of course I know Miss Bannister. You'd better come in. There's never very much in the place on a Sunday, but I could probably run to a cup of tea.'

The prisms were quite dazzling now, and the light seemed to flow over Hermione as she stood, still panting for breath, at the top of the staircase, like a molten stream.

'Actually,' Tyler Kent said, 'we thought you might like to come out some place with us. So dull to be sitting at home on a Sunday when you could be gadding about.'

Again, he managed to invest the words with an almost paralysing suggestiveness. There was no knowing, he implied, where he and Hermione might take her, or the delights that might be awaiting her when they got there. Like Mrs Kirkpatrick, in pre-war days, before disillusionment had set in, the force of his personality was quite overwhelming. Cynthia went to get her coat and hat.

Lucy had gone out an hour ago, leaving a note that said: *unexpectedly called away: back later.* 'Unexpectedly called away' stood high on the list of Mrs Kirkpatrick's forbidden excuses, on the grounds that it could mean absolutely anything.

When Cynthia got back to the landing, Tyler Kent and Hermione had gone into a little huddle: Tyler's face still sardonically amused; Hermione's faintly resentful. The once-molten light had faded away almost to nothing.

'If you haven't the energy to walk down four flights of stairs and then get as far as the taxi-rank in Halkin Street, there wasn't a whole lot of point in bringing you,' he said.

There was some doubt as to how Hermione might take this. In the end she gave a meek little nod and they went downstairs in triangle formation, Tyler Kent leading the way, the girls following. Each landing that they passed turned out to have a range of obstacles to negotiate. Next to the Catholic charity's vestibule, someone had left a perambulator filled with flannelette nightgowns. Outside the literary agent's door, there were half a dozen parcels spilled over the mat. The entrance to the embassy was almost blocked by cane chairs piled to a height of six or seven feet.

'Now, a fellow I know who lived in a rooming house in Baltimore once came downstairs and found a stiff in the hallway,' Tyler Kent said.

However long he had been in England, he was still entranced by its peculiarities. As they passed the ballroom on the ground floor he threw a longing glance towards the high, plate-glass doors. 'I'd certainly like to take a look in there some day,' he said.

There was a difficulty about taxis. Tyler strode jauntily off down Halkin Street to summon one and she found herself standing on the kerbside with Hermione. The illusion of normality brought by the staircase and the coruscating light had disappeared: she looked weirder than ever. At the same time it was hard to work out exactly what this weirdness consisted of.

Anthea's oddity—and it was remarkable how Anthea had become the point of comparison for every other person she met—rested on her clothes, and the way she wore those clothes, and her sulky demeanour. Hermione's oddity, on the other hand, lay in everything about her being faintly out of proportion. If her head seemed too large for her body, then her feet, conversely, looked too small for the legs they supported. She seemed ready to fall over at a moment's notice.

Over the years Cynthia had developed a technique for dealing with the Hermiones of this world. It consisted of attending to their more outrageous pronouncements in a spirit of tolerant irony, not taking any nonsense, and jollying them along.

'Actually, we came by your address because Mummy knows Mrs Yeoward and they happened to meet at a sale of work for the Serbian refugees,' Hermione said, all in a rush, and Cynthia registered another absolutely vital odd-girl's characteristic: a habit of *blurting things out*.

Seeing that Tyler Kent was still thirty yards away, although now negotiating with a taxi man, and there was no knowing what Hermione might come out with next, she said, 'It must be rather nice to have Mr Kent taking you round London.'

'Oh, we're seeing a great deal of each other,' Hermione said, almost roguishly. 'And Mummy doesn't mind a bit,' she added. It was impossible to work out exactly what was meant by this: whether the seeing a great deal of each other was Hermione's idea, or Tyler Kent's, or why Mrs Bannister might have been expected to mind about it, but now didn't. There were worse things, surely, than having your daughter paying Sunday morning calls in Belgrave Square in the company of a man who worked at the American Embassy.

The taxi was now moving down Halkin Street towards them, slowing as it approached. For some reason, Tyler Kent had preferred to walk. He was about twenty yards behind, brow furrowed, hands plunged in the pockets of his overcoat. She could not work out whether he was good-looking, or, if he was good-looking, in what kind of way. When he saw she was staring at him, he took one hand out of his pocket and made a little gesture at the cab.

Nobody had troubled to tell her where they were going, but Tyler Kent gave the man an address in Soho. The asphyxiating smell of mothballs that pervaded the cab turned out to come from Hermione. There was not much traffic about. Beyond the window, London sped by. Grosvenor Place. Hyde Park Corner. Piccadilly. Lumbering army vans. Dig for Victory signs. This reminded her of the Bloomsbury square, flattened into bare earth a month ago now. Some of the letters printed in *The Times*, Desmond's copy of which she sometimes read in the afternoons, had got very cross about the Bloomsbury squares.

The taxi dropped them in Brewer Street and they walked down some steps into a kind of subterranean tea-room-cum-drinking-den whose walls were hung with marginally surrealist paintings. She had been to this kind of place once or twice before and was not much shocked by it. There was an epicene old man behind the bar whose high colour was accentuated by the spots of rouge on his cheeks, and some younger men in purple-and-green suits whom Mr Kirkpatrick would have described as 'nancy-boys.'

They ordered gin-and-Italians but there turned out not to be any Italian, so they had to settle for orange juice. The old man with the rouge spots had a pet monkey in a tarboosh, sitting on the bar beside him, who sometimes leapt up onto his shoulder.

'A fellow at the Embassy brought me here once,' Tyler Kent explained as they sat down. He was grinning with delight. 'Isn't it the greatest place?'

He was definitely good-looking, Cynthia had decided, and in the right kind of way.

Hermione, meanwhile, was doing her best to appreciate this new milieu. 'When my uncle was Commissioner of Police,' she said, 'this is exactly the sort of club the Home Secretary would have wanted him to close down.'

'I guess he was the most respectable old guy in Christendom, wasn't he, sweetie?' Tyler Kent broke in, allowing himself to sound vastly more American than he had done on the staircase or in the taxi. 'Now, why don't you drink the nice drink I've just bought you and then we'll be interested to hear what you've got to say.'

To her surprise, Cynthia discovered that the first unwritten law of female solidarity—that if one of your number was suffering even the mildest of hard times from a man, you instantly combined against him—no longer applied, and that she hadn't the faintest desire to come to Hermione's aid. They drank their gin-and-oranges in silence, while Tyler Kent cast an appreciative look or two around the bar.

'Do you know,' he said, 'the monkey's name is Joynson-Hicks? After some minister or other who made himself unpopular around here in the '20s. How about that?'

Looking at him as he said this, Cynthia decided that the adjective which best described him was 'natty.' As used by Mrs Kirkpatrick, this was not quite a compliment. It meant observing routines of dress and deportment to the point where they became ostentatious. Among other things, Tyler Kent was wearing a double-breasted waistcoat and a pair of diamond links.

There was a minor commotion as Hermione got up to go to the Ladies'. When they had reset the stools and retrieved the ashtray that had clattered to the floor in her wake, Tyler Kent said: 'She's a nice girl, Hermione, but, what would you say, a little *distraite*?'

Until then it had not occurred to Cynthia that their relationship might be a case of Hermione taking Tyler Kent up rather than the other way around. Now, when she thought about it, this explained rather a lot. But Tyler Kent seemed not to want to talk about Hermione.

'I hear great things about *Duration*. Isn't that right? And this fellow Sylvester Del Mar that Desmond's discovered. He sounds quite a find.'

'How did you know about Desmond and Sylvester Del Mar?'

'Oh, Des knows someone at the Embassy. You'd be surprised how these things get talked about.'

It was becoming unbearably hot and the old man with the rouge spots had rolled up his shirtsleeves to expose wasted white arms that were the texture of cold chicken. At his side the monkey ate peanuts studiously out of a bowl. One or two people were drinking Pernod at the bar and there was a strong smell of aniseed. Hermione came back from the Ladies' and there was another rearrangement of furniture.

'You'll never believe it,' she said, rather excitedly, 'but just now, as I was going into the lavatories, there was a *man* coming out of them. At least, I think it was a man.'

'Ah, Bohemia,' Tyler Kent said, clasping his hands behind the back of his head. 'There's nothing like it.' It was impossible to tell whether he was joking or not.

Outside, rain fell on the basement windows. There was something unreal about the situation in which she found herself, Cynthia thought: the red faces; the monkey's burrowing paw; the old man's thin white arms. She had a feeling that if she snapped her fingers the scene would instantly dissolve, prior to reconfiguring itself in a different shape.

The trip to the Ladies' turned out to have had a lowering effect on Hermione's spirits. While Tyler Kent told them, in quite merciless detail, about a visit he had paid to some people in Hampshire, her face grew steadily more woebegone. Finally, as he was explaining the idiosyncrasies of a pheasant shoot, she made a little gurgling noise in her throat and said: 'This place is getting on my nerves. I never smelled so much aniseed. And that dreadful old man. Can't we go somewhere else?'

Tyler Kent looked at her interestedly, not with any concern but in a spirit of scientific detachment. 'I thought you liked coming to dives like this,' he said mildly. 'Seeing a bit of life. That's what you always say. I've smelled worse things in my time than aniseed. What's the matter with the place, anyhow?'

Most, but not quite all, of the fight went out of Hermione. She said, a bit dramatically, lowering her voice: 'Well, you never take me anywhere I really want to go.' She raised her voice again. 'Just these dreadful, dreary dives.'

If Hermione had hoped by this gesture to raise any kind of sympathy in the people looking on, she was mistaken. Clearly, the basement was used to scenes. The shirtsleeved old man gave a little shrug of his shoulders, as if to say that the tribulations of the world should be philosophically borne. The monkey chattered furiously. Tyler Kent gave a sharp, decisive little smile, leaned over the table, and grabbed Hermione's wrist.

'I think I get it,' he said. 'What time did you say you were meeting your cousin?'

'About three o'clock. But . . .'

'Well, why don't you get off now? That way you'll have plenty of time to arrange things, and not have to hang about in dreary dives. You needn't worry about me. I'll be fine with Miss Kirkpatrick here.'

There was nothing in the least discourteous in the way Tyler Kent said this. Equally, it was clear that he expected Hermione to agree with him, that resistance was futile, that there was nothing for it but for her to go off calamitously ahead of schedule—it was now about half-past one—and get ready to meet her cousin. Though he continued to hold her wrist after he had stopped talking, Hermione did not try to remove his hand. Instead, she said, 'Perhaps you're right, and I really ought to go.'

'That's the spirit,' Tyler Kent said. He was still holding her wrist. 'While you're at it, could you give your father a message from me?'

'What sort of a message?'

'Tell him I can see him and Ramsay on Tuesday. Wednesday morning if it's more convenient. Tell him to give me a call. But not on the Embassy number if he can help it.'

'Not on the Embassy number?'

'That's right. Now, off you go. Want me to get you a taxi? No? There's a rank down at the end of Wardour Street.'

Again, there was no way in which Hermione could have resisted this. She went off rather brightly, convinced that it was for the best.

'The thing I've discovered about Hermione,' Tyler Kent said, in a spirit of mild enquiry, as if he were formulating some behavioural law for which humanity would later want to thank him, 'is that you should never stand any nonsense. English people are like that, I find. Well, women anyway.'

All her life, Cynthia knew, she had been impressed by men who behaved, or spoke, like this. Men who sized up situations and dealt with them, whose stealthy psychological pressure paid off. Men who managed to impose their personalities on a dinner table or a crowded room without the imposition being noticed, much less resented. Men who, meeting another car halfway along a narrow lane, always contrived, without the least hint of unpleasantness, to secure the *pas*.

She was even more impressed with Tyler Kent's behaviour in the moments that followed. He did not simply imply that now they had disposed of Hermione, they could have some fun. Rather, he began to talk about things that had not been discussed while she was there, while hinting that the conversation had moved on to a higher intellectual plane to which Hermione, even had she been there, could sadly not have aspired.

In particular, they talked about the war.

'I give it three months,' Tyler Kent said. 'Time for Desmond to bring out three numbers of his magazine and then have to call it something else.'

'But everyone says'—*everyone* was Peter Wildgoose—'that the Germans wanting peace talks is just a bluff.'

'Well, that's not how we see it. The way I look at it is: how did the whole thing happen at all? What's it to anyone here whether the Germans have a piece of central Europe where a whole lot of Germans happen to live anyhow? This isn't a war that anyone wants. No one in America wants it, and not a hell of a lot of people here either. Do you know who the person was who put himself out most to stop it? I'll tell you—the King.'

'You're part of the King's Party, aren't you?' Cynthia said. 'The . . . what is it . . . the Faction?'

'Oh, so you've heard about that, have you?' Tyler Kent grinned. He did not seem at all put out by this. On the other hand, when he started speaking again his voice was not so loud as it had been. 'Well, I wouldn't say I was a Kingsman, being the citizen of a republic. But I'll have to admit that's where my sympathies lie.'

It was on the tip of her tongue to ask something about Captain Ramsay, and even Norman Burdett, but she decided not to. Instead, she said, 'How did you come to be so thick with Hermione?'

'The deuce if I know. A couple of dinners at the Bannisters' and suddenly I'm a kind of brevet son-in-law. No, that makes it sound worse than it is. I'm sure Ma and Pa Bannister were just as surprised as I was. Nothing to do with me, you understand. It's just that whenever I pick up the telephone, there's Hermione on the other end. Do you know, just the other day she told me I could call her Hermy?'

Suddenly female solidarity renewed itself. 'You should take that as a compliment,' Cynthia said.

'I guess I should. She's a nice girl, Hermione,' Tyler Kent said. 'But you know what I'd do if I were her? I'd stop getting my hair fixed in that ridiculous way, and I'd stop rearranging the furniture every time I walked across a room. And most of all I'd stop bawling out people who don't always appreciate the bawling. That's what I'd do. But she's a very nice girl.'

Outside the rain beat on the windows. The monkey, balked of his peanuts, gave an almighty snarl and then subsided.

When she got back to Belgrave Square, it was gone four and there were dense pools of shadow over the sitting-room carpet. Lucy sat in one of the armchairs eating a biscuit.

'My dear,' she said, 'you absolutely reek of gin. If this goes on I shall have to tell Mother and Dads you aren't at all the kind of young woman I should be sharing a flat with.'

'How were they?'

'Frightful. They want me to marry Hector Kilbannock.'

This was a new one. 'Who exactly is Hector Kilbannock?'

'He's Lord Kilbannock's son. He runs their estate up in Aberdeenshire and spends his spare time tossing cabers in the garden.'

'He doesn't sound very suitable.'

'No, he doesn't. But I keep being told there's a war on and all us young women should be grateful for anything we can get.'

Later they had an omelette made from the eggs that Mrs Yeoward had sent home with Lucy, listened to *Dance Cabaret* on the radio, and tried to repair some of the pieces of brown paper that had come away from the window. It seemed the most natural thing in the world that Tyler Kent should telephone three days later to ask if she wanted to go out for a drink and that, after a moment or two's prevarication with a bogus engagement diary, she should say yes.

PART TWO

CHAPTER 7

All the Conspirators

They were drinking coffee in Hegarty's office. This was at the end of a long corridor, which looked out onto an enclosed green space, where in summer astonishingly pretty girls sometimes came to eat their packed lunches. But it was deep into autumn now, and the pretty girls had all disappeared.

Hegarty said: 'I stuffed one of the secretaries in B.3 the other evening.'

'Who was the lucky girl?' Johnson asked politely.

'That tall blonde with the coil of hair that looks like a rope twisted round her head. Nancy Oglethorpe.'

'I thought she was married.'

'She very possibly is,' Hegarty said. He was a tall, thin man in his early thirties who shook with nervous excitement as he spoke. 'All I can say is that it didn't seem to make much difference.'

'No?'

'Quite the reverse. Went off like a firecracker.'

'And where did this meeting of true minds take place?' Experience had told him that you had to talk to Hegarty ironically.

'Actually it was in the kitchen down at the end of the B.3 corridor, if you really want to know.'

Hegarty was always saying things like this. The fact that the kitchens were locked up at five when the charwoman went home, and that everybody knew they were locked up, meant nothing to him. The war had been going on for eight weeks now without being able to extinguish the essential hedonism of his temperament.

He said: 'What are you doing this morning?'

'I'm going to that meeting of the League of St George,' Johnson told him. 'At the place in Bayswater.'

'On your own?'

'With the girl who acts as secretary. Miss Frencham.'

'That's turning into quite a romance.'

'Not if I can help it.'

'Don't do what Inkerman in B.2 did. He went away for a weekend with that woman he met at the Nordic League—the one who had a picture of Adolf in her bedroom—and there was the hell of a row.'

'Well, I don't think I shall be going away for a weekend with Miss Frencham.'

'More's the pity.'

It was not true, as some of Hegarty's fellow-workers in B.1 alleged, that he was only interested in sex. In fact, he had several other hobbies. They included dressage and US Confederate Issue postage stamps. But it was always sex that predominated. He had a genius for recasting the area of the department in which he worked in his own image. Before his arrival in B.1 it had been a model of probity, where even a sprig of mistletoe hung over the typewriting console had been frowned upon. Now it seemed to sprout moral laxness from every tuber.

Oddly enough, as he went back along the corridor he met the blonde girl from B.3 walking the other way, carrying a couple of correspondence files pressed close to her chest, and they exchanged nods. There was not the slightest chance that Hegarty had done anything with her, either inside the B.3 kitchen or beyond it. Outside, rain rattled on the window and taxis clashed their gears on the building's asphalt forecourt.

When Johnson got to Bayswater Station she was already waiting for him by the cigarette kiosk at the top of the step: a spare, dark-haired, expensively dressed girl with over-bright eyes. Her father was a rear-admiral, or something. When she saw him she gave a little tremor of recognition—the wire-rimmed glasses on the bridge of her nose shook—came over and touched him lightly on the arm.

'It's very good of you to come, Charles, especially in your lunch-hour.' She had taken to calling him 'Charles' rather than 'Mr Blessington.' This was a bad sign, although neither name was his own.

'Oh, I wouldn't have missed it,' he said.

'I think I heard some of the BUF people were coming. They don't usually, but their secretary said that the situation was so serious it was important to set ideological differences aside.'

'I'm sure that's the best way of looking at it.'

There were times when the act of dissembling alarmed him, and times when it was possible to regard it as something fundamentally humorous. The trouble came when, as now, this bogus conviction stirred an emotional response. Worse, as well as deceiving Miss Frencham, who in peacetime had gone to parties at the German Embassy and, under her father's auspices, shaken hands with Herr von Ribbentrop, he felt sorry for her, appreciated that her fanaticism was only English moral seriousness gone sour.

As they went off together down the Bayswater Road he knew that he could have taken her hand, had he wanted to, and she would not have resisted. The problem was that he didn't want to. The fact that she liked him was, at any rate morally, about the one point in her favour, and his awareness of this made him ashamed.

The meeting was in a frail, broken-down building that had once belonged to a Theosophical society: high-windowed and with sagging rafters. In the vestibule an old lady sat guard over a jam jar full of sixpenny bits and a collection of pamphlets with titles like *The Alien Menace*, *Leese on Peace*, and *Statement on the European Crisis*. There was also a placard carrying the slogan THE TIME TO NEGOTIATE IS NOW. He was a connoisseur of gatherings of this sort and knew their routines: the red glow of the paraffin heater; the trestle-tables pulled together to make a platform; the old men asleep in the back row. This was no exception.

'Who's speaking today?' he wondered.

'I think Miss Harris-Foster first. And then Captain Ramsay. They said Mr Leese might be here, but he doesn't seem to have arrived.'

'Is he the man who wrote that article about the Alien Occupations Bill?'

But what Miss Frencham said in reply was lost in a clatter of thrown-down walking sticks and colliding chairs as a fresh knot of people came into the room. There were about forty of them altogether: grim old characters in sober suits; a white-faced boy or two; elderly ladies in ancient fur coats plundered by moth. The light cast by the two electric bulbs was insufficient for the space, and this gave the room an oddly subterranean look, grey-tinged and inert. An imp-like woman, not more than five feet tall, had risen from her chair next to the trestle-tables and begun to speak: shrill-voiced yet compelling, like the governesses bidden to subdue the children's parties of his youth.

Notebook to hand, neatly and dispassionately, like a doctor taking down symptoms, he found himself registering individual phrases:

'. . . Not a question of giving any secret information to the Germans, unless events reach the stage they did in Spain . . . Don't want to be ruled by the Nazis, or any foreigners, but even that is preferable to being ground to pulp under the heel of the Jewish financiers . . . Really only one war-aim: *we are fighting the Jews* . . . Poland and Czechoslovakia not British interests, but Jewish interests . . .'

He knew Miss Harris-Foster of old: Miss Harris-Foster who, if truth were to be believed, had once taken tea with Hitler, and had a letter addressed to the *Führer und Reichskanzler Adolf Hitler, Reichskanzlei, Berlin* returned to her by the censor a day or so after war was declared. At his side Miss Frencham sat gazing raptly in front of her, but with an oddly vigilant look, like an inquisitor in search of heresy. One false word from Miss Harris-Foster, you felt, and she would have risen to her feet to denounce her.

All this went on for some time. He wondered, as he so often did, what the people who came to meetings of this kind did when they were over. Did they go home and tell the other people they lived with that they had just heard Mr Chamberlain denounced as a warmonger, and that we were at war to preserve Jewish interests? Did they discuss the advantages of granting self-determination to the German-speaking peoples of Europe with the same matter-of-factness that they brought to the night's radio programmes or pub opening hours? Miss Harris-Foster, he knew, lived in a service flat in Kensington with her widowed sister. Did the Führer come in with the breakfast tray, as it were, and go out again with the tea-things?

He was tolerant of what the newspapers rather gaily called the psychology of Fascism—he could understand that—but not of what hardly anybody called the psychology of appeasement, that irrepressible urge to give someone something that it was pretty clear he ought not to have. When he had first met Miss Frencham—Alicia—he had wondered whether she thought the whole thing a gigantic game, like the Girl Guides on a grand scale. Finding out that, on the contrary, she regarded it with an immense seriousness was both exhilarating and disappointing: the one because it confirmed his professional judgement; the other because it made clear to him the kind of person he was dealing with. There was no getting away from this.

Eventually it was over. The gust of applause that saw off the speakers surprised him with its intensity: like a football match won in the last minute; an unfancied horse turning the tables at the final fence. There was a retiring collection, to which he contributed a shilling and Miss Frencham a pound note. He looked round the room to see if there were any more faces to add to the half-dozen or so already recognised.

With what was clearly something of an effort, Miss Frencham said: 'If you liked, we could drop in at my house for a glass of sherry. It's only a street or two away. My father would be delighted to meet you.'

'It's awfully kind of you,' he said, 'but I really must be getting back. The New York market will be opening, you see.'

There was a fiction that he worked as a stockbroker.

'Well, perhaps another time.'

He knew that he had no earthly reason ever to attend a meeting of the League of St George again.

'That would be very nice.'

She nodded seriously, as if they had just sealed some holy compact, perishable only by death. 'Here,' she said, 'you must take some of these to distribute.'

'Thanks,' he said, without looking at the little pile of handbills she dropped into his palm, 'I'll do that.' He gave her a valedictory tap on the arm. He had not meant to do this, but somehow he did—and once again the wire-rimmed glasses fell forward onto the bridge of her nose. When he looked back she was standing by the pamphlet stall, one hand poised over the jam jar full of sixpences, white-faced and traumatised, like a girl in a medieval painting.

In the Bayswater Road it was getting colder and the people seemed less manic. The doggerel poem on the handbill turned out to be an old one from the early days of the war.

> Land of dope and Jewry
> Land that once was free
> All the Jew boys praise thee
> Whilst they plunder thee
>
> Poorer still and poorer
> Grow thy true-born sons
> Faster still and faster
> They're sent to feed the guns.

He kept one of the bills and stuffed the rest down a grating in the street. Miss Frencham would soon be drinking her glass of sherry in Powis Square, with the parlourmaid hanging up her coat. He did not find this incongruous. It was how a certain part of the English world worked: Captain Ramsay at the Eton–Harrow match; Mosley in his fencing gear. The carriage he sat in was empty and the war might never have been, and he occupied his time in writing an account of what he had noticed at the meeting.

> **Miss Harris-Foster.** Much more virulent than when last seen. Denounced Chamberlain. Said that 'world Jewry' was responsible for 'misunderstandings' between Germany and Britain, instigators of present war. Maintained that no one should be willing to bear arms.

But important that nothing should be done which might prejudice this country's interests. League members should play part in civilian defence/humanitarian work while striving to enlighten those with whom they are in contact as to the 'real' nature of factors which brought about the war.

Miss H-F received mixed reception. E.g. remarks about not bearing arms strongly applauded. Much less enthusiasm for comments about war-work.

Others present already known to B.1:

Captain Ramsay. Polished speaker. None of Miss H-F's suppressed hysteria. Well received. Intends to proceed along lines of: (a) distribution among MPs, in clubs, services, etc., of memorandum aimed at refuting Prime Minister's statement that Hitler can't be trusted, dealing with issues of Austria, Bohemia and Poland and designed throughout to show that 'world Jewry' instigators of the war; (b) leaflets, placards and labels bearing anti-Jewish propaganda. Said had been in touch with Mosley with view to 'arriving at a basis for co-operation.' When pressed by BUF members as to how far this co-operation might go, slightly evasive. Otherwise frank, open, made no secret of beliefs i.e. war result of Jewish 'ramp,' our real enemy Bolshevism, etc. Talked about 'peace feelers,' idea that these might be extended through neutral embassies, messages sent out in diplomatic bag. Would not criticise those who bore arms against Germany.

Lord Lymington. Made his usual speech. Admired the 'new spirit' emerging in Germany. War of benefit to none but 'Jews and international Communists.' Has links with Peace Aims Group. Solution lay in conference prior to negotiated peace. The King's role crucial. HM had worked for peace before war declared; declaration against his wishes; should now be encouraged to work for peace again. This statement loudly applauded.

Alicia Frencham—

But the train had reached Piccadilly, and Johnson decided to leave the problem of Miss Frencham until later.

Back at the office the B.1 corridor was nearly empty, and he stood in his room with the door open, smoking a cigarette and turning over some papers about a meeting of the Liberty Restoration Committee in Acton. He was not even sure if the Liberty Restoration Committee needed an eye being kept on it. But you could never tell.

The B.1 corridor was at its worst in the early afternoon. The cigarette smoke hung in the cornices and the strip-lighting made the faces of the secretaries who passed beneath it look like pieces of cold boiled veal on a butcher's slab. A full colonel in red tabs came crashing down the row, peering suspiciously through the open doorways as he went, and then disappeared into B.3, where his voice could be heard loudly asking directions. The place was full of these bewildered migrants: civil servants sent after files; emissaries from the services publicity departments. Security was lax. 'One of these days,' Hegarty had said, 'I shall hand over a file to some messenger boy with a chit and he'll drop his bloody parachute on the floor as he goes out.'

It was about three o'clock. From one of the nearby cells sounded a snatch of dance music, which meant that someone was (illegally) tampering with a short-wave radio. The suspicious colonel's voice had disappeared now, swallowed up in the clatter of tea-trolleys being bumped into each other and the smash of filing cabinets. Just when it seemed that everything had grown too intolerable to be borne, there was a sound of whistling from along the corridor and Hegarty came into the room. He was wearing a mackintosh buttoned up to the neck and there was a small red mark on the side of his face that had not been in evidence before.

'Been back long?' Hegarty was always terrified that his regular absences from the office would be made more conspicuous by the sight of other people tethered to their desks.

'About a quarter of an hour.'

'Splendid. If anyone asks, you can say that we came back together.'

'But nobody ever does ask.'

'That's as may be. I heard Davenport say only the other day that he thought time-keeping was getting damnably slack. His words. I didn't think people used expressions like "damnably slack" anymore, but apparently they do. How was the League of St George?'

'Appalling.'

'Why so?'

'I wouldn't mind it so much if they genuinely thought they had the country's best interests at heart. But as far as I can see most of them are actively pro-Nazi.'

'Who was there?'

'The usual lot. Miss Harris-Foster. Ramsay. Lymington. That chap from the BUF we saw with the undercover agent in Sloane Street the other week.'

'Mrs Tanqueray-Smith?'

'Not that I recall. Now you come to mention it, I wondered why she wasn't there.'

Hegarty's face showed the same delight it had worn when a visiting major-general had spilled a cup of coffee over his dress uniform.

'The reason, my dear fellow, why Mrs Tanqueray-Smith wasn't there, or at the monthly meeting of the Christian Patriots, or the British People's Party's fortnightly committee, is that according to intelligence that came over the wire this morning she has recently accepted a position at the German Air Ministry.'

'Well, I never. How on earth did she get out?'

'I don't know. How do any of them get out? Travel through some neutral territory and apply at the border, I suppose. At least my conscience is clear. I told you about Mrs Tanqueray-Smith months ago.' He looked unexpectedly crestfallen, as if suddenly reminded that the work they were engaged on was not a glorious game, but something impenetrable and serious. 'Anyhow, what will you say about the League of St George in your report?'

'I don't know. I can't get very worked up about Miss Harris-Foster.'

'Leipzig Lil? Why not?'

'I looked up her file. Do you know she joined the Imperial Fascist League as far back as 1929 when there were just half a dozen of them sitting in a room in Craven Street with Mussolini's photograph on the wall? And somebody who had tea at her flat said she had an antimacassar with the words "Perish Judah" embroidered on the back. I can't get very worked up about Miss Harris-Foster.'

'And the Honourable and Gallant Member for Peebles?'

'Ramsay? I'd say he was definitely unbalanced. Thinks the *Protocols of the Elders of Zion* came down from the Mount with the Ten Commandments. And then there's his line about "peace feelers" going out through the neutral embassies. If anyone should be putting out peace feelers it's Lord Halifax, not a back-bench MP. Apparently he and Bannister and some of the others had a grand confabulation down at Bannister's place in Sussex just the other weekend. When does an honourable and legitimate desire for peace turn into collaborating with your country's enemies?'

'He's got a son in the army.'

'He's got a chap in the American Embassy telling him the contents of Roosevelt's telegrams, if what I hear's true.'

'And what about the seductive Miss Frencham? Did she ask you back for sherry again?'

'A harmless fanatic.'

'No such thing. She's Rear-Admiral Sir Gervase Frencham's daughter, and we all know about him.'

'We do?'

'"The man who has Hitler's photograph on his desk," as the *Daily Mail* so regularly reminds us. So, what shall you tell Davenport?'

'What I said. Ramsay certainly can't be allowed to go around London saying that kind of thing. And the BUF chap we saw in Sloane Street definitely ought to be picked up.'

'I'm with you there.' There was a laborious, thundering noise in the corridor, like a *Tyrannosaurus rex* in flight, and the afternoon tea-trolley went by. 'But will Davenport be, too? That's the question.'

'Why shouldn't he? It's his job.'

'Just a hunch,' Hegarty said. The skin of his face was pale to the point of translucence, blue-tinged like skimmed milk. 'One of life's little mysteries.'

'Talking of life's little mysteries, how did you get that mark on the side of your head?'

One of the things about Hegarty—one of the many things—was that you could never tell precisely what the expression on his face meant. Just now it could have been panicked, chastened, bashful, quietly triumphant, or a combination of all four. He said: 'Let's just say I got an unexpectedly poor reception. Like the one you're going to get from Davenport, I shouldn't wonder.'

'I doubt he'll leave a mark on the side of my face.'

'But he might put one on your file,' Hegarty said. 'It amounts to the same thing.'

As a general rule the higher you climbed into the building, the less hospitable it became. Mostly this was to do with the absence of people. There were no secretaries' consoles beyond the third floor, and no messengers, and even such piecemeal symbols of civilisation as wastepaper baskets unexpectedly gave out. Quite who typed the memoranda circulated there and where they were ultimately disposed of, only the section heads knew. Nearly always deserted, but rarely soundless—frequently alive with the tramp of feet moving in counterpoint far out of sight—the corridors had other ways of emphasising their detachment from the ordinary course of human life.

Two floors below, the noticeboards advertised rugby teams, lost property, departmental soirées. Here they carried information so abstruse as to almost be in code, full of odd jargon and jagged truncations. *Mtg 26 ult. General purps. Authorised personnel to attend. B.B.O. (ops).* Presumably people who wrote and pinned up such notices knew what they meant. Hegarty had once said: 'Someone could make a great deal of money by printing a guide to departmental shorthand. I mean, what does *Exp. Gen. B.B.D.* mean? I've seen half a dozen things like that on memos since I got here and never had the slightest idea what they're about. It's the same with people's titles. Who is the *Asst P.B.C. (Div.)*? He could be the Deputy Head of Intelligence or the man who staffs the first aid post for all I know.'

On the other hand, whoever had designed these infinitely sinister backdrops, laid down the pale, threadbare carpets, applied the lemon-yellow paint to the peeling walls and been responsible for the carbolic soap smell that hung over the corridor from dawn to dusk, had not lacked all aesthetic sense. You could see this in the clumps of photographs that turned up every so often in the lobbies, or flanking lift-shaft doorways. They had nothing to do with the work of the department, but depicted ancient colonial scenes: a dozen men in solar topis and khaki shorts gathered around a dead tiger; an elephant rolling a log with its trunk; Eastern temples; pagodas glinting in the Burmese sun. 'Ghastly things,' Hegarty had commented. 'The white man's burden and some of its incidental rewards. Makes me think of being read Kipling at prep school. I wonder how Davenport can stand looking at them.'

No one quite knew how Davenport had become a section head. He was supposed to have been a National Government MP who had lost his seat in the general election of 1935, and then to have worked in Naval Intelligence. None of this inspired confidence. 'Probably filed the VD returns at Portsmouth Military Hospital,' Hegarty had said.

Davenport was a stoutish, red-haired man of fifty, who preferred to go about in military uniform rather than the dark suits that most people of his rank put on, and was famous for two idiosyncrasies. One of these was to smoke cigarettes through an amber holder. The other was to affect to forget the faces and even the identities of people that he came into contact with on a daily basis.

Davenport's room was not easy to find, as it lay at the far end of the right-hand side fourth-floor corridor, at the point where the rows of offices petered out into a kind of no man's land of broom-cupboards and store chests, from which it was sometimes possible to pilfer stationery. It was a tiny, bare-walled cubicle whose only ornament, apart from the desk, was a gunmetal filing cabinet and a photograph of Davenport standing on the House of Commons terrace with Stanley Baldwin, and conveyed an air of studied impermanence, as if Davenport had come there under duress, disdained to unpack the things he had brought with him, and was hard at work negotiating better quarters.

'Good morning, sir.'

'Good morning.' It was one of Davenport's habits not to look up if anyone under the rank of major came into his room. 'Do I know you?'

'Johnson, sir. B.1. I believe we've met several times.'

'Well, you obviously remember them better than I do. What do you want now?'

'You sent a message that you wanted to see me, sir. About that subversives report.'

'Did I? Did I indeed?' Davenport looked horribly glum. The skin of his plump, shiny face was full of odd abrasions, far too deep to have been made by a razor. 'Oh yes, the League of St George. In which, I seem to remember, the very first paragraph contained a faulty subjunctive. If it *were* possible to invoke the Defence of the Realm Act, not if it *was*.' It was another of Davenport's habits to trump initial vagueness about any document sent to him with total recall of its contents.

The redness was spreading to all parts of his face now, like red wine leaching into a tablecloth. He picked up the report, which, as anyone who had dealings with him would have been able to predict, lay an inch or two from his elbow beneath the amber cigarette holder, and began to riffle through it, all uncertainty gone.

'Miss Harris-Foster, now. Has a Nazi flag in her sitting-room and thinks the PM's real name is Mosieski. I don't know what you want me to do about her.'

'Nothing, sir.'

'Well, that's a relief. For let me tell you, at this stage there's nothing that can be done, nothing at all.' Davenport raised both hands dramatically in the air to emphasise this point. 'What about Captain Ramsay?'

'We've been monitoring him at meetings of this kind for nearly two months, sir. You can see the sort of thing he says. We've taken legal opinion. The Home Office lawyers think that statements of this kind may very probably be regarded as treasonable. As for his supporters, we know the whole thing is organised. One of our people has been following the membership book around London, but we haven't yet been able to get a sight of it.' You had to be careful about involving the Home Office lawyers with Davenport, but it was sometimes the only way.

'Home Office lawyers, eh?'

The people who regarded Davenport as a figure of fun were those who had no dealings with him. Subordinates knew better.

He picked up the amber cigarette holder and took a puff of smoke, then slowly exhaled, so that it hung round the corners of his eyes. He was intensely irritated. 'I can't let you go after Ramsay. Absolutely no question of it. I don't care if he is in cahoots with Mosley. As far as I know, Mosley is urging all patriotic Englishmen to do their duty. If he were sending cables through the neutral embassies it would be a different matter. As for what he thinks about the Jews, you can read pretty much the same thing in the letters page of the *Daily Telegraph*.' Then, seeing that he might have gone too far, he said: 'Not that I want to disparage what you've done, Johnson. Not at all. Highly commendable. But between you and me, I think we have other things on our plate beyond half a dozen lunatics in a church hall in Bayswater.'

According to all the best-tried methods of dealing with Davenport, this would have been the moment to retire. But he could not resist asking: 'Are you personally acquainted with Captain Ramsay, sir?'

Davenport could get very angry when asked direct questions. Now he simply took the amber holder out of his mouth and tapped the end on the topmost page of the report. 'I don't think that's any business of yours at all . . .'

'Johnson, sir.'

'Johnson. And Lord Lymington's correct title, for future reference, Johnson, is Viscount Lymington.' The stretched damson skin of his face had almost returned to normal. There was supposed to be a Mrs Davenport, although no one Johnson knew had ever seen her.

What did she make of the amber cigarette holder, the abraded face, and the studied incomprehension? You could never tell.

'I'm very sorry, sir. B.3 borrowed our copy of *Debrett* and we haven't been able to check things in the usual way.'

For some reason Johnson was thinking about his school days: lumps of suet pudding on blue-and-white plates; the liniment reek of the changing rooms; fog hanging low over the Sussex Downs. One of the masters had looked rather like Davenport, which explained the trick his mind had played.

'What about Denison, sir?'

'Denison?'

'The BUF man, sir. Been liasing between Mosley and the Right Club since the war began. Anthea Carey saw him last week with a chap that Special Branch are positive is a German agent.'

Davenport spread the papers on his desk into a kind of star, shuffled them together and then slapped them down. It was a mournful gesture, the gesture of the man cut out for better things, the man who has followed enticing trails into the jungle only to see them disappear, the man who has worshipped gods that turned out never to have existed. He said: 'Oh, well, if that's the case you'd better bring him in.'

'Today, sir?'

'Today. Tomorrow. This minute if you feel like it. It's all the same to me. Just make sure that the usual protocols are followed.'

'Yes, sir.'

'Naturally I shall want a full report of everything he says. If he does say anything, of course. Some of them don't.'

'Of course, sir.'

He waited for the nod of dismissal, but it never came. Davenport had picked another file out of the stack on his desk and was examining its cover with a kind of desperate seriousness, like an actor auditioning for the part of an intellectual.

Going back down the corridor, past the stationery cupboards with their broken locks, and desolate cubby-holes from which furious-looking men stuck out their heads at his approach and then disappointedly drew them back, he found that he was still oppressed by the memory of his school days: whitewashed corridors smelling of disinfectant; sawdust piles in the joinery shop; gulls flying overhead towards the Channel. The department's resemblance to a minor public school had occurred to other people. Hegarty had once said: 'It's not just that Davenport and his pals behave as if they were the prefects and we were the lower fourth, it's the eternal feeling that you're about to be blamed for an offence you didn't even know you'd committed.'

Back on the B.1 corridor, everything was just as he had left it, except that a stack of files nearly a foot high had appeared on the carpet outside Hegarty's door. Hegarty sat at his desk with one hand pressed to his forehead and the other dangling a half-smoked cigarette. 'Any news?'

'You were right about Ramsay and Lord Lymingon—sorry, *Viscount* Lymington. We're not to touch them. But we can go and get Denison whenever we like.'

'Where does he live?'

'Highbury way, I think. Near the Arsenal football club.'

'There's a directory on the chair,' Hegarty said. He was thoroughly galvanised, as if an electrical current had just started to shoot through him. 'I'm going to enjoy this. Or perhaps not. At any rate, for the moment we must give Davenport the benefit of the doubt.'

'What do you mean?'

'You'll see. . . . What about reinforcements?'

'Davenport said to follow the usual procedures.'

'Ah, but what are the usual procedures? That's what I'd like to know. Everyone talks about them and then does exactly what they like, as far as I can see.' He picked up the telephone receiver on his desk and, after a moment or two, said in an impossibly languid voice: 'This is Mr Hegarty from B.1. I know there are meant to be proper channels, but this is an emergency. I should like to order a couple of constables to attend a little event that my colleague Mr Johnson and I are planning.' Hegarty always spoke to the police sergeant as if he were hiring waiters for a party. 'We'd better go in my car,' he said, when he had finished making the arrangements, 'and they can meet us there.'

'Why do you always speak in that affected voice to the duty sergeant?'

'Because they think we're all pompous idiots who swan about while they do all the heavy work.'

'But isn't that more or less true?'

'It may well be, but the last thing we want is those people at West End Central getting above themselves.'

Outside there were faint striations of mist floating in from across the Whitehall battlements, so that the passers-by walking down Jermyn Street seemed more than usually wraith-like and sinister. Hegarty's car was at the far end. Seated at the wheel, he turned unexpectedly glum, as if the expedition had been a mistake from the start, was bound to end in failure. All this meant, as those familiar with Hegarty's temperament well knew, was that he had temporarily lost interest in his professional duties and returned to the permanently engrossing subject of his personal life.

Sure enough, they had barely reached Piccadilly when he said: 'Did I tell you about Julia?'

'I don't think you did. Is she the one you met in the Lyons?'

'No, that's Sally-Ann. Julia's the one whose aunt was a friend of my aunt's at school. It sounds unlikely, I know, but there you are. Now I come to remember it, I did tell you about her. That afternoon when we were writing the report about the White Knights of St Athelstan. Well, that girl will be the death of me. It's not that she won't let you stuff her. Far from it. It's just that everything has to be, well, I suppose the word would be *choreographed*. You know. Smart restaurant. Decent show—if there is a show. Taxis both ways. Do you know, the other night I'm pretty sure the reason she wouldn't let me come back with her was because when she wanted a cigarette in the cab I chucked a box of matches over rather than waving my lighter under her nose as I believe a civilised gentleman is supposed to do.'

It was one of Hegarty's better monologues about women.

'Never mind about Julia. What about Denison? Will there be any rough stuff?'

'Bound to be,' Hegarty said. Hegarty liked rough stuff. 'Don't all those BUF chaps keep knuckledusters in their sock drawers? I've a good mind to leave the policemen outside so I can really have a go.'

The really disturbing thing about the department, Johnson had long since decided, was its propensity to violence. It was full of gentlemanly young men in dark suits and Toc H ties with hockey-club fixture-cards on their desks, just itching to cause serious damage to the people they came across in the course of their duties. Hegarty had once broken a suspect's arm while bringing him back for questioning.

As they sped along Upper Street, he said again: 'What did you mean about giving Davenport the benefit of the doubt?'

'You'll see,' Hegarty said. 'Do we take a right here, or turn at the top? I don't think I've been this way since I was chasing that Pilkington woman. Which was a tremendous mistake, I can tell you.'

The street was in sight of the Arsenal football ground, treeless and non-descript, thirty or forty terraced houses jammed together in comfortless profusion. The two policemen were already loitering at the kerb. It was Hegarty's policy on these occasions to spend a very long time in parking the car. When he finally stepped out of it, he said, 'I'm very glad to see you men here. A very significant operation. It's important we co-operate at a time like this. Have you established the address?'

The policemen were not impressed by Hegarty. The taller of them said: 'They divide into flats down this end. Looks as if it's on the top floor.'

'Excellent,' Hegarty said. He glanced to left and right, as if a huge invisible crowd had gathered along the pavement. 'Well, what are we waiting for?'

The front door of the house was unlocked. They went rapidly up the staircase, drumming their feet deliberately on the bare boards. A cat went scampering down to safety in the hall. The staircase brought them to a solitary, blue-painted door whose letter-box looked as if it had been stuffed up with brown paper. There was no answer to their repeated knocks.

'Better break it down,' Hegarty said. His eyes were staring out of his head. 'There's a hammer in the car. Hang on, though. Might as well have a go myself. These things are never very well secured. Stand back there, will you?'

In the end the door gave way with surprising ease. The uplifted frame fell into the hallway but there was no one behind it. The flat was empty.

'Poor sort of place,' Hegarty said. He strode into the tiny kitchen, pulled open a cupboard or two, stared at an ironing board that had been propped against the window, and then picked up a paper bag that had been left on the kitchen table to see if anyone had written a telephone number on it. Nobody had. Something caught his eye. 'Look at that,' he said. He put his hand out to touch a kettle that lay on the gas-ring. 'Still hot. Can't have gone far.'

The policemen were more interested, now they had broken into some-body's property. 'Perhaps he'll be back,' one of them said. 'No telling where people come and go, is there?'

'No,' Hegarty said, a bit wearily. 'He won't be back.' His eyes had returned to normal: grey, distant, and faintly mad. 'He won't be back,' he said again. There was a pound weight lying on the kitchen table, next to a set of scales, and with a sudden dramatic movement he picked it up and hurled it through the kitchen window. A fragment of glass sprang out and stuck in the back of one of his hands.

'You won't be needing us, then?' the taller of the two policemen asked respectfully. Hegarty had gone up in his estimation by smashing the window.

'No, we won't. But thanks very much all the same.'

While they listened to the noise of the policemen's boots receding down the stairs, Hegarty took a cotton handkerchief out of his pocket and began to bind up his bleeding hand. He looked horribly self-righteous.

'Well, no more benefit of the doubt,' he said.

'What do you mean?'

'Think about it. Who knew we were coming here? Apart from the desk sergeant at West End Central?'

'That's easy. You, me, and Davenport.'

'Well, I didn't tip Denison the wink and neither did you. So that leaves our man on the fourth floor.'

'Why would Davenport want to tip off a member of the BUF known to be fraternising with Nazi agents?'

'A very good question,' Hegarty said. 'And one I've been asking myself for some time.'

They went back through the empty flat, through the shattered doorway, and out into the silent street.

CHAPTER 8

Palace Days

At Buckingham Palace the wind is blowing in against the high windows. It does this with an extraordinary force, as if someone were throwing lumps of invisible concrete. The frames buckle and shift and make ominous cracking noises, like a ship at anchor, battened down before the approaching storm. Like the war news, the weather is uncertain. No single pattern prevails. Like the war, again, nobody quite knows where they are with it. From fifty yards below comes the sound of a sentry's boots crunching up the gravel. At this distance the noise is oddly insubstantial, like the rasp of a match, an ant passing the Queen of Brobdingnag in her tower.

Head down over his square mahogany table, the King feels the wind rather than hearing it. Oddly enough, it reminds him of his time at Dartmouth: a world of creaking spars, the smell of salt, the grey arm of the Channel. Even now, walking down one of the endless corridors in which the palace abounds, he sometimes finds himself reaching out a hand to steady himself on a phantom ship's rail. His old midshipman's uniform is in a cupboard somewhere, mouldering into dust.

It is half-past ten in the morning and he is examining his correspondence. Not the official letters, the ambassadorial requests, and the episcopal appointments—these have been borne away on a salver by a footman half an hour since—but what his private secretary calls the 'unsoliciteds': the great tide of expostulation, entreaty, and advice that rolls in every morning from country rectories, suburban villas in the Greater London sprawl, and mean little houses in the industrial north.

His father, the old King, never saw these effusions. He had a digest of the opinions expressed in them drawn up by an equerry, which he considered, or did not consider, at his leisure. But the new King is fascinated by them. He likes their variety, their deference, the occasional irruptions of temperament.

Some of the correspondents write in strangely coloured inks. Most of them are faintly ashamed of their effrontery, one or two of them even fearful, as if presuming to address one's sovereign were an offence punishable by law. Their language is unexpectedly archaic, as if the writing of them was a step backwards into a landscape of knights and troubadors, pageboys in the banqueting hall and seneschals at the gate.

Not wishing to intrude upon Your Majesty's valuable time . . .

Wanting to suggest that if Your Majesty will submit the matter to his kind consideration . . .

Sometimes the King wonders how the people who write these things actually envisage him. Christ's representative on earth? A benign but somewhat distant uncle? A managing director? It is difficult to tell.

The wind bangs against the windows, which rattle in their frames. At Osborne, on the Isle of Wight, there was a particular window in which his great-grandmother used to sit to command a view of the terrace. He can still summon up her image—a kind of compound of widow's weeds, black bombazine, that curiously indignant face—but it is all nearly forty years ago and there are other faces come to superimpose themselves.

His correspondents—those respectful housewives, those retired majors of infantry, those dotty vicars, those unemployed men from Salford—are writing to him about the war. A few of the letters are openly pro-German. They remind him of his ancestral ties and the Bolshevik menace. Others wonder why England should be involving herself in a foreign quarrel.

There are people who want him to take a lead—*a word from Your Majesty would, I am convinced, snuff out this unhappy conflagration*, a brigadier has written in green-ink letters half an inch high on the headed paper of the Harrogate Conservative Club. On impulse he takes down a copy of the Army List from the shelf above his desk and riffles through it, but there is no sign of the Harrogate brigadier. Not all the people who petition him, alas, are authentic. Sometimes the ingratiating town clerk and the aspiring Lord Lieutenant can be traced back to mental institutions and reformatory common rooms. It is all very odd.

Just now there is a rustle of movement at the room's further end: not made by the wind, this time, but by Mr Nichols readjusting his trouser-leg with one hand as the other sets down a teacup. The King is not quite sure what he thinks of Mr Nichols, whose fourth or even fifth visit this is. He is a tallish, cherubic, and impossibly juvenile-looking man of forty who writes sprightly newspaper articles and books about his country garden and at one point—so the people who assemble these budgets of intelligence assure him—used to contribute to Cochran's revues. Other details have been vouchsafed about Mr Nichols's private life, none of them exactly creditable. These, curiously enough, the King thinks he can imagine for himself.

He has a memory of Mr Nichols in his salad days, staying with his comptroller, Sir Sidney Greville, a gracious old bachelor with a weakness for pretty young men, and having to be kept out of sight whenever Queen Mary came to call. In fact, the King is relaxed about homosexuals. It takes all sorts. Wallis was always amused by them. Besides, theatrical people—artists, writers—are known to be that way inclined. His father, on the other hand, would not have given Mr Nichols the time of day.

'May I pour you a cup of tea, sir?' Mr Nichols asks, with the immense, self-conscious solicitude that is his signature mark, but the King shakes his head. He is still thinking about Hitler, *Kristallnacht*, the quarter of a million marching men practising their manoeuvres beyond the French frontier. There are people known to him—people at whose houses he has been entertained—who regard Hitler as an instrument of destiny, the saviour of Europe.

The newsreel films that come back from Nuremberg and other ceremonies always strike him as triumphalist and un-English, though admirable in their discipline and fervour. He has dined several times with Herr von Ribbentrop, now returned to Berlin, and found him conceited. Hitler he thinks slightly mad, obsessed, an ex-corporal with a grievance, but such people are all the rage these days. Mussolini, the Italian, is an hysteric. Stalin he can never forgive for Grand Duchess Olga, Grand Duchess Tatiana, Grand Duchess Marie, and Grand Duchess Anastasia—four little girls in muslin dresses and white bonnets who came to Barton the year before his grandfather died, only to be shot by the Bolsheviks in 1917.

On the drawing-room wall at Fort Belvedere there is a photograph of the two families together on the terrace. The Tsar sits next to grandpapa. His father has his arm around Grand Duchess Marie's slender waist. The girls called him 'Cousin David.' One does not forget such things.

'Then of course there was Hartnell's party, sir, at which I believe you were present,' Nichols suggests. They are talking, or rather Nichols is talking, about the entertainments of the 1920s: parties in Sussex orchards and discarded champagne corks bobbing gently downstream. Just now people seem to be very interested in the '20s. The vastness of the gulf between Norman Hartnell's parties and Mussolini does not seem to have occurred to them.

But the past is a bran tub, he thinks, filled with nothing but bran. Half the royal families in Europe are living in bed-sitting rooms in Biarritz and Menton. There is no going back. Grand Duchess Olga and her sisters had long, untethered hair that hung down the seams of their muslin frocks. Even here everything is quietly stagnating, or rolling away like the champagne corks to the distant sea. His mother is at Badminton, quartered on the Duke of Beaufort. There are tales of her going out to tea in the neighbourhood and demanding to be given antiques that take her fancy. Bertie, Elizabeth, and the girls are at Sandringham: he has seen none of them for months.

'No,' he says suddenly—it is the first time he has opened his mouth for five minutes—'I don't think I was ever at one of Hartnell's parties,' and Mr Nichols bobs his neatly brilliantined head.

'I have no doubt, sir, that you have a better memory than I,' he gamely concedes. Mr Nichols is very punctilious about his 'sirs' and 'Your Majestys.' The newspaper columns he writes are full of deferential accounts of the duchesses he has danced with and the celebrated people he has encountered at dinner.

In his time the King has met any number of literary men. Once when he was on a tour of the West Country they sent him to see Thomas Hardy. It was not a success. Hardy's small-talk was limited. He spent most of his time upsetting and then rearranging the fire-irons. The King wonders if there is anything that connects Mr Nichols, in his natty three-piece suit, with a Charvet handkerchief rising from its breast-pocket, to the little bald man by his frugal hearth, and thinks that probably there is not. But then people, he assumes, are all too ready to confound the expectations one has of them, or there would not be ex-corporals in the Chancelleries of Europe. It is all very strange.

The wind is dying down again now. The creaks from the window-frames have become less ominous. Outside in the Mall the plane trees quiver, as if gripped by an electrical current. Mr Nichols is drinking his tea, casting appreciative little glances around the room as he does so. His delight in the honour being done to him is almost tangible. People's reactions to the fact of the royal presence differ enormously, the King has found. Some are abased, others beatific. A few carry their refusal to be impressed to immoderate lengths. Women are the worst. In America the senators' wives say extraordinary things, the confusions of their inner lives laid bare in a sentence or two.

Mr Nichols, he sees, is admiring the framed photographs in which the room abounds. Some of these are family portraits going back to the age of crinolines and side-whiskers—there is a terrific one of his great-grandfather ponderously astride a donkey—but one or two of them are representations of himself brought back from foreign trips: as 'Chief Morning Star' in a Red Indian feather-bonnet in Calgary; inspecting the Buddha's tooth at Kandy. There was a time in his life when he did nothing except tour foreign countries. He has difficulty remembering in what year and to what effect.

Mr Nichols has given up on the '20s, Norman Hartnell's parties, treasure-hunts, and *fêtes champêtres*, and begun to talk about Captain Ramsay. The King knows about Captain Ramsay. He has met him at garden parties and read of his doings in *The Times*, and thinks him slightly unbalanced. Most of these people are: Mosley in his ridiculous high-necked sweaters; Admiral Domvile with his portrait of the Führer on the mantelpiece next to his daughter's riding trophies. There is a strain of fanaticism in upper-class English life that never quite goes away. The letters he receives confirm this.

The world is in the grip of a Zionist conspiracy. The Aryan race is threatened. There are Jews, Freemasons, and Bolsheviks working in harness to defraud the Briton of his birthright. The King, who is a Freemason himself, does not seriously believe any of this, but he can see why certain people might do so. As for the war, to which Captain Ramsay and his friends are so strenuously opposed, he thinks they have a point.

None of this, though, solves the problem of what to do with Mr Nichols, in his natty dove-grey suit, cup of tea now balanced by his elbow, who clearly sees himself as an emissary between the forces of reason and their Godhead, a forger of alliances between like-minded people whom only an absurd series of protocols keeps apart.

Just now Mr Nichols is talking about an attaché at the German Embassy in Dublin, and certain pieces of intelligence that may or may not be conveyed through him; but this is dangerous territory, and both of them know it. 'Mr Nichols,' he begins to say, 'I really cannot . . .'

And Mr Nichols stops, almost in mid-sentence, with the ghost of a smile dodging around the corners of his mouth, as if to say that he knows, understands, sympathises, assumes that what the King sincerely believes cannot be decently uttered. The King's private secretary has his doubts about Mr Nichols, whom he believes to be a demoralising influence, but in the matter of private invitations a king may do as he pleases.

Perhaps, Mr Nichols now proposes, the wave of his hand partly obscuring the picture of Chief Morning Star in his headdress, he would like to meet Captain Ramsay? But the King shakes his head. The problem of kingship, he thinks, is that your neutrality, in theory impregnable, is in practice liable to endless compromise. It is one of the things—the only thing—that Wallis never understood. He can see her now, demanding why, if he is a king and an emperor, he should be compelled to dine with the Duke and Duchess of Westminster rather than the people he really wants to see.

The 'unsoliciteds' are still strewn all over his desk. He wonders how many of them are from fifth columnists. There is a woman in Northumberland who writes to him every week alleging that all the newspaper proprietors in England are Jews. What do you do with such people? And what do you do with Captain Ramsay and his kind?

For some reason he thinks of Hardy again, rattling his fire-irons. One of the questions he had asked at Max Gate, intended to settle an argument with his mother, was whether Hardy had written *Tess of the D'Urbervilles*. But it is possible to envy Hardy, who died before the age of dictators, lofted flags, marching men, and *Lebensraum*, and whose books—he has looked into them since—are not about the neuroses of the modern world but the amours of peasants and elemental tragedies.

'Nichols,' he says unexpectedly—they have left off the Dublin embassy and are talking about the proposed peace petition, a subject in which he thinks he can at least take an unpartisan interest—'did you ever meet Hardy?'

And Mr Nichols looks, for the first time in their dealings, faintly surprised, and says that no, he never did, but keeps the gleam of enquiry in his eye so that the King is compelled to recount the story of his trip to Dorchester and the conversation about *Tess*.

'Rather an odd chap,' he says, and Mr Nichols smiles, back on more familiar territory—the plain man discountenanced in the presence of art—and says that literary people very often are odd, buttressing this statement with anecdotes about Shaw, Wells, and Edith Sitwell, each of whom he has apparently met and sparred with. There is no end to Mr Nichols's repertoire. He has met everyone—President Coolidge, Dame Melba, Noël Coward—and has a story about each of them.

The wind is dying away now. There are equerries at the door, the sound of movement in the corridor. He suspects that Mr Nichols would like an invitation to luncheon, but Mr Nichols will be disappointed. He wonders for a moment what Mr Nichols's motives are in all this. Is he one of those courtiers *manqués*, who get a kick out of the whole royal apparatus, its grave-faced attendants, its damask draperies, its bizarre embodiments of the myth of Albion? Or is he simply a patriotic citizen doing his best in difficult circumstances?

As with all human motivation, it is difficult to tell. There were people who thought Wallis was a gold-digging Yankee seductress. They were, of course, wrong, but he can see why they might have thought it so. Mr Nichols is looking at him expectantly, like a dog who refuses to believe its afternoon walk is at an end, and that no further sticks will be thrown. The King can see no attraction in the life he leads, but no doubt Mr Nichols regards it differently.

The really dreadful thing about the past, he thinks, is that it can never be subdued. The patterns it makes are quite unforeseeable. The little Russian girls spoke English, but of an impossibly arch and archaic kind, as if it had been translated from the French by a Victorian governess. Their servants were extraordinary—old *babushkas*, fled from the story books. He can see Grand Duchess Marie's hair escaping down the back of her neck as she sits in the crook of his father's arm, as if she stands in the room before him now.

Mr Nichols, hat in hand, is getting up to leave. And then a thought occurs to him, so that the spectre of the Russian royal family on the terrace at Barton momentarily recedes and he is left with this impossibly juvenile-looking middle-aged man genuflecting on his carpet. 'Mr Nichols,' he says, and Mr Nichols waits, looking so thoroughly poised and *affairé* that it is rather comical to behold, 'Mr Nichols, there is one task with which you might be able to help me.'

And Mr Nichols listens, fascinated, while a swarm of footmen buzzes into the room to abstract its tea-things and rearrange its furniture, while outside the wind falls away to nothing, the grey clouds gather, and the plane trees in the Mall stand motionless in the bleak, early December light.

CHAPTER 9

Bishop's Park

In this part of London the gardens had not been dug up for vegetables, and the view from the upper storeys of the houses that adjoined the park was the same as it had always been. Standing at one of these high windows you could see canopies of evergreens, a children's playground, picturesque lozenges of bright green grass, a line of elms flanking the tow-path: none of them precisely demarcated—at one point the grass ran as far as the water's edge—but giving the impression of order, design, meaning wrought out of herbaceous chaos that might otherwise have risen up and blocked the thoroughfare to Putney Bridge.

Further off, beyond the evergreens, lay the Bishop's Palace and its walled garden, where Cynthia remembered being taken as a child for picnics. There was nothing reassuring about this familiarity. People already talked about 'before the war' as if the phrase was a guillotine, severing at a stroke any connection that the past might have with the present. This gave even quite recent stretches of time an oddly phantasmal quality, the memory of it not rendered more precious but somehow soured.

In the distance, cut off by lumps of foliage or intrusions of the tide wall, the river lay quiet under weak, late-November sun. Like practically everything else in London it seemed diminished, ground-down and languid. On the Surrey side, sometimes blocked off by the Port of London Authority barges, more often than not open to view, rose much else that was recognisable: Star and Garter Mansions; the Harrods repository; the curve of the Thames as it went down to Barnes and Richmond. Again, there was no satisfaction to be got from these landmarks. In some ways an unknown landscape would have been better: less oppressive; less weighed down with personal baggage; much less frightening.

Tyler Kent's flat was high up in a mansion block at the road's easternmost end. The immediate view was of a rectangle of burnt-cinder tennis courts—out of commission now, with the nets folded in neat piles under tarpaulins—so that by late afternoon a vast pool of blackness seemed to extend in all directions beyond the window. Like the *Duration* office, it had the disadvantage of never catching the light, so that, even at midday, with the blinds drawn back and the lamps on, there was a sense that the people who wandered through its half-dozen rooms were faintly subterranean, struggling to find an exit route that would lead them back towards the sun, while other creatures, less keen on escape, toiled menacingly in their wake.

A previous tenant had had it refurbished in a vaguely modernist way with white-painted circular tables and chairs with supports made out of metal tubing. To this Tyler Kent had added such refinements as a life-sized American eagle, moulded in brass, that sat on a plinth inside the front door, framed maps of Montana and Wyoming showing the progress of the Indian wars, and a portrait of Babe Ruth. Otherwise, nothing in the decor offered any clue to his personality, unless it was that the whole scheme, with its clanging juxtapositions and its discordant notes, was supposed to reflect the coming together of two worlds that his presence in London might have been thought to symbolise.

Privately, Cynthia reckoned that this sort of calculation was slightly beyond him. Apart from this it was quite a nice place to spend time, convenient for bus and underground routes, and with several radiators.

Three months into the conflict, the newspapers had started to run surveys under the heading WHAT HAS THE WAR DONE TO YOU? The people who responded to them wrote of the inconveniences of the blackout, of the privations of food rationing, of the grave uncertainties that lay ahead, of personal lives in which what had once been vague plans had been turned into hard and fast reality. Cynthia would have answered, truthfully, that the war had brought her into contact with people like Tyler Kent, a kind of person of whom she had no previous experience, and the inconsistencies of whose outlook on the world she found entirely baffling. Mrs Kirkpatrick would have looked Tyler Kent up and down, asked him a question or two about origins, antecedents, and acquaintance, and found him wanting. Possibly this was part of his attraction.

On the one hand he was like every young man about London Cynthia had ever met: a wearer of well-cut Anthony Eden suits and black Oxfords from Lobb's in St James's, a hailer of taxis and a bullier of waiters. On the other hand there were gaping compartments of English life that had somehow passed him by. Part of him was so raptly attuned to the new environment in which he found himself that the impersonation was barely noticeable, or, if detected, to be warmly applauded as a mark of his determination to fit in. But there were other parts which suffered from exposure to the detail of everyday life. The general effect was like a Professor of Medieval History, who in preparing his definitive study of Scholasticism had somehow managed to forget the date of the Battle of Hastings.

All this made him an odd person to be with: confident about some things, flustered by others, at all times liable to flare up at the least provocation. He said once, quite sincerely: 'I've a very efficient and reliable character, you see. And whenever I come across people who aren't that way inclined, I pretty soon lose my temper.' There was something exhilarating about these explosions, and also something alienating. Like the map of Custer's last expedition, they hinted at a border that was better not crossed.

One crucial boundary had already been breached. Cynthia was used to pink-faced subalterns who sat in taxis holding her hand as if it were a lump of marble. Tyler Kent, on the other hand, regarded sex as a kind of endless lunch-counter where all the snacks were free. She was not much shocked by his matter-of-factness, but preferred to keep some of its implications at arm's length.

As a general rule they met at the flat on Saturday afternoon: the sun long since disappeared beyond the park, the tennis courts already gathered up in shadow. There was always something faintly theatrical about these occasions, a sense of everything being pre-arranged, gestures stylised to the point where it was odd to think that human beings had contrived them. Afterwards they would lie across the big divan bed, beneath the photograph of Tyler Kent and his fellow Princetonian sophomores, and talk. Or rather he would talk, and she, coverlet pulled up to her neck, eyes fixed on a rather dramatic crack in the whitewashed ceiling, would listen.

Curiously, Cynthia never minded the one-sidedness of these interludes. She had spent her life listening to men laying down the law: it seemed almost morally wrong that Tyler Kent, his proprietorial rights established by her presence under the sheets, should be denied his chance to impress, instruct, and edify. There was also the fact that the subjects Tyler Kent thought it his duty to lecture her on had a definite air of novelty.

Once, in the course of one of these harangues, she said: 'Does this kind of thing happen in Baltimore?'

'What kind of thing?' Tyler Kent's really elemental quality, and the one that separated him from all the Englishmen of her acquaintance, was his suspicion.

'Young men from the diplomatic service taking ladies back to their apartments and seducing them.'

The Princeton sophomores looked glassy-eyed, like rabbits that had lain too long on the ice. Some of them wore risible bow ties. Tyler Kent, whom she had located in the second row, was weighed down by a kind of heavy-duty sports coat. To anyone used to looking at Oxford college photographs, the effect was unutterably bizarre: as if Anthony Eden had appeared on a newsreel dressed as a costermonger.

'I guess they might,' he said, the suspicion gone. 'It's a long time since I was there. Things could have changed.'

Before arriving in London, Tyler Kent had worked in the embassies at Paris and Vienna. These formed the subject of most of his lectures.

'It's not that I don't appreciate the challenges of diplomacy,' he said. 'Far from it. But there's a line that diplomats shouldn't be expected to cross. Take dear old Fred, Ambassador Bullitt, promising support to the

French, or the fellow in Warsaw advising the Polish government. That kind of thing is just as likely to promote war as Hitler marching into the Sudetenland.'

'I suppose it depends what you think about Hitler,' she said.

'It depends what you think about the international policy of your government, which in this case is to keep out of a European war.'

'It sounds very odd to hear you, of all people, saying you're an isolationist.'

It was a good joke, for it had to do with the freight of Tyler Kent's mantelpiece. Here, at any given time, could be found eight or nine stiff-backed invitation cards advertising soirées in South Kensington or bridge parties in Pont Street. Half of Belgravia, it seemed, wanted Mr Tyler Kent to come and dine with them. Cynthia, whose social antennae were finely tuned to social distinctions of this kind, had been impressed.

'Don't mind my asking,' she said, after one of these inspections, 'but how do you know Lady Colefax?'

'Sybil?' An Englishman would not have called Lady Colefax 'Sybil,' but Tyler Kent liked having his egalitarian cake and eating it too. 'I suppose I just met her someplace.' Tyler Kent had a genius for meeting people someplace.

'And the Honourable Mrs Pemberton-Green. Where on earth did you come across her?'

'Is that the little old lady with the sausage curls?' Tyler Kent asked, with absolutely unaffected sincerity. 'I think I met her at the Huntercombes. Or played bridge with her somewhere.'

'I think you're a dreadful *arriviste*,' she said, half-mockingly.

'In America,' he said, still with the same unaffected seriousness, 'we go where we like and don't mind about the people.'

Sometimes these society women rang up the flat demanding to speak to him. They seemed abashed, not quite themselves, as if they suspected the impulse that had led them to the receiver in the first place, fearful that some infinitely superior intelligence might be having a little game at their expense. There had been a moment once when, lying on the divan bed while Tyler Kent, half-dressed, hunted a lost cuff-link, she had wondered whether the whole thing might not have been an imposture, the Princeton sophomore chosen for his phantom resemblance, the trail leading back not to the Baltimore brownstone but to squalor and despair.

But this was an imaginative leap too far. No, Tyler Kent was indisputably who he said he was, a cipher clerk who had swum self-confidently out of his depth and found the other bathers friendly. There were other callers, too, beyond the orbit of Lady Colefax and the Honourable Mrs Pemberton-Green. Once, picking up the telephone when he was out buying cigarettes, she found herself talking to a sharp, high, male voice that instantly returned her to the autumn pinewoods and Sussex-by-the-Sea.

'Is Mr Kent at home? This is Captain Ramsay.'

It was on the tip of her tongue to say that she knew who he was, that she had listened to him reciting Andrew Lang in the antique shooting brake, but for some reason she did not do this. She had not liked Captain Ramsay, and wanted him kept as far away from her as possible. He could make his own identifications. When she heard the noise of Tyler Kent's feet coming up the staircase—he managed to invest even the job of walking upstairs with an intent, sober seriousness—she went out onto the landing in her, or rather his, dressing gown and said, 'Captain Ramsay was on the telephone for you.'

The cigarettes were in a brown paper bag, borne with a certain reverence, like a votive offering. 'Oh yes? What did he want?'

'He didn't say. I told him you'd call him later.'

'Ah, the joys of diplomatic immunity,' Tyler said mysteriously. Voluble about society hostesses, he was unexpectedly silent when it came to Captain Ramsay. 'You want to stay here and eat or go out someplace?'

The flat usually got on Cynthia's nerves after an hour or two, or perhaps it was being with Tyler Kent in it that produced this effect. He was a restless host, forever picking things up and putting them down again, or seizing up piles of papers and locking them away in cupboards. In the end she got dressed, pulled down the front of her skirt in the hope of disguising a rent that had appeared in the knee of her stocking, and they went out to a party in Redcliffe Gardens given by some people who had made their money in the Baltic timber trade and were understandably cross about its cessation.

They went to a lot of parties in that winter—it was a relaxation from sex and ambassadorial failure—not all of them as grand as the Belgravia routs of the Bishop's Park mantelpiece: drinks parties in odd, subterranean flats in North Kensington given by spinster ladies with their hair marcelled like Queen Mary's; a party in a house in Pimlico where the host had placed a framed photograph of Mussolini on the piano; a party in the East End where half the guests seemed to be Blackshirts in roll-neck jumpers and whipcord breeches. If there was anything that brought these entertainments together it was the conversation, which was profoundly defeatist. Had there ever been quite so many English people who were quite so thoroughly ashamed of themselves? Cynthia wondered.

There was talk about approaching the Germans through the neutral embassies, about British regiments who would refuse to fight, about dear departed Margaret and her job on Berlin radio, about the King and what he might do if the politicians *would only leave him alone*. It was all very daring, and very self-conscious, and difficult to believe a word of, and turned yet more fanciful by being caught up in the usual chatter about blackout curtains and servants and the price of stewing steak.

Once, at one of these parties—at the higher end of the scale, with a band and hired waiters and people in dinner jackets—they came across a tall fair-haired woman in a sea-green evening dress smoking a cigarette balanced in a pair of tiny brass tongs.

'Anthea,' Cynthia said, 'what on earth are you doing here?'

Cynthia was always telling herself that she had lost her awe of Anthea, and that the way to proceed was to give as good as you got. So far this had produced quite promising results.

'Odd as it may seem,' Anthea said, 'our hostess and my mother were brought out at the same time. If one can imagine Mrs Featherstonehaugh ever being brought out anywhere. God knows I have few enough family obligations, but this is one of them. This must be your American friend that I've heard so much about.'

The party was in its later stages. There were bald old men with damson faces in paper hats jigging gamely with their daughters on the dance floor, and the fog of cigarette smoke had risen almost to the ceiling. A waiter went by carrying the wreck of a salmon, into which someone had amused themselves by jabbing twenty or thirty cocktail sticks.

'This is Mr Kent,' Cynthia volunteered.

'Charmed, I'm sure,' Anthea said, in a tone so languid that at the *Duration* office it would immediately have been taken as a joke. 'How are they all in Grosvenor Square? Is Frank Thistlewood still on the strength, or did he finally make the place too hot to hold him?'

'Oh, Frank's still on the strength, all right,' Tyler Kent said, not exactly goggling at her but making plain by his expression that this wasn't at all the kind of thing he was used to. 'For all his little failings.'

'I must come down there and look some of you up one of these days,' Anthea said. The band was playing 'In a Mountain Greenery' now, at foxtrot pace, which was too much for the damson-faced old men.

'Yes, you must,' Tyler Kent said. His face was showing the strain. 'How's Desmond? I ought to come over to Bloomsbury and look him up.'

'Oh, Des,' Anthea said, as if Desmond was the greatest joke that anyone had ever minted, but that no one else had ever seen his comic possibilities. 'He's like an old hen just about to lay an egg again. Well, I must be going, Mr Kent. Very nice to have met you. And please don't keep my friend Miss Kirkpatrick up late. She has a great deal to do in the morning.'

The oddity of this conversation, Cynthia decided, was simply unfathomable. It was not possible to establish from it what Anthea and Tyler Kent knew about each other, what assumptions they had made about each other, what traps they might have been laying for each other's discomfort. As she could not crack this code, and knew that no one involved would give her any help, she contented herself with quarrelling with Tyler Kent on the way home.

As his habit of losing his temper with people who disagreed with him was sometimes anaesthetised by a studious gallantry towards members of the opposite sex, this was not as easy as it looked, but happily the party had provided her with ammunition.

'I suppose you're one of those people who want us to lose the war?'

'I wouldn't say that,' Tyler Kent said. The taxi had declined to take them any further than the bottom of the Fulham Road. 'It's more that there shouldn't have been a war in the first place.'

'But now there is, you don't want us to win it? Isn't that just being defeatist?'

'I don't think you want to win it yourselves. Otherwise something would be happening out in Europe, rather than the fellows just staring at each other over the parapets. It's the weirdest thing. Three months into an armed conflict, only there's no conflict, no arms, and anyone with any sense knows it could be stopped tomorrow if only the right people were calling the shots.'

'But what about if there was a conflict? What about if the Germans invaded? Surely half the people you meet at parties would end up in prison? Come to think of it, you might easily end up in prison yourself.'

'You know what I think?' Tyler Kent said. As he grew crosser he became more saturnine in appearance, more genuinely alarming. 'I don't think anyone's going to invade anybody. I think there'll be a new government and a peace settlement, and all that stuff about gallant little Poland can be shut in the drawer again. And all us cipher clerks can just sit at our desks and go on with decoding our cables. . . . Say,' he said, 'who is this Anthea woman, anyhow?'

'I told you. She works at *Duration*.'

'I met her someplace before, I think,' Tyler Kent said seriously. He could not disguise the fact that he knew more about Anthea than he was telling. They were walking past the tennis courts now, and the cinder surfaces welled up like black ink. 'And fancy her knowing about Frank Thistlewood. She must get around, all right. Frank's a great guy, but I guess he's one of the crosses we have to bear.'

And in this spirit of new-found amity they came back to Bishop's Park, its slew of taped-up box-files, its life-size American eagle, its map of Custer's last journeyings around Montana, and its divan bed.

In Bloomsbury the fog was slowly settling over the plane trees. This gave the passing traffic of the square a sinister look: other-worldly, drowning in the murk, like a Turner painting gone horribly wrong. A file of children, led by a cadaver in an overcoat, went skulking round the furthest corner, up to no good. There was no one in the *Duration* office but herself, although a double sheet of grey page proofs had been laid out lengthways on each of the desks. Setting down her bag, and shaking her scarf out in the space between the top of her typewriter and the hat-stand, she discovered that it was Desmond's editorial for the first number.

The artist, in time of war, cuts a lonely figure. The combatant has his regiment, his orders and his duty; the civilian has his anxiety, his ration-book, and his sense of ulterior purpose; but the artist has only his art. The ivory tower from which he once looked out over a landscape that was less and less to his liking has gone. In its place rises only an ivory shelter, in which, cheek by jowl with people who resent his freedom, such as it is, and question his relevance, he wearily subsists. For him to write, or to paint, or indeed to say anything at all, is a paradox, for war is the enemy of creative autonomy, and writers and painters are right both to ignore it and to concentrate their talents on other subjects.

Once Mr Eliot's waste land was a prophecy: now it is a reality. Soon it will be a memory, an elegiac recollection of a world that, however resonant its despair, was not yet ruled over by autocrats and commissars. For ten years we have been adrift on a sea of 'commitment.' For the artist this war is an opportunity to fling back this tide, to restate the conviction that writing is an art, that it is an end in itself as well as a means to an end, and that good writing, like all art, is capable of producing a deep and satisfying emotion in the reader, whether it is about Mozart, the flora of the Antarctic, or the habits of bees. . . .

There was quite a lot more of this: Marxism; Auden's flight to America; almond blossom; shabby streets—rolling periods, dulled by familiarity. All over London, it seemed, sensitive middle-aged men were reaffirming the quality of their *Angst*, writing open letters to younger cousins in the Navy, or pondering the artist's duty in wartime. But she was a dutiful girl and she read on to the end.

Out in the square the wraith-like children had disappeared and the fog was growing denser. She was just putting the proof sheets back on the desk when there was a rasp of shoe-leather and she looked up to find Desmond emerging from the doorway of his office.

'Hello, Des. Would you like a cup of tea?'

The *Duration* tea was unexpectedly good. It was genuine Pekoe Points, delivered each Thursday morning by the Harrods van and charged to Peter Wildgoose's mother's account.

'It'll be the first nourishment I've had this morning,' Desmond said, rather vaguely. He gave a faint impression of having spent the night in his clothes. 'One gets out of the habit of doing normal things, don't you think?'

She resolved not to be embarrassed by Desmond, who had begun to flap his arms weakly against his sides, like an outsized bird deprived of the powers of flight, and went off to boil the kettle. The war had made some men more purposeful, less ground-down by the circumstances of their lives. Desmond seemed somehow more fraught.

She put the teacup on a tray and carried it through into the office. Here a sea of proof sheets covered the floor, like a dull grey blanket, and there was a copy of the contents page lying on the desk. *Letter to a combatant. Death of the Georgians. A Symbolist manifesto.*

'Did you like it?' Desmond asked. His fist had closed around the cup, almost concealing it from view.

There would be no quarter here. 'Did I like what?'

'The editorial letter.'

'I thought it was very good,' Cynthia said, who actually thought it was surprisingly feeble. There was an unspoken agreement among the editorial assistants that whatever Desmond believed about the magazine he should be informed was true.

'Not too much like what Connolly writes in *Horizon*?'

'Not really.'

'Peter thinks we ought to compete with them. You know, have articles about sculpture and the latest gallery openings.'

There was no knowing how long this might go on. Desmond had once kept Lucy prisoner by the stationery cupboard for twenty minutes while he talked about Mallarmé. The nearest of the proof sheets had a mouse-dropping on it, Cynthia noticed. She wondered what Tyler Kent was doing in Grosvenor Square and whether he had anyone like Desmond to contend with.

'Do you know,' Desmond said finally, after what seemed like an eternity of silence, 'I heard some extraordinary news the other day?'

Desmond's revelations were always quite unforeseen. It could be anything from the literary editor of the *Sunday Times* losing his job to sugar going off the ration.

'You're always hearing extraordinary pieces of news, Des,' Cynthia said, consciously modelling herself on Anthea. 'What was this bit?'

'It's about Sylvester. Sylvester Del Mar,' Desmond elaborated, as if there were half a dozen other people called Sylvester clamouring to write short stories for his magazine. 'Actually it's Peter's scoop, not mine at all. You know how he always said that he'd come across Sylvester before, but couldn't remember where? Well, apparently the other night he was going through some old variety-hall programmes—you know he sometimes likes going to the Holborn Empire for the second house—and there was Sylvester on one of them, third on the bill.'

'What sort of thing was he doing?'

'Plate-spinning, I think. Or it may have been paper-tearing. Some kind of novelty act, at any rate. Peter was quite impressed.'

'Does Sylvester know his cover's been blown?'

'That's the odd thing. We had a drink last night. He had a couple of new pieces he wanted me to see. I thought he'd take it quite humorously, Peter finding his name on the programme, but do you know he was almost distraught? Said it was a part of his life that was inexpressibly painful to him. In the end he practically begged me to promise not to mention it to anyone.'

'And shall you?'

'Certainly not,' Desmond said virtuously. He had stopped flapping his arms against his sides and was rubbing his forefingers up and down his chin—possibly, Cynthia thought, to establish whether he had remembered to shave or not. 'I shall keep absolutely *schtum*. It's Peter who always seems to forget what one can and cannot say.'

This was such a travesty of their respective attitudes to confidential information that Cynthia assumed it was meant as a joke. She was bored with Desmond. It was not that he lived in his own world, but that he failed to realise that the other worlds he so blithely infiltrated had their own admission charges. She wondered what it might be like to be married to Desmond, and found her mind instantly occupied by a series of paralysing visions: Desmond lying in the bath smoking a cigar; Desmond making a spill out of an income tax form; or eating a plate of jellied eels that had been left out for the cat. Behind her she could hear the noise of other people arriving: a clatter of footsteps, the sound of someone taking off the cover of a typewriter.

'I think I ought to help Anthea with the post.'

Desmond looked disappointed. Of all things, he required an audience. Even hell would be tolerable, he sometimes said, if the demons took an interest in one. And then, as she moved back into the doorway with the teacup, tugged unwillingly out of Desmond's scarlet paw, in her hand, there came another noise of a door being flung open and someone moving rapidly over the carpet of the ante-room.

'Peter, my dear fellow,' Desmond said anxiously. 'What on earth's the matter?'

'Did you see that note I left on your desk last night?' Peter Wildgoose said. He was immaculately dressed, in a bowler hat and a British Warm overcoat, half-open and exposing the blue pinstripe suit beneath. The only hint that he might be seriously upset came in the exasperated little nod he sent in the direction of the page proofs.

'I can't say I did. There are so many things get left about there. Was it something special?'

'Well, it might interest you to know,' Peter said, 'that I received a telephone call yesterday evening from a director of the Norwich Press. The six thousand copies of *Duration* that they printed and had bound up yesterday are lying on the floor of their warehouse at Sevenoaks. And that is where they're going to stay. The Norwich Press has printed them, but they are not—I repeat, *not*—going to distribute them.'

'Why's that, then?' It was possible, Cynthia thought, that Desmond had not realised quite how annoyed Peter was.

'It's that story of Del Mar's. They say the shops won't accept it on moral grounds.'

'"Miss Harrington Hunts the Hairbrush"? But that's absurd. There isn't a line in it that anyone could take the faintest exception to. You went through it twice yourself.'

'For Christ's sake, Des,' Peter said. 'It's not that one they're complaining about. It's the other story about the car-smash in Delhi. The one that begins: *Fact is there was bugger-all I could do about it.* The Norwich Press say they've just signed a contract with the MOI for printing government stationery, and the last thing they want is to be involved in an obscenity case.'

'But they've already printed the bloody thing,' Desmond said.

'They may have printed it. But they are under no legal obligation to distribute it if, as they firmly believe, it contains material that anyone who purchases it may find objectionable.'

'Well, we'll just have to distribute it ourselves,' Desmond said. He had a rapt, ingenious look on his face. 'It shouldn't be too difficult if we hire a couple of vans. The ones for the London book-shops we could take round by hand.'

It was not immediately obvious that Peter Wildgoose had lost his temper. For a moment or two he stared hard at various objects that lay to hand—a reproduction Cézanne that hung on the wall behind Desmond's desk, a copy of a book called *The Modernist Dilemma* that stuck out from the shelf next to it, and a postcard lying face-up on the desktop sent from Biarritz from someone called Brian—as if each of them somehow symbolised the awful, bottomless depths into which Desmond had dragged him. Then he said very briskly: 'I shan't argue with you. There's no point. There never is. You'd just start whining about the sanctity of the artist. At times like these you couldn't organise a piss-up in a brewery. Anyway, I've settled it with the Norwich Press. They're going to bring the copies up here by lorry later this morning and you—we—are going to alter them.'

Desmond looked thoroughly baffled. 'But you know as well as I do that we haven't got any printing equipment.'

'I didn't say that we had. We are going to alter them by hand.' Some of Peter's bad temper had begun to recede: one or two of the situation's comic possibilities had perhaps occurred to him. 'And you can oblige me, Des, in the midst of your many, onerous duties, by coming up with an acceptable substitute for "bugger-all" . . . oh, and Cynthia.'

'Yes, Mr Wildgoose?'

'I owe you an apology. Barging in here like a helot without so much as a good morning. Do you think you could find it in yourself to make me a cup of tea?'

Being married to Peter Wildgoose would be a very different thing: a town house in a Chelsea square; a solid oak table beneath the dining-room napery; sepia-inked maps of the English counties hung on the wall. Humbled and a little exalted by these imaginings, she went off to make the tea.

The rest of the day passed as Peter had foreseen. At twelve a van arrived from Sevenoaks bringing the copies of *Duration* in two dozen cardboard boxes, and they set to work. At Anthea's suggestion 'bugger-all' became 'damn-all.' Desmond took half a dozen unaltered copies and locked them in the drawer of his desk. 'A hedge against old age,' he explained. 'In twenty years' time I shall be able to sell them at Sotheby's.' Come the early afternoon, when Peter had gone out to the bank, he began to cheer up.

'You might not think it,' he said, 'but Peter can be very theatrical at times. I can remember once at school when he had some kind of a row with the Lower Master, and do you know what he did?' Nobody knew. 'He got hold of one of those toy engines that you can buy at Gamages and took it into chapel hidden under his jacket. Then, just as we were about to sing the hymn, he sent it off in the direction of the choir stalls. The Lower Master nearly had a fit.'

Outside the fog had grown denser still. There was no sign of the bar-rage-balloon. A man from a solicitors' firm came and tried to serve them a writ relating to an unpaid bill for a set of filing cabinets, but they sent him away. There was a queer but rather comforting sense of camaraderie about the afternoon that followed. The girls sat on the floor with the copies piled up around them and half-empty teacups threatening their skirts, their fingers black with printer's ink. So far Anthea had not referred to their meeting at the party, but finding a moment when Lucy had gone off to wash her hands she said: 'So that was your interesting American friend.'

You had to be non-committal at these times.

'Yes, that was him.'

'I always think, don't you,' Anthea said, 'that the Grosvenor Square manner takes some getting used to? At least I never met anyone in the Foreign Office who was at all like that. But, take it from me, there are one or two things you ought to know about your Mr Kent.'

'What sort of things?'

'Well, the company he keeps, for a start. Don't say you haven't wondered about that, or I shall think you won't ever confirm the good opinion I've formed of you.'

But they were interrupted by Peter Wildgoose coming into the room to say that the Norwich Press expected to return for the corrected copies by half-past five, and whatever it was that Anthea wanted to say about Tyler Kent had to wait. Priorities, as Desmond liked to say, were the first rule of magazine publishing.

It was an odd time altogether. The war news was curiously sporadic: rumours of troop movements in North Africa; submarines in the North Atlantic; Russians in Poland. A passenger ship was sunk off Galway, but without great loss of life. A motion calling for a peace conference brought to the House by a pacifist Labour back-bencher was defeated by a hundred votes.

From Portugal came picture-postcards: the Escurial in bright sunshine; peasants in national costume; cathedrals; donkeys; schoolgirls in First Communion frocks. It was hard to connect them with her parents. Mr Kirkpatrick was said to be doing well. Of Mrs Kirkpatrick's hopes, fears, and mythological projections there was not the faintest hint.

Advertised, finally, on news-stands, on sale in book-shops next to copies of *Horizon* and old novels left over from before the war, *Duration* sold briskly. An extract from Desmond's editorial was broadcast on the radio, and a *Times* third leader maintained that he had demonstrated the essential integrity of the artist, however unpromising the political circumstances that surrounded him. Still, though, Cynthia thought, there was something unreal about all of this. A great stretch of time seemed to have passed before her in which nothing had happened. It was hard to believe that she had ever sat in the Ritz Bar talking to Anthea and Norman Burdett, harder still to imagine that she had ever sat in the shooting brake by the Sussex beach listening to Captain Ramsay recite poetry.

Captain Ramsay turned up quite a lot in the parliamentary news these days, asking questions about the war's effects on the Scottish woollen industry and how many servicemen enlisting in the armed forces were of Jewish ancestry. But the odd, phantom quality of the world she inhabited seemed to extend to the people she knew. Like the PLA lighters, glimpsed sometimes from the window in Bishop's Park, they were moving away downstream, borne on the tide. There was no knowing where they might be washed up. The Escurial palace; a *Times* third leader; Tyler Kent's divan bed—who could tell?

And there were people other than Anthea who wanted to talk to her about Tyler Kent. She was walking through Bishop's Park to the Underground one Saturday afternoon when a woman who had been lurking under one of the dripping elm trees scurried over and clawed rather belligerently at her arm.

'Oh, hello, Hermione. What are you doing here?'

'You've ruined everything,' Hermione said, unexpectedly, in her high, desperate voice. Her head sat more awkwardly than ever on her shoulders, and she had exaggerated the effect by wearing a tiny pillbox hat and having her hair done in a kind of deranged bob that allowed the tendrils to fall over her cheek-bones like giant commas. 'I should never have introduced you to him in the first place.'

'Introduced me to whom?' For one brief, disturbing second Cynthia thought of Henry lying in his jungle tomb.

'To Tyler, of course.' There was a flurry of movement at about the level of her waist, and Cynthia realised that Hermione was trying to hit her with her handbag. 'You rotten, rotten bitch.'

So that was it. The part of Bishop's Park they were standing in abutted the church, and they scuffled there for a moment or two beneath a placard advertising the next day's services, until finally Cynthia managed to wheel Hermione towards her—it was curiously like manoeuvring a dustbin you wanted to fill with refuse—and administer a single, sharp slap to her cheek. She could deal with Hermione Bannister.

The pillbox hat fell off onto the asphalt path, and for some reason Cynthia stamped her foot on it. As it turned out, this was the right thing to do. Clearly the hat had a symbolic value to Hermione. All the fight instantly went out of her and she collapsed against the church railings. A young man with a hard, bony face went loping by on his way into the park and Cynthia caught the sardonic glint in his eye.

'Come on, Hermione,' Cynthia said. 'You can't go around behaving like this.'

'No, I can't, can I?' Hermione said. After this she began to cheer up. It was as if some point had been proved. 'Actually, it wasn't you I wanted to see. I was going round to the flat.'

'Well, there wouldn't be much point in that. There's no one there. Why don't you come and have a cup of tea?'

The way to deal with hysteria, Mrs Kirkpatrick had always said, was to stand no nonsense. It was one of her better pieces of advice. Hand clasped firmly in Cynthia's—the skin of her knuckles was scratched and earthy, Cynthia noticed, as if she had been digging far underground—pillbox hat jammed brokenly on her head, Hermione allowed herself to be propelled across the Putney Bridge Road.

'I suppose the places round here are rather awful, aren't they?' she said meekly.

In the end they found a café across the street from Putney Bridge Station. It was a broken-down establishment, smelling of bacon fat and full of tram-drivers, and their arrival had the effect of a pair of flamingos alighting on a starling-strewn lawn, but Cynthia, having dealt with Hermione, thought she was equal to this challenge. She ordered two cups of tea and a bun and took them back to the table by the window where Hermione had arranged herself.

'I'm awfully sorry,' Hermione said. 'I really don't know what came over me. It must be my Bannister blood, I suppose.'

The tea was the colour of tan boot-polish. 'What does your Bannister blood have to do with it?'

'Wasn't there a Bannister who fought a duel with Lord North? I forget his name. Father's always talking about him.'

All this, Cynthia thought, could not be tolerated. Not because it was ridiculous, but because it took the vacant space in front of her and filled it with Bannisters: Mr Bannister standing in the drawing room in Colombo; terrier-faced Mrs Bannister proudly unveiling the memorial stone. She had had enough of the Bannisters, and she wanted redress.

'Don't mind my asking, Hermione, but when did you last see Tyler?'

'A week ago. Ten days. We had tea at the Ritz.'

There were advertisements on the wall for variety theatres and greyhound puppies: hints of the teeming, human life that presumably went on in this part of London, and far more interesting than Hermione.

'No, you didn't. At least I don't believe you did.'

'No, we didn't,' Hermione said. The look of cunning on her face had yielded up to a pained awareness of some of the starker realities of life. 'I'm sorry, Cynthia, truly I am, but you don't know how awful it's been.' There was something unexpectedly drastic about this return to rational thought, like a light-switch going on in a darkened room. 'We seemed to be getting on so well. And then he came to Ashburton. And Father liked him so much.'

'Does he still see your father?' Cynthia asked.

'Oh, they're frightfully thick. What with this business of the Faction and the peace settlement. Father says he's a godsend. I think he was at Ashburton last week. Not that I care about that. I thought we were going to get engaged.'

'Honestly, Hermione,' Cynthia said. 'I had no idea.'

'No,' she said. 'I suppose it would have been too much to expect you would. And it was very foolish of me to think he cared for me. Men are so thoughtless in the way they behave sometimes, aren't they?' For some reason the pace at which Hermione spoke increased with every word she brought out. 'I'm so glad we've had this talk. And you must promise that you'll do me a little favour.'

'What's that?'

'You must come and stay at Ashburton again. Mother and Father love having you there. They often say so.'

'I'd like that,' Cynthia said untruthfully, thinking what an incalculably odd girl Hermione was.

The tea was almost finished now, and the tram-drivers were taking a prurient interest in them. Silently, they got up to go.

Late at night, the flat in Bishop's Mansions grew less forbidding, more tolerable to inhabit. Snatches of dance music pulsed through the party walls. Beyond the park odd protrusions of light bounced off the houses on the Surrey side, as if there were alien spacecraft about to land, untroubled by the blackout. In the deep wells of darkness beneath the kitchen window, cats fought in the wild gardens. There were supposed to be a dozen other people living in Tyler Kent's block: Cynthia had never seen any of them. Tyler Kent's gregariousness was external, not domestic.

'I saw Hermione Bannister,' she said, at one of these times.

'You don't say. The redoubtable Hermione. I guess she was just the same as ever. Isn't that right?'

'Exactly the same. She seemed very cross that you didn't want to marry her.'

There was a joke, or at least a compliment, to be made here, but Tyler Kent ignored it. 'I can never get the hang of girls like Hermione,' he said. 'It's one of the great mysteries of dear old England. Paying any attention to them is a piece of effrontery, but then not paying any attention to them is worse. And then they stare at you as if you're the chauffeur who's forgotten to bring in the bags.'

'She was wearing one of her hats.'

'The hell she was,' Tyler said, less neutrally. 'No question about it. If the Nazis sailed up the Thames, Hermione would be running out to meet them in one of her hats.'

After interludes in other parts of the flat, they had come to rest in the drawing-room. Here, shirt-sleeved and desk-bound, with a ledger balanced on his knee, Tyler Kent was cutting pieces out of the evening newspaper with a pair of scissors.

'Just be a honey, now, would you,' he said, 'and fetch me that copy of the *Star*?'

Men were always bent on this environmental staking-out, Cynthia thought, these accumulations of paraphernalia. Desmond's office at *Duration* was a kind of junk shop of tobacco jars emblazoned with his college coat of arms and penknives bestowed on him by long-dead nannies. Perhaps Mr Chamberlain sat in Downing Street surrounded by monogrammed umbrellas and photographs inscribed to him by world leaders.

She went over to the other side of the room, picked the paper off the floor—the headline said HOUSE QUESTIONS CONDUCT OF WAR—and brought it back, looking at Tyler Kent as he sat at the desk, one hand shading his forehead. She detected a faint resemblance to Henry. The most tedious thing about men was that you always fixed on variations of the same quintessential type. Here the resemblance was not physical, but gestural, or rather it had to do with assumptions. It had never once occurred to Tyler Kent that she might not like to perform any of the tasks he proposed for her. Like Hermione's hats the pattern was fixed, not to be altered by complaint or evasion.

On the other hand—and here, too, there was a connection with Henry—there were worse things than Tyler Kent. Another girl would have been irritated by his absorption in the contents of the desk, especially if, like her, the girl was wearing only a pair of silk pyjamas. Besides, Tyler Kent had information she had begun to take an interest in. There was a rapid shuffle of feet above their heads, like a ballerina executing a pas seul.

'What is it that you're doing with Hermione's father?'

Tyler took this in his stride. 'Mr Bannister?' He tapped the copy of the *Star*, with its headline about the conduct of the war, and stared at his finger, as if it was responsible for all the burdens he had to bear. 'We're trying to get this thing stopped.'

'You personally?'

'Even cipher clerks have their secrets,' Tyler Kent said. 'You'd be surprised. Plus there's the fact that I work at a foreign embassy. That helps too.'

'What about Captain Ramsay?'

'Oh, he's a kind of chairman. Makes sure everyone involved is pulling their weight.'

'Does anyone know you're doing this?'

It occurred to her that Tyler Kent was flattered by these questions, and that a sharper operator would have been less keen to answer them. 'There are people who know it and people who don't. Generally it's better that the people who don't know carry on not knowing. Needless to say, I shouldn't care to find out that they knew any more because of what you told them. Hey,' he said, not quite leaving a bridge between the two sentences and not in the least drawing the sting out of the rebuke, which rather frightened her, 'who was that girl we saw at the Featherstonehaughs? The one who works with you.'

'Anthea Carey.'

'What does she do at *Duration*? I can't see her bringing in the lunch-pail.'

Cynthia was still registering the information about Tyler's plans for the war. 'The other day she spent the whole afternoon altering the first sentence of a short story from "bugger-all" to "damn-all".'

'She comes to parties at the embassy,' Tyler Kent said. 'I've heard of her.'

There was a sheet of paper, grey from the jellygraph, that he seemed to be protecting with the curve of his arm, and some instinct prompted her to go and examine it.

'Where did you get that?'

'A souvenir,' Tyler Kent said.

'Will it help to get the war stopped?'

'Not in itself. Listen,' Tyler Kent said, 'it's all very well your being dressed up like Hedy Lamarr in the second feature, but you're in severe danger of outstaying your welcome.'

Not long after that the air-raid siren went off and the newspaper cuttings and the copy of the presidential telegram were returned to their box-file. The next morning Mrs Bannister rang to say that Hermione had been taken into a nursing home somewhere in Barons Court and was 'not at all well.'

CHAPTER 10

Beverley Nichols's Diary II

25 November 1939

Lunched with Noël. Very gloomy. Said that the war would ruin the theatre for the next two years whether it went on or not. Says he is thinking of writing a play called *The Patriot*. He seems to envisage patriotism as a kind of *stance*, wholly unequivocal. I said: Surely the days of 'My Country Right or Wrong' were over? He laughed at this, but I had the rather disagreeable sensation that we no longer see eye to eye.

Later. As Gaskin is in Cambridge visiting his sister I invited *y* to spend the evening here. *Not* a success. On the other hand, one must remember that if one entertains a pretentious young man, desirous of a helping hand, then one was a pretentious young man oneself once. And yet there is a thing called charm . . . *y* seems to have no idea that there is a war on. Said: 'Oh, we don't bother with these,' when I began to wrestle with the blackout curtains. He seems to have got in with a lot of repertory actors who produce plays that nobody goes to see at the uttermost extremity of the Finchley Road. Managed to get him out of the house by the time that Gaskin returned, only to discover that one of the silver-backed shaving brushes had gone from the bathroom. Really!

27 November 1939

Another summons to the Palace. Well, that is putting it grandly. What happens is that Hardinge, the private secretary, telephones to say that 'His Majesty is at leisure' and wonders if I would care to 'wait upon him.' Rather nicely put, I thought. Found the King surrounded by what he calls his 'unsoliciteds.' I enquired: how many letters did he get? He said two or three hundred a week: a proportion from obvious lunatics, but the majority quite respectful and sensible. I asked him how he dealt with them all, and he said that the secretaries have a standard form of words for replies. He reads them merely to get an idea of public opinion.

More general impressions: Tired and frequently petulant. Footmen coming into the room with messages sometimes quite insufferably patronised. I suppose they regard it as part of their job, to be discussed with amusement in the servants' quarters. Struck by asceticism, compared to tales one heard twenty years ago. Eats, when permitted, off a tray. No hint of any lady companions, hardly even of any social life. Very keen on the Americans, whom he thinks 'vulgar but also go-ahead. They get things done' &c. I daresay this is Mrs Simpson's influence working from beyond the grave. Constantly harping on Mrs S, her sound judgement, vitality, respect in which she was held, &c. All this rather tiresome, not to mention example of myth-making at its worst. I remember Victor telling me that he was at a supper party attended by the Yorks when news of her death was brought in and there was very nearly a round of applause.

Well-informed but erratic. I asked: did he get on well with the PM. Replied: 'Oh, he comes round from time to time, you know.' Devitalised. Often gets up from his chair as if about to reach for something in the room only to sink back into the cushions. Complains of inertia, sidelining by Government. 'All they want me to do is to go and inspect gun emplacements. It is just like being in Flanders again.'

Polite. Solicitous. Thanks me repeatedly for coming to see him. Talks of what he calls his 'political isolation'. Churchill once a great supporter, but now divided from him on account of war. Only friends in the Cabinet one or two of the younger ministers. Told me one very interesting thing. Apparently a week ago Beaverbrook asked to see him privately and asked: What did he think of the idea of a negotiated peace? This is extraordinary, if true. When I asked how he had replied, would not say. Did he think anyone else knew of this? He thought not. Once again, noted his absolute subservience to Hardinge.

Says things like 'I don't think Hardinge will care for that' or 'I should hardly dare propose that to Mr Hardinge.' At one point Hardinge came into the room and commenced on a regular dressing-down—some appointment that the King had failed to keep—only to catch my eye and think better of it.

Very anxious that I should come again. Said: 'There is no one I can talk to. Absolutely no one.' I got the distinct impression that there were several things he burned to tell me, schemes he was desperate to impart, but could not bring himself to. Victor, whom I talked to later—and who does not, of course, know of these meetings—says there are worries about his 'stability.' Says he is still very much liked by some of the Labour members on account of his tours of the distressed areas &c. and 'could do anything with them.'

28 November 1939

Wrote my column for Drawbell. Given that on the last occasion I wrote anything controversial I got into hot water, I confined myself to the meaning of St Andrew's Day. As if anyone is interested in St Andrew's Day at a time like this!

Thought of all the things I might have been, had I applied myself to them when I came down from Oxford. A serious composer, certainly; only to be that, one needs a private income, which I never had. A politician? But then again, who in their right mind would want to dominate the mediocrities who currently infest the House of Commons? The Bar? But the barristers one meets are such frightful bores. So here I am, twenty years later, writing my books and my newspaper articles and acting as a highly unofficial royal confidant. There are worse niches to occupy.

29 November 1939

Faction meeting at Ramsay's house in Kensington. All arranged in conditions of utmost secrecy, e.g. no use of telephone, merely printed card saying 'The circle will convene.' Cloak-and-dagger atmosphere reinforced by Ramsay's butler who absolutely demanded 'password' before admitting me. Of course did not know it. Turned out to be 'Excalibur' and Ramsay had to be summoned from the drawing room to vouch for me. All rather foolish.

One never quite knows with Ramsay whether one is in the presence of something horribly serious and well-organised or simply a lot of interfering ladies who in a happier world would burn off some of their surplus energy in the Girl Guides. Here, on the other hand, I had a very definite sense of being in the company of people who meant business. One of Gort's staff officers talked about the 'mood' at Staff HQ, which is apparently 'volatile.' 'Everyone is waiting for a lead,' whatever that means. Didn't see why I shouldn't tell them about Beaverbrook's appeal to HM, so did. This produced very gratifying response.

Ramsay, in particular, almost wild with excitement. What could be done? Should he make a personal approach to Beaverbrook? Privately I could not think of anything worse for the cause of peace than Ramsay, of whom the *Express* has in the past been highly critical, blundering around in Fleet Street, but did not think I could decently say this, so muttered something about HM's remarks being confidential.

'Clearly,' Ramsay returned, 'Mr Nichols is our conduit.' Whereupon, having been conspiratorial and sinister, the meeting descended into an absolutely ludicrous discussion of how to attach propaganda stickers to lamp-posts under cover of the blackout. The fanatical ladies impossibly serious about this. Apparently one of them has written a little booklet about the best means of proceeding. All this attended to with the gravest expressions of interest, but I think Gort's staff man had his doubts. I had a definite sense that the fanatical ladies were merely camouflage for something that is a great deal more capable than it may look on the surface.

Afterwards Ramsay got hold of me in the hallway. Asked: would I be prepared to carry a letter from himself to HM? I said—what I truly believe—that I did not think this would help, that I had no idea of the King's true position, that any direct approach would probably be refused. Ramsay accepted this, but seemed disappointed, I thought.

Then to a late supper at Barbara Back's. Reflected, as I went there, that I was exchanging the company of some of the most serious people in England for some of the most frivolous. And so it proved.

1 December 1939

The palace again. My visits now a recognised part of the weekly routine. The footmen grin at me in corridors. Hardinge looks up from his desk and nods as I wander by. All very pleasant, but there is something vaguely Ruritanian about it, the thought of paper-thin scenery that could blow away at any time. Also a tremendous sense of desuetude, to use a rather nice word. If this were eighteenth-century France I should be greeted by half a dozen flunkeys and escorted through brocade-hung corridors to some sumptuous orangerie. As it is England of 1939 I am taken to a tiny room with a threadbare carpet that cannot have been decorated for thirty years and given a cup of tea and a penny bun.

Today HM less tired than usual and much more forthcoming. Had *The Times* open on his desk and was shaking his head over the news from France. Said that Gort was right to be playing a waiting game, but in the circumstances that was the only game he could play. I got the impression of a terrible nervousness, eagerness to talk about anything rather than the subject closest to his heart. Again—this very often happens with HM—spoke of personalities he had met: Chaplin; the Japanese Emperor; Woodrow Wilson. Asked me: did I know Crown Prince Hirohito? I replied that I had not had the pleasure of making his acquaintance.

All this went on for nearly half an hour, and I began to think of my article for Drawbell, not to mention a luncheon party at Lady

Londonderry's that I had half promised to drop in on. When I come to write my memoirs—if we still inhabit a world in which memoirs are written—I shall certainly include a section explaining that it is perfectly possible to be bored even by royalty.

Finally, after a great deal of hesitation, half-finished sentences, &c., HM dropped his bombshell. Would I care to assist him in the preparation of his speech to the Empire this Christmas? Naturally I said that I should be delighted. Apparently he has had other helpers in the past, but none of them has proved satisfactory. Anxious that the job should not get in the way of my own work. I assured him there was no danger of this. Asked—this was something I thought best to establish at the outset—if Hardinge and his advisers know about this, he said they did, and had raised no objection. And what were the protocols surrounding it? For example, did the text have to be cleared in advance with the Government? HM said—rather stiffly, I thought—that the monarch's choice of words when addressing his subjects were naturally his own, but that Hardinge generally supplied the PM with a broad outline of what he intended to say.

So there it is, and I am to write the King's speech for him! I can't say that I experienced any sense of false modesty, for I shall do a very good job, certainly better than anyone else in London whom the King might have asked. Evelyn Waugh would have been too stiff; Hugh Walpole too pompous. We are to begin our confabulations in two days' time.

Came away exulting in my good fortune, and did not go to Lady Londonderry's for the excellent reason that I did not think I should be able to stop myself from talking about it. In fact, HM has been rather subtle. He knows that I am in touch with Ramsay and the peace party, but in the nature of things cannot be seen to receive him. By employing me he will be communicating with them by proxy.

Got home to find a telephone message from y asking if I wanted to come to dinner. Ignored this, and instead settled down into an armchair with a large whisky, back numbers of *Spectator*, *New Statesman*, &c., to think how I might set about what, it scarcely needs saying, is the most exalted commission of my career.

3 December 1939

To the palace. All very winter-ish. Guardsmen's breath spouting in the frozen air. Unswept leaves piling up against the sentry boxes. Had assumed that we would begin work straightaway, but when I arrived found myself taken off to Hardinge's office. Cordial but faintly suspicious, like a schoolmaster who fears his prize pupil may have disgraced himself but has no real evidence to prove it. Asked: was I aware of the very grave responsibility that had been placed on my shoulders? I decided to enter into the spirit of the interrogation, smiled my blandest smile and said that I was fully aware.

After that Hardinge relaxed a bit, said the King could be difficult in these matters. Above all, needed *guidance*. Was prone to make passionate statements which then had to be qualified. Apparently last year he ventured some remarks about unemployment in the distressed areas about which Downing Street nearly had a fit. I said I should do my best to curb this impetuousness, but in the last resort he was the King and I merely his humble subject. Hardinge, whom I suspect of having a sense of humour behind his impassive exterior, remarked that this went without saying. If I had any problems, he concluded, I should bring them to him immediately. Meanwhile, he would be glad to see a draft of the speech as soon as it became available. Naturally I agreed to this, while thinking that I wanted as little to do with Hardinge over its contents as possible.

Difficulties of working with HM. (1) His enthusiasm. (2) His vagueness. (3) His terror of offending Hardinge. (4) His lack of stamina. Rushes about like the youngest member of the backstage staff at the school concert, full of good notions, arresting phrases, &c., but no idea of what he wants to do. Then loses interest, grows petulant, drops cigarette ash all over the paper and asks: 'Well, how far have we got, then?' when a child could have told him that we have not got anywhere. Sulks. Says, when gently chided, 'If that's your attitude, I don't think we shall get anywhere at all.' Then instantly repents, declares that the job couldn't be done without me, I shall have his eternal thanks, &c. All very tiring and *much* worse than anything I ever experienced with Cochran.

I began by asking him: what, in a sentence, did he wish the speech to convey? This produced such a torrent of windy rhetoric that I tried again. Was there anything that he thought he should *not* say? He replied that he would not wish to contradict, or call into question, the policies of the Government. Very well, I agreed, but did he consider it acceptable to offer the Government advice, not to seem to influence political decisions but to reflect on them, as it were, from the impregnable vantage point of experience and hindsight? 'Yes, that's exactly it,' HM said. His line, as I take it, is that his memories of the Great War have convinced him that military conflict is an inconceivably bloody thing, and the sooner this one ends the better. The real problem, of course, will come when he gets on to how this might be brought about.

Anyway, I sketched a couple of paragraphs about his sympathy for the men dragged away from the comforts of hearth and home to serve their country in distant lands afar, to which he appended one or two trivial corrections—HM always has to make at least one annotation on anything given to him to sustain the illusion that he is in control—and then said that he approved and we ought to meet again in two days' time.

Struck by the terrible incongruity, not to say the bathos, of it all. This slim, sad little man with his butter-coloured hair going grey and a permanently bemused expression on his face dashing off for notes he has written on scraps of paper and now mislaid, or sending footmen off to find back numbers of *The Times*, in a great high-ceilinged room with white-panelled walls from which the paint is flaking away, and equerries bouncing in every so often to announce that the Spanish ambassador will be here directly, with Hardinge's tread always sounding beyond the door, and the footmen looking like schoolboys and reverential undertakers by turns, and oneself imagining that one has walked by mistake onto the set of an immensely ill-conceived stage play, but smiling all the while like the Cheshire Cat, for, as Hardinge has several times reminded me, HM is prone to lowness of spirits and likes to have people around him who are zealous and enthusiastic. As if one could not have worked *that* out for oneself.

And here is another problem, which has nothing to do with HM. Why have I not yet told Ramsay about this? Answer: because Ramsay will make difficulties. For a start, he will try to interfere. And I suspect—no, I know—that he will make demands it will be impossible to fulfill. The task, as I see it, is to do the best I can and present Ramsay with a fait accompli. If not, I shall simply end up as a telegraph-boy going back and forth between the two of them.

Still, there is a certain quiet satisfaction in these endeavours. Half a dozen times in the past week someone has telephoned me with a 'Beverley, darling. Where have you been? Your friends say you are becoming a recluse.' Well, before very long I shall be able to tell them!

4 December 1939

Three letters from friends in New York during the past week urging me to join them. Apparently the pages of the *American Sketch* and other periodicals will be 'open to me' if I choose to do so. All very gratifying, but I flatter myself I have important work to do here.

Another session with HM. This one lasted two hours. This constant attendance on the royal person is dreadfully exhausting. For a start, one always has to be on one's best behaviour, which is a bore. After all, if one is working on a libretto or a musical comedy, one can always turn round to one's collaborator and call him a bloody fool. I daresay if I called HM a BF I should end up in the Tower with the key thrown away.

Then there is the necessity to indulge every little foible and vanity that raises its head. This morning, for example, I had to listen to a frightful rodomontade about HM's prowess on the ski-slopes—the kind of conversation which, had anyone begun it in a gentleman's club, would simply have been laughed down. Still, at any rate he means well. Came up with a phrase about his being 'a soldier of the last war, whose most earnest prayer was that such a cruel and destructive madness should never again overtake mankind.' This I put into the text unaltered.

Hardinge a touch less suspicious. I daresay HM has shown him a paragraph or two. Greeted me in the corridor with a nod and the remark 'Good work, Mr Nichols.' As if one was a bricklayer who had just put up a new wall in the palace grounds!

The way in which we go about our work would make an interesting psychological study. If I am cautious, HM is suddenly in favour of bold statements and forthright expressions of his opinion. If, on the other hand, I decide to inject a little ginger into the proceedings, HM instantly backtracks, says the Government 'wouldn't like it' and there will be 'no end of a row.' Just at the moment we are stuck on the question of whether it would be proper for him to express a desire for peace—this in the most general sense. At first HM fears this may seem 'defeatist.' Then, when I insert some bromides about the efforts of men of goodwill being concentrated on a speedy resolution to the conflict, &c., says that this is not tough enough and should be pitched stronger.

All very difficult.

5 December 1939

Thinking that I deserved some relaxation from all these strenuous efforts on my country's behalf, and not having had any word from *y*, who I suppose is hard at work designing scenery for plays that will never be produced at the Everyman Theatre, Finchley, I picked up a Guardsman in the park and took him back to the room I keep for such purposes in Maddox Street. Gave him £2, which was well worth it. In fact, felt practically torn in half, so much so that it was all I could do to hobble to the taxi-rank and get myself driven back to Hampstead.

Sitting drinking the extraordinarily weak China tea which HM will insist on having served up to him, six hours later, I found myself marvelling at the incongruity of it all, and what HM might say if he knew what I had been doing. On the other hand, one has heard the most lurid tales of HM's youth, turning up at 'that' kind of party dressed as a geisha, taking the frankest interest in goings-on his father would have had people shot for, &c. He is, I note, completely incurious about all aspects of my life beyond this room—that royal self-absorption of which one hears so much. On reflection, perhaps this is just as well!

Finally decided that I had to grasp the nettle and tell Ramsay what was afoot. As I anticipated, he was hugely excited. Said that I was a national saviour and ought to have a knighthood. Then, as I had also anticipated, came up with a list of points which the speech ought to contain. 'The King must call for an immediate cessation of hostilities and a peace conference to be held on neutral territory—Switzerland, say.' I told him there was not the slightest chance of the King saying this in an address to the Empire, and we had to proceed by stealth.

After a while Ramsay calmed down—he is extremely nervous, I notice, jumps at the slightest noise—and saw the sense in this. 'Well, he can at least say the war was a mistake? Simply the result of people believing foolish propaganda?' I said I did not believe there was any chance of this, either. Ramsay looked rather crestfallen. 'Well, if he is not going to say anything at all, I don't see the point of it.' Tried to explain that there are more ways of getting what one believes across than a direct statement, and that it might be possible to convey a very strong impression of HM's position without its being a kind of giant advertising hoarding. In the end Ramsay accepted this.

The problem, of course, is that one is caught between two rampant egotists, neither of whom has an ounce of subtlety in his head.

Began to appreciate—not that I did not realise it before—that I am playing a very dangerous game. If it fails, I shall make an enemy of Ramsay. If, on the other hand, it succeeds, I shall make an enemy of a great many other people, as well as setting in train something whose ultimate consequences can only be guessed at.

Well, that is a risk one will have to take.

6 December 1939

With the help of certain acquaintances at the BBC, I have been investigating the circumstances in which the broadcast is made. In the old days it was recorded at Sandringham, to which the King traditionally retires in the middle of December. But of course HM loathes Sandringham and won't go there—apparently he has only set foot on the estate once since his accession, and stayed only long enough to order that all the peach blossoms from the hot-houses be sent to Mrs Simpson. At one point he announced that he wanted to spend Christmas at Fort Belvedere, but Hardinge argued against this and so he will be at Windsor.

The important thing is that the broadcast will be relayed 'live,' meaning that whatever is written down in advance, and whatever may have been shown to Hardinge, or indeed to the Government, need not actually be what HM says. Not sure if HM is aware of this, but think I ought to make it my business to let him know.

Interested to find, in this regard, that Downing Street has expressed a keen interest in what the King intends to say. In fact, Hardinge tells me that he has twice been asked for a preliminary synopsis, and that Churchill—who apparently used to advise HM on his speeches in earlier days—has volunteered his services. Told Hardinge that a synopsis should certainly be forthcoming and that we should get on very well without external help.

7 December 1939

At long last, and to the neglect of all manner of professional duties, not to mention one's social life, we have an outline. Or at any rate an outline suitable for Downing Street. HM will begin by reflecting on the dark period in which we find ourselves. He will recall his own experiences of military service in the Great War and offer sympathy and encouragement to those engaged in the current conflict. He will then consider war's privations for those on the home front—families kept apart from their loved ones and so forth. He will stress the value of our Imperial ties, and how such a conflict brings together people in far-flung corners of the world united only by their fealty to the British flag. Finally he will express his confidence in the ability of our armed forces, on land and sea and in the air, and express a pious hope for a speedy resolution.

Left a copy of this on Hardinge's desk.

8 December 1939

As I foresaw, synopsis did the trick in spades. Hardinge now apparently disposed to regard me as an ally. There is talk of the 'signal services' one is performing. If Hardinge really knew what was going on, he would have a seizure, but never mind.

HM's attitude like that of a schoolboy bent on an immensely laborious practical joke. The conspiratorial air he maintains at these times is extremely comical. Not sure, amid all these clandestine goings-on—there was a moment the other day when Hardinge came into the room unexpectedly and a particularly incriminating sheet had to be hidden under a copy of *Debrett*—that I like him very much: petulance, high-handedness, small-mindedness, slightly virtuous air of the reformed rake, &c., all rather tiresome.

At his best, inevitably, when he forgets who one is for a moment and talks about his early life: his naval training at Dartmouth; Queen Alexandra feeding him toffee out of a paper bag; experiences on the staff in Flanders. Uses army slang expressions that went out twenty years ago. No *interests*, so far as one can see, beyond his relatives, society high life, its ramifications. Will say, with appearance of great curiosity, 'Isn't she related to the Duke of Milford Haven—on her mother's side, that is?' Amusing, and of course important, as all this is, it will be a great relief when it is all over.

And the greatest difficulty is not HM, or Hardinge, with his ponderous confidences and his 'signal services,' but Ramsay, who will not let one alone and sends three or four telephone messages a morning demanding to be 'kept in the picture.' Thinking that a certain amount of haughtiness might now be in order, I told him that I really must be given a free hand, and that the thing most likely to upset the apple-cart was extraneous interference.

One other thing. I shall certainly *not* be attending a meeting of the Faction in the near future. Victor says the entire organisation is riddled with informers and that at least two of Ramsay's fanatical young ladies are working for MI6! Imagine the indignity of having every casual remark that one utters at one of these gatherings earnestly recorded for the benefit of some tough young man in Jermyn Street!

And so we press on. Ramsay quietly furious that his suggestions are not being given more weight. HM schoolboyish and, I infer, not having the faintest idea what the consequence of all this may be. Hardinge pitilessly deceived. Myself modestly confident that some real shift in our national destiny may be achieved, and—let us be honest about this—horribly afraid of what the outcome may be if it all goes wrong.

CHAPTER 11

Party Chambers

Three weeks before Christmas, against all expectation, Desmond decided to give a party. There turned out to be several reasons for this. One was that the first issue of *Duration*, though selling well, needed a further stimulus that only the arrival of several dozen people to drink cheap red wine on its premises for three or four hours at a stretch could provide. Another was that Desmond had chalked up so many social debts in the course of putting the magazine together, eaten so many free lunches, and performed so many semi-comic turns in so many hospitable drawing rooms, that he now felt under an obligation to pay some of them off.

But there was a third explanation, more abstract, in the last resort even philosophical. As Desmond put it: 'There haven't been any parties since I don't know when. Everyone's morale needs a boost. There are any number of one's friends who won't be in England three months from now. And Christmas is coming, too. I think we owe it to ourselves to let our hair down. Those of us that have any, that is.'

And so eighty or ninety invitations had been sent out—to literary editors in Fleet Street cubby-holes, to the denizens of Chelsea basements mouldering in the late-autumn fog, to elderly society hostesses whom Desmond had cultivated in the halcyon days of his '20s youth—and forty bottles of a fiery Algerian procured from a wine merchant with whom Peter Wildgoose was on friendly terms.

Of the *Duration* staff, only Anthea positively disapproved. She said: 'I think it's a perfectly terrible idea. One of Des's very worst. Nobody will come who's the slightest use to the magazine, and it will get into the gossip columns and make Des look even more foolish. And then there's the money. I shouldn't wonder if it costs poor Peter £50, just for the privilege of watching a lot of people he doesn't know getting drunk at his expense and trying to steal things.'

The party was due to begin at seven o'clock on a Friday night. At half-past five Cynthia found herself closeted with Anthea in Desmond's office—newly swept for the occasion and with the desktop cleared—cutting up carrots and spring onions for a dip.

'This is unbelievably awful,' Anthea said. She was in the worst mood that Cynthia had ever seen her, and had earlier that afternoon sent a girl from the advertising agent's away from the office in tears. 'Why Des couldn't get hold of some smoked salmon or canapés rather than ransacking somebody's market garden, I shall never know.'

'I don't think you can get smoked salmon at the moment,' Cynthia said, rather apologetically. 'I went out to dinner the other evening and they'd taken it off the menu.'

'With your American friend, I'll be bound,' Anthea said. She sliced into a chunk of carrot so viciously that a piece of it broke off and slammed against the foot of the bookcase. 'You know, I really am going to have to have a serious talk with you about him before too long. Is he coming this evening?'

'He has to stay late at work. He said he might try to get along around nine.'

'Well, take it from me, he won't be missing anything.' Anthea threw the handful of carrot pieces and spring onion fragments onto a plate and began to arrange them into a curious kind of mosaic. 'Have you ever been to one of Desmond's parties? I gather they used to be quite something ten years ago when he was living with that Carrington woman in Montpellier Square. Now they're just dreary. *Bloomsbury*-ish, if that's still possible. Poor old Peter stands in the background wringing his hands with misery, and then just when you think Des has forgotten about it altogether he'll turn up with some extraordinary old personage who was dandled as an infant on Dickens's knee.'

'I think somebody said he was bringing Mrs Gurvitz.'

'I shouldn't be surprised.'

'Who is Mrs Gurvitz?'

'I think she was "the toast of 1927," whatever that means. Desmond knows such a lot of odd people. Have you seen these?'

'What are they?'

'They're letters that have come in about the first issue. You know how Desmond made a point of asking anyone who read the magazine to tell him what he thought. Well, that's what people said.'

Cynthia removed the paperweight from the little pile of correspondence on Desmond's desk and looked at a page or two. The first letter was from a clergyman in the West Country diffidently correcting a misused classical tag. The second, from a serving soldier, complained about 'a lack of genuine engagement with the real issues of the war.'

'Poor old Des,' Anthea said. Her tone had softened a little. 'He doesn't realise how unpopular you make yourself by sitting on the fence these days.'

'Is that what Desmond's doing? Sitting on the fence, I mean.'

'Oh no. Far too conspicuous. Skulking around somewhere underneath, I should say. Do you know, as soon as the war began and he got Peter to put up the money for *Duration*, he rushed round to the MOI and got himself classified as "Reserved Occupation"? One or two people were very cross about that.'

Outside in the square there was a sound of lorries turning: the mechanised hum of another world. Moving in counterpoint there came a second noise of footsteps on the staircase. Cynthia returned the letters to the desk and shifted the paperweight back on top of them, but not before Desmond, moving hastily into the room, saw her do it.

195

'So you've been reading the subscribers' letters?' he said cheerfully. 'What did you think of them?'

Cynthia wondered what she thought about the subscribers' letters. Like the progress of the war, or the fragments of embassy gossip that Tyler Kent occasionally let fall into his conversation, it was difficult to know what view to take, or whether, if it came to it, you had to take a view at all.

'I think they want to know where you stand, Des,' Anthea said.

For some reason Desmond seemed delighted to hear this. He rubbed his hands together enthusiastically. 'I think we could all do with knowing where we stand,' he said. 'I think that at this point in time it's an absolutely fundamental human requirement.'

Desmond often said things that were meant to be taken humorously. But this had precisely the opposite effect. All three of them looked at each other dumbstruck for a moment, as if not knowing where one stood was a crime of unimaginable seriousness, shameful to acknowledge, impossible to evade. Cynthia wondered exactly where she stood, and what this lack of precise definition implied. She was not at all happy, and suspected that the fault was Tyler Kent's.

'Are you allowed to bring this kind of thing home with you?' she had enquired about the copy of the presidential telegram.

'Maybe not,' Tyler Kent had told her, 'but sometimes there are risks you just have to take.'

There had been something deeply intimidating about him as he said these words. She found herself staring hard at Desmond and wondering why, when it was a party and she and Anthea had bothered to put on frocks, he was dressed more oddly than ever in a kind of furry jacket, grey flannel trousers, and a pair of tennis shoes that seemed several sizes too large for his already substantial feet.

Taking her cue, Anthea said: 'You didn't tell us it was fancy dress, Des. And I thought you were bringing Mrs Gurvitz.'

'I am,' Desmond said. He looked even more flustered, as if he suspected that this combination of the subscribers' letters, not knowing where he stood, and having fun poked at his clothes augured badly for the evening ahead. 'She'll be along in a bit. She's had to go to one of Sybil Colefax's cocktail parties, and there's no knowing how long everyone will be kept hanging about.' Something seemed to strike him and he went on: 'But what I meant to say was, has either of you seen the *Star*? Somebody was telling me there was a huge article in it about Del Mar.'

'What? About the first line of his story having to be censored by hand?'

'Not that,' Desmond said, looking unexpectedly stern. 'About his being a variety-hall performer before he took up writing. There was even a picture of him doing his act, next to a girl in sequins. And all across a couple of pages, my informant said.'

'I think someone's left a copy in the waste-paper basket,' Anthea said. 'I'll go and look.'

The misery of not knowing where they stood had passed. Unexpectedly, they had a purpose. The dim lights of Desmond's office gleamed fitfully down upon their enterprise. The newspaper, unfurled across Desmond's desk, confirmed his summary. There was a photograph of Sylvester, picturesquely attired in cape and evening suit, a cane in each hand, on the top of which rested a revolving plate, and a third cane balanced on the bridge of his nose. A woman in a bathing dress and high-heeled shoes looked on with reluctant admiration.

'"The Amazing Del Mar",' Cynthia read, genuinely stirred. 'I wonder if she's his wife.'

It was Anthea who discovered the final paragraph, tucked away at the foot of the second page, in which 'Mr Desmond Rafferty, editor of *Duration*, London's latest highbrow monthly,' welcomed the arrival of 'a prodigious literary talent.'

'Des,' she said soberly, the governess chancing upon an upturned pot plant, fragments of glass, an incriminating stone, 'did you do this?'

Desmond had lost interest in the newspaper, and was trying to decipher a message that someone had left on his desk written on the back of a matchbox. 'Did I do what?'

'Did you ring up the *Star* and tell them about Sylvester?'

'I don't see why I should be held responsible for every scrap of publicity this magazine manages to attract, though heaven knows we can do with it.'

'You did, didn't you?'

'I may have done,' Desmond said, not obviously abashed. 'At least I think I mentioned Del Mar as the new writer I was keenest on.'

'But you know how put out he was when Peter found his name in the programme. How on earth do you think he'll react to this?'

'Del Mar is a man of the world,' Desmond said, without much conviction. 'I'm sure he'll see the amusement in it, Anthea, even if you don't.'

What Anthea began to say in return was cut short by the arrival of Peter Wildgoose in the room. He was so immaculately turned out that he and Desmond might have stepped from the advertisement in which the well-dressed man and the badly-dressed man debate which fifty-shilling tailor to try. He said, 'I was just coming up the south side of the square in the blackout when I saw a girl fixing a sticky-back to a lamp-post. She ran off as I got near, but I brought it with me.'

He put the yellow flyer face-up on the table next to the open pages of the *Star* and they all lowered their heads and looked at it.

YOUR NEW YEAR'S RESOLUTION

We appeal to the working men and women of Great Britain to purchase the new Defence Bank and Savings Certificates, thus keeping the war going as long as possible. Your willing self-sacrifice and support will enable the Jew war-profiteers to make bigger and better profits and at the same time save their wealth from being conscripted. Help to defend the right of British manhood to die in a foreign quarrel every 25 years. Don't be selfish! Save for sheds and slaughter. Forget about the slums, the unemployed, the old age pensioners and other social reforms your money could be invested in. Just remember that your savings are much more usefully spent on the cause of death and destruction. Be patriotic! Come on— we confidently await the first million pounds!

'Fifth columnists, I suppose,' Desmond said. He did not seem particularly interested. 'There are enough of them about.'

'I saw another one the other day that went: *Land of dope and Jewry/Land that once was free/All the Jew boys praise thee/While they plunder thee,*' Peter Wildgoose said. 'What on earth's that on the desk? It looks like Sylvester.'

They explained about Desmond's conversation with the journalist on the *Star.*

'Des, you are a bloody fool,' Peter said, not crossly as he had done about the unbowdlerised story, but with an infinite weariness. 'You know how sensitive Sylvester is about all this. And now you go and encourage a newspaper to crack it up. Well, I shan't be answerable. You'll have to tell him yourself.'

'That's exactly what I intend to do,' Desmond said peevishly. All the high good humour of his first appearance had vanished. He looked like a music-hall comedian at whom the audience refuses to laugh. 'I shall discuss it with him as soon as he arrives—he said he'd be here quite early on—and I guarantee you there won't be any trouble.'

As if at a given signal, the quartet broke up. Desmond stood staring unhappily at the newspaper with one hand clasped dramatically to the top of his head. Anthea went back to her vegetable mosaic. Peter dragged a chair out into the centre of the room and sat miserably on it. He said, 'Anthea. Cynthia. You must think I didn't notice, but those are very elegant dresses you're wearing. It was very good of you to make the effort.'

Really, Cynthia thought, looking at him as he perched uneasily on the chair-end, still brooding about Desmond's indiscretion, she could think of no more desirable outcome to her life than being married to Peter Wildgoose. There would be no presidential telegrams lying around any mansion flat inhabited by him, nor any telephone calls from the likes of Captain Ramsay. All would be order, restraint, and punctilious transparency.

For a moment she wanted to leap over to the chair and fling her arms around Peter, but she knew that she could not do this. Instead she thought about the painfully thin line that seemed to separate the comic things in her life from the sinister ones. She had started off being amused by Tyler Kent and his intrigues and the curious parties he had taken her to, and now she was alarmed by and slightly ashamed of them. What had been mildly ridiculous had become definitely ominous. Worse, it was no longer possible to separate the Tyler Kent with whom, quite gratefully and enthusiastically, she lay on the divan mattress from the Tyler Kent who talked about isolationism and American ambassadors sticking to their script, for they were essentially the same person.

All this, she knew, made her unhappy, but she felt that taking any decisive step to extricate herself would make her unhappier still. It was the war that had done this to her, she thought bitterly, the war that had turned Tyler Kent into the kind of man whose flat she visited three evenings a week rather than the kind of man her mother liked to escort her to golf-club dances and 'look in' for supper on Sunday nights. All over London, presumably, there were people silently regretting things that the war had pushed them into doing, a great tide of moral insalubrity sent rushing across the city by a single telegram to Berlin.

It was about a quarter to seven now, and the first of the guests had begun to arrive. They were a mixed lot. One or two of the older people were in dinner jackets, and looked around them with faint bewilderment, fearing that they had misjudged the gathering's tone. The younger ones wore duffel coats or bohemian motley. At least a quarter of them were unknown to the *Duration* staff.

'The odd thing about parties,' Desmond said, surveying this tatterdemalion horde, 'even the ones that one gives oneself, is how few of the people one actually recognises. I suppose they must have had the invitations passed on.' His good humour had quite returned, and he made occasional stately progresses across the outer office, wineglass in hand, altogether conscious of the figure he cut.

'Des is good at parties,' Anthea said, appearing suddenly at Cynthia's elbow. She, too, seemed less cross than before. 'There's a man on the telephone asking for you.'

Cynthia went into Desmond's room, where two or three people were picking avidly through the pile of review copies and a bearded man in an Inverness cape had got hold of Desmond's address book, and grasped the receiver. Tyler Kent's voice said: 'Everyone having a good time, I hope?'

'It's not so bad. Will you be able to come over?'

'I don't think so. There's a bit of a flap on. The old man's cancelled his dinner engagement. We've all got to stand to. Shall I see you later?'

'I don't see why not.'

'Till then, then.'

'That's right, then. Till then.'

She put the receiver back on its cradle and went into the main room, where some more people were coming in. Somebody had had the bright idea of hanging paper streamers down the sides of the blackout curtains, but the general effect was not prepossessing. Cynthia thought of the Christmases of her childhood, which had nearly always taken place abroad: plum puddings made with *ghee* instead of butter, eaten in bright sunshine under the winnowing fans; old men in topis bending to inspect the nativity scene; *Adeste Fideles* sung before a backdrop of palm trees.

Lucy, who was a good-natured girl, had sent invitations to the London representatives of the printer, the distributor, and the advertising agent. These men, who wore dark suits and had anointed themselves with hair-oil, stood in a suspicious knot by the door. Later they would go back to their homes in the suburbs and tell their scandalised wives what they had seen.

'There's Sylvester,' Anthea said suddenly. 'Somebody had better go and get Des.'

If there was any kind of harmonising factor about the party, it came by default, which was to say that all the people who came to it were surprisingly ill-sorted. In these circumstances an individual guest would have had to make a very great effort to stand out from the crowd.

Even so, Sylvester Del Mar looked far more incongruous, far less sure of himself, than the printers' representatives in their subfusc suits or the grey-haired women in knickerbockers and pince-nez. As well as wearing his usual mackintosh and trilby hat, he was carrying a large brown-paper envelope with the words D. RAFFERTY ESQ. EDITOR DURATION written on it in letters so large that they could be seen halfway across the room. When he saw Cynthia and Anthea, he gave a little nod of recognition, clicked his heels smartly together, and made a mock-salute.

'Evening, ladies. Nice to be with you again. Very charming dresses you've got on, if you don't mind my saying.'

'Good evening, Sylvester,' Anthea said. 'I expect you'll be wanting to say hello to Des.'

'If Mr Rafferty has a brief moment to spare I should be very grateful to talk to him.' Sylvester was definitely worse at being obsequious than hail-fellow-well-met. 'I've brought those other stories he wanted to see. In fact, I spent the whole night sitting up to finish them.'

Cynthia wondered if he had brought the same intense absorption to his other career. She had a vision of him sitting in his digs at Finsbury Park, dance music blaring from the radio, spinning plates deep into the night. Desmond had seen him across the room and began to shoulder his way into view, waving as he came.

'Sylvester! It's very good to see you. We were wondering if you'd be able to make it.'

There were dark, purplish patches under Sylvester's eyes, Cynthia noticed. She wondered if he had any other life beyond the commissions that Desmond threw his way. For all his jauntiness, his respectful compliments, and his mock salute, he gave off a sense of huge discomfort, of not fitting in with any of the arrangements other people saw as necessary for their survival.

'I nearly didn't come,' he said. 'Not had any sleep for thirty-six hours, as a matter of fact. Been trying to finish those stories you said you wanted to see.'

'Well, that's splendid,' Desmond said, not quite mock-heartily. 'Really splendid, Sylvester. I wish all my contributors were so committed to their craft. Why don't we go into my office and have a talk about it, eh? And why don't we have something to drink?'

'What I'd really like,' Sylvester deposed, 'is a cup of tea.'

Anthea volunteered to make the tea. Cynthia wondered if Desmond was losing interest in Sylvester. Anthea said: 'I feel sorry for Sylvester. He's got about another fortnight basking in Desmond's shadow and having his stories accepted, and then it'll all be over. He should enjoy it while he can.'

'Why's that?' Cynthia asked, less interested in Sylvester's undoing than in the reason for Desmond's capriciousness.

'Oh, Des doesn't like to be *harassed*. And then he gets tired of people. His ideal contributor would be a fighter pilot who produced a sheaf of absolutely wonderful poems and then went off and got himself killed somewhere, leaving Des to write a memoir of his life. I daresay he'll find one soon if the war goes on. Now with women it's exactly the other way round. He gets fixated on them and can't leave them alone. I knew a girl who was having a walk-out with him, and he used to send her a note every other morning saying she'd broken his heart.'

As if on cue, the office door swung dramatically open and a large, platinum-haired woman came into the room. Here was someone else whose presence in the *Duration* office seemed wholly outlandish. She was wearing a fur coat—chinchilla, Cynthia thought—and the platinum hair was arranged in a style that she remembered from the bound volumes of *Punch* that had lain in the Government House library at Colombo.

Unlike Sylvester Del Mar, who had shuffled onto the premises with the greatest unease, the woman glanced across the room with a rather complacent air, as if to say that while this might not have been the world to which she was accustomed, she had some experience of it and would not be shocked by anything she found there.

Catching sight of Anthea and Cynthia, she said, rather in the manner of a headmistress questioning a couple of her prefects: 'Is this the party for *Duration*? I'm Mr Rafferty's guest. I'm afraid I was delayed. The taxi driver got lost in the blackout. Perhaps you could tell Mr Rafferty I'm here?'

There was something altogether mesmerising about Mrs Gurvitz, if this was what the apparition was: kindly but giving off an air of faint menace, like a monstrous carp passing sedately through a pond full of goldfish. Anthea, conscious that here, finally, was another woman who might be somewhere near to her own fighting weight, decided to bestow on her what was very nearly respectful attention.

'I think he's in that room over there. Would you like me to fetch him for you?'

'Not at all,' Mrs Gurvitz said. She looked as if she might be about to divest herself of the fur coat, which shimmered a little in the light, but thought better of it. 'This is a democratic age, or so everyone tells me. We've got past people being *announced*. I shall go and find him.'

They watched her make her way, politely yet insistently, through the banks of duffel coats and girls in trousers. Peter Wildgoose came up, almost shaking with suppressed laughter.

'So Esme Gurvitz has come, has she?' he said. 'I never for a moment thought she would. I just assumed it was Des getting intoxicated by the fumes of some cocktail party he'd been to where she turned up.'

'Who is Mrs Gurvitz?' Anthea asked. 'I don't think anyone's ever explained to me quite why she's so famous.'

Peter Wildgoose looked his best when he laughed. His face lost its worried expression and his surprisingly even teeth were displayed to advantage. He said, rather thoughtfully, as if this was an interesting anthropological question that ought to be gone into with the greatest rigour: 'I don't know that she's so very famous. She was Augustus John's mistress, I think, or was it the Prince before he took up with Lady Furness? And then she married an insurance broker called Gurvitz who died and left her a lot of money. But I shouldn't have thought she was one of Desmond's girls.'

'What makes you say that?' Anthea asked, sounding genuinely interested.

'Well, Des likes to be dominated by women but not exactly trampled on, if you see what I mean. But perhaps he's decided that what he really wants from life is to be ordered about.'

Desmond came out of his room. There was no sign of either Sylvester or Mrs Gurvitz. He touched Peter's arm just above the elbow. 'Have we got any champagne?'

'You know very well we haven't.'

'Only I can't offer Mrs Gurvitz a glass of Algerian red wine. I'd never hear the last of it.'

'She'll just have to put up with it,' Peter said. 'Tell her there's a war on.'

'That's what she's just been telling me. She had dinner with Winston the other night. I don't know how she manages these things, but there it is.'

'What did Winston have to say?'

'Oh, apparently they're very worried about the King. They think he's about to say something foolish. . . . Isn't there a bottle of Bordeaux left over somewhere?'

'No, there isn't,' Peter said.

He was being brusquer than usual with Desmond, Cynthia thought. Perhaps the sight of Mrs Gurvitz had emboldened him. A foot or so of the blackout curtain had come away and she could see the dark outlines of the plane trees in the square quivering in the breeze.

'How did Sylvester take it?' Anthea asked.

'How did Sylvester take what?' Desmond wondered, immersed in his brand-new world of champagne, Mrs Gurvitz, and bottles of Bordeaux that might have been left over somewhere.

'The story in the *Star.*'

'Oh, about as well as could be expected,' Desmond said. He was looking nervously over his shoulder at the wall, as if there were invisible guests standing there whose presence was discernible only to himself. 'He agreed with me that these kinds of things were more or less inevitable. Said he quite understood the paper could do with the publicity.'

'So you told him that it was your fault?'

'I won't say I went quite that far,' Desmond said. One of his fat red hands was wrapped so tightly around a wineglass that only the stem was visible.

'Where is Sylvester?' Cynthia asked.

'I don't know,' Desmond said. 'I really can't be personally responsible for all my guests. Emerald Cunard does that, you know. She follows them from room to room and match-makes. I expect Sylvester's gone to the lavatory or something. I really hope he isn't going to start turning into a pest. Do you know, he brought in another six stories just now? I looked at the first and it seemed to be a dialogue between various parts of an internal combustion engine.'

Cynthia yawned. A great stretch of time seemed to have elapsed since she and Anthea had stood in Desmond's office cutting up the vegetables, but, looking at her watch, she discovered that it was only half-past seven. She had not been to many literary parties in her life, but she had a feeling that this one had a very long way to go.

A man she did not recognise, wearing a blue, collarless shirt and with streaks of paint on his fingers, came over and said, 'I say, didn't you sit for me once?'

Cynthia could deal with this sort of thing. 'I don't think I did.'

'Oh, but you did. You were the girl who always wanted the heater turned up because you thought the studio was too cold.'

'No, I wasn't.'

'Well, if you ever did feel like sitting for me I'd be absolutely delighted to oblige.'

A yard or so away, Desmond, Mrs Gurvitz, and Peter Wildgoose, all of whom seemed to be getting on very well with each other, were talking about definitions of happiness.

'Easy,' Desmond said. 'Writing a tolerably good book while travelling south in the company of someone your conscience permits you to love.'

'Do you know?' Mrs Gurvitz said—her high colour had grown higher still—'I think it's to do with people not making demands on one. If I woke up one morning in the knowledge that nobody was going to write to me, send me a bill, or ask me to lunch, then the rest of the day would be a pleasure to contemplate.'

'And what would you do?' Peter Wildgoose said, who looked as if he wanted to burst out laughing but was constrained by a sense of social obligation. 'I mean, if nobody wrote or sent in a bill or telephoned to ask you to lunch?'

'Well, I don't know,' Mrs Gurvitz admitted. 'I expect in the end I should read the *Sketch*, smoke three cigarettes instead of two, and go for a walk around Kensington Gardens. But it's the principle of the thing.'

'Yes,' Peter Wildgoose was saying absently, 'yes . . . yes.' And Cynthia gazed at him so intently that for a moment the world was composed entirely of this dapper little man in his dark suit, straw-coloured hair neatly parted at the side of his head and a quizzical expression on his face.

There was a sudden commotion at the far end of the room, a quick, purposeful displacement of bodies, a noise of glass smashing on the carpet, and Lucy came hurrying towards them.

'Des,' she said urgently. 'It's Sylvester. You'll have to come and talk to him.'

'Why?' Desmond wanted to know. He was still travelling south in the company of someone his conscience permitted him to love. 'What has he done?'

'He's locked himself in the lavatory and won't come out.'

'Why has he done that?'

'I don't know. But he says that it's all your fault.'

The lavatories were on the further side of the landing: two cubicles preceded by a Spartan ante-room containing a washbasin, a mirror, a pair of hand-towels and a poster warning that coughs and sneezes spread diseases. As they made their way through the crowd, Lucy supplied further details.

'I'd just gone in there to wash my hands, and then I heard the sound of someone, well, *crying*.'

'He's not doing any harm,' Desmond said. They had reached the ante-room by now. 'Don't you think it would be better to leave him there until he feels like coming out?'

'No, I don't,' Peter Wildgoose said. He looked horribly pale. 'I think that's a dreadful idea. We'll have to talk to him. Sylvester,' he said, in a voice too loud for the room, 'are you all right in there? Lucy said you weren't feeling too well. Is there anything we can do to help?'

'What an awfully squalid place,' Mrs Gurvitz said, who had accompanied them over from the office. 'I hope it's not the one you girls have to use.'

The cubicle door ended about six inches from the tile floor. Anthea bent down slightly and lowered her head, as if she was attempting to perform a piece of old-fashioned physical jerks. 'Is he actually in there at all?' she demanded. 'I can't see his feet.'

'Sylvester,' Peter Wildgoose said. 'You really ought to come out of there. It won't do you any good to stay in, and it will inconvenience anyone else who wants to use the place. Now what is the matter?'

'When I was a girl,' Mrs Gurvitz said, reminiscently, 'whenever anyone locked themselves in the lavatory it was always to take cocaine.'

'Christ,' Peter Wildgoose said suddenly. 'Des, you'd better give me a hand. Anthea, would you take Cynthia and Mrs Gurvitz outside please? And whatever you do, don't let anyone else in here.'

They went and stood on the landing as directed. Almost immediately there came a noise of smashing wood and shouted instructions. This was followed, shortly afterwards, by what sounded like the rush of water. Peter Wildgoose's head appeared in the doorway. He had taken off the jacket of his suit and was breathing hard.

'Someone go to the office and telephone for an ambulance, please.' There was a sharp and faintly inhuman cry behind him. 'Oh, and a plumber too. I think the cistern's about to come down.'

They brought Sylvester—purple-faced and with staring eyes—out on the lavatory cubicle's shattered door. He had attempted to hang himself with his braces from one of the overhead pipes. After a short while he was able to sit up and drink a glass of water. There was a terrible red mark round his neck where the braces had caught. Desmond stood staring at him with an odd mixture of bewilderment and resentment.

Within a moment a quantity of water began to leak out of the washroom door and flow down the staircase. Presently three ambulancemen—not best pleased at having to climb the flights of stairs—arrived on the landing bearing a stretcher. When they saw Sylvester their faces brightened.

'Tried to do himself in?' they asked.

'It really is none of my business,' Desmond said. And Cynthia knew that whether he lived or died, won the Nobel Prize for Literature or sank into obscurity, no more of Sylvester's stories would ever appear in *Duration*.

'Someone ought to turn the water off,' one of the ambulancemen said.

There was no knowing how long this might have gone on. In the end, Peter Wildgoose managed the business. He was adroit in a crisis. Five minutes later the ambulancemen and their burden had disappeared down the staircase, the stopcock been run to earth in an obscure cupboard on the next landing, and the water turned off.

To the duffel-clad youths who came out onto the landing to see what was going on, Peter said: 'I'm afraid one of our guests has been taken rather ill. Sylvester Del Mar, who writes those brilliant short stories. Perhaps you've heard of him?' Each time he moved his feet, standing water rose up from the carpet over the tips of his shoes.

But even Peter Wildgoose's sangfroid could not save the party. Too many people had seen the ambulancemen arrive, too many people heard the shouted instructions from the lavatory cubicle and the thud as the cistern went down. A presentiment of doom was in the air. Within another quarter of an hour the office was almost empty.

'It really is too bad,' Desmond said. He was still treating Sylvester's attempt at suicide as a personal insult. 'Why did he have to do a thing like that? After all, plenty of people get written about in the newspapers, and for more disagreeable reasons than this. Perhaps he has a mythological view of himself. So many people do these days.' Nobody paid him any attention. Mrs Gurvitz, who might have offered some consolation in the circumstances, had disappeared along with the duffel-clad hordes.

Cynthia washed up some of the wineglasses desultorily in the sink. She felt sorry for Sylvester Del Mar, who seemed to her in some incalculable way a victim of the environment in which she imagined herself to reside: not up to his opponents' fighting weight; brought down by secrets he struggled all too vainly to conceal. The outer office had an altogether debauched air, as if some unimaginable orgy had been held in it. Clouds of cigarette smoke hung under the ceiling and there were carrot slices all over the floor. An effort was made to clear them up.

Then Anthea said, 'There's no point in staying here. The only thing we can do is leave the windows open. I think I'll go. Come on, Cynthia.'

There was no way in which this invitation could be refused: the look on Anthea's face confirmed it. Cynthia tried to accept it in one of those all-girls-together invitations one heard flung out half a dozen times a day in Lyons cafés and cinema queues, but failed miserably. Together they went off down the pitch-black stairs. Halfway down the second flight, Cynthia's foot struck against something soft and yielding. It was Sylvester Del Mar's hat, dropped there by the ambulancemen.

In the square the wind was still up and the plane trees writhed. A few cars went by, showing tiny streaks of light. Somewhere in the distance there was a booming noise, almost hydraulic, like water rising in some ancient plumbing system. They went westward in silence towards the Tottenham Court Road. Anthea said, 'If I do go home, there'll only be bread-and-butter and sardines. Besides, I need to talk to you. Let's go and have something to eat.'

A hundred yards further on they came to a tiny café, set back from the street and advertising its existence by tiny traceries of light behind the rims of the shutters. Inside, a fat woman lurked behind the chromium counter, polishing teacups.

'Gracious,' Anthea said. 'Straight out of Ed Burra. Look, there's some cheese. I wonder if one could get some Welsh rarebit.'

They negotiated with the fat woman for a while and then went and sat down at a table aggrandised over by two outsize, high-backed chairs.

'Well, that was a depressing evening,' Anthea said. 'Desmond's parties are always like that in the end. Rain or shine, war or peace. It makes no difference. But someone trying to hang themselves from the lavatory cistern is hitting a new low, even for Des. But that's not what I want to talk to you about. Tell me about your American friend.'

Cynthia had been prepared for this. 'About Tyler Kent?'

'About Mr Kent. Unless there are other American friends you've been keeping under your hat. Don't think me brutally inquisitive, but what is his attraction?'

Something told Cynthia she did not have to answer this. Something else told her that, mesmerised as she was by Anthea's personality, she was incapable of remaining silent. The Welsh rarebits came, and proved to be a great disappointment.

'Well?' Anthea said.

'I suppose,' Cynthia found herself saying, 'it's because he's not English.'

'You don't mean he's feeding you silk stockings and packets of Lucky Strikes? That sounds a bit mercenary.'

She could not tell if Anthea was joking or not. 'That's not what I meant at all. I meant that he's different from anyone else. He doesn't work for a timber firm, or talk about where he went to school, or play tennis, or drink pink gins when the sun's behind the yardarm. You can't imagine how awful Englishmen are in the East. After all, they wouldn't be sent there if they were any good at anything.'

'Rather a comment on our colonial system,' Anthea said. 'And I can see all that being fairly dreary. But do you know what he's *like*?'

For God's sake, Cynthia found herself wanting to say, *I go to bed with him three times a week and twice on Sundays. He says 'nice to see a couple of old friends again' when I take my brassiere off. I think I ought to know what he's like.* And then she remembered that, with the exception of certain easily grasped essentials, she did not really know what Tyler Kent was like at all.

'Let me tell you what he's like,' Anthea said briskly. 'He's a cipher clerk at the American Embassy. How he leads the life he does on a cipher clerk's pay is a very interesting question. But he spends his time going to defeatist parties where everyone stands around saying that of course they didn't approve of *Kristallnacht* but at least Adolf's giving the Germans a *lead*. He's great friends with Captain Ramsay. As for what he does with the information that comes his way at the Embassy, well, it rather pains me to tell you.'

Cynthia remembered the presidential telegram, with its superscription: *W. S. Churchill. First Sea Lord.* 'How do you know all this?'

The fat woman had disappeared on some errand in the back parts of the café. Anthea made sure she was out of earshot. For the first time in their acquaintance, Cynthia thought, she looked a little less assured, a little less certain that the ground beneath her feet could not possibly give way.

'Cynthia. Why do you think I go off to the Ritz to see people like Norman Burdett? What do you think I was doing at that party you turned up to with Kent? What do you imagine I do at *Duration*, if it comes to that?'

'I don't know. What *do* you do at *Duration*?'

'Well, for one thing I keep an eye on Des.'

'Keep an eye on Des?' This seemed extraordinary. 'What on earth for?'

Anthea laughed. 'Poor old Des. He's not much of a security risk, but he's been CP since 1934. Probably not much in it, but one likes to know. I expect he only did it to impress his left-wing friends. Only you can never tell with Des.'

'You mean you're *spying* on him and Peter?'

'My dear, you've been reading too many newspaper articles. Nobody is spying on Des, and certainly not on Peter. It's just that there are certain things one's supervisors like to know about him. I'm sorry, is all this very shocking?'

'No, not really.'

'Yes, it is. But you needn't alarm yourself about it. Des isn't a complete idiot. I expect he has a pretty good idea what I'm up to. I should think he finds it all rather funny. But it's not Des I'm interested in. It's your Mr Kent.'

'What has he done?'

'If I didn't think you might be able to help me, I wouldn't be telling you this. Now, you've heard about the King's Party, the "Faction" they call it? The people who want a negotiated peace? Well, it's certainly not treasonable to want there not to be a war. It's what everybody wants, apart from a few armaments manufacturers. But it probably is treasonable to assume you can do the negotiating yourself. I think—we think—Mr Kent is up to his neck with Captain Ramsay and your Mr Bannister in this, that he's giving them copies of telegrams from foreign embassies, that he's allowing Ramsay to make use of his diplomatic immunity.'

'How can he do that?'

'Very easily. For one thing, the Faction has a membership book. I haven't seen it. Nobody has. But I can tell you that it's spent several weeks in a safe in Grosvenor Square where no one can get hold of it, and there's a man whom your Mr Kent pays to carry it around London. It's probably been brought to the flat. Have you seen it?'

'No, I haven't, Anthea.' Cynthia was close to tears. 'You know I haven't.'

'It's all right, darling. Nobody's accusing you of anything. Not anything much, that is. You're just—how do I put this officially?— spending a lot of your time with a foreign national who is known to be associating with people who, according to a strict definition of the term, are traitors to the Crown. The only question is: what are you going to do about it?'

Half of Cynthia thought that the men she slept with were her own affair. The other half was dimly aware that, without in the least intending to, she might have morally compromised herself. 'What do you want me to do about it?'

'Do you know,' Anthea said suddenly, 'I haven't the least idea what you think about any of this? None at all. You might think Hitler's a jolly good thing. You might think Mosley is just the kind of chap we want in *these difficult times*. You might think that if there are Germans living in Poland, then lots of other Germans are perfectly entitled to invade it. I mean, where do your parents stand on this?'

'I don't know. Mother always said she could never take Hitler seriously since someone took her to see Chaplin in *The Great Dictator*. Father says that he's a perfect expression of one side of the German temperament, but that was never any reason why you should quarrel with him.'

'And what does Mr Kent say?'

Cynthia thought about the many—the very many—things that Tyler Kent had said about Hitler, Chamberlain, and Roosevelt, late at night in the flat, head bent studiously over his desk, scissors poised above the litter of press cuttings.

'He says it's nothing to do with America. That it's just the Jews making mischief, and if somebody took the trouble to go to Berlin the whole thing could be settled quite happily.'

'Just at this moment there are a dozen army divisions right behind the German border,' Anthea said. 'Does that make it sound as if the whole thing could be settled quite happily by Lord Halifax or someone taking a plane to Berlin?'

At various stages in her life, quite a few people had tried to lecture Cynthia in this way. Mrs Kirkpatrick had done it in high-walled Eastern gardens, with the sun flaring over the rhododendron bushes. Henry Bannister had done it in yachts tracking across the Solent. Schoolmistresses had done it in gloomy South Kensington basements, with the smell of gravy haunting the passageways beyond. This eternal sense of being kept up to the mark, of being told—kindly, condescendingly, or encouragingly—that she was failing to fulfil the expectations that other people had of her had always grated. It grated on her now, here in the Bloomsbury café, with the steam rising from the urns and the hideously contorted reflection of her face gleaming off the burnished chrome.

Without caring what the consequences might be, she said, 'I don't think you have to speak to me like that, Anthea, and I don't think I have to listen.'

'Fair enough,' Anthea said, not sounding in the least put out. 'But do you know, Norman Burdett nearly died that night in Jermyn Street? And even Desmond is going about saying he needs to know where he stands. Fancy that of Desmond, who never knew where he stood in his life before. Well, I shan't say any more. But there are things that you might do for us. Things that only you could do for us, if you take my meaning. And things that have to be done soon. If you won't do them, then I dare say we shall have to find someone else. Which will be a great bore, and an inconvenience, and quite frankly a disappointment.'

The moral arbiters of the Eastern gardens, the Solent yachts, and the Kensington basements had all dealt in disappointment. There seemed to be no other form of rebuke. Looking at Anthea as she leaned across the table, not exactly craftily but with an immense and inscrutable guile, Cynthia wondered if she had always been like this. In the nursery? In the schoolroom? She was supposed to have had a husband. What had he thought about it? She had a swift and rather embarrassing vision of Anthea, stark naked on the marital bed, still offering up these witty remarks as some eager bridegroom plunged gamely into her. Glancing at her watch, she saw it was nearly half-past nine.

'I really think I should be going.'

'I shouldn't dream of keeping you for a moment,' Anthea said. 'Just think about what I've said. It's not your fault. I'm sure Mr Kent makes a nice change from all those dull young men one comes across. I know the ladies in Belgravia who send him invitations think he's a dear. Do you know, Sybil Colefax had him to lunch at the Ritz the other day? It's like something out of Henry James. He'll be marrying an heiress if this goes on much longer. And whatever you do, don't worry about Mr Kent. He can take care of himself. It's the people like Des that I agonise about. People who don't know where they stand.'

When she got back to Tyler Kent's flat, it was a quarter-past ten and there was light spilling out in a long, yellowish bar from under the door and the sound of a radio playing faintly in the background. Her first thought was that Tyler Kent was back early from the embassy, but when she stepped into the drawing room the first thing she saw was Captain Ramsay sitting at the desk, with a pair of spectacles pushed up to the crown of his balding head. There was another man standing at the side of the desk, younger and tough-looking, dressed in a mackintosh with a brown-paper parcel under his arm, smoking a cigarette, who looked at her incuriously.

With his semi-detached spectacles and his bald head, Captain Ramsay looked almost comically sinister, like someone doing an impression of a man up to no good. He said, 'Do excuse me, Miss Kirkpatrick. I had no idea you would be arriving. Mr Kent sometimes lets me do a little work here of an evening. Don't let us disturb you. Please do whatever you want to do.'

There was something rather subtle about this. It implied that someone—possibly Tyler Kent—had been seriously remiss in not letting Captain Ramsay know of her arrangements for the evening, while hinting that whatever she might now want to do was bound to be almost dangerously frivolous. The young man took the cigarette out of his mouth.

'I was just going meself,' he said. He had a northern accent, like some of the comedians one sometimes endured on the radio, and she had a vague suspicion that she had seen him before. 'You mustn't mind me.'

'I won't,' Cynthia said. She went and made herself a cup of tea and, for want of any better location, took it into the bedroom and drank it sitting beneath the faces of Tyler Kent and his Princeton classmates. A moment or two later the front door slammed shut and there was a sound of footsteps rapidly descending. The blackout curtain had not yet been lowered, and she went across to the window to fix it. She had just finished the tea and was wondering about making herself a piece of toast when there were further noises from outside—a door opening, a snatch or two of conversation—and Tyler Kent came into the room.

'Sorry about Ramsay,' he said. 'Guess I should have told you he'd be here.'

'Who was the other man?'

'Which other man?'

'The one with the parcel.'

'That would be Rodney. Was he here long?'

'I don't know. He said he was just going when I arrived.'

'How was the party?'

Cynthia explained about the party: Desmond and the *Star*; the raw, red mark around Sylvester Del Mar's neck; Mrs Gurvitz. Tyler looked interested.

'I've heard of Esmé Gurvitz,' he said seriously. 'Wasn't she that painter's mistress? And didn't her husband die and leave her a lot of money? She sounds quite a girl. I wish I'd been there.'

Waking next morning, she was gripped by a suspicion that Captain Ramsay might still be sitting in the drawing room with his spectacles pushed back over his forehead, but there was no sign of him or indeed any hint that he had ever been there.

She wondered just exactly what she did believe in. That remark had stung. She was not at all sure that she believed in Tyler Kent, either personally or politically. She supposed that, when it came to it, she believed in people's right to be left alone, and not be made to do things they didn't want, not to be picked up by the tidal waves of other people's scheming and deposited on alien beaches, far from home, and with no prospect of a return passage. But her suspicions had been roused and she was determined to pay more attention to the world laid out before her.

At the *Duration* office everybody was in the foulest imaginable temper. Cynthia and Lucy spent the morning picking up shreds of carrot from the carpet and dealing with the ashes of a small fire that seemed to have been lit in the corner of Desmond's room. The latest news on Sylvester Del Mar was that he had gone away somewhere for a rest.

'Poor old Sylvester,' Desmond said cheerfully. 'On the other hand, I daresay that in twenty years' time somebody will write it all up in a book called *Literary Life in Wartime London* and we shall all be interviewed for the Sunday papers.'

All that morning Cynthia waited for Anthea's arrival, not because she wanted to say anything, but because she had an expression ready for her that would say: *yes, I will do what you want.* But it turned out that Anthea had telephoned in to say that she was ill.

It was a strange time: everyone agreed. The landlord, keen to apportion blame for the flood, the damaged carpet, and the wrecked cistern, sent in a bill for £59 7s. Captain Ramsay asked a question in the House about the percentage of Jewish personnel known to be serving in the armed forces. A reconnaissance plane crash-landed on the sands at Beachy Head and its pilot, a minor German aristocrat who was popularly supposed to have brought a sheaf of peace proposals with him, was taken away for questioning.

In early December, the newspapers began to wonder what the King might say in his Christmas Day speech to the nation, in a world where, it was quickly established, spruce trees, mincemeat, turkeys, and mistletoe were in chronically short supply.

CHAPTER 12

December

It is too early to go home, but nonetheless Cynthia goes. There is nothing much happening at the office—the New Year issue is with the printer—and in any case since Sylvester Del Mar tried to hang himself Desmond's behaviour has become erratic.

She wanders back to Belgrave Square through the Knightsbridge side-streets, where the winter light is turning grey and dusk-ridden and the Friday afternoon sounds of children playing on area steps and errand-boys' bicycles are borne on the air behind her. There are soldiers walking back and forth from the Knightsbridge barracks, red-faced and curiously unmartial, as if their proper destiny was to swell an operatic chorus rather than pick up a rifle.

The landscape has been familiar to her since childhood: spacious, anonymous, and barren. From the basement windows, fenced in behind area steps, come glimpses of dozens of miniature, fenced-in worlds, like the dioramas at the Science Museum: a maidservant ironing shirts; a double row of small girls in gingham frocks having their tea; a man staring balefully at a typewriter. Some of the houses are shuttered up and have FOR SALE boards in their upper windows. The old tribes are in retreat, gone elsewhere. There is no traffic except for the errand-boys' bicycles and a Rolls-Royce, carrying an old lady with yellow-white hair the colour of piano keys, which steals softly round the corner of West Halkin Street and moves off in the direction of the park.

Just lately there have been articles in the newspapers hazarding that the age of the little old lady in the Rolls-Royce is dead, and that the war, whatever its outcome, will have a 'democratising influence.' Cynthia isn't so sure. But she would like to know where the other old ladies, with their fox-furs and their feathered hats, have gone. Perhaps there are colonies of them camped out in the Yorkshire stately homes, twenty to a butler. Who can tell? The Rolls-Royce is fifty yards away now and gathering speed, a bullet shot from one world into another.

She stops at a kiosk on the corner of the square and buys a newspaper. Here the weekly and monthly magazines are piled up in long, rippling mounds, like brightly coloured roof tiles. *Cage Birds. John O'London's. Blackwood's.* Her father subscribed to *Blackwood's.* She has a memory of it lying on the veranda table at the villa in Colombo next to the tea-brokers' catalogues and the back-numbers of the *Island News.*

Belgrave Square is so dark that the plane trees at the further end can barely be seen: the ghosts of old sentinels marching through fog. She rolls the newspaper up into a taut cylinder and holds it wedged under her elbow like a swagger-stick. There will be no one in the flat, she thinks, and she can enjoy something that has lately been rather denied her: a little private time. Everybody is feeling the strain, of course. Like democratising influences, the privations of the home front are a newspaper staple. There is a whole new iconography made up of tired housewives, overworked machinists falling asleep at their lathes. If there is one consolation, it is that we are all in this together.

Sometimes Cynthia thinks she is marshalling her inner resources; at other times she despairs of her inability to cope. Just now she is thoroughly demoralised by the conversation with Anthea and the responsibility it brings. In fact, the memory of the evening in the Bloomsbury café has been nagging at her for days, an instant rebuke whenever she hears Tyler

Kent's voice on the telephone. She suspects that this kind of life is not good for her. Late nights in Bishop's Mansions and rackety Knightsbridge parties take their toll. Better to lie fallow: the Bachelor Girl taking her ease. When she first heard that phrase she imagined a woman in a pinstripe suit with a burnt-cork moustache, like an actress in a musical comedy.

The pavement in Belgrave Square is unnaturally sticky. There are traces of slime on its surface, as if somebody has dropped a tray of chicken-fat. There is no one about.

She walks up the flight of steps to the front door and passes through it, the heels of her shoes sticking in the holes of the coconut matting, and stops awkwardly just inside the doorway, half with the aim of freeing her feet, half out of sheer exhaustion.

On the far side of the vestibule the ballroom gapes grey and ghostly. There is talk of turning it into a regimental recruiting office, but no decision has yet been made. Here in the late afternoon, the lower parts of the house are still prey to human traffic. On the first floor, in sight of the embassy's brass plate, a crisis presents itself. A swarthy man with odd tints of ochre in his face sits half-tumbled on the topmost stair, attended by two other men so similar in size and skin-tone that they look like middle-aged triplets.

'Is he all right?' Cynthia asks briskly, in the tone her mother used for childhood injuries.

'A little faintness, that is all,' one of the attendants tells her in impeccably accented English. 'It is kind of you to enquire,' the other adds. The seated man is making odd little growling noises that are practically canine in their pitch. Clearly it is not only tired housewives and machinists at their lathes who are feeling the strain.

Courteously, and with a practised economy of gesture, the triptych rearranges itself to allow her to pass. On the second floor there is a light behind the frosted glass of the literary agency, a smell of cigar smoke and a pair of silhouetted figures in conversation. The book trade is in the doldrums, Desmond says—the second volume of his autobiography has been mysteriously stymied—but here, it seems, some kind of business still precariously survives. On the third landing the bags of old clothing piled up before the quarter-open door of the Catholic charity reach halfway to the ceiling. A middle-aged nun with a pair of tennis shoes sticking out from under her vestments is gravely inspecting them.

'Are you from the Red Cross?' the nun asks as Cynthia heaves into view. She has curiously milky eyes, like those rogue marbles that disintegrate at the pressure of a thumb.

'No, I'm not,' Cynthia says, with the same briskness she brought to the fainting diplomat. 'I live upstairs.'

The nun does not answer. Perhaps Cynthia's appearance is somehow a symbol of the working-out of divine providence? Some of the bags have rents in them and are disgorging soiled underclothes onto the polished floor. At the same time there is something comforting about this transit of four flights of Belgravian stairs, the presumption of harmony. Diplomacy, commerce, charity—each has had its say. Now domesticity awaits.

On the topmost stair of the topmost flight, one of the ribs she cracked in Henry Bannister's car gives a twinge, and she thinks of Ceylon: the green jungle canopy beneath Sigiriya Rock; parakeets screeching in the tree-tops; Jaffna, Kandy, and Trincomalee; the flying fish in the bay at Colombo. Five months gone, it seems a lifetime away.

The nun, a dozen feet below but still visible in the murk, is singing quietly to herself, like the nuns in story books. London is full of these solitary entertainers: old men with the medals of the Great War on their chests playing the mouth-organ at the Tube entrances; picturesque charwomen holding forth on the tops of buses. Half of her is still in Ceylon, hearing the detonation of the holiday fire-crackers that sound uncomfortably like small-arms fire, watching the bright chips of colour that are the saris of the Tamil tea-pickers moving up and down the hillside. The other half is thinking about Tyler Kent.

Being somebody's mistress—and this is the category in which she presumes herself to reside—is primarily a matter of gesture: a series of coded signals sent out to observers who may or may not be in the know, a private joke that half of you wants to keep to yourself and half of you wants to share with other people. There is a particular way in which Tyler Kent leaps forward with his lighter whenever she takes a cigarette from the packet and places it in her mouth that symbolises all this—its confidences, its conspiracies, its bleak assumptions. She assumes that doing what Anthea wants her to do will be a betrayal of a sort.

But what exactly is being betrayed? Tyler Kent is not going to marry her. That much is abundantly clear. In a year, or eighteen months, he will get another posting, and the maps of the Indian wars and the photographs of the Princeton sophomores will move on to Rome, or Madrid. Tyler Kent, as he is fond of pointing out, is a man without ties. Or rather a man whose ties can be severed whenever Tyler Kent feels like doing the severing. He was engaged once, to the daughter of a Delaware real-estate tycoon who owned half the properties in Martha's Vineyard. He talks about it as the tightest of tight spots. Beating an honourable retreat needed all his dexterity to accomplish.

Cynthia puts her key in the door, which is full of rust and makes a crackling sound, like old leaves trampled underfoot. The flat is supposed to be empty. Lucy has gone off somewhere with her squadron leader. There will probably not be any food in the kitchen cupboard. Unexpectedly the door opens onto voices: Tyler Kent's and Lucy's. Walking into the sitting-room, she finds them both ensconced in armchairs. There is a bottle of wine, half-empty, on the table before them and the atmosphere, if not conspiratorial, is at any rate faintly exclusive, as if the joke Tyler Kent might have been about to tell before Cynthia's arrival will still be told, but without the same level of attack.

'Hi, Cynthia,' Tyler Kent says. He has taken off the jacket of his charcoal-coloured suit to reveal fanciful light-blue braces that run over his shoulders in an inverted Y and looks far more natty and self-possessed than any Englishman found in the same circumstances could ever do. 'I was just passing and thought I'd come by.'

Lucy, still wearing the thoroughly sensible coat that people in the office sometimes make jokes about, has a slightly far-away look in her eyes, as if the bottle of wine is a prelude to some Barmecidal feast that will suddenly drop from the rafters onto a dozen gleaming gold plates.

'I thought you were going away somewhere with your chap,' Cynthia says, who cannot quite remember if the squadron leader's name is Roger or Rupert.

'I was,' Lucy says, 'but he got called off to Biggin Hill on an exercise. He says he might be able to get up to town tomorrow.'

RAF officers lead erratic lives, Cynthia knows. There are stories in the press about their being thrown out of nightclubs and overturning cars, late at night, in the Sussex back-lanes. Their professional slang—'kites' and 'prangs' and 'crates'—has been taken up by radio comedians. There are also jokes about 'joysticks.'

Having established what Lucy and Tyler Kent are doing here at half-past four on a Friday afternoon, Cynthia's gaze falls on the wine, which is not, as she first assumes, from North Africa but spectacularly ancient, the dust at its neck almost cobwebbed, as if it were first ordered up to celebrate the news from Trafalgar. 'Where did you get that?' she wonders.

'The wine?' Tyler says. 'Oh, I was lunching with Logan. The old fellow's taken a shine to me. Why don't you have some?'

Logan is an elderly American expatriate, almost as ancient as the wine, whom Desmond sometimes talks about. It is extraordinary how many people end up taking a shine to Tyler Kent. The Belgravia hostesses aren't the half of it. Extraordinary, too, how often they end up giving him things. Novels from Heywood Hill's book-shop, ripe to be appreciated for their 'Englishness.' Gewgaws from the Burlington Arcade. Cynthia is not quite sure how much of this Englishness Tyler Kent wants. Essentially his attitude to England is that of the tourist, interested in these little sideshows got up for his diversion, but whose real concerns lie back across the border just crossed. He can take it or leave it.

But she accepts a glass of the wine which is, as she anticipated, quite astonishing: dense and mellow—practically the colour of blood—and containing countless little scents and intimations of other things. 'It's quite something, isn't it?' Tyler Kent says. He seems genuinely impressed, which is unusual. With Captain Ramsay he looks calculating, the New World bringing its managerial skills to right the deficiencies of the old. Logan's wine cellar, on the other hand, has made him humble.

Wineglass in hand, Cynthia goes into the kitchen, which looks faintly ramshackle and unlived-in. What with Lucy's squadron leader and Cynthia's nights in Bishop's Mansions, the girls are not often here. The cupboards are nearly bare, and the drift of flour on the square table has been there a week. Beneath her, the house is turning quieter. 'I've no idea what we have to eat,' she says, going back into the sitting-room, where

Tyler Kent is explaining something to Lucy about the situation on the Franco-German border. 'There's hardly anything in the kitchen and the rest of the shepherd's pie is definitely off.'

'Then I shall insist, I shall absolutely insist,' Tyler Kent says, who has drunk two glasses of the red wine, 'on taking you young ladies out to supper.'

'That would be a wonderful idea,' Lucy says, for whom even one glass of wine is a dangerous incitement, and Cynthia bows her head meekly at the derailment of her evening.

'I shall absolutely insist,' Tyler Kent says again, with a little flourish of his cupped hands—a new gesture which Cynthia wonders if he has borrowed from Logan.

This is another difference between Tyler Kent and Englishmen: the fuss about hospitality given and received, the gratification involved in standing treat. Sometimes she imagines America as a kind of gigantic restaurant full of people desperately trying to pay for each other's meals.

None of this, she acknowledges, is getting her any nearer to solving the problem of Tyler Kent who, if Anthea is to be believed, is in league with people whose activities could be regarded as treasonable. She wonders what some of the Belgravia hostesses whose invitation cards lie on Tyler Kent's mantelpiece would say if they knew. But perhaps some of *them* are engaged in activities which could be regarded as treasonable. It is hard to tell.

There is post on the doormat: a postcard to a previous tenant with a picture of St Moritz on the front in which not one of the words is intelligible, and an air-mail letter with a Portuguese frank. Cynthia puts this aside to read later. In the past few weeks Mrs Kirkpatrick's letters have grown terse and unrevealing. Cynthia has no idea whether her mother finds Portugal congenial or what she does there, but she knows that she has read a great deal of Trollope. She wonders what she would say if her mother were there in the room with her now and concludes that she would keep her information—and her suspicions—to herself, and that her moral judgements are for her alone.

Tyler Kent, meanwhile, has jumped up from his chair and is handing round the rest of the wine. He is nowhere near drunk, but there is definitely the air of a performing seal about these manoeuvres: a precariously balanced ball that may plunge to earth at any moment. The neck of the bottle clinks against Lucy's glass as he pours. Lucy's squadron leader has a Theology degree from Cambridge and a manner to match. It is difficult to imagine him at the controls of a Fairey Battle. 'What happened at the office this afternoon?' Lucy asks.

'Oh, nothing very much,' Cynthia says. 'A solicitor's clerk brought round a libel letter about that piece Teddy Chambers wrote called "London After Dark," but Desmond says he thinks it will all blow over. Oh, and Anthea came in wearing one of her hats.'

'What was it like this time?' Lucy asks, whose awe of Anthea is even less qualifiable than her own.

'Oh, like one of those Lalique glass lanterns. Desmond practically bowed to her when she came through the door.'

'That Anthea is quite a lady,' Tyler Kent says, winding a little trail of irony around the word 'lady.' It occurs to Cynthia that, such is Tyler Kent's absorption in his chosen milieu, he very probably knows what Anthea is. 'Do you know,' he goes on, 'when I first came over here she used to be Ramsay's secretary? But she was always more of a *literary* kind of a girl.'

The faint air of tension does not recede. It is a quarter to five now, far too early to go out. Seeing Lucy's face bent over the rim of the wineglass, and her own wrist torpid on the chair-arm, she realises how painfully thin they have become. London is full of skimpy, undernourished girls queuing palely at bus stops. Even the women in the bakers' shops have this wraith-like quality.

Tyler Kent, on the other hand, has grown sleek and prosperous: the embassy dinners and the late suppers with Lady Colefax seem to suit him. At night he complains about Cynthia's sharp bones poking into his flanks. He is a restless sleeper, throwing out unexpected arms and legs, like a man trying to swim the backstroke, and, if woken, not above sending Cynthia to the kitchen to fetch him a glass of water.

There is a catchphrase doing the rounds—it began life in a variety-hall sketch and has now migrated to the newspapers—in which a woman exchanging confidences with her friend asks, 'But, my dear, what do you *see* in him?' Cynthia wonders what she sees in Tyler Kent. What she said to Anthea in the Bloomsbury café was not, of course, meant to mislead. The greater part of Tyler Kent's attraction does lie in his not being English, in not having been to Winchester or Merchant Taylors', in not being a subaltern in a Guards regiment, or having parents who wear stiff, formal clothes and sit all day in a villa near Goldalming hoping that the weather will soon be fine enough for a walk.

A bit more to it, she thinks, is to do with sophistication: that feeling of a series of dense, occluded worlds, each with its chain-link of secret protocols, whose end result is Tyler Kent ordering an exotic cocktail from a startled waiter, or stamping into a restaurant not quite as if he owned the place but as if the owner had asked his advice on decor and cuisine. Plus—and this is in marked contrast to every Englishman she has ever met—he not only likes her, but takes the trouble to tell her so. The only problem about Tyler Kent—in addition to the things that Anthea has told her about him—is that it is impossible to conceive of an English life for him other than the one he lives. She has tried to imagine him playing golf on the links at Brancaster or walking through the Wiltshire back-lanes, but it is never any good. Sophistication, she thinks, can only take you so far.

'Goodness,' Lucy says, plunging back into the chair from which she has half risen, 'I do feel *peculiar.*' Her skin is so white as to be almost translucent: the veins visible beneath it are like blue wires. There is a letter on the table next to the three-quarters empty wine bottle from Lucy's parents enquiring about arrangements for the festive season. Mrs Kirkpatrick, too, always refers somewhat archly to the 'festive season' rather than Christmas. It is a caste-mark, like calling make-up 'face powder.' Lucy, it seems, with or without her squadron leader, will be going to her uncle's in North Yorkshire. Cynthia wonders where she will end up.

There has been talk of The Bell at Aston Clinton, which is Tyler Kent's idea of the country. Otherwise there is nowhere to go. Cynthia wonders what Christmas at The Bell at Aston Clinton will consist of. Tyler Kent, meanwhile, is relishing his captive audience. Possibly the other cipher clerks at the embassy are not so accommodating. Just now they are talking, or rather Tyler Kent is talking, about the tides of history, the incremental shifts in power and perspective that are changing the way the world works.

'In thirty years' time, even twenty years' time,' Tyler Kent is saying, 'the whole idea of empire will be pretty much outdated. The white man's burden? Well, the white man will have to start laying his burden down. And pretty soon he'll find there are easier ways of getting what he wants out of the subject races. Now, America woke up to that fact a quarter of a century ago. It's odd that Europe still thinks that if you want another place's natural resources you have to go in and *organise* it. Take it from me, the new empires will be run at arm's length, by invisible strings. They'll cost less, and sometimes people won't even know they're there.'

Cynthia, having heard this kind of thing before, is not impressed by it, but Lucy, whose squadron leader presumably keeps to safer topics, is profoundly stirred. 'But surely,' Lucy says, 'empires aren't just about natural resources, oil and cotton and so on?' (*And tea*, Cynthia thinks stoutly, remembering her father.)

'Sure,' Tyler Kent says, 'they're about territorial influence. But the time when fellows in pith helmets could come riding out of the jungle to scare the natives is over.'

'I'm sure you're right,' Lucy says, wide-eyed. 'Roger says independence is the price we shall have to pay for keeping India on our side in the war.' And Cynthia thinks of her mother's worst nightmare, which is a procession of coolies, intent and evil-eyed, marching on their bungalow beneath lofted torches.

There is something not quite right about Tyler Kent as he finishes up the dregs of Logan's wine in that practised oenophile's sniff of his. Perhaps something has happened to him that nobody else knows about, some grandmother dead on the Pennsylvania porch, some ruined cipherene's father making his presence felt. Helping the girls with their coats as they set out for the restaurant, he is unusually solicitous.

The staircases are sunk in gloom, and the push-button switches on the landings click back after a few seconds. Nun, literary agent, and diplomat: all have disappeared, and the locked doors are ghostly with reflected twilight. The mice run away at their approach: they can hear them scampering off into the darkness. In Ceylon the mongooses came out of the garden and lay by the veranda door all night, hoping for snakes. But there are no mongooses now, just Tyler Kent buttoning up his gentlemanly ambassador's overcoat, and giving her one of those quizzical, semi-adroit looks that presumably in another world are used to subdue cipherene and ambassadorial eminence alike.

Down in the hallway it is bitterly cold and the traffic surges in the square. 'I do think,' Lucy says, with an unexpected screech of feeling, 'that Roger could have got out of going to Biggin Hill.' And Cynthia divines that someone else is prey to doubt, uncertainty, and rank suspicion.

'Let's not mind about Roger,' Tyler Kent says, and Cynthia thinks his flamboyance is assumed in the same way as his Aquascutum overcoat and that beneath it is something much more vulnerable and compromised. Out in the square he commandeers a taxi—one of the countless taxis he has commandeered for her in the past six weeks—hailed, subdued, and bent to his will, like a cowboy lassoing a steer, and they are bouncing away in the direction of Soho, where for some reason, when not enslaved by the Belgravia ladies, Tyler Kent nearly always ends up having his supper.

For an isolationist, Tyler Kent is remarkably cosmopolitan in his attitude to food. He likes gay little Italian restaurants with salami hung up in the window, French cafés with Napoleonic waiters. Just now the gay little Italian waiters have grown nervous, on account of Mussolini, and display notices that read BRITISH OWNED or ONLY BRITISH STAFF EMPLOYED HERE.

Tonight's destination is some sort of culvert off Wardour Street, behind boarded-up windows but vouchsafed for by an article Tyler Kent read in the *Evening Standard*. It is horribly dark and all the light seems to come from candle-stubs mounted in the necks of old wine bottles. They have not been there a moment when a voice says 'Cynthia,' and there is a tall girl, with a nose so *retroussé* that it barely disturbs the planes of her face, coming up effusively to clutch at her wrist, while a man in army uniform who is peeling off a pair of gloves that are too tight for him smiles benevolently in the background.

The girl is called Theresa Sinclair-Haddon, and at some infinitely remote point she attended the day school in South Kensington to which Cynthia was sent during Mr Kirkpatrick's furloughs. There was nothing memorable about her except her nose, and there is nothing memorable about her now, but still they shake hands, and Cynthia is introduced to Simon, her fiancé and a captain in the RAMC. He has one of those spectacularly chiselled faces like the Spartan athletes in Lord Leighton's paintings, as if he ought to have a laurel wreath over his forehead rather than a service cap.

'Heavens,' Cynthia says, when all this has been explained to her, twice, 'didn't you have a sister called Honoria?' and a damp yet enticing blanket of complicity settles over the proceedings, and Simon, tugging off the final finger of his glove, gives a thankful nod, as if to say that here, in the depths of Soho, against pretty considerable odds, lurks some faint vestige of a world, and its citizens, with which he is familiar. Tyler Kent stands at the back, mutely attentive. He has taxi-fleets and ambassadorial telegrams at his command: he can cope with a noseless girl from Borehamwood and her statuesque fiancé.

There is, of course, no question of their not dining together. Theresa has begun on one of those mythologising performances that Cynthia has previously associated only with her own mother, in which quite ordinary incidents are blown up into events of profound symbolic significance, and girls Cynthia can hardly remember are roped into a vast, panoramic frieze of confabulation and triumph in which she and Theresa are the undoubted stars.

'And then that time,' Theresa says, 'when somebody sent the toy mouse whirring into the cloakroom and Miss McNab was so cross she made us go without our luncheon.'

Who was Miss McNab? Where was the cloakroom? For a moment Cynthia wonders whether she isn't the victim of some extravagant practical joke. But no, there is a look of absolute, seraphic conviction on Theresa's face. Simon, meanwhile, is nodding, glad to see the girls amused. Tyler Kent, head bent over the menu card, black Oxfords drumming on the linoleumed floor, has grown quiet. Perhaps there are areas of English life that even he finds difficult to infiltrate.

Cynthia is untroubled by this detachment. She likes Simon, the silent RAMC captain, and she is prepared to put up with Theresa Sinclair-Haddon who, she is pretty sure, pinched a gold-tipped fountain pen from her bag in 1935, long before the era of Chamberlain, before lofted torches in market squares and marching men.

Lucy is talking about Roger, whose studiousness, not to mention his military responsibilities, is apparently a trial to her. 'He started talking to me the other day about Maimonides. Whoever's heard of Maimonides?'

'Now, *I've* heard of Maimonides,' Tyler Kent says, looking up from the menu card, but somehow this intervention, however theoretically reasonable, is not what the company wants. They want an atmosphere of good fellowship, in which alien boarders can be repelled, and philosophy is the smile on a dog.

It is about half-past seven: early for Soho. There are anti-aircraft guns a mile away in Hyde Park and ambulances rushing down Shaftesbury Avenue. The restaurant turns out to be one of those in which chorus girls and nightclub hostesses come to recruit themselves before the real fun of the evening kicks in. There are six or seven of them eating frugal suppers at a long table by the window. In the half-light their faces are like death's-heads.

Tyler Kent's expression, as he puts down the menu card, suggests that a mistake has been made. For once the complex intelligence network that sustains his life has let him down. 'Odd kind of things they have to eat here,' he says.

'Oh, I don't know,' Simon returns. There is a faint suspicion that he has not taken to Tyler Kent. 'All looks fairly decent to me.' His face is so finely chiselled that it looks almost greenish in the candlelight, like decaying limestone.

'Ah,' Tyler Kent says, 'the time-honoured spectacle of the Englishman not caring what he eats.'

'Welsh, actually,' Simon says, and indeed there is a faint Cambrian lilt somewhere behind the solid Home Counties vowels. They order grilled sardines on toast, which everyone seems to think is amusing and provokes Theresa into a reminiscence of the fish they had for lunch at Kensington.

'Now in America,' Tyler Kent says, 'we don't have this all-consuming interest in what people did at their schools. Of course there's that Class of '29 stuff, but I guess nostalgia for your schooldays is an English thing.'

'I think it's a question of heritage,' Simon says, with just a faint implication that this is a benefit that Tyler Kent, for all his black Oxfords and his natty tie-pin, does not possess.

'Ah, dear old *heritage*,' Tyler Kent says mock-seigneurially, and Cynthia divines not only that the two men dislike each other but that her sympathies are with Simon, the feigned innocuousness of whose steely resolve appeals to her. She wonders, not for the first time in her life, whether she has made a terrible mistake with Tyler Kent and in nailing her colours to one mast she has forgotten the comforting solidity of another. 'Heritage,' Tyler Kent says again. 'Queen Mary's coach and the dear old Beefeaters.'

'And the dear old Atlantic Ocean,' Simon says, with outright satirical intent, 'keeping the dear old barbarians at bay.'

Seeing that no further entertainment can be got out of the Kensington day school, its staff, cloakrooms, and fish luncheons, Theresa Sinclair-Haddon settles down to eat her sardines. She looks faintly disappointed, as if this reunion of old friends, with its lavish mythologisings, has not quite lived up to her expectations. Lucy is half-asleep.

'Now, about *heritage* . . .' Tyler Kent says, returning fire. And Cynthia, fork in hand—the sardines are the size of dace, soused in Worcestershire sauce and quite horrible—thinks that all this—Tyler Kent, Belgravia flat-shares, late nights in Bishop's Park, compromise and drift—cannot, realistically, go on. Outside there are more ambulances tearing down Shaftesbury Avenue. The showgirls and the nightclub hostesses are squabbling over their bills. Behind the restaurant's battened-down shutters, searching and incorrigible, the wind lifts.

CHAPTER 13

A Departure from the Script

In his study at Windsor, head down over the mahogany desk, with its profusion of paperweights, its framed portraits of Wallis by Beaton and Madame Yevonde and its pile of unread documents, the King is thinking of Hitler.

There is nothing so very unusual in this. All over Europe, he supposes, people are thinking about the ex-corporal with the toothbrush moustache, with varying degrees of affection, alarm, and contempt. For his own part, the King believes that not enough is made of the Führer's mystical side—the mad, starry look in his eyes, the sense of utter detachment from the world around him.

There are Christmas cards on the mantelpiece, drawn up between the fronds of festive evergreens sent down from Balmoral, and the King stares at them for a moment. But the fir-trimmings and the inscriptions of seasonal goodwill are a poor substitute for the enigma that is Herr Schicklgruber, to give him his correct name, about which the newspapers have been appropriately satirical.

He remembers the little Russian girls again at Barton: Grand Duchess Tatiana, Grand Duchess Anastasia, Grand Duchess Marie, and Grand Duchess Olga, with their serious expressions and their muslin flounces. There is something that connects the little man from Berlin and these long-lost children—some monstrous and indefinable tide sweeping across the old world of his youth and laying it waste.

For several days running he has woken just before dawn with the memory of that day oppressing him. Every last detail is there: his father and the Tsar, as alike as Tweedledum and Tweedledee; the ladies ghost-like behind their veils; himself sweating in his midshipman's gear. It was thirty years ago and as bright as yesterday.

Hitler himself is known to be fixated on the British Royal Family.

Von Ribbentrop, before his departure, used to convey the most unctuous expressions of his regard: birthday greetings; gifts (of varying degrees of appropriateness); invitations. Curiously, there is further evidence of this in a letter that fell out of the morning's post and which lies now on the table top next to the portraits of Wallis and a paperweight which, if shaken, encourages snow to whirl around a representation of Westminster Abbey. The letter is from Prince William of Celle, a distant relation, but not so distant that a photograph of him could not be turned up in one of the family albums.

The King has not kept up with the Celles, who have fallen on hard times. Prince William's mother, the old duchess, is thought to be inhabiting a bed-sitting room at Biarritz. Nevertheless Prince William is cheerful, or affects to be. The family estates are mostly gone, and his sisters married to businessmen, but the Nazi Government, he maintains, is 'not hostile to people of our kind.' The King wonders exactly what is meant by this. Are the people of Prince William's kind the people of his kind? After all, he is a King and an Emperor, and his relative—they are second cousins, he calculates, once removed—is a dispossessed Palatine prince. It is difficult to tell just what thread may now connect them.

Prince William, with his Christmas greetings and his hopes for the coming year, believes that the war is a mistake, and that the whole thing could be brought to a satisfactory end if 'men of sense' were brought around a table to debate it. Again, the King wonders what exactly is meant by this. Who, when it comes to it, are men of sense? He suspects, without being in the least able to confirm the hunch, that he is being got at, and that Prince William, in expressing this pious desire for reconciliation, took notes from someone in Berlin. He will have to show the letter to Hardinge.

Meanwhile, there are more pressing problems than disingenuous letters from Prince William of Celle, a man whom the King believes he last met in 1913. Out in the corridor and the large room behind it there are footsteps manoeuvring and the sound of raised voices. Footmen have been roaming the passageways with trays of teacups for the past couple of hours. Mr Wood, the impresario of these performances, is in his element. In half an hour it will be time to proceed to the microphone and address his subjects, or rather that proportion of them which has access to a radio, or that proportion which can be bothered to switch it on. The Corporation is always very bullish about the audience for royal addresses. On the other hand, there are thought to be streets in northern cities where not a single person listens in.

As with Hitler, and his distressed German relatives, the King is not sure what to think about radio broadcasts. His father regarded them as vulgar but necessary, the monarchy projecting itself to the modern world, a flaring advertisement for the merits of tradition, sentiment, and duty. His stammering brother Bertie is, he knows, ready to faint with horror should a microphone be put in front of his mouth. The King, when speaking, is conscious not of the words he delivers but the voice delivering them: *wiv*; *deloightful*; as vulgar to him as the medium was to his father.

For some reason the room seems smaller the longer he sits in it. Christmas cards; paperweights; Wallis's portrait—all of them seem to be crowding in on him, diminishing him in size as they grow larger. He wonders what Wallis would have made of all this. Sometimes she was fascinated by the protocols of the life he lived; at other times merely bored. He woke up the other morning trying to remember the last words she ever spoke to him. He has a feeling they were 'I'm not having that bitch Lady Carpenter to dinner.'

Hitler. Prince William of Celle. Lady Carpenter. The tide will wash them all away, just as it washed Grand Duchess Olga and her sisters. It will even wash away Hitler, who may be said to be responsible for it, or at any rate its willing accessory.

Out in the corridor all the appurtenances of a royal broadcast are in place: Mr Wood and his technicians; Hardinge and his vigilant eye. There is only one absentee, and that is Mr Nichols, who, despite the most dignified representations, has been kept away. The King thinks he has had enough of Mr Nichols. Also there is the danger that his presence at the proceedings may offer some hint of the deception that is about to be practised. The King has considered the implications of what he has decided to do and is not much troubled by them. Surely, in the last resort, short of handing over his domains to an enemy, a king may say what he likes? Hardinge, he knows, will be furious. But he thinks he can put up with Hardinge. It is all horribly serious and yet, in the end, rather a lark, like the practical jokes they used to play on the new recruits at Dartmouth, the up-ended hammocks and the soapy cups of tea.

As for the deceiving of Mr Hardinge, there is no great mystery to it. A typed copy of the script has been circulated to interested parties: the Cabinet Secretary; the Prime Minister; Mr Wood at Broadcasting House. Hardinge's copy, with a few punctilious annotations, lies on the desk before the microphone at which he will speak. When he sits down he will discreetly replace it with a second version concealed in the pocket of his jacket. It is as simple as that. As for what may happen afterwards, who cares?

One question interests him, though, and that is for whose benefit this gesture is being made. Prince William of Celle, who is not the first distantly connected German aristocrat to write to him stressing the value of ancestral ties? The authors of the unsoliciteds, who continue to petition him from their country rectories, their grimy terraced houses and their bijou suburban retreats? Himself, even? The King is not sure about this. The tide is sweeping us all away, he thinks. The old order is disappearing. Who knows how best to resist it?

For some reason he remembers that immeasurably tedious afternoon spent in the house outside Dorchester. What would Hardy have made of this? The King has an idea that he would not have noticed it, or would have ignored it (which is not the same thing). But this is not something you can do in 1939, not anymore. We are all in it, he thinks, Hitler and Prince William of Celle and Lady Carpenter, up to our necks.

He can feel the piece of paper in his inner pocket, subtly distorting the line of the suit. Mr Nichols's assiduousness in the writing of the speech has been extraordinary. There have been moments when the thing has bored him, when the magnitude of the scheme he has embarked on rather scares him with its immensity, but always Mr Nichols has seen him through. There is a footman beckoning from the doorway. Mr Wood lurks behind him: half-deferential; half-triumphant. His father swore by Mr Wood's expertise, while regretting the necessity for it, just as he regretted the Labour Party and democratic movements in the Dominions. Mr Wood; George Lansbury; Gandhi. Ultimately they were all the same to him.

As he strides along the corridor, men in morning suits snap to attention. Momentarily his reflection stares back at him from a mirror: butter-coloured hair going brindled; quizzical expression. There is apparently a man who does impressions of him on the stage of variety halls. The King has seen a photograph, and is not convinced.

'A minute, sir,' somebody says as he reaches the desk. Hardinge is somewhere in the corner of the room, whispering to an underling, Adam's apple jerking up and down as he speaks. The papers are there in front of him and he spreads them in a fan, draws in his breath and slowly lets it out. 'Thirty seconds, sir,' says another man. A part of him—the part that has grown tired of Mr Nichols, subterfuge, the slow crawl of pen over paper—is urging that the whole thing be given up while there is still time. He picks up the first of the sheets of paper and clears his throat.

The end of a year is naturally a time for reflection on the events which have taken place in the previous twelve months. But it is also a time to look forward to the year which will follow. These necessities are especially important to us at a time such as this, when our nation—the country that each of us knows and loves—is beset by such grave dangers, and by such an unprecedented threat to all the things that we hold dear.

I speak to you not only as a King but as a veteran of the last war, one who remembers the unimaginable horrors of the conflict in Flanders that claimed so many lives, snuffed out so many bright and blameless futures, and indeed has spent a great part of his time campaigning that such a conflagration should not be repeated. It is my earnest wish, and I think the wish of every civilised person, in this great Empire of ours and beyond it, that this should be so.

Yet now, despite all our best efforts, despite the urgent solicitations of our leaders, we are at war, with all the consequences for our national destiny, our identity and well-being that this implies . . .

Hardinge, the King sees, is looking at him keenly. He has not yet diverted in any key regard from the original.

War's privations, of course, are twofold. They affect not only the men who forsake home and hearth, and not only the family and friends they leave behind. For every soldier doing his duty in far-flung corners of the world there are a dozen other people intimately connected to him—his wife, his sons, his daughters, his mother, his father—fearful for his safety, anxious that he may return to join them once more with his duty done. In this conflict, as in the last, I have been heartened by the messages of support I have received from around the world and also by the splendid efforts of our Dominions to raise men and munitions to sustain a struggle in which, above all, it is vital to preserve our identity, our sense of who we are . . .

Hardinge is staring openly at him now: the copy of the text he was attempting to follow has fallen from his hand.

But if this is a time of war, then it is also a time to remember what we have forfeited by going to war. 'Blessed are the peacemakers,' Scripture says. But how does one obtain peace, when it is not there? And how does one guarantee that, if it returns, it may be preserved? This, we are told, is a war to defend the interests of those who cannot defend themselves. But might not those interests be better defended by war's cessation?

These are not questions for me to answer. They are for governments, for the democratically elected representatives of free nations to consider. But I put it to you that they should be considered, that the duties which lie before us may not be as straightforward as they seem to be . . .

All over England these words are heard and considered. Cynthia and Tyler Kent hear them in the bar of The Bell at Aston Clinton, where they are festively but, if truth be known, not very happily recruiting themselves.

Desmond and Mrs Gurvitz hear them in the lounge of Claridge's Hotel, where they have just eaten a solitary Christmas dinner amid gangs of aristocratic old ladies in paper hats.

Peter Wildgoose hears them over brandy cocktails with three or four gentlemen friends at somebody's flat in Chester Square.

Anthea hears them standing stark naked halfway between the kitchen and the bedroom of her maisonette, with a Bath Oliver biscuit in one hand, while a man's voice asks what the matter is.

Beverley Nichols hears them at a snug little theatrical party in Earls Court, next to a mantelpiece full of portrait photographs signed by their subjects, 'Ivor' and 'Noël' and 'Gertie.'

Lucy and her squadron leader hear them issuing from an ancient crystal set in North Yorkshire with a view of snow-covered dales beyond the window.

Captain Ramsay and his wife hear them in a baronial pile somewhere in Peeblesshire, staring at each other under the points of an antique candelabra.

Each in their various ways registers some element of shock, surprise, disquiet, or disapproval.

'Heavens,' Mrs Gurvitz says, 'I daresay the fat will be in the fire now.'

'Sheer defeatism,' Peter Wildgoose tells the epicene young man sitting next to him.

'There's something so deliciously *grave* about Royalty, don't you think?' Beverley Nichols's companion coyly declares.

Tyler Kent smiles, the jaunty smile of a race-goer whose horse, backed at long odds, moves inexorably towards the finishing post as more fancied names labour grimly in its wake.

Cynthia, who has had rather too much to drink and has spent part of the morning in tears, stares at the faces of the people in the bar, which are pitched at various points between exaltation and despair, and wonders what will happen to them all, and to her, and to everyone.

PART THREE

PART THREE

It is very many years since a British sovereign has intervened in the public affairs of his nation. Nevertheless, His Majesty's Christmas Day broadcast may be counted as such an intervention. Whatever one may think about the King's Speech to his subjects and dominions, one or two points should be made clear.

It is not true, as certain persons have suggested, that in delivering this address His Majesty has exceeded his constitutional powers, for in this matter he has no constitutional powers to exceed. The King's Speech is one of the few occasions on which the Sovereign is permitted—in fact encouraged—to express a personal opinion. Neither is it accurate to insist that the sentiments conveyed to a listening Empire were in any way 'defeatist.' As a veteran of the Great War, and the patron of numberless charitable organisations, the King's sympathies clearly lie with the armed services.

Not the least poignant aspect of his address was the high degree of fellow feeling extended to those members of the British Expeditionary Force at present serving in France. Neither could it be possible for anyone seriously to object to His Majesty's principal theme, which was the horror of war and the misfortune of those caught up in it.

The King is not a defeatist. He is perfectly entitled to hold the views attributed to him. And yet it is not difficult to believe that the unguarded expression of them is a grave error of judgement. The gap between what a man may say in private and what may decently be uttered on a public platform is known to every individual who plays a part in our national life. In supposing such a gap not to exist, the King has not only—albeit inadvertently—offered comfort to our enemies; he has played into the hands of certain persons on the Home Front who would like, against considerable evidence to the contrary, to be considered our friends.

No one can doubt that, acting in good faith, His Majesty has been badly advised, and it behoves the authorities both to determine how this advice came to be tendered and to ensure that it shall not be repeated. As for the wider impact of these remarks, it has been suggested—though not by this newspaper—that the King has 'lit a candle,' to which all those opposed to the conduct of the war, or indeed to its very existence, may rally. We do not believe this to be the case, and we maintain that the events of the next few months will bear us out.

Daily Telegraph, 27 December 1939

A. HARDINGE TO CABINET SECRETARY, 28 DECEMBER 1939

. . . Clearly the fault and the responsibility for what occurred are mine. In slight mitigation, I was grievously misled, not only by the King, but by Mr Nichols, the amanuensis whom His Majesty had engaged to assist him with the speech. By the time the full extent of the King's duplicity—and I can only call it that—had become plain, it was, of course, far too late to act. Mr Wood, whom I naturally consulted about halfway through the proceedings, confirmed that there was not the slightest chance of preventing the King from continuing to speak or of conjuring some pretext for going 'off air.' I should be very glad if you could lay this information before the Prime Minister, and convey to him my sincere apologies for the debacle that has ensued . . .

Yours very sincerely,
A. Hardinge

CABINET SECRETARY TO A. HARDINGE, 29 DECEMBER 1939

The Prime Minister has noted your comments, and has asked me to convey his sympathy for the extremely difficult circumstances in which you have been placed. He believes that further investigation of what occurred, both during the broadcast and before it, would serve no useful purpose. Given the extremely volatile nature of the political situation, the Prime Minister thinks it imperative that His Majesty should be persuaded to leave London at the earliest opportunity, and be set to work at some task at which, and in a location where—to be perfectly frank about the matter—he can do no more harm.

Yours very sincerely,

A. L. du Quesne, Cabinet Secretary

A. HARDINGE TO CABINET SECRETARY, 30 DECEMBER 1939

. . . The Prime Minister will perhaps be aware of the King's extreme reluctance to leave London at the present moment, or indeed to do anything that he does not wish to. But I have placed before him the recent invitation from the Lord Lieutenant of Lancashire—I believe that your office was privy to this—to undertake an inspection tour of military hospitals in the north-west of England. I should say that I think it highly unlikely he will agree to do this.

Yours very sincerely,

A. Hardinge

CABINET SECRETARY TO A. HARDINGE, 31 DECEMBER 1939

. . . The Prime Minister has asked me to tell you that he thinks the north-western tour will do very well, and that the King should be informed—insofar as is consistent with the respect due to his position—that this is not a suggestion, but an order.

CHAPTER 14

Beverley Nichols's Diary III

1 January 1940

Never have I known such a to-do—perhaps the proper word is *furore*—over a few words spoken over the wireless! Apparently on Boxing Day several hundred people gathered outside the gates of Buckingham Palace bearing placards announcing that WE SUPPORT OUR KING and END THE WAR NOW. Naturally, all mention of this kept out of the newspapers.

As for one's own part in the proceedings, I feel increasingly like the proprietor of a Punch and Judy show who occasionally peeps beyond the curtain to see how his effects are being received by the audience. Certainly all through Christmas Week when people were discussing the speech, it was all I could do to refrain from jumping up to correct them on points of detail! Thankfully I managed to prevent myself, otherwise who knows what cats might have been let out of the bag.

General reactions to the speech, based on the persons one has spoken to, in descending order of approval:

(1) The King has shown great courage in stating his views in this way, and his opinions should be listened to and acted upon.

(2) The King has shown great courage in stating his views, but also a distressing naivety. There is a danger that the speech may be misinterpreted, both by our enemies and our friends.

(3) The King has been foolish ('Very foolish'—a Labour MP) and also badly advised. What on earth did he, and those around him, imagine they were doing?

(4) The King is pro-Nazi, and should no longer be allowed to speak in public.

There is also a fifth theory, which is that the whole thing was orchestrated by the Government with the aim of discrediting the King.

All this highly amusing, and also deeply alarming, given one's own involvement. The disagreeable sense of having leapt onto a conveyor belt which none of the levers one grasps seem capable of halting. No sooner had I arrived back at Hampstead than Ramsay telephoned, practically beside himself. Said it was *imperative*—one of Ramsay's favourite words—that we should ascertain the King's views, how he intended to act, &c. I replied that it was quite probable the King had no views other than those he had expressed, certainly did not intend to 'act,' as Ramsay put it. Ramsay then insisted that I should try to make contact with the King through Hardinge. My protest that Hardinge would probably want to have me hanged for treason if the law would allow it brushed aside, and in the end I said that I would do this.

As I foresaw, the minion who answered Hardinge's telephone about as frosty as it was possible for a human being to be, if not actually seated in an ice-box. Said that there was not the slightest chance that Hardinge would see me. If there was anything I wished to communicate it should be put in a letter. 'But this is disgraceful,' Ramsay complained, when I told him. 'It amounts to nothing more than a conspiracy.' Well, I can think of other conspiracies that are afoot, but forbore to tell him this.

Deeply ambiguous leading article in *The Times*. Having read it half a dozen times I could not establish whether the writer supported the King, with certain reservations, or reprobated him, also with certain reservations. Ramsay, on the other hand, triumphant. 'The press is on our side,' &c. For an intelligent man, he can be woefully obtuse.

3 January 1940

Extraordinary to relate, when I came downstairs at 10 A.M., wishing that I had not indulged so freely in what a Victorian novelist would call 'spirituous liquors,' it was to be told, by an imperturbable Gaskin, that the Palace had telephoned, and would telephone again. Was so unnerved by this that I retired to the study for a brandy-and-soda, whereupon the telephone bell rang again and I was instantly summoned back to the drawing room.

Not Hardinge, but a factotum whose voice I did not recognise. Said that the King was most anxious to see me. Would it be possible for me to call at the Palace at 3? Naturally I said I would do this. Thought about consulting Ramsay, but in the end decided against this. It would simply mean his giving me a lot of orders to follow. Besides, I have no idea why the King wishes to speak to me, and it may all be perfectly innocuous.

Rather surprised, when I put down the telephone, to find that my hand was shaking. It is all the consequence of too much worry and too many late nights, I daresay.

Later. Had determined on taking a taxi to the Palace, but grew so nervous that when we reached the Tottenham Court Road I decided to get out and walk. A cold day with the remnants of last night's frost still on the pavement. A few people examining the frontages of shops which did not seem to have a great deal to sell. Policemen on traffic duty in the Mall blowing into their cupped hands to keep warm.

Atmosphere at the Palace very subdued. A little black man in a morning coat and a silk hat, no doubt some foreign plenipotentiary, being driven off in a carriage. Found HM not in his usual eyrie but in a tiny study, no more than a cubby-hole, crammed with ancient postage stamp gaz-etteers—the old King's, apparently, which have never been cleared out. Oddly animated, but also worn-looking. The chevrons at the corners of his eyes are turning into deep grooves.

I asked how had he spent Christmas? 'Oh, there are relatives one has to see, don't you know?' When I commented on the rather emphatic tie he was wearing he said: 'Oh yes, my niece Lilibet gave it to me.' It appears Hardinge is ill with bronchitis. Struck once again by the King's hesitancy, inability to get to the point.

A footman brought in a tray of tea-things for which there was scarcely room on the cramped, paper-strewn table. One of the newspapers dated 10 September 1937. Eventually, after a great deal of beating about the bush, including a pitiless account of one of Noël's plays that he had been taken to, the King dropped his bombshell. He wishes to see Ramsay. How might this be accomplished?

When I remarked that he was the King of England and nothing, surely, could be easier than to arrange a meeting with one of his own subjects, he frowned. There could be no question of his inviting Ramsay to the Palace, or of Hardinge finding out what he was up to. Very struck by this spectacle of a King and Emperor going in fear of his lackeys. In that case, I proposed, we should find some neutral territory.

Eventually the King said that there was a gallery in Bruton Street where he sometimes went to meet people (which people, I wonder, and for what reason?). We agreed on a time at which I should bring Ramsay there. No indication of what he intends to ask Ramsay, or what schemes he has in mind. Asked for details of Ramsay's associates. These I supplied as truth-fully as I could. Again, noted the tangential way in which his mind works. 'Wasn't he married to the Duke of Beaufort's daughter?' &c.

Left just after four and walked back along the Mall, where ice was forming on the plane trees, sky a curious blue-grey colour, all impossibly melancholy and ground-down.

On my return to Hampstead, telephoned Ramsay with the news. An interesting psychological contrast. Ramsay exultant—'Now we are finally on to something,' &c. Myself pessimistic, unable to believe that anything will come of this, convinced that unseen powers at work to frustrate the King's intentions in this or indeed any other matter.

Later. Had arranged to play bridge with Victor and Alistair Forbes—smart young man who writes for the newspapers. As I had foreseen, so nervous that completely unfit for duty and revoked three times. Twitted for this by Victor. Naturally it is impossible for one's friends to appreciate the strain one is under, particularly as one is unable to supply details, but really, I do feel one could expect a little more consideration! Forbes, for example, pocketing two guineas without the slightest compunction.

Came home to discover that Ramsay had sent round a 'memorandum' of all the questions he intended to ask the King. Felt like telling him that it was not our duty to ask the King anything but merely to listen.

7 January 1940

To Bruton Street. An extraordinarily conspiratorial air. Ramsay, arriving at precisely the same moment as myself, casting suspicious glances up and down the pavement to see if he were being followed. In fact, the street entirely empty.

Gallery one of those quietly plutocratic redoubts—only half a dozen pictures in the window but the cheapest of them priced at fifty guineas. Greeted in the vestibule by a polite young man in a Guards' tie who enquired: had we an appointment with Mr Windsor? We said that we had. Having established our bona fides, we were hastened away into a room rather like a dentist's ante-chamber: anonymous furniture; wax flowers in vases; occasional tables bearing copies of *The Field, Tatler,* &c. I asked the polite young man if many people had appointments here with Mr Windsor and received the blandest of smiles.

The King arrived shortly afterwards. *Horribly* nervous, like a schoolboy who fears that his absence from the dormitory will soon be detected by matron, but also affable, urbane, giving the impression that the back room of a Bruton Street *gallerie* with its Zoffany prints much more his natural milieu than the palace. Said: 'The Windsor Faction, I presume?' as we shook hands. Smoked incessantly, the polite young man arriving every so often to take away his ashtrays with an almost comical reverence.

Small-talk—which one can never avoid with the King—painfully thin. Ramsay did not seem to know whether to treat the King as his oldest intimate friend or a public meeting he had been bidden to address. Still, once we had got beyond marchionesses the two had in common, the most extraordinary conversation ensued. He seems to want to place himself entirely in our, or rather Ramsay's, hands. Said he had been 'gratified beyond measure' by the response to his speech. Asked if it could be arranged for him to meet 'like-minded people' who shared his views. Enquired of Ramsay: what was the state of pacifist opinion in the House of Commons?

At no point did his nervousness abate. Examined his watch perhaps a dozen times. At one point, when a car's exhaust back-fired in the street outside, he gave such a start that the chair in which he was sitting positively rocked on its castors. Ramsay by this time had become grandly avuncular, seemed to think that the morning was his, that he could take the King off for luncheon at his club without anyone turning a hair. But not more than half an hour had gone by before the King, flinging the last of his cigarette butts down on the table—the polite young man not yet having returned with his ashtray—declared that he had to leave us: 'You see, gentlemen, my time is not my own.' Left us amid a profusion of hand-shakings, expressions of mutual regard, resolved to meet again in three days' time.

Ramsay almost purring with satisfaction, seemed to think he would be summoned forthwith to Downing Street to state his terms and so forth. 'Make no mistake, Nichols, we have started something here that the country will thank us for finishing.' For my own part, I could not help but wonder what the upshot might be when Hardinge was recovered from his bronchitis, but did not like to say this.

8 January 1940

Infinitely tedious morning writing my article for Drawbell. Did this almost somnambulistically: could not remember, ten minutes after completing it, what I had written about. Several times interrupted by Ramsay telephoning for advice with drafts of a letter he is composing to associates.

Warned him to proceed with extreme caution. After all, one has no notion how this business will turn out, whether in fact the whole thing will not prove to be some kind of chimera.

10 January 1940

And so, not altogether to my surprise, it proved. Convening once more in Bruton Street, we were met by the polite young man with a message to the effect that 'Mr Windsor' had been 'unavoidably detained elsewhere.' All Ramsay's efforts to convey a message, solicit further details, courteously repulsed. The only means of contact available to us apparently 'the usual channels.' Ramsay convinced that the whole thing 'a plot,' insisted on waiting twenty minutes in the ante-chamber lest the King should merely have been delayed. This the polite young man accepted with a shrug of his shoulders: I expect he has worse to deal with than Ramsay.

Ramsay then urged me to telephone Hardinge with the threat of 'questions being asked in the House.' I pointed out that Hardinge would certainly not speak to me, and one could not protest at the fact of the King of England's having broken an appointment with two of his subjects. 'Well then, you must write to him,' Ramsay said. 'Write to him and tell him that we will not stand for this behaviour.' There is a rather fanatical glint in Ramsay's eye on these occasions, which is intensely disagreeable.

Photograph of the King in evening papers inspecting troop of Boy Scouts outside gates of Buckingham Palace, with fatuous letterpress. Never have I seen a man seem so wretchedly unhappy with the task on which he was engaged!

15 January 1940

After sending three letters, all unacknowledged, and making half a dozen telephone calls, I finally receive a note from Hardinge. Glacially formal and written in the third person. Presents his compliments, acknowledges my assistance, conveys His Majesty's grateful thanks and offers to defray any out-of-pocket expenses that I may have incurred. Really! At first

immensely cross about this, but then began to see amusing side, in particular the spot in which my bamboozling of Hardinge has placed him.

Sent back note saying that as His Majesty's faithful subject, I hoped
that I had done my duty. No doubt this will make Hardinge even angrier
than he already is. Naturally, no information on the subject in which I
was really interested, viz. what has happened to the King? No reports of
his whereabouts, or any official engagements, in the newspapers. No one
I know of has seen him. They can hardly be keeping him prisoner in his
own palace!

I continue to note down comments about the speech, which show no
sign of diminishing.

Middle-aged woman in theatre queue: 'I'm surprised he didn't just
invite Adolf to fly over and form a government. We should have got rid of
him when we had the chance in 1936.'

Young man on street corner: 'I don't hold with Royalty, but he's the
only one who's on our side. The only one who'll save us from the f——g
politicians.'

Letters in newspapers, I notice, about evenly divided for and against.
Of course, it may very well be that the newspaper proprietors—who are
nearly all pro-war—are suppressing some of the unfavourable ones.

Later. Curious encounter at Criterion Bar, which, among other things,
answers the question of what has happened to the King. Had barely
been there a moment when a spotty-looking young man came over and
remarked: 'You're Mr Nichols, aren't you?' Remembering that one has to
be careful about the kind of people who accost one in the Criterion Bar,
I indicated that I was indeed Mr Nichols. 'Well,' he said, 'we haven't seen
you for a week or two at the old shop.' It then dawned on me that he was
one of the Palace footmen.

When I suggested that this was hardly surprising in the circumstances,
the young man ('Call me Cyril') almost burst his sides laughing. 'No more
it isn't. Do you know, Mr Hardinge wanted to have your guts for garters?
Never seen him so cross. Heard him on the telephone telling someone we
had "a viper in our midst." One of the equerries reckoned Mr Lascelles
told him it was all his fault and he should have had more sense.' Naturally,
all this fascinating to hear.

Apparently the King has been despatched to the north of England at the personal request of the Prime Minister to inspect military hospitals, regimental barracks, etc., officially to 'boost morale' but in fact to get him out of the way. 'Cyril' a mine of Palace gossip. Revealed that the footmen's nickname for Hardinge is 'Sound of marching footsteps.' Several of the footmen 'that way' and call each other by feminine nicknames— 'Myrtle,' 'Denise' and so forth. I asked: what did they think of the King? To which Cyril replied that he 'wasn't a bad sort' but thoroughly idle, vague, directionless. Very respectful of one's efforts. 'We all listened in, sir, and thought it was jolly good.'

Resigned myself to the inevitable appeal for funds and eventually gave him two pounds, but was worth it for the fun.

18 January 1940

No war news. A War Office general quoted in today's *Times* to the effect that current 'stalemate' (an odd expression for a conflict in which neither side wants to fight) could continue 'indefinitely.'

To Faction meeting at Ramsay's house. Had not wanted to attend, as convinced that meetings are under covert surveillance, but Ramsay insisted. Perhaps two dozen people collected in Ramsay's drawing room: Mrs Ramsay, supervising the maids as they brought in tea; 'Commandant' Allen, the very sight of whom always makes me want to roar with laughter, talking loudly about communications received from Berlin, &c. Ramsay, whom I had not seen since Bruton Street, thanked me publicly for 'signal services' to the cause. This was very gratifying, but can't say I enjoyed myself—they are all so horribly fanatical.

Ramsay, as is his custom, had one or two new recruits ostentatiously in tow. These included a Dr Clavane, a Cambridge don, middle-aged and with a high forehead, who talks superciliously about the need for 'European regeneration,' and a man named Amery, son of the Cabinet Minister: thin, nervous-looking character with a pencil moustache and a prodigious stammer. Really, this sort of thing makes one question Ramsay's judgement. Amery, so far as one knows, a thoroughly bad lot. Talks to anyone who will listen about his 'contacts' in the Cabinet, friendships with various continental politicians one has never heard of. Ramsay, I noticed, immensely proud of this lion, but also slightly wary, as if fearing the new boy might disgrace himself at any moment.

Bad impression made by Clavane, Amery junior, Allen in her police-woman's gear, confirmed by business of meeting. According to Ramsay, definite contact has been made with the German Embassy in Dublin, the idea being that somebody (who?) will canvass the idea of a peace conference to be held on neutral ground (where?). This scheme will be taken to Halifax, the suggestion being that Ramsay's parliamentary allies—not to mention sympathetic army officers, &c.—will turn very nasty if it is not given serious consideration. Looking at the matter objectively, it seems to me that whoever goes to Dublin will be committing a treasonable act.

Struck, once again, by faint note of hysteria in some of the interventions. Ramsay immensely courteous and grateful. Wants me to lunch with him at the House. Thought to myself that this is the last thing I ought to do in the circumstances. In another month's time things may be very different, of course, but at the moment I get a definite feeling of people playing with fire who do not realise that fire burns. If all this goes wrong Ramsay will end up behind bars. And then what will happen to the people who are seen to have been his friends?

21 January 1940

Struck by the very odd atmosphere in London at the moment. Policemen nervously moving passers-by on, soldiers much in evidence. Victor told me that three officers in one of the Household regiments had been detained by the Secret Services the other day, but there is no proof of this. Curious sense of there being something about to happen, but nobody knowing quite what. Meanwhile, one has a living to make. Wrote piece for Drawbell saying that whatever happened our national spirit would win through, which, queerly enough, I happen to believe.

Later. Intensely disagreeable experience, which I thought I ought to set down in full. I had arranged to meet *y* at the Turkish baths in Swallow Street. There is never anyone much there after midnight and it is *very* discreet. *Y*, whose behaviour is extremely tiresome when one thinks of all one has done for him, arrived late and insisted on reading a poem he had written. The most awful rubbish, but charitably forbore from telling him this. All this is by the way.

Emerging from my cubicle into the ante-room an hour or so later, I saw a sharp-faced man seated in the corner give me the merest imaginable glance and immediately begin dressing himself. Leaving the premises a few moments later I saw him again, settling his bill at the reception desk. Lo and behold if he did not then follow me into Regent Street, only giving up his pursuit when I hailed a providential taxi. Thinking it over later, I am *sure* that this has something to do with Ramsay, and that someone is taking an interest in me who would better be kept as far away as possible.

Y, to whom I later confided these fears, without of course admitting the full extent of my association with Ramsay, said airily: 'Oh, one is always getting blackmailed these days. It is something people like ourselves have to live with.' This must be one of the most vainglorious remarks I have ever heard.

24 January 1940

A story in *The Times* about troop movements beyond the German border. Ramsay, to whom I mentioned this when he telephoned—he is still avid for me to lunch at the House—absolutely denied it had happened. Quite 'out of the question' and 'simple scaremongering' on the newspapers' part. How does he know?

Convinced this morning that I was being followed along Hampstead High Street by a bespectacled man in a Trilby hat. Finally plucked up enough courage to confront him. What did he want, &c? Naturally, the man denied everything, claimed to be a teacher of the pianoforte en route from one lesson to another and even produced a business card to this effect. There is no doubt that this business of Ramsay and the King is playing havoc with my nerves. . . .

CHAPTER 15

The End of Something

At Buckingham Palace there is snow falling against the great high windows: stealthy and insistent, covering the ledges with incremental zest. The King is not much interested in snow. In Canada, once, on one of his Imperial tours, he was invited to inspect a drift twenty feet high which had engulfed a steam train. These things are always a matter of scale.

Instead he is thinking about the photograph taken on the lawn at Barton. When the Revolution came, his father hatched a scheme to import the Russian Imperial family to England and to place one of the royal residences—it may even have been Sandringham—at their disposal. In the end, to nearly everyone's considerable relief, the plan was dropped. His father, the King thinks, was nothing if not a pragmatist.

It is four years since the old man died. He can remember his face on the deathbed, as white as piano keys, and also some of the things he said about Wallis. Things, he thinks, that are not to be forgotten or forgiven, even at this remove. The little Russian girls, he imagines, symbolise the end of something, that vast net that his great-grandmother threw out to pinion the crowned heads of Europe. His father was not a clever man—even in his lifetime the newspapers made jokes about his stamp collection and the hetacombs of slaughtered grouse—but he knew his worth, what he could expect to give to the world and what he might expect to receive in return. It is a good thing to know one's value, and the King wishes he knew his.

A cough sounds somewhere in the region of the door, which is Hardinge's way of announcing his presence. Hardinge has always signalled his arrival in rooms by way of coughs. In his current post-bronchial state they are practically percussive, great claps of laryngeal thunder that break upon the air like gravel stirred in a bucket. Perhaps, like himself, the cough symbolises something. Just lately the King and his private secretary have been communicating in a kind of code. Nothing has been said about the speech or the volume of correspondence provoked by it, which the King has insisted on reading with an ostentatious concern.

On the other hand, silence has its own eloquence. The King knows that he has offended Hardinge, offended him mortally, and that he can expect to pay. Just now there is a plan afoot to induce him to tour the military hospitals of the north-west. There is scarcely anyone to be found in these establishments—not a shot having been fired in the last three months— but still the Government is sure the King's presence will boost morale.

'How are you, Hardinge?' the King asks, as Mr Hardinge glides forward onto the carpet before him. One must always be affable with one's retainers, however much one distrusts them. Mr Hardinge nods his head. If there is one thing to be said for Mr Hardinge it is that his respect for the institution he serves is never compromised by his opinion of the man on whom its resources are concentrated. In these cases the individual is nothing; the tradition all.

The King notices that Hardinge has a letter in his hand: not one of those large foolscap documents by which official business is transacted, but a tiny, insignificant scrap through which, paradoxically, the real pulse of government is allowed to beat. 'The Prime Minister requested that I give you this, sir,' Hardinge remarks, and the King wonders why it is that Hardinge, with his smile, his punctilious manners, his innocuousness, is so irresistible, so impossible to gainsay. The letter is about those military hospitals in the north-west, those caverns of much-laundered sheeting, linoleumed floors, and tenantless beds.

'I really think, Hardinge . . .' he begins, and Mr Hardinge waits to see what his sovereign thinks, one hand gripping the letter with such force that it is as if he half expects it to try to escape his grasp, go sailing off the chimney flue, the other making little undulating movements, as if he is stroking the fur of an invisible cat. 'I really think,' he begins again, and Mr Hardinge smiles: conniving but attentive, suggesting that there is no difficulty that cannot be overcome, no royal whim that cannot be conciliated once the truth of their relationship is acknowledged.

He has made enquiries, Mr Hardinge now proposes, and the accommodation in Lancashire looks as if it will be eminently suitable. Although still white around the gills, he is as determined as ever. The King has a sudden vision of himself trying to escape, of running full tilt across the Palace gardens, in sight of the distant gate, and being rugby-tackled by Mr Hardinge, brought down in a tangle of descending limbs and returned to the building in disgrace.

There is nothing to be done, nothing at all. He had thought that making the speech would be a dramatic throwing-over of the traces, a galvanising act from which all manner of spectacular events would follow, but somehow it has not happened and he has sunk back into torpor. The things that mattered most to him—the past, the old dead world before the age of revolutions and marching men, Wallis's face beyond the teacups, and the Fort Belvedere table set for two—have gone and will never come back.

Outside the snow continues to fall against the quivering glass.

Captain Ramsay (Con. Peebles and South Midlothian) asked if the Home Secretary was aware that, as a result of his recent address to the nation, His Majesty the King had been requested by certain persons in authority to limit the expression of his sincerely held views, and to undertake engagements which, he had on good authority, His Majesty regarded as detrimental to the war-effort, that, in fact, His Majesty's wholly legitimate interventions in a matter of crucial national importance were regarded as an embarrassment by the Government and had led to an attempt to remove him from the public sphere?

The Home Secretary replied that he feared the question was not only unparliamentary but disingenuous, but that he could assure the Hon. and Gallant Member that no attempt had been made to limit the expression of any sincerely held views, let alone those of the King, and that the King's current tour of the north-west had been arranged with His Majesty's enthusiastic consent.

Hansard, 27 January 1940

CHAPTER 16

Some of the Time

'Well, at least we seem to be getting somewhere at last,' Anthea said. 'And not before time, I can tell you.'

There was not very much one could say in response to this. The glass of gin-and-orange lying on the wooden table top before her had no answer. In the end Cynthia said, 'Is this what you have to do in your job? Persuade people to do things they don't want to, I mean.'

'Oh no,' Anthea said. 'Most of the time it's much less exciting than that. You'd be surprised.'

They were sitting in a pub in Percy Street, whose door kept coming away from its catch so that paralysing shafts of cold air tended to over-whelm the single-bar electric heater in the corner. It was about five past two in the afternoon and theoretically they should have been back at the *Duration* office, but Desmond had ceased to care about time-keeping.

There were some Polish airmen at the far end of the bar who would clearly have liked to come and talk to them, but were equally clearly put off by the look on Anthea's face. As to whether the Polish airmen would have been better than the conversation they were having, Cynthia could not quite decide. Mingling with the gin and the smell of sawdust on the floor came the faint scent of ammonia.

'What on earth have you got in that bag?' Cynthia wondered.

'The tiniest piece of salmon you ever saw. The fishmonger in Warwick Way saved it for me. He usually has something if you go at the right time of day and don't put on any airs.'

Magazine articles of the kind that Cynthia sometimes came across in dentists' waiting rooms often analysed the factors that separated one woman from another. Beauty, intellect, and charm all had their supporters. Here in wartime, in a world of shortage and blight, there were plainly other distinctions at work. Cynthia knew that no fishmonger in London would ever save *her* a piece of salmon. Rather than inspiring any resentment, this confirmed the awe in which she held Anthea. At the same time she thought that she was her own woman. Anthea might get the things she wanted from her, but it would be because *she* wanted them too.

'Do you know,' Anthea said out of the blue, 'this phoney war is getting on my nerves? Things happening are so much easier to deal with than waiting for them to happen, don't you think? Never mind allowing all the defeatists to wander about saying the Germans don't really want a war and why don't we get together and stop it before there's any serious harm done.'

'Is it true,' Cynthia asked, 'that Hitler offered to meet the King?'

'Who knows?' Anthea said, so loudly that one of the Polish airmen looked up hopefully from the bar. 'Mind you, the chances of the King meeting anyone above the level of a Territorial Army colonel are pretty slim these days. They scarcely allow him out in public after that speech, I believe. But never mind about that. The point is that we know where the Faction membership book is.'

'How did you find out?'

'We managed to intercept the man who was carrying it around,' Anthea said. 'He didn't have it, but he knew the last person he'd given it to.'

'Is it at the Embassy?'

'Happily, not. No, your other friend Mr Bannister has it down in Sussex.'

One of the Polish airmen now detached himself from the group at the bar and came shambling across. He was not bad-looking in a rather haphazard way, but did not seem to have shaved.

'Hello to you, ladies,' he said in surprisingly good English, making what looked like a series of semaphore signals with his hand. 'My hospitable friends were wondering if you would care to join us.'

'Absolutely not,' Anthea said. 'Go away.'

The Polish airman went back to the bar, shrugging his shoulders. Perhaps he was used to these rebuffs. It was well known that London's womenfolk were not interested in Poland, and would have preferred America to join the war.

'It's perfectly simple,' Anthea said, as if Cynthia had complained about the complexity of the enterprise. 'Bannister and Ramsay know their errand boy was stopped. They need to keep it as far away from London as possible. The Embassy isn't safe anymore, diplomatic immunity or no diplomatic immunity. So it's down at Ashburton in Bannister's study.'

'Why can't you just go and take it?'

'We'd need a search warrant. By the time we'd got one, the thing would have gone. No, much better to rely on you.'

'What on earth do you mean?'

'You can go down there and liberate it. Isn't that the word the Russians used whenever they stole anything from the bourgeoisie? What could be more natural? An old friend of the family come for the weekend. Ring up Hermione and sort it out,' Anthea said. 'I hear she's out of the bin, or whatever they call that nursing home in South Kensington, and feeling a great deal better. I'm sure she'd be delighted to see you.'

She found that the prospect of stealing around Ashburton Grange with a torch, bent on ransacking Mr Bannister's study, filled her with terror.

'You're not being serious.'

'Believe me, Cynthia, there is one person in London uniquely qualified to perform this act, and that person is you.'

'Anthea, I *can't*.'

'Yes, you can,' Anthea said. 'It will be the best piece of war-work you ever did. Much better than typing Des's letters to print-brokers or running down the stairs after Peter when he's forgotten his hat. Just think, it will be practically heroic. In twenty years' time young men will come up to you at parties and ask you to tell them about it.'

'I don't want young men coming up to me at parties in twenty years' time,' Cynthia said, tears starting up in her face. 'And I don't want to go down to Ashburton Grange ever again. I can't so much as look in a mirror without Henry's face staring back out of it. You have no idea.' The enormity of the plan baffled her. 'What will happen if I bring the book back?'

'As things currently stand,' Anthea said, 'I should say that Captain Ramsay and your chum Mr Bannister will probably be interned for the duration. I can't imagine you'll find that any great loss.'

It was twenty past two now, and the pub was almost empty. The floor was full of shiny little blue-green rectangles that turned out to be empty cigarette packets stamped into the sawdust. Quite of its own accord the door flew open once again to reveal a vista of grey pavement, passing feet, a shop window advertising a New Year sale.

January had got becalmed somehow, Cynthia thought, like the cigarette packets in their sawdust. At Bishop's Mansions the fog hung so low that it was impossible to see the tennis courts, and the Palace might not have been there at all. The task Anthea had outlined for her did not sound in the least heroic. It was more like a practical joke that one schoolboy might play on another.

'And how *is* your American friend?' Anthea asked, as if the express purpose of this lunch-hour flight from the Bloomsbury square had been to discuss Tyler Kent, his habits and inclinations.

'Perfectly all right, thank you,' Cynthia said. 'Friend' as in 'gentleman friend' had been one of Mrs Kirkpatrick's code words, and implied distrust of motive. Henry Bannister, significantly, had always been 'Henry.'

'That's the thing about sugar,' Anthea said mysteriously. 'It's only sweet some of the time.'

They took up their bags and went out into the street, past the pub's dismal frontage and a large hole surrounded by lanterns and charcoal braziers at which a group of workmen were desultorily engaged.

'I suppose,' Anthea said, 'that you've got *scruples* about all this? Well, you can forget about them, I can tell you. Bannister and Ramsay don't have any, and neither does your Mr Kent. Nor that boy who hit Norman on the head in the blackout. It's not a *game*, for all it might sound like one. If you won't do it I shall think you're a poor fish who only wants a quiet life. Just like poor old Des.'

The wind blew in against their legs as they turned onto the Tottenham Court Road, and Cynthia nodded her head, modestly surprised at how heroic and unscrupulous she felt.

Back at the office things were at a surprisingly low ebb. Lucy was stuffing a pile of rejected manuscripts back into their envelopes.

Desmond was having what sounded like quite a serious conversation with Peter Wildgoose about Mrs Gurvitz.

'The thing I like about Esmé,' he said, as Anthea and Cynthia came into the room, 'is that she really has seen a bit of life. One doesn't have to keep explaining who people are, for example.'

'You mustn't mind my saying this, Des,' Peter Wildgoose said. He was wearing a suit that was marginally less smart than usual. 'After all, you know how keen I am on candour. But really, I can't for a moment imagine what she sees in you.'

'You know, people are always saying that,' Desmond said, with what for him was unusual humility, 'and yet I've had some surprising successes with women in my time.'

'I expect she sees you as her long-lost son, Des,' Anthea said. She slapped her canvas bag down on the desk and the scent of ammonia began rapidly to pervade the room.

After that, some semblance of industry returned. Lucy took the stack of rejected manuscripts in their envelopes and dumped them unceremoniously in the post sack. Anthea began to proof-read some translations from the Chinese that Desmond had had set up in type but could not decide whether or not to print. Peter Wildgoose got up hastily from his chair, took out his pocket-book, and started hunting for somebody's telephone number.

Only Desmond seemed disinclined to apply himself. He stood rather forlornly in the centre of the room watching the activities going on around him with a suspicious look. Finally he said: 'Where are all the war poets? People say they exist, but I never seem to see any.'

'I believe Sir John Squire had a sonnet in *The Times* the other day,' Peter Wildgoose suggested, not quite able to keep himself from laughing.

'It's an important cultural point,' Desmond said, sounding much crosser than he had a right to, 'and not something to have jokes made about.'

There were times, Cynthia thought, when Desmond and Peter Wildgoose could barely tolerate each other, but were restrained by the solidarity of their upbringing. Desmond went back to his office and shut the door behind him. Once things had quietened down, and Anthea was safely out of the way, Cynthia picked up the telephone and had herself connected to the American Embassy. Outside it had begun to rain, and there were coin-sized blobs of water beginning to streak the surface of the window.

'Hello there,' said Tyler Kent's voice. He was always superbly unflappable on the telephone, but also faintly impersonal, like a Hollywood actor trying out his lines. It would not have been surprising if he had said the words several times over, giving them different inflexions as he went. 'How are you? What have you been up to?'

'I'm very well,' Cynthia told him. It was the first time they had spoken since the weekend. 'I've just been having lunch with Anthea.'

'The redoubtable Miss Carey? I guess there are worse ways of spending your lunch-break. Do we have an appointment tonight?' It was a mark of Tyler Kent's absorption in the protocols of the Old World that he said 'appointment' rather than 'date.'

'I thought we were going to that film,' Cynthia said. She did not particularly want to see the film, but she had an old-fashioned notion that social agreements ought to be stuck to.

'No can do,' Tyler Kent said, still sounding as if he were reading from a script. 'There's a lot of work on here. Half a dozen things just come in from Paree. You know how it is.'

Cynthia knew how it was. The downward curve in her relationships with men rarely surprised her, for she had always been adept at seeing the warning signs. There was a piece of foolscap paper on the desk in front of her, and she began to draw a series of concentric circles with a fountain pen on it to distract herself while she talked. Part of her resented Tyler Kent for his off-handedness, but the other half, curiously enough, was anxious to grab at any lifeline that offered itself.

'Are you sure you can't get away? I think I saw in the newspaper that there was a showing at half-past eight.'

'No can do,' Tyler Kent said again. He sounded a little less like an actor reading from a script. 'I shall be here until at least nine.'

'Oh well, it can't be helped then.'

'That's the only way to look at it, I guess.'

'Yes—I suppose it is.'

'After all,' Tyler Kent said, without the least shred of irony, 'there is a war on. Why don't you come over on Saturday? No, wait. A fellow from the Italian Embassy's asked me to go to Greenford to see the trotting races. Why don't you come over on Sunday and we'll have lunch somewhere?'

'As it happens, I'm rather busy on Sunday,' Cynthia said, thinking that she really could not put up with any more of this, 'but I'll see.' After that she put the phone down.

Five minutes later, while typing up one of Desmond's garbled letters to the printer, Cynthia considered her relationship with Tyler Kent. It was not so much Tyler Kent she was angry with, she decided, but the process of which he was a symbol: an environment in which the Tyler Kents of this world danced through a succession of parties and mansion flats, dallying with women when they felt like it and on terms that were theirs alone.

At the same time she had a feeling that she was just as bad as Tyler Kent, on the grounds that people only treated other people in this way if the person encouraged or permitted them to. There were other girls of her age—girls from the Kensington day school, girls met on the boats plying back and forth from the East—who were settled down with nice young men they would shortly marry. The problem was that the nice young men tended to be horrible bores whom no girl of any spirit would want to go anywhere near.

There was no getting away from this conundrum, or resolving it, and when she finished Desmond's letter, with its complaints about the typesetter's inability to reproduce Greek epsilons, she sat at her desk and cried silently for twenty minutes, while Lucy stared anxiously at her from behind her typewriter keys, and Peter Wildgoose, whose tact in these matters was immense, fetched her a cup of tea and stood vigilantly over her while she drank it. After a bit she felt better, and for some reason curiously resolute, convinced in some indefinable way that if anyone was to blame for her difficulties it was Tyler Kent and the Bannisters and people like them, and that in stealing the membership book from Mr Bannister she would be taking the first steps towards reparation.

She came out of this reverie to discover that Desmond had emerged from his study once more, and was talking to Peter Wildgoose about the King's speech.

'Actually I was tremendously impressed,' Desmond said. He had a cup of tea in his hand and was standing against the mantelpiece in a rather flamboyant attitude. 'It's so rare that a member of the Royal Family takes any kind of stand. I should imagine the Government was livid, which makes it all the better.'

'Sheer defeatism,' Peter Wildgoose said. 'Playing into the enemy's hands. I can't imagine what he thought he was doing. But they say he's been very odd ever since Wallis died.'

'Honestly, Peter,' Desmond said. 'Do you really think that? You aren't just trying to unsettle me?'

'Yes, I do. No, I'm not,' Peter Wildgoose said. He gave the impression of not really being interested in what Desmond had to say, but still determined, for auld acquaintance's sake, to conciliate him. 'But if there's another confidence vote in the House, I shall know who to blame.'

'So shall I,' Anthea said, looking up from her desk.

'You know, I sometimes think that if Anthea had been living at the time of the French Revolution she'd have been the kind of girl who went round in a muslin fichu stabbing people in their baths,' Desmond said. It was meant as a light remark, but nobody laughed.

Eventually the afternoon wore on. The rejected manuscripts in their brown-paper envelopes were taken away by the postman. Desmond went back to his study to telephone various of his friends. Anthea left early with her parcel of fish.

As for the weekend at Ashburton Grange, it turned out to be the easiest thing in the world to organise. Hermione, tracked down to the Bannisters' town-house, and betraying no memory of the altercation in Bishop's Park, proved thoroughly amenable, and a date was set forthwith.

CHAPTER 17

Goodbye Mrs McKechnie

Yellow light, slanting in through the cracks in the blinds, gathering in odd patches on the ceiling and burning off the polished surface of the oak bedstead, gave the room an oddly medical air, as if an operation was about to be performed in it. Or perhaps the operation had already taken place, and this was its aftermath. In her own idiosyncratic way, Mrs McKechnie—sitting up in bed, cardigan half-askew over her bony shoulders, one hand reaching for her spectacles on a bedside table crammed with ashtrays and patent-medicine bottles, like a grey still-life from the Camden school—was a part of this imposture.

Languid and resentful, temper clearly not improved by what had been, or was about to be, done to her, she looked every inch a hospital patient, confined against her will, anxious to pick a quarrel with her nurses. Outside in the square, in a long series of preliminary shocks, volcanic detonations, and sinister after-tremors, another train went by.

Mrs McKechnie, her spectacles now retrieved from beneath a bottle of Parrish's Health Food, the creased skin of her nose livid against the merciless light, said, 'I don't like those trains. They get on my nerves. I'd sooner live in the country. *There* all you'd get would be cows and cockerels.'

'Just as soon get a bomb fall on you in the country as here,' he said. 'That's if they ever drop any.'

'Nonsense,' she said. 'What's the point of dropping a bomb in the countryside? I'd go and live there tomorrow, only Edgar says he couldn't stand not being in London.'

Without dramatically proclaiming the fact, the McKechnies' bedroom was like an extension of their shop. There were calf-bound editions of Jane Austen's novels flanking Mrs McKechnie's dressing table. Two reproductions of paintings by Sickert balanced against the lamp-stand.

Recumbent among this clutter, Mrs McKechnie looked less dangerous than when downstairs prowling the shop, but still not completely tamed. She said: 'What is there to make a noise outside where *you* come from, anyhow?'

'I don't know. Trolley-buses. Trams. The mills start early. Most days there's no sleep after five.'

'I wonder you don't go back there,' Mrs McKechnie said, with a terrifying dispassionateness. 'A boy like you. What is there for you here?'

'It's a point of view,' he conceded. The room smelled of sweat and face-powder, and the light was exhausting to look at. From twenty feet below came the sound of a locked door being tried.

'Somebody trying to get into the shop,' he said.

'The shop!' Mrs McKechnie said. 'Who cares about the shop? I don't. It could burn down tomorrow. *I* shouldn't care.'

Rodney caught sight of his reflection in what, from its position between a razor-strop and a pot of brilliantine, was presumably Mr McKechnie's shaving mirror, and saw that two of his shirt-buttons were still undone. It was the third occasion on which they had done this. The first and second time Mr McKechnie had been out at sales. This time he was visiting his aunt in Roehampton. Trying to determine exactly how it had happened, he could find no explanation, no heightening of the emotional atmosphere, no causative chain, no evidence that the idea had been either hers or his.

'I've a good mind to burn the place down myself,' Mrs McKechnie said, with slightly less conviction. '*That* would show him.'

Mrs McKechnie was always saying things like this. Sticks of dynamite quietly fizzing behind the pewter pots. Sickerts and Winterhalters in bright conflagration. The brass ashtrays melting into the gutter, and flaming disarray. Downstairs the shop door rattled again.

'How long have you been married?' he demanded. He didn't care in the least how long Mrs McKechnie had been married, but it was preferable to her talking about the shop burning down.

There was a little cluster of birthmarks on her shoulder, drifting away into the buffer-zone of her cardigan. In a great rush, as if there was only a limited amount of time in which these confessions could be made, she said, 'I met him when I was seventeen. I bet that surprises you. A young girl like me falling for an old man like that. I daresay I was a fool. We used to have a shop in Camberwell. And after that we sold horse-brasses in Ewell village. But Edgar said they were all stuffed shirts and retired majors and so we came here.'

He was lost in this world. Camberwell. Ewell village. It might as well have been the moon. The American had not come for a week now, and the five-pound notes had been spent. Mrs McKechnie was still talking, but in a more mannered style, like a film-star dictating her memoirs to a stenographer.

'Edgar's not such a bad old sort in his way. His own sweet way. I won't have you making jokes about him. He's been very good to me. There are some women don't have half the freedom. I daresay he takes a drop too much sometimes. I don't hold that against him. We can't all be perfect. Last Christmas he took me to Denbighshire and we stayed in a hotel. I call that nice, don't you?'

He was about to make his way onto the landing when he realised that he was still in his stockinged feet. Somehow his shoes had ended up under the bed. There was comfort in putting them on: a return to routine; a way out of Mrs McKechnie's mottled boudoir, her sinewy clutch. He would not go there again, he thought. There was something voracious about Mrs McKechnie, some deeper hunger that went beyond physical desire, which alarmed him. Mrs McKechnie was still talking about her Christmas in Rhyl.

'Poor old Edgar,' he said suddenly. 'What's he going to say about this, then?'

'What a dreadful thing to say,' Mrs McKechnie protested, trying to be imperious but divining that the moral high ground had crumbled away beneath her. 'I don't know who on earth you think you are.' Once, she had hit him slap-bang in the face, like a welterweight, with such venom that he could hear his teeth rattle.

'What the eye doesn't see, the heart doesn't grieve about,' he tried. He didn't care about Edgar. Like the old women who left their baking out to cool on window-sills and came back to find it gone, he had only himself to blame.

On the wall beyond the lampshade there was a photograph of Mr McKechnie, gnome-like and insubstantial, standing in the entrance to a marquee in which towering clumps of antique furniture were ranged against the canvas like ancient burial mounds. He had met other Edgars in his time and marvelled at their lack of gumption, their eagerness to leave their windows open and their sills unguarded.

'I really think you had better be going,' she said, unexpectedly regal behind the off-white counterpane, and he realised that you did not say things about eyes seeing and hearts grieving to Mrs McKechnie.

The light was less oppressive now and he made his way out onto the linoleumed landing, past the door to the kitchen, where Mr McKechnie had left a bucket of potato peelings ready for dispatch, and down the squeaking wooden staircase. Something she had said caught in his mind—he could feel it hanging there like a burr—and he wondered what there was for him here. Mrs McKechnie. The American. The fair-haired girl in the Soho pub who had taken such an interest in him. He could take them or leave them.

The shop, whose electric light had yet to be switched on, was more aquarium-like than ever. He lit a cigarette and went over to the window to smoke it, listening to the dispersed yet elephantine sounds from on high of Mrs McKechnie dressing herself. Outside the light was slowly receding and there were patches of shadow silting up the corners of the square. It was about half-past eleven. The summons from Mrs McKechnie had been unexpected.

He had been opening up the shop, realigning the displays of pewter pots, stacking the brass ashtrays, when she had materialised at the foot of the stairs as Lord Leighton's nymphs stared sympathetically on. One of them looked uncannily like the girl in the Soho pub. The McKechnies' bed had smelled uncomfortably of Mr McKechnie: a comb choked with thin, cinnamon-coloured hair had fallen out from under the pillow. It could have been worse.

When he opened the door a man who had been standing a few yards along the street outside the shop that sold fishing tackle—youngish but hard-eyed—came looming up into view and he saw that of all people it was Ikey. He was about to tug the door to when the futility of this gesture occurred to him and he wedged himself in the doorway with one hand stuck in his pocket and the other protectively around his chin.

'What are you doing here?' he demanded. He had decided several years ago, on no very good evidence, that he wasn't frightened of Ikey.

'I could ask the same of you. Christ, you took some finding. Chap at the last address wouldn't tell me where you'd gone until I told him what it was you were wanted for.'

He still had his hand in front of his chin. 'So you've been up to Islington, have you?'

'Islington. Hammersmith. Every-bloody-where. Makes no difference to me. Anyway, now I've found you, so you'd better collect your traps and we can be off.'

He did not want to turn his head, but he knew that Mrs McKechnie had come down into the shop and was watching him from the till. To play for time he lit a second cigarette off the end of the first and ground the butt under his foot. There was another train going past in the corner of the square and he wished it would pass right by the shop's front door so that he could be picked up by it and borne away.

'I'm prepared to let bygones be bygones,' Ikey said, not quite as decisively as he had intended. He had worked underground once, and there were still little bluish scars running over his forehead like the veins in a Roquefort cheese. The serge suit sat uncomfortably on him. 'Edna says the same.'

'Suits me.' Rodney was still half-in and half-out of the door, his mind miles away, out on the moors above Glossop: Edna's face a blur in the bright spring sunlight, the crocuses out and sheep huddled by the fence-posts. 'But there's a problem about that.'

'No problem that I can see,' Ikey said. His real name was Philip: no one could remember how the 'Ikey' had supervened. 'Going back to where you're wanted. Where you've responsibilities. Never mind what's owed. No, no problem I can see.'

Mrs McKechnie was definitely in the shop. He could hear her taking the cover off the till, the click of an ashtray as she emptied it into the bin. She could not be allowed to speak to Ikey. That much was certain.

Thinking about Edna, half a dozen images sprang fully formed into his head to do battle with the demons of the present: cherry blossom descending onto green grass; smoke rolling out of the bakery chimney; the Royal Antediluvian Order of Buffaloes plaque on the public-house door; grey brickwork smouldering under a wide sky. All as extinct as the first volcano.

'No problem I can see,' Ikey said again. It was London, Rodney thought, that made Ikey so nervous. A hundred and fifty miles beyond his natural orbit, he had lost his poise. The serge suit and the scars on his face betrayed him. This was not his milieu. He belonged in an older world: the world of clogs and trolley-buses and chapel hymns. Not here in London. The realisation emboldened him. He could deal with Ikey.

'The problem is I'm not coming with you.' The last words came out as 'wi' you.' That was how far it had gone. In case there should be any doubt about this, he went on hurriedly: 'I came on my own account, and I'm [ah'm] not going back again.'

'Try telling that to Edna,' Ikey said. But he looked resigned, diminished in his serge suit. Had he any other card up his sleeve? It was difficult to tell. 'Me father says he'll have the law on you.'

'Can't see how he could do that.'

There were phrases Ikey had armed himself with. You could see him summoning them up. He said: 'Breach of promise, for one thing.'

'Don't remember promising anything to anyone.' There were other pictures crowding into his head: a Salvation Army band playing; speedway riders waiting for the flag; the smoky twilight beyond the flaring gas lamps. 'Listen, Ikey,' he said. 'I'm not coming back. Can say anything you like. Can hit me if you fancy it. But I'm not coming, and that's that. I don't care what anyone says and that's the end of it.'

'You'll regret this,' Ikey said, with infinite bitterness.

'Daresay I will. Up to me, though.'

For a moment he thought Ikey was going to rush at him, pull him out of the shop doorway and drag him into the street. But this was Maida Vale, not Lancashire. The shop's dim interior, the henge of pewter pots and Mrs McKechnie's Queen-of-Hearts face at the till was too much for Ikey, who shot him a queer and not quite intelligible glance—half-disgusted, half-imploring—and went off down the street.

Inside the shop Mrs McKechnie was totting up the petty cash. She had the curious ability to move columns of coins together without their clinking. She gave him an amused but critical look.

'Someone you know?'

'Used to.'

'Seemed to want quite a conversation.'

'It's nothing,' he said. Again he was struck by the idea that they might be on a stage together, like Nervo and Knox or Flanagan and Allen. There was comedy in their dealings if you looked for it, under the freight of menace. One of the cylinders of farthings was about to collapse: the topmost three or four coins had formed a kind of precipice. In the distance another train went by. But he had lost the desire to leave with it. He could have been on a station platform in the north, watching the Wakes week excursions set out, making his own plans for the ghost-town left behind.

'Strapping great boy like you,' Mrs McKechnie said. 'You ought to be in the army. Out there with the BEF.'

'I'll go when I'm wanted,' he shot back. He had no intention of going anywhere. Something that had lain dormant in his mind during the past half-hour, with its smells of sweat and face powder, the odd pallor of her face against the pillow, suddenly blossomed to life. 'Do this often, do you?'

The top two farthings lost their battle with the laws of gravity and went skidding away over the counter.

'What on earth are you talking about?'

'Lie in bed when Edgar's off seeing his aunt.'

'It's really not something I care to talk about.'

It occurred to him that he had never met anyone like her. If he had he might have been able to deal with her better. There had been women who resembled her—publicans' wives, mostly, or adventurous widows—but they were more subdued, kept in better order. A man came into the shop with his eye full of bright, acquisitive purpose, bought one of the brass ashtrays, and went out again. Thinking that it would be a kind of test, he took half the money and put it in the till. There was no response.

Perhaps she didn't really care about the shop, Edgar, the piles of pewter plates, Lord Leighton's nymphs in their frames. All this begged the question of what she did care about. There he was stumped. The thought occurred to him that he was getting tired of all this, that perhaps he ought to go somewhere where no one—not Ikey, or Mrs McKechnie or anyone else—could find him.

Thinking about this he lit another cigarette and blew the smoke out of his nostrils directly above his head, like a narwhal's spout. The two farthings that had tumbled down from their precipice still lay on the counter, and he picked them up and put them in the till. With a sudden decisiveness, as if she had been brooding about the matter for days and the sight of the scooped-up farthings had galvanised her into action, Mrs McKechnie said: 'I can't stand hanging around here anymore. I'm going out.'

'Fair enough.' He was quite happy to be left alone in the shop until Edgar came back.

'Don't go shutting the place up and disappearing somewhere.'

'You can trust me.'

'That's one thing I'm determined not to do,' she said.

There was a copy of the local weekly paper next to the till and he began to flick through it: a dead baby pulled from the Regent's Park Canal; the Women's Institute knitting scarves for the troops; a photograph of the ARP wardens' headquarters. At the back there was a page of job advertisements for gas-fitters and car mechanics and bright lads wanted to apprentice themselves to butchers' shops or explore openings in the furnishing trade. Was he a bright lad? It depended what you meant by bright.

There was a noise of high heels in precipitous descent, and Mrs McKechnie came back down the staircase. She was wearing a hat he had never seen before and had her handbag clutched against her chest.

'What shall I tell Edgar?' he asked.

'It's nothing to me,' she said, 'what you tell Edgar.' He really hadn't met anyone like her before. The shop door jangled and she was gone.

In her absence the *Maida Vale and Kilburn Gazette* had inexplicably lost its savour. Its flower-beds dug up for cabbages and its teenage tearaways hastened off to the juvenile court meant nothing to him. There were other parts of London waiting for him to explore. Silently he ran the names over his tongue. Deptford. Lewisham. Camberwell. And dominating them all, the grey flood of the river running on to the sea.

He folded the newspaper up into a quarter-size oblong, the way his mother dealt with tablecloths, and jammed it against the side of the till, just as the door-frame rattled again and the American came jauntily into the shop. He had an umbrella under his arm and, seeing Rodney at the till, grasped it in both hands like a gun and made as if to spray him with imaginary bullets.

'I'm not disturbing you, I hope?'

'There's nobody here but me,' he said. A small part of him would have liked Mrs McKechnie to see the American.

'That's fine then. Quite a long time it's been.'

'Depends how you look at it.'

'Everything depends how you look at it,' the American said. He had something in his hand, white and diminutive, a miniature envelope of the kind you might use for Christmas cards. 'Look. I brought you a souvenir.'

Inside there was a sheet of newsprint, folded up very small, offering an account of the incident in Jermyn Street. He read it through twice, impressed by its talk of unprovoked assaults and unknown assailants.

'Doesn't mean anything,' he said, evenly. 'Anyone can write anything if they want to. It stands to reason.'

'I'm sure it does,' the American said. He was wearing an overcoat above his dark suit, and a natty silk scarf. It occurred to Rodney that he had never met anyone like the American either. 'Busy tonight?'

'Embassy Club,' he said. 'Conducting the band.'

The American laughed. 'I like that,' he said. 'Maybe we ought to pay a visit to the Embassy some time. An ambassadorial visit. As for tonight, it would simply be an hour of your time.'

He was still looking at the press clipping. 'It's not fair,' he said. 'Coming up behind people in the dark.'

'No, it isn't fair, is it?' the American said, as if this was a tremendously funny remark. 'But no one wants you to come up behind anybody in the dark. Not this evening. It's just an errand in the usual way.'

He wondered what was so enviable about the American, and decided that it was not his accent, or his clothes, but simply his whole way of behaving and the pictures it conjured up in his mind: soda-jerks in white jackets dispensing twists of popcorn; girls in high heels daintily alighting from sidecars; sleepy midwestern sidewalks patrolled by Buicks and Oldsmobiles; jazz bands starting up. For a moment the antiques shop was a Burbank film lot, garish and ramshackle, a work of limitless possibility where anything might happen and anyone—Chaplin, Hitler, George Formby—walk in.

He said: 'I don't like these errands. They get on my nerves.'

'They're pretty well-paid, as errands go,' the American said. 'What do you want? A coach-and-four to take you?'

He was glancing out of the window, but there was nothing there: just a schoolgirl or two going home to lunch. The bright vision of Hollywood faded away to nothing.

'Where is it this time?' he asked.

'Just the usual places,' the American said. 'Westminster and then back to mine. A child could do it.'

'Why don't you get a child then?' He could not resist saying this. 'Or why don't you do it yourself?'

The American was still smiling, but not quite so luxuriantly. In the corner of the square another train was going by. The clatter of the wheels and the sharp current of movement made him think of Ikey, who had taken just such a train to be with him that morning. Ikey, Edna, Mrs McKechnie, and now the American. They could never let you alone.

'All right,' he said. 'But it'll have to wait till seven. I've things to do.'

'Seven o'clock, then,' the American said. The smile was gone, along with the soda-jerks, the dainty girls, and the fleets of Oldsmobiles. Behind him the pewter pots and the Winterhalter reproductions gleamed dully in the pale light.

Slowly the early afternoon passed. Whether it was Ikey or the memory of Mrs McKechnie staring at him from her nest amid the pillows, something had put him on edge. He looked out of the window several times but there was nobody much in sight. A policeman went by and he shrank instinctively into the shadow thrown up by the till. Once or twice he went and stood outside and smoked a cigarette, but it was too cold for gestures of this sort.

At two o'clock Mrs McKechnie came back, rather pink in the face and walking with quick, deliberate steps. He had never been able to work out whether Mrs McKechnie was relatively abstemious or simply drank as much as Mr McKechnie but was better at concealing it. When she saw him she said, 'Still at your post? When they get you in the army they'll want you to stay at your post.'

Her eye fell on the press clipping that still lay next to the till and she picked it up and stared at it rather belligerently, as if it was a summons for rent or an unpaid bill.

'I suppose you did this, didn't you?' she said. 'I wouldn't put it past you.'

'It's just a piece of paper,' he said. He couldn't care less what Mrs McKechnie thought he'd done.

'"Premeditated assault,"' Mrs McKechnie read. She was not holding her drink quite as well as she had done in the past. '"Unknown assailant."' She mistook the gleam in his eye. 'I don't mind,' she said. 'I don't mind at all. It's all the same to me.'

After a bit she went upstairs and he heard the sound of small objects being thrown about and what might have been a chair falling over. This was followed by a profound silence. It was about half-past two. To judge from past experience, Mr McKechnie would not be back from visiting his aunt for another four hours. He had a vision of the two of them sitting before a table crammed with miniature gin bottles.

The sense of unease was dragging him down into some dim, subterranean vault where unimaginable horrors lurked. After another ten minutes, when the noise from upstairs was an ancient memory, he took his coat from the stand to the right of the till, stepped out into the street, locked the door, and pushed the key through the letter-box. The movement made him feel better.

He walked up to Maida Vale Underground Station and took a bus to the West End, only to find that the promise of freedom had deceived him. The bus was full of fat women with canvas bags who stared at him angrily as he stepped on board. Their breath rose in steamy clouds to the off-white ceiling: the roof of the bus was wet with condensation.

He sat at the back and smoked a cigarette until it was time to get off, looking backwards and forwards along the aisle of the bus, measuring the potential threat of the people he saw. There was a man with a gas mask reading the *Daily Sketch* who let him walk down the gangway in front of him and the gesture terrified him and he ran to get away.

Oxford Street was crowded, with heat spreading out from the shop entrances and expensive-looking women in fur coats coming in and out of doorways, and he went gladly into the throng, as if it was a football crowd assembling for match day. Here he could disappear, far away from Ikey, the American, whoever else might be on his trail. There was a bottleneck of people halfway along all trying to get into a radio shop as another group tried to get out, full of old ladies with monstrous black hats and coats that made them look like crows, and he bumped into the man with the *Daily Sketch*, who seemed somehow to have accompanied him down the street.

He knew now that the man with the *Daily Sketch* had him in his sights, and the realisation made him increase his pace, only to find that the man increased his own pace to keep up with him. He went another fifty yards along Oxford Street without looking back, but the sensation that he was being followed burned up in him. There were shop doorways crying out for him to hide himself, but he could hear the footsteps behind him and knew that an enclosed space would be his ruin.

Suddenly there were fewer people around and the evil old ladies seemed to have disappeared. He had a sudden feeling, cancelling out all his previous schemes, that he ought to stow himself away somewhere, that he was too conspicuous out in this street with all the shoppers passing by and staring at him, that something dreadful and unnegotiable lurked around the corner ready to destroy him.

Just then another man stopped in front of him and said in the pleasantest possible way, 'Excuse me, sir, I think you dropped this,' and as he turned to look—Mrs McKechnie was in his mind somewhere, and Ikey with his Roquefort-veined forehead, and the American with his mock-machine-gun spray—the man with the *Daily Sketch* came up behind him, jerked his arm up behind his back in an agonising twist, and held him fast.

CHAPTER 18

Returning

On the morning of the afternoon on which she was due to travel down to Ashburton Grange, two disagreeable things happened, each of which involved, in one way or another, the shattering of an illusion. The wonder was that neither of these had anything to do with Tyler Kent. But then, as Cynthia later reflected, most of her illusions regarding Tyler Kent had long since been blown into fragments.

Since the beginning of the New Year a change had come over the Bloomsbury square. It was as if, to put the matter mechanistically, the life of the quarter had somehow rattled on while most of the personnel involved had been redeployed or moved to subsidiary establishments far away. The crocodile of schoolchildren and their attendant wraith had gone, no one knew where. In their place came squads of tall, blue-chinned foreigners, thought, like the Poles in the Percy Street pub, to be foreign airmen, who practised extraordinarily vigorous physical jerks on a patch of bare earth in the corner of the square gardens. Meanwhile the army lorries continued to thunder past at the rate of six or seven an hour.

All this realised an air of purposeful activity whose implications, to the onlookers of the *Duration* office, were practically moral. As Desmond had once put it, with his hand curved guiltily around a bottle of Algerian red wine left over from the party: 'Looking out of a window and finding something going on in which one isn't directly involved always makes me uneasy. It's as if one is being judged for absenting oneself. Like watching the fifteen in training at school when one had a sprained ankle. I like a landscape to be a landscape. Half the reason the Romantic movement in art collapsed is to do with motorised transport. Constable could never have painted a charabanc.'

There was a suspicion, never openly voiced either inside the office or out of it, that Desmond was losing his grip.

It was about a quarter to eleven, and neither the editor of *Duration* nor its proprietor had yet arrived. Mr Woodmansee, on the other hand, had been at his desk for the past hour and a half. He was a tall, spare, austere-looking man, dressed unselfconsciously in a morning coat and striped trousers, whose task, as Peter Wildgoose had put it, was 'to make us all a little more aware of our financial responsibilities.' Whatever his achievements in raising fiscal awareness, Mr Woodmansee's arrival in the outer office had had one unlooked-for effect, which was to dispel the faint air of moral laxity that had hung there since the previous autumn. In fact, the girls were quite daunted by his presence.

For some reason nobody, seeing him at his desk in the far corner of the room, felt like discussing the party they had been to the previous night or the man they had danced with the previous weekend. Conversation either became anodyne or lapsed altogether. For his own part Mr Woodmansee ate occasional pink-wafer biscuits out of a tin kept in his briefcase, looked at the cartoons in *Punch* with an expression of absolute impassivity, and did his best to laugh at jokes.

Brow furrowed over her desk, a pile of booksellers' invoices to hand as camouflage, the light from the bulb above her head making queer patterns on the arms of her dun-coloured cardigan, Cynthia thought about Ashburton Grange, the Bannisters, and the task that loomed before her. The difficulty, she knew, lay in choosing a context in which to frame her part in it, and denied this resource she alternated between finding it irresistibly funny and horribly sinister. It was like a Ruritanian romance, except that the figure in coloured tights at the end of the drawbridge, cutlass raised and knife clenched between his teeth, was Mr Bannister.

None of these imaginings had been helped by the postcard that Hermione had sent her yesterday, which read: *Longing to see you. So much to tell you about.* What had Hermione done in the weeks since they had last met that she had to tell her about, she wondered? Joined a glee-singing club in Hampstead Garden Suburb? Engaged herself to the butler? Anything was possible. She had a vision of Hermione's fat, discontented, over-sized face—like a woman in a modernist painting, where all the proportions were deliberately mismanaged—and felt appalled at the prospect of having to spend time with her.

The thought oppressed her so much that she tipped over the tray of invoices—white, melancholy documents addressed to Bumpus and Heywood Hill—and had to go down on her knees to retrieve them, while Anthea and Lucy—anchorites now, insensible to diversion—stared at the space above her head. As she straightened up and returned the invoices to their tray, she heard a male voice speak her name.

'Yes, Mr Woodmansee?'

'I was wondering, Miss Kirkpatrick,' Mr Woodmansee said—he looked more than ever like the bursar at her old school—'if you could identify this signature for me?'

'I'll do my best. Where is it?'

But Mr Woodmansee did not like relinquishing documents from his grasp. He laid out the bill—it was from a wine merchant, and six weeks old—reverently on his desk, and let her look at it over his shoulder. Close up he smelt of mothballs, Churchman's pipe tobacco, and, incongruously enough, patchouli.

'I think it must be Desmond's—Mr Rafferty's.'

'I confess that that was my assumption,' Mr Woodmansee said, giving a little vulpine grin to show that he meant to be humorous. 'But this is an exceptional specimen, surely, even for him?'

This was a new side to Mr Woodmansee: a bright, capering spirit come to confound the workaday accessories of bank-book and cash-tin. Cynthia was wondering if he knew any more tricks of this kind—might be about to jump on the mantelpiece or sing a comic song—when there was a noise of footsteps on the stair. Instantly Mr Woodmansee seized up the sheet of paper in both hands and looked for a file to stow it in. Clearly the smile had been a mistake. Any levity that had passed between them was at an end. The dust-motes swarmed in the air and the outer door rattled in its frame.

'That'll be Des,' Anthea said. 'Provided he's managed to tear himself away from Mrs G.'

Desmond's courtship of Mrs Gurvitz was the great joke of the office. People waited for him to start talking about her, like auxiliary firemen anticipating the sirens' call. She was supposed to be putting up the money for a galleries supplement. But it was not Desmond. Instead a dark-skinned young man with extraordinarily white teeth and wavy, blue-black hair came sidling into the room.

'Hello, Tambi,' Anthea said, with the air of one who sees the pulse of life quickening around her. 'How are you?'

Just as the staff of the *Duration* office had been added to in the four weeks since Christmas, so had its extraneous personnel. Sylvester Del Mar was a distant memory, entombed behind the hospital wall. In his place came a tribe of aspiring writers Desmond had met at parties or had pointed out to him in Soho. Tambi was one of these. He had arrived in England on a boat from Ceylon six months before with a letter of introduction to T. S. Eliot, wrote colourful articles about the poetry of the New Apocalypse, and was, as Desmond remarked, more adept at borrowing money than anyone he had ever met.

'I am very well,' Tambi said, a bit stiffly. He was wary of Anthea. 'But it is very cold. I do not find it at all conducive to my work.'

'You should wear more clothes,' Lucy said encouragingly. 'An overcoat, or one of those nice duffels that Jaeger sells.'

All the girls were solicitous of Tambi, far more so than they had ever been of Sylvester Del Mar.

'That is an excellent suggestion,' Tambi said. He spoke precise, old-world English, like the natives in E. M. Forster. 'In fact Mr Rafferty has kindly offered to bestow upon me a greatcoat for which he has no further use.'

'Good old Des,' Anthea said. 'I expect he borrowed it from someone else, but it's a kind thought.'

'Yes . . . yes,' Tambi said. He looked hopelessly woebegone, as if no material comfort could ever soothe the spiritual oppression from which he suffered.

'But what about your work?' Lucy asked. 'Have you met anyone interesting?'

Tambi perked up immediately. He liked nothing better than to be asked about his adventures in literary London. 'It is kind of you to ask, yes. I attended a most fascinating evening at the house of Mr Charles Morgan, in the course of which Sir Hugh Walpole did me the honour of saying that he had read and admired my poems.'

For her own part, Cynthia was bored with Tambi. In all her years in Ceylon, she had never heard of the Sinhalese dynasty whose heir he claimed to be. Instead she thought about Tyler Kent, who on the last time they had met, a week ago now, had shown a certain amount of interest in her trip to Ashburton Grange.

'Why on earth are you going there?' he wondered. 'I thought you couldn't stand Hermione.'

'Oh, I don't know,' she had said. 'She's rather amusing in small doses, don't you think?'

There was something mysterious going on at the Embassy, about which Tyler Kent could not be drawn.

'And then,' Tambi continued, 'I was most fortunate to be asked to the house of the Honourable Mrs Pelly, and to read some of my work to her guests.'

There was no knowing how long this might go on. On a previous visit Tambi had spent twenty minutes discussing a fancy-dress party he had been to at Cyril Connolly's flat. Glancing at Mr Woodmansee, Cynthia saw that he was staring at Tambi with a look of absolute bewilderment, as if he could not comprehend the lineaments of a world that set him to work in a room where a Sinhalese prince with blue-black hair talked about Hugh Walpole. It was Anthea who decided to break the spell.

'I'm afraid we're all rather busy, Tambi,' she said. 'You'll have to come back later. But do give me anything you want to leave for Mr Rafferty and I'll make sure he sees it.'

Sylvester Del Mar would have found half a dozen ways of prolonging this interview, of minting some satirical remark that would have kept the ball rolling for another minute or two. But Tambi was not in this category of pest. Reluctantly, as if a small part of his soul was being yielded up in the transaction, he took a wad of grimy paper out of the inside pocket of his jacket and passed it across.

'And if Desmond should come up with that greatcoat,' Anthea said, 'I'll be sure to let you know. It's the Meard Street address, isn't it?'

'Yes, yes, Meard Street. Please to give Mr Rafferty my humble good wishes.'

'I'll do that,' Anthea said.

After he had gone an air of gloom settled over the office.

'The worst of it all is that the people Tambi thinks it wonderful to meet are so *passé*,' Anthea said, 'and one never dares tell him.'

There was no getting away from this: its implications hung in the air like a gas-cloud. A bit later she went into Desmond's office and left the wad of grimy paper on the desk next to an invitation card for a reception at the Danish Embassy and a pamphlet entitled *War Never Pays*. Cynthia, her mind still roving through the corridors of Ashburton Grange, found that the absurdity of what she proposed to do now terrified her. On the other hand she knew that if she did not do it Anthea would never forgive her: Anthea had said as much.

It was about a quarter-past eleven, and great stretches of time seemed to be passing before them. Somebody went out and bought a paper which said that 140 Conservative MPs wanted to put down an early day motion criticising the Government's conduct of the war, and which had a picture of the King inspecting ARP wardens in Stoke Poges. A man from the printers brought a box containing early copies of the February number and left it on the carpet next to Cynthia's desk. Outside it began to rain, and the water raised thin, snail-like trails on the window panes. In another half-hour, she thought, if the going was good, she would fetch her suitcase—this was propped up against the coat-stand—and make haste for Waterloo.

There was a conspiratorial glint in Anthea's eye and Cynthia glanced back. Anthea had put her up to this. Anthea had made her aware of her moral duty. Anthea would reap whatever displeasure it threw up. Whatever it cost her, Anthea would pay her share.

The invoices to Bumpus and Heywood Hill were all in their envelopes now, awaiting dispatch, and nothing could be done with Desmond's last lot of letters until he signed them. The light was still splashing off the sleeves of her cardigan, and for some reason she thought of her mother's green, sea-horse face bobbing around the Colombo kitchen. The box containing the advance copies of the February issue was half-open, and she reached into it and drew one out. The funeral urn with its attendant cupids and incidental inscriptions (*Duration: A Monthly Review of Art and Letters: Edited by Desmond Rafferty*) stared up at her.

Most of the contents were advertised on the cover: 'The Symbolist's Challenge'; 'Two New Poets'; 'Kierkegaard versus Kafka.' There would be no surprises here. Not quite knowing why she did it—boredom having long since descended—she turned to Desmond's editorial, which was about the shame of being a non-combatant when all one's friends were in uniform, and found, to her surprise, that it was not about this subject at all.

From any kind of progressive standpoint, Desmond had written in his final paragraph, *the monarchical prerogative were better not exercised at all. But on this occasion we can thank His Majesty for giving a lead where one was sorely needed.*

For a moment she thought that this transformation was simply a piece of magic. Then she realised that Des must have jettisoned the existing editorial at some late stage in the proceedings and substituted the stuff about the monarchical prerogative and its exercise. Cynthia found that this piece of duplicity shocked her profoundly, and that it seemed to her on a level with forging someone's signature. She read the paragraph above it and discovered that Desmond thought the war almost entirely a bad thing and called for 'progressive forces'—whatever they were—to work for its being brought ('honourably') to a halt.

She wondered what Peter Wildgoose thought about this, and realised that it diverged so markedly from his own view of the war that he could not possibly have seen it. Mr Woodmansee had disappeared somewhere and Anthea and Lucy were having a conversation about somebody called Marjorie Chevenix-Trench, and the unexploded bomb that lay on her desk sat quietly ticking, unnoticed by anyone except herself. *There will be trouble about this*, she thought, *terrible, terrible trouble.*

Worse even than this was the fact that the trouble was connected to other trouble, to the King's voice heard on the radio that Christmas Day in The Bell at Aston Clinton, to Anthea's pale, serious face bent over the table of the Bloomsbury café, to Norman Burdett with his head smashed in on the Jermyn Street pavement, to the pearl waiting to be plucked from the oyster of Mr Bannister's study, and to the small matter of herself. The rain swept in against the window, a little scream broke from above the ceiling as the dentist's drill did its work, and she thought of Mr Bannister, wax-faced and malign, looming over her in the Colombo drawing room, and what might happen if the plan went wrong.

And trouble there was, though it was preceded by a different kind of trouble that had nothing to do with *Duration* and was exclusive to herself. A moment or so after she had put the copy of the magazine back into its box, Desmond came into the office. There was some doubt, what with the arrival of Mrs Gurvitz in his life, as to where Desmond might currently be living, who was looking after his clothes, whether, in fact, he had any kind of settled domestic existence at all.

'Poor old Des is worse than when he was at school,' Peter Wildgoose had pronounced. '*Much* worse. At least then he had buttons on his shirt.'

This particular morning he was wearing a pair of green corduroy trousers, patent-leather evening shoes, and an overcoat so decrepit that there was a hint of verdigris on its collar. White-faced, but with patches of red, tomato-coloured skin on his neck, he looked horribly ill at ease, but also completely indifferent to the effect he might have on the people around him.

'Peter's just coming,' he volunteered. 'At least I think I saw him in the distance behind me.'

'You've just missed Tambi,' Anthea explained. 'He said you'd offered to lend him a coat. Is that the one you're wearing now?'

'Oh, he's been here, has he?' Desmond said. He did not rise to the bait about the overcoat. 'Do you know, I never really believe that story about his being a Sinhalese prince. A fellow I met the other night who'd been in Ceylon had never heard of him.'

It was a mark of the state Desmond was in that he could say this about one of his protégés. Sylvester Del Mar had been allowed to make almost any statement about his personal life and have it respectfully attended to. He hung the overcoat on a peg above Cynthia's suitcase, gave a despairing look around the office, as if there was something he desperately wanted to say but feared the consequences of doing so, and disappeared into his office. Cynthia, deciding to visit the washroom, walked out onto the landing.

There were voices on the stairs, and as she stood there inspecting a ladder which had just appeared in one of her stockings, Peter Wildgoose came into view, together with a younger man—jaunty and debonair—whose features seemed vaguely familiar to her.

'Hello, Cynthia,' Peter Wildgoose said. He was unexpectedly jolly. 'Do you know my friend Christopher? Chris, this is Miss Kirkpatrick, who works on the mag.' She saw now that it was the young man from the fish restaurant in Wilton Street.

'Now, you'll have to excuse me, Chris,' Peter Wildgoose said, clearly not expecting any response from her, 'because I really cannot spend any more time in your all too delightful company.'

Thinking her presence superfluous, Cynthia smiled politely and went into the washroom, where the sound of them talking offered a ringing counterpoint to the rush of water and the noise of the roller towel. When she came out it was just in time to see Peter Wildgoose, poised at the summit of the staircase, with Christopher a step or two beneath, reach down and brush his cheek with the fingers of his right hand. There was no mistaking this gesture.

Like the final piece of a fretwork castle fitted into place, a last machicolated turret glued above the outer wall, it confirmed one or two pieces of gossip that had come her way in the past few months. The odd thing about these assumptions, she realised, as Peter Wildgoose straightened his head, turned round, and only then became aware of her presence, was that they had been perfectly capable of existing side by side with the vision of Peter Wildgoose in his Chelsea drawing room, and needed this kind of context to take coherent shape.

The vision now seemed to her the most foolish daydream she had ever indulged in, and she gave a furious little shake of her head, so that Peter

Wildgoose, looking at her keenly, said, 'Are you all right, Cynthia? You look dreadfully pale.'

'I'm quite all right, Mr Wildgoose,' she assured him, which was the truth. There were worse things to happen to one than the discovery that Peter Wildgoose was a pansy. One had to be tough about these revelations. It occurred to her that the events of the past six months might have been more tolerable had she brought less delicacy to them.

All the same, as they stepped through the office door, she was conscious of a shift in whatever social relationship existed between them: a change made all the more distressing by the fact that Peter Wildgoose could not possibly be aware that it had happened. And yet in some ways this was less disconcerting than the scene which greeted her on the other side of the door: not because it had changed in any spectacular way, but because its outlines seemed exactly the same— Lucy attacking her typewriter with curious downward strokes of her fingers, as if it was an old-fashioned shop till; Anthea staring into space; Mr Woodmansee silent behind his invoice tray. It was Anthea, once again, who broke the spell.

'Hello, Peter,' she said, producing the exclusive smile that Desmond had so often complained about. 'We wondered if you were looking in at all today. Can I get you anything?'

'I should like a cup of tea very much,' Peter Wildgoose said. The spotless carapace of good manners that he presented to the world could never quite disguise the pleasure he got out of Anthea's solicitude. 'But not if it's any trouble.'

'It's no trouble,' Anthea said, ignoring the telephone that now began to ring beside her. 'Did you have a good time at the Old Boys' dinner?'

'These things are always a trial. One tries to think well of the companions of one's youth, and they all turn out to have developed such disagreeable habits.'

'Did Des turn up in the end?'

'Not all the companions of one's youth were able to make it, alas. But I should have enjoyed seeing Des there. He would have been so utterly unlike anyone else at the table that it would have been a pleasure to behold.' Taking the cup of tea from her and contriving to suggest, with his wonderful manners, that nothing less than the freedom of a city had fallen into his hands, he went and sat in a chair next to the window.

Anthea scooped up the telephone, which had continued to ring through her conversation with Peter Wildgoose, listened briefly to whatever the person at the other end had to say, and then slammed it down without comment. There was a commotion from the inner office and Desmond came out of it holding Tambi's wad of poems in his outstretched hand.

'I must say Tambi's done us proud this time. Listen to this:

Like a leaf a-tremble, life twists on its precipice. And Bodhisattva
His grim face astir, sheds bitter tears for a world tossed out
of kilter
While pale yellow butter-coloured Buddha lazily reclines
Next to the darkling snow of yesteryear . . .'

Peter Wildgoose glanced up from the February number. He was looking over the list of contributor biographies on the inside front page, Cynthia saw. Soon he would get to the editorial. 'Is he one of your discoveries, Des?'

'I wouldn't put it quite like that,' Desmond said. 'Tom Eliot sent me a note about him.'

'Tom Eliot is a very polite man,' Peter Wildgoose said. He gave a quick, grim little laugh that might have been prompted by Tambi's poems, T. S. Eliot's sponsorship of them, or some other subject quite unknown to them all. 'I expect he thinks you're just the man to give Tambi the rope to hang himself.'

He was not really concentrating on Desmond, Cynthia thought, but reading the first paragraph of the editorial. Then the fat would be in the fire, and no mistake. Desmond, seeing what he was doing, looked uncomfortable.

'They're not *bad* poems,' he said. 'You might even say that kind of souped-up romanticism was an inevitable part of the times we live in.'

'The times we live in,' Peter Wildgoose echoed. There was definitely something going on in the room now, a series of incremental adjustments to its temperature of which only Cynthia, and to a certain extent Desmond, seemed aware. Peter Wildgoose had turned over a leaf and was on the second page of Desmond's editorial. 'How many times have I heard that? Do you know, I think it's extraordinary that at a time like this we should be debating the merits of a poem about pale yellow butter-coloured Buddhas. Don't you think so too?'

'But that's the point, isn't it?' Desmond said eagerly. 'It's really because things are in such a state that people are taking up romanticism again. Do you know, Esmé came down to breakfast yesterday saying that she felt like writing a sonnet?'

'I'm sure you were happy to help,' Peter Wildgoose said. He had turned back to the first page of the editorial again. His face betrayed no emotion. 'Do you realise they're debating the conduct of the war in Parliament this afternoon? All kinds of curious people are making speeches about what a mistake it's been. And here we are with our pale yellow butter-coloured Buddhas.'

The tension in the room had communicated itself to Anthea and Lucy now, both of whom, reasoning that he could only be the source of it, decided to stare at Desmond.

Only Mr Woodmansee seemed oblivious to what was going on. Supposing that Peter Wildgoose had said all he wanted, he shifted the angle of his body in its chair and addressed himself to Desmond with an absolutely awful gravity. 'I wonder, Mr Rafferty, if I might have your opinion on this bill?'

'Which bill?' Desmond said nervously.

'This bill for a cigar humidor. Mr Wildgoose said that I was to make a point of asking you about it.'

'Oh, *that*,' Desmond said. 'I really think . . .'

'Desmond,' Peter Wildgoose said. 'What happened to the editorial?'

'I don't know what you're talking about,' Desmond said.

'The letter to an officer from a non-combatant, in which, among other things, you mention the complacent look you detect upon the faces of young men in uniform. I don't seem to see it here.'

'That's because I decided to put something else in,' Desmond said. He was breathing heavily and making agitated little movements with his hands.

'So I see. Did it occur to you that I might like to be consulted about this change of plan?'

'I'm editor of this magazine,' Desmond said, with what might just have passed for dignity. 'I think I have a right to decide what goes into it.'

There had been a moment, Cynthia thought, when the situation might have been resolved, calmed, brought to an end in some kind of compromise. But that moment had passed. Despite her sympathy for Peter Wildgoose, she felt sorry for Desmond, who was clearly having trouble keeping this level of self-justification going.

'And so,' Peter Wildgoose said, '—stay here, Lucy, I absolutely forbid you to leave the room—you decide to substitute these pages of defeatist nonsense. I shouldn't mind if it were something new, but it's *exactly* like the rubbish being spouted in the House this morning. Did Esmé Gurvitz put you up to it?'

'She certainly did not,' Desmond said, all caution gone. 'I never spoke to her about it. I suppose you think people like me can't take a stand on issues they feel strongly about without being told to do it.'

Englishmen were bad at losing their tempers, Cynthia thought. They preferred writing letters to each other, dropping coded intimations of their displeasure. Cutting someone adrift was a kind of social sleight of hand, so subtly performed that sometimes neither side grasped the implications of what had happened. Tyler Kent would have wrapped the business up in a couple of sentences. Neither, by extension, were Englishmen any good at taking a stand. Stands were for the people in Europe, people in torch-lit squares and on crowded railway platforms, not for the likes of Desmond and Peter Wildgoose.

'Des,' Peter Wildgoose said, with a sort of infinite weariness. 'I expect that somewhere in an old drawer, probably covered up by a couple of Charvet ties, you have that old Communist Party membership card you got in—when was it?—1934. I'm sure it must be some consolation to you. But let me tell you that you have the least amount of political awareness of anyone I have ever met. What did you think you were doing?'

'I've told you,' Desmond said. He had stopped looking furtive and now seemed thoroughly pleased with himself. 'I was taking a stand. Somebody has to.'

'I'm not interested,' Peter Wildgoose said, in his high, polite voice. 'I really am not. If I thought I could redeem you from all this, then it might be worth taking the trouble. It's simply a betrayal of trust. Like several others I could mention but won't. You're sacked, Des, and that's all there is to it.'

'You can't sack me,' Desmond said. He looked utterly astonished, like a conjuror who, feigning to saw his sequinned assistant in half, hears a genuine scream. 'You absolutely cannot.'

'But I just did,' Peter Wildgoose said. 'And when I pay your salary to the end of the quarter, as your contract obliges me to, you'll find that I've deducted the cost of that cigar humidor. Now go away.'

Even then there was a feeling in the room that the situation could somehow have been saved, that a snap of Peter Wildgoose's fingers might reveal the whole thing to have been an imposture, a bizarre, half-sinister routine got up to raise everyone's spirits on a dull winter day.

But it turned out that both actors had meant what they said. Peter Wildgoose continued to sit in his chair reading a copy of *The Times* that someone had left there. Desmond retired into his office, shut the door, and could be heard moving things about. Mr Woodmansee reapplied himself to his invoice tray as if what he had just heard was the most natural thing in the world. Not long after this the clock in the far corner of the square chimed the hour and Cynthia tidied her desk, repossessed herself of her suitcase, and left for Waterloo.

Sussex in February was not Sussex in October: that much was clear. The train rattled south through clumps of frail-looking larch trees, pale and ghastly beneath the red disc of the sun. All signs of mist and mellow fruitfulness had vanished. There was still snow on the ground, and the hedgerows ran off over the slowly ascending fields like piping on a dress. The sheep were gathered together in the field bottoms, silent and resentful. They had not bargained for this.

There was a copy of a London evening paper on one of the seats which said that the Government would probably win a no-confidence motion by a good 80 votes, and she put it across her knees and sat looking out of the window at the gorse thickets. By the time she reached Arundel the light had almost gone and the train was full of schoolgirls in elaborate winter bonnets practising French conversation. Blundering out into the semi-darkness of the station forecourt, where there were packing cases stacked up in towering ziggurats and what looked like half an armoured car concealed under a tarpaulin, she found not the Bannisters' Daimler with its less than respectful chauffeur, but a decrepit Ford with Hermione's big moon face staring keenly out of the facing window.

'I wasn't doing anything this afternoon,' she explained as Cynthia got in beside her, 'and Mummy needed some more bran for the pullets in case they start laying again. So I said I'd come and fetch you.'

'What happened to your chauffeur?' Cynthia asked.

'Ricketts?' Hermione gave a high-pitched laugh, so artificial that it would have done credit to a drawing-room comedy. In the confines of the car her head seemed bigger than ever. 'Oh, he had a falling-out with Father. And then Father said what was the point of the Daimler anyhow, and if he wanted to go to London he might as well bicycle to the station.' Her plump, roly-poly hands quivered on the steering wheel. 'Father's started saying a lot of things like that. Isn't it a scream?'

The car barrelled on through the Sussex back-lanes, a cyclist or two skidding in its wake. The owls were already out in the fields, off-white bundles crossing at tree-height, with occasional darts below. Thinking that she ought to make an ally of Hermione, and that her mission required as much sisterly solidarity as possible, Cynthia said: 'What was the exciting news you were talking about?'

'What exciting news was that?'

'You sent me a postcard saying you had something wildly exciting to tell me.'

'Did I? Well, if you really must know, I'm engaged to Walter Partridge.' This was a new name. 'Who's he?'

'Oh, you must have heard of Walter. He's getting the nomination at Haslemere, now old Mr Symes is retiring. He's with RAF Coastal Command at Greenock. I shall probably go and live up there.'

It was hard to define the dramatic new landscape into which Hermione's oddity had now moved, but it had something to do with long pent-up emotions, narrowly held in check. For a moment she had a dreadful feeling that Hermione might be about to purposely drive the car off the road and into a ditch, and that if Hermione did this she would simply pick herself up and run back to Arundel Station. Then the expression on Hermione's face relaxed a little. The rest of the journey passed without incident.

'Walter's a sweet boy,' Hermione volunteered, 'but he says he finds the language the NCOs use rather a strain.'

Ashburton Grange was sunk in gloom. The only vehicle on the forecourt was a butcher's van making a delivery, whose rear wheel Hermione managed to clip as she came to rest alongside it. As she got out of the car, and the light from the flung-open front door illumined the gravel, she said:

'Do you like my shoes? Walter simply adores them.'

They were black-and-white co-respondent's shoes, of the kind that people had worn to go to parties or play golf a dozen years ago, and as out of place on this winter night in Sussex as a hula skirt or a pair of Lido trousers. But Cynthia saw that they had captivated Hermione, suborned her imagination, meant everything to her, and that whole parts of her life would now be projected through them.

Moving on towards the house, they found Mrs Bannister regarding them rather doubtfully from the doorstep. She had a fur coat draped over her shoulders, hopped nervously from one leg to the other, and was clearly feeling the cold.

'It feels terribly odd to be opening one's front door,' she explained, 'but Gladys is visiting her mother in the village, and I think Eunice is feeding the chickens.' If Hermione was odder, then Mrs Bannister was more subdued. She contrived to suggest that there was something shameful about a gentlewoman being found on a doorstep deputising for an absent parlourmaid.

'Where's Father?' Hermione demanded. She had put on her mother's old fox-terrier look and was rooting through a pile of parcels that lay just inside the door. 'Only I had something I particularly wanted to tell him.'

'I think the House is sitting until five,' Mrs Bannister said. But Hermione was already off into the main body of the house, the heels of the wonderful shoes clacking like castanets. As Cynthia went to follow her, Mrs Bannister laid a restraining arm on her elbow. 'My dear, you mustn't mind Hermione. She isn't quite herself.'

This warning had been uttered so many times during Cynthia's adolescence, had been pronounced over so many variegated female heads, that its implications were unguessable. It could mean that the person referred to was clinically insane, mildly unwell, or simply in a bad temper. Cynthia had no idea what it implied in relation to Hermione. But she said, rather gamely in the circumstances, 'You must be very glad about Walter.'

'Oh, *that*,' Mrs Bannister said. They could hear Hermione's footsteps rattling away on the staircase, like some Pied Piper calling her charges to destruction among the attics.

It was difficult to tell what had gone wrong with Ashburton Grange in the three months since she had last been there. The glass still sparkled on its mahogany sideboards. There were still the photographs of ancestral Bannisters, posed athwart slaughtered tigers, to divert the eye. The Carlton Club lecture list and the hunt-ball invitations still marched *bras dessous, bras dessous* across the mantelpiece. But not even the arrival of Mr Bannister at his most piratical, so that one almost expected to see a cutlass rather than a watch-and-chain dangling from his waistcoat, could dispel the faint air of desuetude that hung over the place.

It was a moot point as to whether Mr Bannister had been warned of Cynthia's arrival, but at any rate he took it like a trouper, came skilfully to attention on the drawing-room carpet and made a kind of pawing motion at her shoulder which, had it come from a man thirty years younger, would have been rewarded with a slap round the ear.

'Cynthia,' he said. 'You are always welcome here. We were lamenting just the other day that we saw so little of you.'

There was a terrible bogusness about this, so much so that she almost expected a trap door to spring open and plunge her into some icy lagoon reserved for those unfortunates on whom the Bannisters had pronounced their curse. But the floorboards were still solid beneath her feet.

Still looking like the heavy father in an Edwardian comedy, Mr Bannister went on: 'And how are your parents? Are they still removed from these shores?' It was extraordinary how Mr Bannister had come by these antique phrases. He must have read them in a book. Or perhaps someone had said something patriotic in the House that afternoon and this had turned his head.

'Father is getting on nicely, thank you,' she said. This was the official line from Mrs Kirkpatrick. 'Of course, they would like to come home. But the Channel shipping is very precarious.'

'Between you and me, danger from that quarter is exaggerated,' Mr Bannister said, who now seemed to be modelling himself on Metternich at the Congress of Vienna. 'I don't think our friend Adolf has much interest in the British merchant fleet.'

Somehow it was not the 'our friend Adolf' that irked but the expressions on the faces of the other Bannisters. Mrs Bannister looked, if not exactly admiring, then comradely, proud to be in this together. Hermione, who had lashed a bandeau round her bulging forehead again, gave a little village halfwit's simper.

'I heard a dreadful story today,' Mr Bannister said. 'Can't think how I wasn't told it before. Lord Falconhurst's girl. Minna, I think her name is. Well, Minna had been spending a lot of time in Berlin. Very keen on Anglo-German fellowship. Might even have been engaged to a German, chap who told me thought. Anyway, when she heard that war had been declared she was so affected that she walked into the *Englischer garten* and shot herself in the head. Only the wound wasn't fatal. Just damaged her brain in some way. They brought her home in an ambulance a week before Christmas. But do you know what I think was a nice gesture? Apparently Falconhurst tried to reimburse the travelling expenses, but the Führer wouldn't hear of it.'

'Poor Minna Falconhurst,' Hermione said, thoughtfully. 'She used to have such lovely hair. But I expect it's all had to be cut off now.'

After that they went in to dinner.

It was in the Bannisters' dining room that what had gone wrong with Ashburton Grange over the past three months came plainly into view, for they dined off grilled anchovies on toast and shepherd's pie handed round by a maidservant, and the bottle of thin claret that lay on the sideboard was uncorked and decanted by Mr Bannister himself.

'We had to let two of the girls go,' Mrs Bannister explained, looking suddenly like her old *burra memsahib* self, back in the gardens of some colonial bungalow. 'I think they're working at the munitions factory outside Chichester. And of course you can't get a footman now for love nor money. Half the agencies have closed down.'

And Cynthia thought of Minna Falconhurst, whom she had seen once at a party, plain and indignant behind her three beautiful sisters, with the blood streaming over her hands onto the turf of the *Englischer garten*. The dinner was so awful, what with the intensity of its silences and the implications of its chatter, that she could have screamed. But then, when she came back to earth, she realised that it was merely the Bannisters at table: Mr Bannister, whom she had known all her life, been chaffed by, waved off in cars by, even, on one dreadful occasion, bought a frock by, playing the heavy father in the company of his wife and daughter.

It was the same with the magnitude of the task she was bent on accomplishing, which in the context of the house and the Bannisters and her relationship with it and them had no magnitude at all and was simply a kind of gargantuan practical joke, like those weekend parties in country houses where you went about at dead of night stealing people's chamber-pots and putting salt-cellars in their beds. Here at Ashburton Grange, with Victorian Bannisters grinning from their frames, with the scent of Henry filling the air like marsh gas, she could not make any connection between the address book—if indeed there was one—lying in Mr Bannister's study drawer and the tumbling world beyond. Someone else could do that. Her own aims, if they were aims, could not be disentangled from the personal resentment she felt. The fate of Europe was one thing. But it had nothing on her hatred for her hosts.

Mr Bannister, meanwhile, was clearly pregnant with some great secret. When the remains of the anchovies had gone out, and the shepherd's pie lay congealing on the plates before them, he said, 'I think I can safely say that within a fortnight's time we shall have a settlement.'

'Good gracious,' Mrs Bannister said, turning over something nasty-looking that had come to rest between her knife and fork. 'You're not saying that Chamberlain isn't safe?'

'I'm not saying that at all,' Mr Bannister said. He could not quite decide whether he was playing the great statesman or the confidential husband. 'Only that I have it on very good authority that a peace proposal will be coming in soon by way of one of the neutral embassies. Something concrete. Of the kind that would provoke an outcry were it to be ignored. Something that would really put the warmongers on the back foot.'

After that the entertainment lapsed, and they had to make do with Hermione, who had clearly decided to turn the second half of the meal into a showcase for her dramatic talents. During the eating of the shepherd's pie she played the part of the young ingénue, confused and chastened by the world's enticing snares. Then, when the dessert was brought in, she switched to the role of hard-bitten politician's confidante, dishing up a row of Cabinet heads on their metaphorical salvers. To all this Mr Bannister attended benignly and Mrs Bannister with what passed for tolerance. But there came a moment when even Hermione went too far.

'Isn't Dr Goebbels nice-looking?' she said. 'I saw a picture of him in *The Times* and thought how nice he looked.'

'I think that will do, Hermione,' Mr Bannister said.

'I don't see why I shouldn't say if I think a man's good-looking.'

'*Hermione*,' Mrs Bannister warned.

'Do you know something?' Hermione said, jumping to her feet in a gesture that was, for once, genuinely dramatic. 'I hate you all. I shall ring up Walter and get him to take me away from all this.'

After she had gone, Mr Bannister said with immense gloominess, grim and predatory beneath the raw light that burned off the wall behind him: 'I think I ought to say, in case there should be any doubt, that Hermione is certainly not going to marry Walter Partridge. Nor anyone else, I should imagine, if she carries on like that.'

Come the morning, Hermione had still not calmed down and Cynthia was left to her own devices. There were blue-black clouds massing towards the sea and the landscape looked as uninviting as any she had seen outside Ceylon in the rains, but she put on an ancient Inverness cape that someone had left parcelled up in the vestibule and trudged gamely around the estate.

Lichen was beginning to grow on Henry's memorial stone and the descent of some heavy object had chipped one of its corners, but she stared at it dutifully for a moment while the wind blew her hair into her face and the dogs howled listlessly in their kennels. Back inside, she did her best to appear unobtrusive. This was not hard, as nobody appeared to want to take any notice of her at all.

For a house with so few people in it, Ashburton Grange seemed extremely chaotic. The telephone bell rang every ten minutes, two telegraph boys arrived within the space of half an hour, and there was an unexpected visit from the Chairman of the Arundel and South Downs Conservative Party. While Mr Bannister dealt with these interruptions, Mrs Bannister sat on the drawing-room sofa, made a nuisance of herself with the parlourmaids, and affected to read the same page of the *Bystander* for two hours at a stretch.

In these circumstances it was nearly inevitable that Cynthia should find herself in Henry's old room: no longer a shrine to his memory, it turned out, but a repository for sets of fire-irons, old packing cases, and other miscellaneous junk. But there were still sufficient traces of Henry's personality to give her pause for thought: a pair of monogrammed cuff-links that had come to rest under a chair; the ancient shotgun he had taught her to shoot with; a row of boys' school stories; Loeb editions of Hesiod and Xenophon that no one had bothered to return to Balliol College library.

In one of them she found what was fairly evidently a draft of a love letter, its subject indisputably not herself, not at all sparing in its physical detail, and the effect was so unsettling that she simply sat on the single high-backed armchair that remained in the room and stared at it: not because she was jealous of the other girl, or angry with Henry for wanting to sleep with her, or shocked by the language that he brought to his anticipation of the task, but because she could not connect the words with the person she knew had written them.

The copies of *The Liveliest Term at Templeton* and *The White House Boys* stared back at her, and she thought that there were whole areas of English life that she had altogether failed to understand, that there was some vital qualification missing from her repertoire that would have enabled her to better comprehend Henry Bannister and his kind, to sympathise with them, and deal with them, and not be so discountenanced by their actions or the letters they wrote to anonymous girls, with (apparently) enormous breasts, that they left lying around in Loeb editions of Xenophon for people to stumble on after their deaths.

At various times during her years in the East, on mildewed verandas set back from the maidan, up-country in Ceylon, in broken-backed armchairs in ships' libraries tacking across the Indian Ocean, Cynthia had read novels about weekends in English country houses, where girls in jumpers and tweed skirts ate chocolates in front of a roaring fire and laid bare their most intimate secrets. But life at Ashburton Grange could not aspire to this exacting paradigm. You either had to listen to Mrs Bannister discussing the rubbish in the *Bystander*, or Hermione talking about nightclubs she had pretty obviously not been to, men she had pretty obviously not met, and the particular man that she was pretty clearly not going to marry. And all the time the momentous task Cynthia was bent on accomplishing hung in the air before her, terrifying her and exhilarating her by turns.

As for the obstacles lying in the way of her expedition, these removed themselves almost at a stroke. Shortly after lunch the sky cleared and Mr and Mrs Bannister declared their intention of taking the car into Arundel on some unspecified errand. Hermione, launched onto another of her roles—that of the galumphing country girl with much to accomplish—announced that she would clean out the kennels. Even Mrs Bannister seemed surprised at this. But the upshot was that at three o'clock Cynthia found herself in the dining room, a half-drunk cup of coffee in her lap, a picture of the Duke of Connaught on Torquay seafront staring up at her from Mrs Bannister's copy of the *Bystander*, and around her an empty house.

Mr Bannister's study was at the end of a serpentine corridor, preceded by various billiard-rooms and store cupboards, on the opposite side of the house. No difficulty there. Remembering a film she had once seen in which a rebellious schoolgirl had robbed her headmistress's trophy cabinet, she took off her shoes to negotiate it. The study door was half-open and she ducked under the lintel and closed it behind her.

Here, as she expected, there was nothing to surprise her. Apart from a few trifling idiosyncrasies of decor and ornament, Mr Bannister's study was exactly like every other gentleman's study she had been into. There was a picture of Henry in a gilt frame on the desk—a toothy and faintly scrofulous Henry who might then have been about eighteen—a group portrait of the Bannister children, out of which Hermione's face stared like a giant vegetable, and several other photographs of Mr Bannister on horses, in the uniform of a Territorial Army colonel, dyspeptic at a banquet and wearing a rather ridiculous cocked hat. She was used to this, reassured by it, so comforted by the ordinariness of it that she found herself examining the bookshelves to see if, among the copies of *The War in the Air* and the memoirs of General Haig, there were smaller, incriminating volumes with titles like *Behind Convent Walls* and *Hard-hearted Hannah*.

But there was nothing like this, and in some ways its absence lowered Mr Bannister a further rung in her estimation. The drawers of the desk were unlocked. Beyond the window rain had begun to lash the Bannisters' melancholy garden. In the third of the drawers, beneath a pile of stationery and a stapling machine, exactly as Anthea had predicted, she found the thing she had come to find. It was a slender volume, no bigger than a diary, bound in red leather, embossed across the spine with the letters 'PJ' in gold, and secured by a metal clasp with a tiny lock. She hunted for the key for a moment, but there was nothing else in the drawer except myriad paper clips. Well, Anthea could worry about that.

She was just replacing the stationery, and balancing the stapling machine on top of it at the same 45-degree angle, when something else nosed out into view from its hiding place between two sheets of notepaper. This was a letter, apparently sent from the Foreign Ministry in Berlin, addressed to Mr Bannister, or rather *Herr* Bannister, dated six weeks before, written in dignified but not absolutely flawless English, and signed by no less a correspondent than von Ribbentrop.

For a second or two she gazed despairingly at the letter. Half of her recoiled from it, found it almost painful to the touch, as if it might burn her fingers if she held on to it. The other half knew that Anthea would never forgive her if she left it there. For this, whatever gloss that *Herr* Bannister might like to put on it, was treason. After another second or two, while the rain continued to lash the Bannisters' melancholy garden and drummed on the window, she stuffed it into the pocket of her skirt.

She found, rather to her surprise, that she was exalted by what she had done and what Anthea would say about it. The book, she now saw, was small enough to conceal in the neck of her sweater, provided she kept a hand in the vicinity. She had reached the end of the corridor, and was almost in sight of the staircase, when there was a rustle of Lisle stockings and one of the parlourmaids—the glamorous, sullen one—slunk into view.

'Were you wanting anything, miss?'

'No,' would have been inadmissible. No one could possibly be returning along the approach road to Mr Bannister's lair unless they wanted something. The book was pressed hard against the gap between her throat and her breast-bone. Instead she said, 'I was looking for Mr Bannister.'

'He's gone out, miss, and Mrs Bannister with him.' It was not, perhaps, meant to sound insinuating, but somehow it did so. 'Can I get you anything?'

'No, thank you.'

Back in her bedroom, with the parlourmaid's tread uncomfortably close on the staircase nearby, she searched for a hiding place. Under the bed was too obvious, she thought. In the end she wrapped the book up in a chiffon scarf and hid it at the bottom of her suitcase. Her hands were shaking and she remembered lying in the wrecked car bawling for Henry while the noise of the jungle fizzed and echoed around her.

When she had calmed down, she decided to read the letter. This was not as easy as it appeared, for it was written in a kind of code, referred to previous communications whose significance eluded her and was light on background detail. On the other hand it seemed to have less to do with peace proposals than with assurances of the high regard in which Mr Bannister was held by the German Foreign Ministry and the opportunities that might be available to him in some vague and unspecific war-free future.

There was also, about halfway through, a curious, and rather slighting, reference to Captain Ramsay, and mention of the latter's 'futile manoeuvrings,' all of which led her to wonder whether Mr Bannister might not be playing some game of his own, infinitely more sinister and deserving of exposure. After a few minutes more she folded the letter up into a tiny square, hid it under the book, went downstairs and returned to the drawing room.

Here, just as she entered it, the telephone began to ring. It continued to ring, parlourmaid or no parlourmaid, and there seemed no reason why she should not pick it up. After a certain amount of scrabbling and the sound of the operator neighing in the background, a man's voice, oddly familiar and carrying some echo of the room in which she now stood, said: 'Is Mr Bannister there?'

'I'm afraid they're all out,' Cynthia said, and then remembering the prescriptions of her upbringing, 'this is Cynthia Kirkpatrick.'

'How do you do, Miss Kirkpatrick?' the voice went on, not uncourteously. 'Delighted to speak to you again. Captain Ramsay here. Could you ask Mr Bannister to telephone me when he gets in?'

'Certainly.'

'Tell him something important has come up.'

'I'll do that.'

'Goodbye then.'

'Yes, yes, goodbye.' There was something so awful about the coincidence of Captain Ramsay telephoning at the precise moment after she had returned from reading von Ribbentrop's low opinion of him that all her sangfroid disappeared and she sprawled on the sofa clenching and unclenching her fists. It was here that Hermione found her when she came back from the kennels.

'Having a nap, eh?' Hermione said. She was still doing her stable-girl routine. 'Do you know, I went and gave the horses a rub-down as well and I'm absolutely certain that Creditor has a spavined hock. Father will be simply furious at having to get the vet out again.'

Later they had tea in front of the dying fire and Hermione talked some more about Walter Partridge and the nature of his duties at RAF Coastal Command, which was all horribly dull but at any rate a relief from Captain Ramsay, the book with the letters 'PJ' embossed on its spine, and the letter from Herr von Ribbentrop concealed in her suitcase.

Meanwhile, there was the rest of the weekend to get through. Whatever Mr and Mrs Bannister had or had not done in Arundel had put them into unimaginably foul tempers, but Mr Bannister cheered up at the news of Captain Ramsay's telephone call, went away to return it and was not seen again until dinner. In the evening they played bezique in the drawing room while the rain beat against the window frames and she thought about the contraband in the suitcase.

What were the chances of Mr Bannister going to examine his study drawer between now and Sunday lunchtime? And even if he noticed the contents were gone, what were the chances of his associating their disappearance with her? She had a feeling they were unwarrantedly high.

There was a train leaving Arundel Station at 11 to which the Bannisters had promised to convey her. She tipped the glamorous but sulky parlourmaid a whole ten shillings, which might have been regarded as an admission of guilt. The wind was raging across the gravel drive, bending the stunted larches at its further end nearly in two, and the Bannisters, father, mother, and daughter, assembled in the hallway to see her off.

'It was jolly good of you to come all this way,' Hermione said, as if, against all evidence to the contrary, it had been a weekend full of late nights and spectacular entertainment. Mrs Bannister was unexpectedly subdued. Mr Bannister teetered on his big, ungainly feet, as if a single push would send him flying. The door was half-open and the car in which Hermione had volunteered to drive her to Arundel twenty feet away on the gravel, so that she could see that the RAC badge was badly tarnished, and she was shaking hands—Hermione's fingers were still whorled with dirt, as if she had spent the night labouring far underground—when Mr Bannister, looming into the space between door and jamb, said unexpectedly:

'It pains me to have to say this, Cynthia, but I think you have two pieces of rather valuable property of mine.'

She had no idea if the other Bannisters were in on the act, nor any way of stopping her face from turning bright red.

'I really don't know what you're talking about.'

'I really am terribly afraid, Cynthia, that I am going to have to ask you to turn out your suitcase.'

'Gracious,' she heard herself saying emphatically, 'I never *heard* anything so ridiculous.'

But Mr Bannister had the case in his hands now. He looked more than ever like a pirate: mad, grim, unappeasable, up to no good.

She gave a little tug at his elbow and had it briskly rebuffed. Mrs Bannister gave one of her mad-terrier barks. In the end the suitcase fell on the floor, disgorging two pairs of directoire knickers, the pot of home-made jam that Mrs Bannister had loftily presented her with at breakfast, the book in its crimson binding, and Herr von Ribbentrop's letter. Henry Bannister's dead face stared up at her from the jungle floor and behind her the door slammed shut.

CHAPTER 19

Emerald Isle

In Dublin it is raining. Relentless, implacable rain, like something out of a Victorian novel. Merrion Square is awash under what looks like off-colour gravy: turning into Mount Street, the taxi sends up a sheet of water four feet high. The Grand Canal gleams beneath them. From the back seat, squeezed in between his two companions, Captain Ramsay eyes the wet streets with misgiving.

Dublin, he suspects, is not his kind of place. There is too much history, but of the wrong kind. Even the street names—Wolf Tone Quay, Parnell Place—carry a freight of mockery, that grinning Hibernian contempt for discipline and order. Gaunt Victorian architecture and rebel posturing: it is like London gone wrong, turned Gothic and sinister. But there is more to his unease than the Catholic cathedrals and memorials to famine, dull Irish faces and newspapers for whom an overturned pony and trap on the Maynooth Road is a very serious business, while the news from Europe rates a paragraph on the inside page.

Something tells Captain Ramsay that he has made a mistake in coming here, this February Sunday, and would much better have stayed away, or sent Bannister in his stead, were it not for the fact that Bannister seemed very anxious not to attend this particular excursion. It is not just the complexity of the journey, and the necessity to hide up incognito in a vile little commercial hotel in Mulholland rather than a respectable establishment in Temple Bar, but something else, not quite frameable, always hanging a little way beyond the taxi as it surges along the Shelburne Road.

Like the Gothic pinnacles, the Dublin cab drivers are a throwback to another world. You can imagine them on the box of a stagecoach, gathering up the traces of a four-in-hand. There is a ghostliness about their vigour, a sense of being fetched up somewhere beyond the place they really want to be. Captain Ramsay thinks that he can sympathise with this. Half the world's problems, he sometimes tells himself, are down to creeping modernity.

Beyond the Shelburne Road there is scarcely any traffic at all. A few ancient touring cars labouring into Mass at St Patrick's. Picturesque provision carts transporting God knows what to God knows where. A handful of girls, be-hatted and wearing long floral skirts beneath their mackintoshes, on bicycles. Dr Clavane, who has previously been half-asleep behind the *Sunday Press*, perks up at this and stares over the top of his thick spectacles.

'The finest peasantry in Europe,' he says, the hint of mischief in this voice daring anyone to take him wholly seriously. 'But the stage Irishman, you know, is self-created. The Victorians came looking for local colour, and by God the natives were determined to let them have it. Just like the agricultural labourers in Dorset. Didn't somebody once say that after Hardy they all went about behaving like artists' models?'

Dr Clavane is always saying things like this—little seeds of quasi-intellectual inquiry, fated to fall on stony ground. Captain Ramsay isn't interested. Amery, on the other hand, still sprawled against his shoulder, is merely ignorant. He has probably never heard of Hardy, although, Ramsay thinks, he could probably claim acquaintance with one or two artists' models.

'Of course,' Dr Clavane declares, 'Ireland is going to have to play its part in the new Europe. It's a pity de Valera can't make up his mind which it ought to be.'

Dr Clavane has some curious ideas about Europe. It is almost like the Federal Union people, yet more atavistic, as if some new Charlemagne is suddenly going to rise up and subjugate a dozen sovereign states from Dublin to Prague to his will. Hitler, to him, is a modern version of Barbarossa. Captain Ramsay wonders what on earth they make of him in Cambridge, or at the various learned societies whose notepaper his name adorns.

The rain is falling away. The dark clouds are moving off to Slane and Monaghan. Queerly, this does not improve the view. The streets—levelling out into suburbs now, with patches of waste ground and occasional scrubby fields—look even greyer and more nondescript.

Perhaps, Ramsay thinks, it is actually the people he has brought along for the ride that disquiet him. Dr Clavane he can put up with. Beneath the bluster and the Billy Bunter trousers and the air of ineffable complacency, Dr Clavane means no harm. This is more than can be said for Amery, the Cabinet Minister's son, still sound asleep at his side, so profoundly unconscious, in fact, that one of his inexpensively shod feet—soleless, Ramsay is pained to observe—is banging metronomically against the floor of the taxi. What is it, Ramsay wonders, about the children of celebrated men? He can think of half a dozen political friends with delinquent heirs still hanging around, jobless, in the parental drawing room, racketing off into the world's unsuitable margins, having to be bailed out from hare-brained business ventures.

They are passing through Donnybrook now: Mortonstown and its beach are only a mile or so away. It is about half-past ten: hopelessly early. Krastner and the other men from the Embassy will like as not wait until eleven. The implications of what he is doing have occurred to Captain Ramsay, but do not greatly concern him. He can brazen it out. There are a dozen reasons why a British Member of Parliament, accompanied by a Cambridge don and a Cabinet minister's wayward son, might be taking the seaside air at Mortonstown. Doesn't Halifax know, or can he not have inferred, that he is here?

Ramsay thinks that, in the matter of awkward questions, he can look after himself. More alarming to him are some of the rumours that are coming out of Berlin. These suggest that, contrary to all expectations, and every speech that Ramsay has made to every political meeting he has addressed in the past six months, the Germans are serious about the war. He wishes that Bannister were here to provide reassurance, but there is something odd about Bannister at the moment, the sense of a mind not fully committed to the cause, or perhaps of someone committed to a cause that is merely his own.

Meanwhile, if the Germans are serious about the war, then a peace-seeking patriot may very well look like a stooge. But still here he is, on a Sunday in February, with the last vestiges of the rain disappearing behind him, far from home, his anxieties about Bannister set momentarily to one side, come to see Herr Krastner of the Dublin Embassy and his associates. Anything is possible, he feels, with a sudden surge of exhilaration. The destiny of Europe is in his hands.

Beside him, Amery is slowly coming awake. There is quite a lot about Amery that does not inspire confidence. One of these things is the fact that, even now, at half-past ten on a Sunday morning, he smells not exactly of gin but of some deeper, more elemental reek. Another is his habit of making grand-sounding pronouncements about European politics and his role in them. On the other hand, Ramsay thinks, as the taxi judders over a pot-hole—the Irish roads are shockingly bad—one can be too fastidious about these things. If Amery is the price of his meeting with Herr Krastner, then it is worth paying.

They are in sight of the sea now: oddly mutinous with great high breakers in the distance. Nearer at hand, the water surges up over the beach like a live thing: blue-black at the peak but descending into brown. The joke about Amery—although this is something that Ramsay would never mention—is that he is a quarter Jewish. Uncoiling his legs, and patting the knee of his trousers with a thin hand—he has managed cuff-links, Ramsay sees—he says out of nowhere: 'Of course, we may be entirely mistaken over the right kind of mediator. If it were left to me, I should try Grandi, that fellow who used to be the Italian ambassador to London, and see if he couldn't get Mussolini to intervene.'

'I think you'll find,' Ramsay says, 'that he's now the Minister of Justice at Rome. How would we reach him?'

'I'd do the job myself,' Amery responds, 'if anyone could put a plane at my disposal. Fly to Switzerland and then get over the Italian border. Grandi would know me, of course. He used to come to the house when we were children.'

This is so fanciful, so implausibly far-fetched, that Ramsay almost laughs. Even Clavane, who is rather in awe of Amery, is grinning. Amery turns his head from side to side, puzzled by the lack of response, as if he has brought an eleventh commandment down from the mountain and yet, queerly, no one is interested.

The taxi is negotiating a small esplanade next to the seashore. There are a few beach-huts, a shed or two bolted up against the summer's return.

'Dear me, what a place,' Clavane says, his dreams of a new Europe come to grief amid half a mile of oily sand, scattered seaweed, and driftwood.

Amery has begun to shiver beneath his trench-coat. He looks horribly seedy. There are gulls crying above their heads, more birds further out to sea moving slant-wise against the wind. 'I think you underestimate Mussolini's capacity for taking effective action,' Amery says seriously. There is no stopping him, no defying his self-belief. He and Mussolini, or Count Grandi, will sort things out, if only the forces that are keeping them apart can be pushed aside.

Ramsay pays off the taxi man, who agrees to wait a little way down the front for their return, and they descend awkwardly onto the sand: Amery in a nervous frenzy; Clavane as if the whole business of movement is deeply inimical to him and back in Cambridge his journeys are undertaken by richly brocaded palanquin. It is then that one of the things Ramsay has dreaded—not the worst thing, but one of them—happens, and a plump, blithe, hatless man who has been bumbling along the esplanade towards them stops by the winded taxi and gives Clavane a friendly pat on the arm.

'Clavvy!' this apparition exclaims. He has odd, protruding teeth, bursting out at an angle from his upper jaw and almost green-coloured. 'Fancy seeing you here. I didn't know you were a Shamrock! What brings you to Dublin?'

'I'm just making a little trip with these gentlemen,' Clavane says, with what in the circumstances is an impressive sobriety. 'But what about you? Are you still at the *Architectural Review?*'

'Not possible, old chap, when your pa-in-law's a retired field marshal. You have to follow the guns. Or at least watch where the guns are being dragged. Right now I'm press attaché at the embassy. I don't expect it will last. These things rarely do.'

'And how's Penelope?' Clavane wonders.

'Oh, couldn't be better. Grand, in fact. Do you know, I think the reason I come here of a Sunday is to work out what I'm going to put in my letter home. But look, don't let me keep you from your friends. We're bound to bump into each other sometime in London, I daresay.'

'I daresay we shall,' Clavane says.

They watch him toddle off into the wind: plump, gammy-legged—like Clavane, he seems to find the whole business of locomotion curiously confusing—but oddly formidable. 'Who was that?' Ramsay demands.

'He's called Betjeman,' Clavane says. 'You wouldn't credit it, but we were at school together. There's not the faintest chance of his suspecting anything. He's the most unworldly man in England.'

A hundred yards ahead of them, at a point where the last cluster of beach-huts gives out, another car has appeared. The wind has reached an astonishing pitch now. A hat worn by one of the men getting out of the car goes racing away towards the breakwaters and he bounds off to retrieve it. Ramsay is still thinking about Mr Betjeman the press attaché with his greeny-grey teeth and blithering chatter, who surely cannot fail to have recognised him. Or perhaps he is quite as guileless as he makes out. It is difficult to tell.

The wind is gusting so violently that there are little eddies of grit moving through the air, lashing the legs of the unwary. Silently the two groups of men move towards each other. Ramsay can recognise Krastner, whom he met once years ago. The other two are unknown to him.

'Gentlemen,' Krastner says, and the word is caught up and flung away by the wind. Six inches shorter than Ramsay, he is not much of an advertisement for Aryan supremacy. But then, Ramsay recalls, so many

Germans are not. Himmler looks like a janitor; Goering as if he ought to be standing behind the counter of a butcher's shop. Perhaps, on the other hand, that is part of their attraction. Krastner introduces his colleagues: again the names go flying off into the breeze.

'This is Dr Clavane,' Ramsay explains. 'And Mr Amery.'

'*Herr Doktor*,' Krastner says, inclining his head an inch or two and clicking his heels. The Nazis like titles, even non-aristocratic ones. But for Amery there is only the briskest of nods. Perhaps Krastner has done his homework on Amery and knows him for what he is.

Amery says something else about it being a pity that official channels do not allow for this sort of communication, and Krastner gives him an unutterably contemptuous smile that would stop any other man dead in his tracks but is entirely lost on the Cabinet Minister's son.

There is something horribly conspicuous about all this, Ramsay thinks, the six of them slowly processing along the Mortonstown shore in the bitter wind. On the other hand, there is no one about. Mr Betjeman, a rapidly retreating dot a quarter of a mile away, shows no interest in them. Krastner, having given up on Amery, stands a foot or two from the sea looking up at the wheeling gulls.

'With whose authority do you attend this meeting, Captain Ramsay?'

'All the authority I need,' Ramsay says equably. 'I am an elected representative of a party which governs my country.'

'Certainly that is so,' Krastner agrees. 'But does that make you a representative of, let us say, Lord Halifax?'

'I can convey any proposals you may care to make to Lord Halifax without delay.'

'And so can my ambassador. What is the advantage to us of dealing with yourselves?'

All this, Ramsay knows, needs careful consideration. It is necessary, above all, to let Krastner know with whom he is dealing.

'There is a great desire for peace in our country,' he says. 'The King wants it. Most of the people want it. The army wants it. Our aim is to open a channel by which it may be brought about.'

'And what would bring it about? After all,' Krastner deposes, 'it was you who began this war.'

'So it was,' Ramsay defers. He does not quite like the way the conversation is going. 'As to what might lead to a cessation of hostilities, we suggest a peace conference, in neutral territory, without preconditions.'

It is impossible to tell what Krastner thinks of this. His face is quite impassive. 'You know as well as I do, Captain Ramsay, that the Führer would not agree to any ceding of territory,' he says. 'Estonia, Poland, Czechoslovakia, or anywhere else.'

'No one is asking anyone to return any territory,' Ramsay says. 'What is needed is some evidence of willingness to negotiate. A guarantee of the liberties of non-German speakers in the annexed territories, perhaps.'

'Do you have Lord Halifax's authority to make this proposal?'

That word again. Ramsay stares at the sea, which is losing its tints as the light fades and turning as grey as the sky above it. 'No, but I can convey it to Lord Halifax should it be acceptable.'

'I could convey it to my father in six hours' time, I daresay,' Amery says, who has been trying desperately to intrude himself into the conversation. Krastner ignores him. He is not interested in Amery.

'What if I was to tell you that such a proposal was made to Lord Halifax—and rejected by him—months ago? What then would you say?'

'I should say that we had the means of exerting pressure on him, which he would find difficult to resist. That we have at our disposal a sufficient body of opinion to make him realise that he can no longer ignore us.'

'And what can a body of opinion, as you call it, do, Captain Ramsay? Can it replace a Prime Minister? Can it make an army lay down its arms?'

The great difficulty in life, Ramsay thinks, is understanding what people want, of fathoming their motives. This process is made yet more complicated when those involved do not know themselves. The people who come to his constituency surgeries—small businessmen, municipal officers, the decently downtrodden poor—are quite thoroughly confused, sure that some hurt has been done to them, uncertain as to what redress is due. What does Krastner want? Does he believe—as Captain Ramsay fervently believes—that there are greater dangers to the security of Europe than Nazi troops in Warsaw, that the real enemy lies to the east? Or is all this talk of peace conferences and Lord Halifax simple disingenuousness?

'The situation in the armed forces is very volatile,' he says. 'There is no doubt pressure can be brought to bear.' Again he wonders what Krastner wants. A detachment of the Household Cavalry marching on Downing Street? A hail of bullets in Whitehall? Neither of these things is in the least likely to happen, for this is England, where politics are done differently. He catches sight of Amery's eye and notes that he is greener about the gills than ever, gasping for breath like a trout hauled out on the river bank.

The wind has dropped a little now. Krastner's companions have drawn back a step. They are only stooges, Ramsay sees, bit-part players there to swell a scene. Amery is making little pawing movements with one of his feet against the sand. As for what Amery wants, Ramsay has not the slightest idea. The taxi waits a hundred yards away.

'The situation is very volatile everywhere,' Krastner says. He looks bored. Perhaps this posting to Dublin is the graveyard of his career. 'Very well, then. You may tell Lord Halifax that I shall refer the proposal for a peace conference to . . .'—there is a pause—'. . . the relevant authorities, and that he is at liberty to make suggestions for the . . .'—again there is a pause—'. . . administration of occupied territories.'

It is at this precise moment that Amery starts to make a series of honking noises and is then dramatically sick onto the ochre sand. The vomit is strangely coloured: like the pink juices that run out of a chicken when it is not quite cooked. On the other hand, there is a great deal of it. Krastner dances nimbly back from this detonation, but not before one or two splashes of vomit have flecked his shiny black boots.

'You had better get him away from here,' he says, not unamused by this. 'I should say that he has been drinking.'

'I assure you, sir,' Amery says between gulps, 'that not a drop of alcohol has passed my lips.' He is practically doubled up on the sand. Dr Clavane dabs ineffectually at him with a handkerchief. He looks more than ever like Billy Bunter, the Fat Owl of the Remove. 'These gentlemen will vouch for me.'

There is something horribly unconvincing about this. Ramsay would like to say something about Russia and the Red Menace and the alliances that lie before them, but he knows that he cannot, not while Amery, the

Cabinet Minister's son, is still disgorging the contents of his stomach over the sand at his feet.

There is a round of hand-shaking. Amery, still crouched on the beach with one fist pressed into his midriff, manages to raise the other to the level of his head. This gesture is ignored.

'If you or anyone else wishes to telephone me at the Embassy,' Krastner says, 'the code is Austerlitz.'

Austerlitz. Waterloo. Balaclava. The names of the great battles of Europe resound in Ramsay's head. He himself fought, and was badly wounded, in Flanders. There will be no more great battles if he can help it, he thinks.

The Embassy car is revving up. Krastner makes a small, faintly supercilious gesture with his hand, like a schoolmaster indicating that the interview is over. Together, Ramsay and Clavane assist Amery to the taxi. The displaced sand runs over the tips of their shoes.

'A sensible sort of idea,' Clavane says. He is still lost in some dream of a reconstituted Carolingian Europe.

Ramsay shrugs his shoulders. He has a lurking feeling that he has wasted his time, that German hordes are massing beyond the Maginot Line and no one can stop them.

Amery gives one final, despairing groan, emits what looks like a squirt of seawater, and falls into his seat. There is sand all over the taxi floor.

Outside there are gulls screaming beyond the breakers. The wind lifts.

CHAPTER 20

A Change of Climate

They were drinking coffee in Hegarty's room again, down at the end of the B.1 corridor. The patch of grass on which in summer the astonishingly pretty girls sometimes came and ate their lunchtime sandwiches was white with frost, and half a dozen rooks were grimly disputing a sausage roll that someone had dropped out of an upstairs window.

'I shall never understand women as long as I live,' Hegarty said bitterly. There was a fervour about his voice that gave even his most hackneyed utterances a desperate conviction. He managed to make it sound as if there was something remarkable and unprecedented about this failure, that questions ought to be asked in the House about it.

'What has one of them been doing to you now?'

'It's that Nancy Oglethorpe,' Hegarty said. It was one of those after-noons when his nerves were giving him trouble, and his head shook slightly as he spoke. 'You remember I told you about our little liaison?' Hegarty had a number of phrases for the sexual act. They included 'inti-mate connection' and 'horizontal Charleston.' 'Well, yesterday morning when I got in I went and left a gardenia that someone had given me the night before at that club Lydia and I go to on her desk. It was perfectly fresh. I'd kept it in water. And then, when I went back half an hour later, there was still no sign of her but the gardenia had been thrown in the waste-paper basket.'

There was something tragic about Hegarty as he said this. The thought of him crouched over the waste-paper basket, perhaps even placing the fragments of the gardenia in the palm of his hand, was painful to contemplate. Despite this setback he looked better than usual, Johnson thought. The pouches under his eyes were less dark than before. Though weighed down by his usual assortment of paraphernalia—two newspapers, a large buff envelope, a paperback book entitled *Aryan Destiny*—he seemed poised, intent, ready to spring.

'Never mind Miss Oglethorpe. How are you getting on with—what's his name—Rodney?'

'I'm going down there directly for a good long session,' Hegarty said. 'Which reminds me. Shillito asked me to give you this. He thought you ought to see it.'

Shillito was one of the section heads, at the same level of seniority as Davenport, but thought to be more au fait with the actual workings of the department.

Johnson put the buff envelope under his arm and got up from his chair. The rooks had finished off the sausage roll and were skidding over the icy grass. 'Is there anything I ought to know about it in advance?'

'It's all perfectly self-explanatory,' Hegarty said. He was not interested in the buff envelope. 'Well, wish me luck with Master Rodney. From what we saw of him when we brought him in, I'd say he looked stroppy but pliable.'

'My thoughts exactly.'

After he had gone, Johnson went back along the corridor to his own room, disposed of a box of training manuals that someone had left on the carpet outside it, and sat down behind his desk. There was a memorandum on it from Davenport about defective grammar in official documents and a surveillance report listing the names of several people who had attended a meeting of the Handmaidens of Albion two nights ago at an address in Ealing. The topmost name on the list was *Miss Alicia Frencham.*

Johnson shook his head. Miss Frencham, he knew, was sailing into dark waters. One day soon she would come home to her house in Powis Square, with its brown sherry in cut-glass decanters and her father sitting in his study over a copy of the *Naval Intelligence Review,* and find a policeman with a search warrant on the doorstep. That was what would happen to Miss Frencham.

He wondered how she would get on in Holloway, or wherever it was they sent them, and decided she would thrive. Upper-class girls usually liked the boarding-school atmosphere of a women's prison and appreciated the discipline. It was the rectors' daughters who were made miserable.

The buff envelope contained a carbon copy of a four-page typewritten report on the King's Party. There was no indication of who had written it, or who might previously have seen it. This anonymity appealed to Johnson. The thought that he was reading something newly minted, without obvious origins, fatherless, wholly detached from the systems of administrative life, was a solace. He had just finished the second read-through when there was a knock at the door and Hegarty stepped into the room. He was grinning broadly.

'How did you get on with Rodney?'

'Rodney?' Hegarty said, as if none of the people he had dealings with could possibly be called by that name. 'He seems harmless enough. In fact, there was a point where I felt positively sorry for him.'

'And when was that reached?'

'Apparently he's in a mess back home in Skelmersdale or wherever it is he comes from. Got some girl in trouble and the devil to pay. Of course, I was able to advise him about that.'

'I'm sure you were. What else did he have to say? It can't all have been about sexual irregularity in Lancashire.'

'No more it was. Well, he owned up to working for Kent straightaway.'

'He could hardly have denied it. We've got sworn statements from the people who owned that shop he worked in that Kent had called there.'

'Naturally, his line is that he simply ran errands. Kent would ask him to take a parcel to the House, or from the House to his flat, and he'd oblige.

As for what was in the parcel, it could have been last week's laundry for all Master Rodney cared.'

'I'm sure it could. But what about the other business? What about Burdett in Jermyn Street?'

'Actually we didn't get that far,' Hegarty said. 'Things were just getting interesting when I got called out by a message from Shillito. He wants to see the pair of us instanter.'

'What's it got to do with Shillito? I thought he was working on illegal aliens. All those nice Italian waiters who're supposed to be sabotaging the water supply on their evenings off and leaving tin tacks on the tram lines.'

'Change of climate,' Hegarty said. 'Shillito's our man now. No one's seen Davenport for a couple of days. In any event, he's off the case altogether.'

'What happened?'

'There was the most corking row. Apparently it went as far as the Home Secretary. But it was thought that Davenport's enthusiasm for the work before him was not all that it might have been.'

'Who told you that?'

'Shillito did. When he gave me that dossier, which I have reason to believe he drew up in his own fair hand.'

In the bleak glare of the electric light, Hegarty looked oddly animated, over-stimulated, wound up, like a music-hall comedian, summoned on stage by his quieter accomplice, who might suddenly stand on his head or start doing the splits. There was nothing particularly unusual in the piece of information he had just conveyed. Changes of climate happened all the time: complex games of musical chairs, sometimes involving as many as a dozen people, played at bewildering speed, so that the documents that authenticated them lagged some way in the rear, allowing for the perpetration of quite serious administrative gaffes.

'We'd better go and see him now,' Hegarty said. 'He can be very nasty when he isn't properly attended to. He hates Davenport like poison, you know. I think he was once overheard calling him a fifth columnist.'

Slowly, and thoroughly alert to the discussions that were going on in the offices that they passed—you could quite often pick up valuable information in this way—they set off along the corridor and up the steps that led to the third floor. Here someone had dropped a banana skin and a photograph of Veronica Lake. Hegarty stared at the photograph crossly. He was in the mood—a comparatively rare one—where women meant nothing to him, might even be considered a snare especially designed to prevent men carrying out their duty.

Shillito's office was on the left-hand side of the third floor. Passing Davenport's office en route, they noticed that it had been cleared of everything bar a couple of packing cases. Seeing this, Hegarty's look of quiet resolve grew even more fixed. 'You can't imagine how I loathed that fat slug,' he said.

They found Shillito in his room, reading a sheaf of telegrams that had just come in. It was impossible to look at Shillito without thinking of the manatees in the Regent's Park Zoo. He was a fattish, middle-aged man, already gone to seed, with a high, bulbous face and wide, blunt teeth, who could easily have been imagined browsing among the vegetable matter of some tropical ocean. But this appearance was deceptive. In fact, Shillito could be crosser than Davenport. Worse, in any argument that arose he had the advantage of being thoroughly conversant with the work that everyone did. Just now he seemed friendly.

'You may be wondering what has happened to Colonel Davenport,' he said. 'It's not something I can reasonably discuss. You can draw your own conclusions. But everything you were working on under him has top priority. Do I make myself clear?'

'Perfectly, sir,' Hegarty said, with no irony at all.

There were one or two files which they recognised as having belonged to Davenport open on Shillito's desk, much decorated with red ink. Shillito said: 'I must say from the outset that I'm not at all interested in the philosophy of all this. As far as I'm concerned, we're at war with a hostile power. Until I'm officially informed that we're not at war, then anyone operating independently of His Majesty's Government to bring that war to a close is a subversive and should be treated as such.'

'Even members of the House of Commons, sir?' Hegarty asked, with what for him was extreme politeness.

'Especially them. Although I'll allow there are problems in that department. As matters stand, we cannot detain Ramsay or that Bannister fellow. Don't ask me why, but we can't. On the other hand, we have a duty to accumulate as much evidence as we can in the event of a situation arising when it might be possible to detain them. Do you understand what I mean?'

'What situation would that be exactly, sir?'

'Well, I suppose there's no harm in spelling it out. As far as I can deduce from the things Ramsay says in the House and the reports that come back from meetings, he believes that Germany doesn't want to fight and has been pushed into a corner by the inflexibility of the Allied powers. If it suddenly turns out that Germany is serious about marching into France, then Ramsay's case disappears. We won't be fighting a war to defend the Jews. We'll be fighting a war to defend the Channel. Now, what have you got on this fellow you picked up in Maida Vale?'

'We know he's been running errands for Kent and Ramsay, sir. Sometimes between the House and Kent's flat. Sometimes to the Embassy. Anthea Carey was keeping him under surveillance. We know the errands involved Ramsay's membership book, and that it went to the Embassy every so often on grounds of diplomatic immunity. We believe it's there now.'

Shillito looked more than ever like some great cetacean intent on getting its lunch. He was once supposed to have played rugby for the London Irish, but no trace of this accomplishment survived. He gave a little shake of his hand at the file in front of him.

'It's not at the Embassy. If it were, we should have very good grounds for going in there and getting it, diplomatic immunity or no diplomatic immunity. To the best of my knowledge it's at Bannister's house in Sussex.'

'Couldn't we just go down and get it then, sir?'

'We should have to get a search warrant. And I very much doubt whether we could. In any case, I don't think it will be necessary. We've another iron in the fire. I know Miss Carey has already been doing sterling work on this project . . .'

'I should say she has,' Hegarty said warmly. Anthea was once supposed to have dislocated his little finger in an incident in a lift.

'Well, just lately Miss Carey has been working at *Duration*. Officially, she's been keeping an eye on that Rafferty fellow—you remember how interested B.3 were in him a couple of years ago when he attended that conference in Sofia? But now it turns out she's persuaded some friend of Bannister's daughter to go down there and retrieve it.'

'Will she be able to do that?'

'I don't see why not. If she's anything like Miss Carey she'll probably blow the place up with thermite. Now, going back to Ramsay, there's a rumour—only a rumour, mind—that he was in Dublin the other day. At any rate a man called Ismay was booked onto the Rosslare ferry last Friday. Ismay is his wife's Christian name, by the way. Also on the boat were a Mr Amery and a Dr Clavane—both names which, as I'm sure you'll remember, are not unknown to this department. We believe that they may have been meeting an attaché from the German Embassy there.'

'Isn't that an indictable offence, sir?'

'It would be if we could prove that it happened. Unfortunately, as soon as he reached Dublin, Mr Ismay went to ground. No one could find him at any of the hotels. The Embassy people went off on some wild-goose chase to Roscommon and made complete asses of themselves.'

'What about the others?'

'I sent a man to Cambridge to interview Clavane. He had the most impeccable bona fides. Spent the weekend with Dr Seamas O'Coughlan, who, as you may or may not know, is an expert on seventeenth-century Irish social history and the author of a standard work entitled *Cromwell and Hibernia*.'

'So what are we to do, sir?'

'What are we to do?' Shillito looked suddenly mournful, as if all the talk of the last few minutes had been dealt out simply for effect and beneath it lay nothing of any conceivable substance. 'We are to monitor the situation, and we shall continue to allow Ramsay to dig himself into a pit from which, with any luck, he will not be able to extricate himself. Bannister I have serious doubts about. As for Mr Kent and the important work he takes home from Grosvenor Square, I think we'll bide our time. But there would be no harm in rounding up a few of the smaller fry, just to show we mean business. Why not the League of St George people? Why not bring half a dozen of them in here and see what they know?'

There was an odd look on Shillito's face as he said this, as if the instructions about the League of St George were merely camouflage, and the really serious business of the conversation lay concealed beneath. Eventually he said, 'I don't mind saying there are some extraordinary rumours flying about at the moment. One report came in which said that in the event of the Germans invading, Ramsay would be appointed gauleiter of Scotland on the spot. There's talk of Bannister having letters smuggled in from Berlin, though we've never set eyes on one. And then we heard just the other day that a platoon at Catterick was refusing to serve, laid down its arms and confined itself to barracks. In the end it turned out it was a dispute over allowances, but the CO was so scared he put in a request for half a dozen armoured cars.'

'What about the King?' Johnson asked.

'The King? The King's on a tour of the northern counties, inspecting troops and visiting regional nursing centres. After that he's doing the same thing in Devon and Cornwall. Best place for him. If he hadn't opened his mouth like that, most of this wouldn't have happened. Which reminds me, what has that fellow Nichols been up to?'

'Very little, so far as we can tell, sir. No contact with the Palace. We did track him to a Turkish bath in Swallow Street the other night, but I'm reliably informed that the only offences he may have committed there were of a kind liable to outrage public decency. We've been looking at those articles of his in the *Chronicle* for code words, but the last one was all about his hardy perennials.'

'I suppose that's the difference between us and the Continentals,' Shillito offered. 'If they want a change of government policy, they get up and start shooting people in the streets. If we want one, it's a question of deciphering what some pansy writes in his newspaper column or working out whether Captain Ramsay went to Dublin on the Rosslare ferry. Makes you glad to be British, I suppose.'

There was a short silence, in which they all felt glad to be British.

'If you don't mind, sir,' Hegarty said, 'I think I ought to finish talking to the Maida Vale suspect.'

'You do that,' Shillito said. 'And tell him we can keep him for as long as we like under Regulation 18b. It's not strictly true, but I don't expect he has any legal training.'

They walked back along the corridor, Hegarty whistling as he went. He seemed in extraordinarily good spirits. When they reached the first-floor landing again, he gave a little mock salute with the fingers of his left hand and continued down into the basement. After he had disappeared, the sound of his feet echoed for a long time on the concrete steps.

When Johnson got back to his room he discovered that someone had left another large buff-coloured envelope on his chair. This turned out to harbour a page cut from a back number of the *Tatler*, showing a series of photographs of the crowd at the Eton–Harrow match. One of them was marked with a cross. Here Captain Ramsay and Davenport were staring bleakly at a woman with a hat like a modernist lamp-shade. A speech bubble had been inked in over Captain Ramsay's head, encircling the words ISN'T THAT HERR VON RIBBENTROP OVER THERE?

He scooped up the sheet of paper and flung it into the waste-paper bin. Best not to leave such things lying around. It was about half-past four and the chaos of the desk oppressed him more than ever. The uppermost file was labelled *White Knights of St Athelstan*. There were perhaps a dozen White Knights of St Athelstan. They met weekly in the upstairs room of a public house in Chiswick and complained of Soviet infiltration of the legal profession. Who cared about these arcane activities? On the other hand, such things might, if allowed to proceed unchecked, have some faint bearing on the political situation. It was hard to tell.

That reminded him of Shillito's order to 'bring in' half a dozen members of the League of St George. By rights, this sample would include Miss Frencham. Try as he might, he could not rid himself of a degree of guilt about Miss Frencham and her white, anguished face. In the end he took a picture postcard of Admiral Nelson that happened to be lying on the desk, wrote *Security investigation imminent. Suggest you leave London. All the best, C.* on it, and sealed it in an envelope addressed to the house in Powis Square.

About half an hour passed before Hegarty came back. His face had a guilty, exuberant look and his hands were trembling.

'Everything go well?'

'Certainly did.'

'Anything to alter your opinion?'

'Not so harmless after all,' Hegarty said. 'Halfway through I realised that no one had searched the beggar. So I did. And guess what turned up?' He unclenched the palm of his right hand, where a newspaper clipping hovered uncertainly, and bent his face over it as if it were a butterfly about to take wing.

That evening the newspapers said that new peace proposals had emerged, which the Government was invited urgently to consider.

CHAPTER 21

A Room with a View

'Where's Cynthia?' Peter Wildgoose wondered at about half-past eleven on Monday morning. 'Is it just my imagination, or haven't I seen her today?'

'I think she went somewhere for the weekend,' Anthea said guilelessly. 'I expect she got delayed.'

'It's not like her to neglect her duties,' said Peter Wildgoose, quite crossly for him.

'No, it isn't, is it?' Anthea said, even more guilelessly than before.

They were in the process of clearing out Desmond's office, and already regretting that such a Herculean endeavour had not been left to someone better qualified to undertake it, possibly even Desmond himself.

'Well, I do hope she turns up soon,' Peter Wildgoose said. He looked irritated and unhappy, as if the high standards he had previously demanded, and obtained, from the world had now been revealed as a desperate chimera. 'It would be awful to lose a member of one's staff two days running.'

'I think it was somewhere down in the West Country,' Anthea said. 'I expect the trains have failed again. Now, what had I better do with all these cards?'

There was something impressive about the room's chaos, as if a single person could not possibly have been responsible for it. Half of the books seemed to have no connection with the magazine's activities at all, and the number of dinner receipts amounted to seventeen. Peter Wildgoose looked at the stack of picture postcards, each with its fervent salutation, its fond valedictory wish and its hope of employment, and shook his head.

'They're Des's personal property. I can't have them destroyed. It wouldn't be fair. You'd better put them in an envelope and send them back to him.'

Outside in the main office Mr Woodmansee, a wafer biscuit clutched in his gnarled left hand, was staring in a terrier-like way at a file of invoices. There was no sign of Lucy.

'Peter,' Anthea said, 'never mind the postcards. What are you going to do about Des's editorial?'

'What do you mean, "What am I going to do about it?"'

'Well, you haven't done anything about not getting this month's number distributed, have you? The Norwich Press's vans will be out on the road by now, I expect.'

'No, I haven't, have I?' Peter Wildgoose said. He was inspecting the pages from a book he had taken from the pile on Desmond's window ledge called *Dawns in Wardour Street*. 'Do you know, I was thinking about this over the weekend, and in the end I decided that I had to let it stand even though I disagreed with it so much. After all, Des was editor of the magazine, so I suppose it was up to him what went into it, and I thought he ought to have the satisfaction of seeing it in print. If it is a satisfaction. Anything else would have been rather letting him down.'

'You know, Peter,' Anthea said, 'you really are awfully scrupulous. Just think of how many times Des has let you down.'

'Am I?' Peter Wildgoose said. He looked surprised, then smiled and dropped the copy of *Dawns in Wardour Street* into the waste-paper basket to mingle with Desmond's discarded cigar butts. 'I sometimes think I'm not nearly scrupulous enough. But thank you all the same.'

They took her upstairs and put her in a bedroom under the eaves of the house. It had once done service as a nursery, and there were pixies romping on the wallpaper and an evil-looking rocking horse in the corner. Mrs Bannister stood at the bottom of the staircase wearing her mad-terrier's stare, wholly disassociated from this act of violence. There was a cacophony of sound—wind rattling against the panes, Hermione's laboured breathing, feet skidding on polished wood, a key turning in the lock. After they had gone she beat at the door with her hands, but the footsteps in the corridor rattled away into silence and did not come back.

There was a chamber pot under the bed, and a water jug on the stand, but no electric light. Beyond the window grey fields sprinkled with sheep climbed into the middle distance. When she had stopped shaking she ransacked her suitcase—thankfully this had arrived in the room with her—ate the bar of chocolate she found there and stared out into the dim February light. The house had gone quiet; the music had stopped; there was only herself, like some castaway on a rock, cruelly exposed.

Presently the warmth generated in her by the struggle wore off and the room grew cold, so she stood by the window stamping her feet up and down and squeezing her arms around her chest. In this way several hours passed. Once or twice she hammered loudly on the door. It began to get dark, but nobody came.

Towards midnight she fell asleep on the blanketless bed. Still nobody had come. Whoever had set out the chamber pot had omitted to provide lavatory paper. In the small hours she thought she heard footsteps in the corridor. This filled her with an all-consuming terror, but the steps—if that was what they were—seemed to patter off in a different direction. The rocking horse's ivory teeth looming up through the shadow frightened her so much that she could not bear looking at them. They would tear her clothes off her while she slept and devour her whole when she woke.

Then in the early morning there was a scrabbling at the door and a tremendous tearing of metal in the lock, and she shrank back in horror, only to find that the black-clad figure which tumbled into the room was not Mr Bannister, bent on embarrassing her, but a parlourmaid with a vague, vacant-looking face bringing in her breakfast on a tray.

For quite a long time, waking up in the early mornings, with bitter white light seeping through the gaps in the bedroom curtains and the rocking horse's teeth poised to bite her, she was oppressed by the thought of something stealing away into the outer margins of consciousness, the vestiges of some memory in which the sights that met her after she woke—the light, the glint of a watercolour painting on the far wall, the bands of shadow beyond—played some part. Eventually she realised that the memory had nothing to do with her present situation but was of living in the East.

Once she had arrived at this conclusion, all the stanchions of this earlier life fell smartly into place: the flying fish in the bay at Colombo; the warm froth of the Indian Ocean; the *Rangoon Gazette* with its stories of leopard-hunts, rogue elephants, and governors' visitations. She was aware, deep down, that the East had not been like this at all—that it had largely consisted of heat and dirt, inedible food, and Mrs Kirkpatrick being tiresome, and the grass seeds from the maidan working their way up the insides of your stockings like little metal burrs—but there was something about the room, and her terror, that encouraged these imaginings and she found as she lay there, with the light getting brighter and somehow more ominous, that she could indulge herself in them for what seemed like hours at a time, and that this daydreaming—if that was what it was—was in some way more important to her than the material challenges that lay in wait beyond it.

The oddest thing about her life in the room, she quickly discovered, was that she had no yardstick to compare it against. It was like being ill, except that the symptoms of illness had been replaced with a permanent sense of anxiety, while the bell on the bedside table was quite likely to go unanswered or bring someone she did not at all want to see.

The routines of life at Ashburton Grange—or her life at Ashburton Grange—were military in their precision. At 8 A.M. the plain but kindly parlourmaid, whose name was Gladys, brought her a cup of tea and carried off her chamber pot. At 8:30 the glamorous but sullen parlourmaid, whose name was Eunice, brought her breakfast on a tray and returned the pot. Each of these operations was constrained by the door having to be unlocked to admit them, shut while they were transacting the business of the visit, unlocked again to let them out and shut again when they were on the other side. The breakfast was always the same: two slices of toast and some ghastly patent cereal that Mrs Bannister took for her digestion.

After them came Mr Bannister.

'I want to know one thing,' he said on the first of these occasions, 'and that is who you are working for.'

'I really don't know that I'm working for anyone,' Cynthia said.

She had decided that she was not going to be frightened of Mr Bannister.

'Was it that woman Carey who put you up to this?'

'I suppose you think I'm too stupid to understand,' Cynthia said. 'Well, you're wrong. I understand it all. And you can't keep me here. The people in the office know where I am. They'll be wondering why I haven't come back.'

'I have telephoned your office and told them you are suffering from a bad attack of influenza.'

'They won't believe you.'

'On the contrary. They wished you a speedy recovery. Tomorrow I shall telephone again and say that it has developed into a very bad attack. Now, where did you meet my friend Captain Ramsay?' Mr Bannister went pompously on. 'What do you know about him?'

'You know very well I met Captain Ramsay at this house,' Cynthia told him. Her voice was cracking into hysteria. 'You must have a bad memory, as well as being quite mad. If you don't let me out of this room, I shall start screaming.'

But there was no point in screaming, for nobody came and nothing was done, and Mr Bannister merely stood there like the demon king on the edge of the underworld, with a pained but slightly malevolent expression on his face, before turning on his heel and stalking away. She tried to run past him and make her escape, but when she did so he merely reached out a fat hand, twisted her arm in a V, and threw her back into her chair, and she forgot her resolve and was genuinely frightened of Mr Bannister.

And there were other visitors, in some ways worse than Mr Bannister. On the second afternoon the key, turning in the lock, brought Hermione, very red in the face and dressed in a pair of blue factory-worker's overalls.

'I just wanted to say that I never liked you,' Hermione said. 'Never at all. You always laughed at me. I could have married Tyler Kent if it hadn't been for you.'

'Hermione,' Cynthia said. There were tears running down her face. 'You know that isn't true. You know it isn't.'

'Yes, it is,' Hermione said, with unexpected venom. 'I hate you, and I hope you starve to death.'

And this was worse than Mr Bannister asking her who she was working for, or the look on the glamorous but sullen parlourmaid's face as she brought back the empty chamber pot.

'I never realised anyone could be so cruel,' she said to Mr Bannister on the afternoon of the third day. 'You can't possibly keep me here any longer. People will be wondering where I am. And then what will you do?'

It was only after she had spoken the words that she wondered just exactly who these people were.

'Here's something,' Hegarty said to Johnson. They were standing in the kitchen at the end of the B.3 corridor watching a pair of charladies manoeuvre a tea urn into place. 'That girl Anthea Carey sent down to Bannister's house in Sussex hasn't come back.'

'How do you know?'

'Anthea rang up Shillito and told him. Apparently someone telephoned to say she'd gone down with the 'flu, but Anthea says she doesn't believe it.'

Miss, or Mrs, Oglethorpe came walking down the corridor towards them coiling up the thick hair on the top of her head as she went, but they ignored her. 'What does Shillito say?'

'He says we have to monitor the situation. He says Bannister is a distinguished public servant and you can't just go down with a search warrant and demand to see one of his guests.'

'Does anyone know what Bannister's up to?'

'This is where it gets even more interesting. Apparently Bannister and Ramsay are booked to see the Foreign Secretary tomorrow morning. There's talk of an all-party delegation going with them.'

'The PM won't like that.'

'The PM won't like all sorts of things,' Hegarty said, 'if what I hear from the War Office is true.'

On the morning of the fourth day she tried Gladys, the plain but kindly parlourmaid, with a little conversation.

'It must be difficult, working all the way out here,' she said. 'Being so far from town, I mean.'

'Yes, miss.'

'Don't you find yourself wishing you had more people around you? I know I would.'

'There are always places to find company, miss.'

'If I gave you a letter, would you post it for me in the village?'

'No, miss.'

'Not even for five pounds?' This was the sum Cynthia had in her purse.

'No, miss, I can't.'

Mr Bannister's questions became more insistent. He gave the impression that during the first few days of her sojourn in the room he had merely been polite, but that now he wanted to get down to business. At the same time there was something apologetic about him.

'I daresay you're wondering why we continue to keep you here,' he said.

There was no answer to this. To say that she was being kept at Ashburton Grange because she knew that Mr Bannister was in league with Herr von Ribbentrop would not have helped either of them.

Mr Bannister continued, more courteously than on previous occasions: 'But it is imperative that I know exactly what brought you here. And the people who sent you. Unless you tell me that, I cannot possibly let you go. There are negotiations going on that a single unguarded word might upset. Do you understand what I am saying?'

'Up to a point,' she said, thinking that it was best to admit to something.

'It is absolutely vital to the well-being of our country that the plans my friends and I are engaged upon should succeed. You must understand that. Surely you must want them to succeed as well?'

'I want a car to take me to Arundel Station,' she said. 'That is what I want.'

'Had I allowed you to walk out of the house with the things you stole from my study, who would you have given them to?'

'I really can't answer that,' she said.

'Then we are going to keep you here until you do.'

'My friends will wonder where I am.'

'Your friends have been told that your influenza was much more serious than was first thought and that you are convalescing.'

At least Anthea won't believe that, she thought.

'Now, let me try again,' Mr Bannister said, still sounding uncannily like the man who had once tried to teach her to say 'Is your mistress in the garden?' in Tamil, but with a dreadful overlaid malignity. 'When you got back to London with the book and the letter, who would you have given them to?'

'It turns out Cynthia's gone down with the 'flu,' Anthea told Peter Wildgoose. 'Quite a bad case. Anyway, she'll have to stay where she is for a while.'

'Poor Cynthia,' Peter Wildgoose said. He was sitting at his desk signing cheques from a book held reverently before him by Mr Woodmansee. 'Send her my good wishes, won't you, and tell her I hope she doesn't get too bored.'

'Certainly,' Anthea said. 'And you really ought to have a look at this morning's *Telegraph*.'

'Not a paper I generally consult,' Peter Wildgoose said. 'What does it say?'

'They're not at all pleased about Des's editorial. There's a lot of stuff about the sanctimonious appeasement of the pacifist conscience.'

'That's what comes of being scrupulous,' Peter Wildgoose said.

Sometimes Mr Bannister was lofty. Sometimes he was ingratiating, at others calculating. There were times when he had clearly been consulting with other people, and the questions he asked did not seem to come naturally to him. There were occasional moments when he seemed uncertain, as if he might suddenly be considering the full implications of the task he had set himself, only for the uncertainty to be replaced by a steely resolve. On balance, these were the worst times.

'It is very foolish of you to give us all this trouble.'

There was no point in answering this and she hung her head to one side, out of range of his glare.

'I suppose you think,' Mr Bannister said, 'that family association will win out. Because it nearly always does. Because we have known each other so long. Because . . .' For a moment Henry's ghost hung between them, vivid and menacing, looming up from the Ceylonese verdure. 'Well, let me tell you that nothing could be further from the case.'

She told herself that she would leap out of the chair and make for the door again, kicking over the rocking horse into Mr Bannister's path, but by the time she had summoned up the courage the door was shut once more and Mr Bannister vanished on the other side of it.

Not having got anywhere with Gladys, the plain but kindly parlour-maid, she decided to try Eunice, the glamorous but sullen one.

'Eunice, I'd be obliged if you'd do something for me,' she said one morning when the breakfast tray had just been brought in and Mrs Bannister's patent cereal, which you made with milk, sat steaming nastily in its bowl.

'What's that then, miss?'

'I want you to go and telephone to the local police station and say that I am being held here against my will.'

'I can't do that, miss.'

'Is there anything I could say to persuade you to do it?'

'No, miss.'

After that she gave Eunice up as a bad job.

In the absence of very much human contact, Cynthia got by on sound.

The maids' shoes on the stairs: a succession of precise, purposeful steps, each following on from the other like some slow-motion tap dance.

Mrs Bannister's voice giving instructions in the hallway: a kind of high-pitched babble, verging on hysteria, like a children's party getting out of hand.

A radio playing dance music in the hall.

The paralysing detonation of Mr Bannister's attempts to shut the front door.

A key turning in the lock.

A monotonous drumming sound, sometimes seeming to come from far away, sometimes uncomfortably close at hand, that turned out to be the beating of her heart.

Something Mr Bannister said once, in the course of his interrogations, stuck in her head: 'It's not enough to say that England will muddle through. England has always muddled through. That has been the problem. What we are fighting for is civilisation. Christian civilisation. The chance to manage our destiny. When have we been allowed to do that, I should like to know? When have we been allowed to do that?'

There were times when her spirits lifted. One of Mr Kirkpatrick's favourite sayings—born of long experience of the East—was that anyone engaged on a tediously repetitive task would eventually neglect their duty. There would be a moment, Cynthia knew, when someone responsible for her welfare would make a mistake.

It came quite unexpectedly one morning when she found that the door of her room had been left an inch or two open. Curiously, this discovery impressed itself upon her first as a lapse in routine rather than a chance to escape. Then she remembered that Gladys, who for some reason had brought her breakfast that morning rather than Eunice, had been summoned down the corridor by a sergeant-major's shout of Mrs Bannister's and for some other reason failed to return. It was about a quarter to nine and the house seemed to have fallen silent, so she went stealthily along the corridor and down the staircase, picking her way between some cardboard boxes that had been left here and there along its lower flight.

There was nobody about, and the pale February sunshine was streaming over the polished oak floor of the hallway. She discovered that this temporary freedom had badly disconcerted her, and that the various possibilities that now offered themselves were a confusion rather than a spur to action. The front door turned out to be locked and there was no sign of the key. Nothing doing there.

She swept off into the back parts of the house and eventually found herself in the kitchen, which was empty apart from a tortoiseshell cat licking up a puddle of milk that had been spilled on one of the surfaces, but the back door was shut too. There were butcher's weights lying on the table, great thick ones weighing two or three pounds, and she resolved to take them into the drawing room and hurl them through the window.

She had just got herself into the room and was levering up the first weight to the level of her shoulder like a shot-putter when Gladys, very breathless and with her maid's cap fallen over her forehead, appeared in the doorway behind her.

'You mustn't do that, miss. You mustn't. The master's out in the garage and he'll hear as soon as the glass goes.'

In its way, this counted as an overture of friendship.

'You go back to your room, miss,' Gladys said. There was an air of authority about her, as if Cynthia was a boisterous younger sister she had decided to face down.

'It's all your fault I'm here, Gladys,' Cynthia said. 'It was you that left the door open for me to get out. I'll tell Mr Bannister.'

'There's no need for you to do that, miss,' Gladys said gravely. 'Least-ways, if you don't I won't say anything about you coming downstairs.'

The weight was still in Cynthia's hand. In the split second that Gladys—moving surprisingly quickly—came towards her she hurled it at the drawing-room window, but it was too heavy for her and went glancing against the frame, bounced away and shattered one of the side panels. The glass burst out and Cynthia screamed, but it was no good, for by the time she reached down to pick up the next weight, Gladys had her by the wrist and the fight went out of her. She tried to wrench her arm away, but it was no good.

'I told you you shouldn't do that, miss,' Gladys said, but there was no malice in her voice.

They took the weights back into the kitchen and the even tenor of the day resumed.

Standing next to the bedroom's solitary bookshelf one afternoon after Mr Bannister had left the room, she discovered half a dozen children's books with Hermione's signature scrawled in the front. The first of these was called *The Snack-boat Sails at Noon*. The book had clearly been dropped in the bath at some point, but that did not lessen its allure. It was about a family of children who lived in a house on the Norfolk Broads, whose mother was dead and whose father, who wrote detective novels, struggled to find the money for their school fees.

The children, though in reduced circumstances, set out for the day in roll-necked pullovers and were prostrated with shame if they broke a plate or threw a tennis ball through the conservatory window. They were conscientious children, who ran errands for their elderly neighbours and went punctiliously to church on Sunday mornings, but at the same time were not above playing practical jokes on such local dignitaries who made themselves objectionable to them or simply got on their nerves.

The most resourceful of them was the eldest, a girl named Myfanwy, and it was she, one hot summer's afternoon, who came up with the idea of the snack-boat: a reconditioned motor launch found rotting in a local boatyard but made seaworthy by a kindly uncle, which, stocked with homemade cakes, punnets of blackcurrants, and flagons of lemonade, plied its trade among the pleasure-cruisers of the vicinity. The book ended with the death of a half-forgotten great-aunt and the bequeathing of a small fortune, the sale of one of their father's detective novels to a film company, and the purchase by Myfanwy of an evening dress in which piece of finery she was able to attend the local hunt ball.

It was a queer sensation, reading this book, curled up in a chair behind the locked door of the Ashburton Grange bedroom, with the sound of the maids' heels clattering on the stair, the chamber pot stinking under the bed, and the wind beating against the window. In her own childhood she had read dozens of similar books, and she was shrewd enough to realise that the childhoods set out here were not so much idyllic as purely mythological. Friendship; solidarity; pleasure; purpose. All the things of which a childhood ought ideally to consist were there.

And yet it struck her that if no one had ever had a childhood like Myfanwy's, then there must be people who had had a childhood that approximated to it, who had been benignly neglected, made the most of their opportunities, and emerged, their personalities all a-glimmer, into the late-adolescent light. Or perhaps such books were merely snares for the unwary, designed to fill their readers' heads with false hopes and unreal expectations. Mrs Kirkpatrick had been very severe on books like *The Snack-boat Sails at Noon*, which she said gave children a highly misleading view of the world.

All this begged the question: how did you stop children forming a misleading view of the world? And, given what was likely to happen to them afterwards, wasn't a misleading view of the world a rather desirable thing to have?

When she had finished reading *The Snack-boat Sails at Noon*, she hid it in a nest of old stockings at the bottom of her suitcase. This, it turned out, was the thing she had really wanted to steal from Ashburton Grange.

She was lying on her bed early one afternoon when the key turned so rapidly in the lock that she barely had time to get up, and of all people Tyler Kent came into the room. He was as sprucely dressed as ever, and if not exactly jaunty then not particularly put out by the situation in which he found himself.

'I was just here to see Bannister,' he said, 'so I thought I'd better come and look you up.'

'Tyler, you've got to get me out of here.'

'You know I can't do that,' Tyler Kent said. He had not turned the key in the lock. He stood there holding it in his hand, which gave a kind of dreadful symbolism to these exchanges.

'Yes, you can, Tyler. You have to.'

'I can't,' Tyler Kent said again. 'Not with the way things are at the moment. You don't understand. It would upset everything.'

'How could it? How could taking me to Arundel and putting me on the train to London possibly upset anything? How could it?'

'I suppose Anthea Carey got you to do this, didn't she?' Tyler Kent said. 'I very soon figured that out. But then she's quite a girl. Enough to make you wish she was on our side. Do you know she used to be Ramsay's secretary? She did such a good job of it that it took him three months to work out that she was passing copies of his letters to Jermyn Street, where her friend Mr Burdett could read them. Social life: that's the trouble with England. Just because somebody's mother was presented at Court with somebody else's mother, they couldn't possibly be a security risk. If there's one thing we have to do, it's to keep you away from Anthea until everything's signed and sealed.'

'What is? What's being signed and sealed?'

It occurred to her that Tyler Kent's defining flaw was vanity, that the impulse that had led him to leave presidential telegrams lying around his flat was sheer vaingloriousness. As it was he reminded her of Johnnie Town Mouse. 'I shouldn't be telling you this,' Tyler Kent said, but sounding as if he very much wanted to tell her. 'But there are people in Dublin right now working on a set of peace proposals. Pretty soon they'll be on Halifax's desk. If he doesn't accept them, I daresay there'll be all kinds of trouble.'

'What kind of trouble?'

'Trouble from people who don't want war. Who think it's feudal.'

'*Feudal?*' she said, getting a sudden vision of knights in chain mail stalking the Ashburton Grange turrets, and Mr Bannister in a crusader's surtout attended by a couple of pageboys. 'How could it possibly be that?'

'Feudal,' he said again, quite furious at having been caught out in this elementary English usage, and she realised that this was how an American pronounced 'futile.'

'What kind of peace proposals?'

'Oh, I daresay something about protecting the rights of German minorities in Czechoslovakia and Poland while respecting the interests of indigenous peoples. I guess there might be something about the colonial territories. Not sure about that.'

'Tyler,' she said, 'there was a letter in the same drawer as the book from von Ribbentrop. It didn't say anything about peace proposals. It was more about what might happen to Mr Bannister after the Germans invaded.'

'That's a good joke,' said Tyler Kent, not quite confidently enough. 'I'm sure your friend Miss Carey would just love to hear it.'

Suddenly she found that she did not care about the colonial territories and what might happen to them, or Mr Bannister and what von Ribbentrop might do for him, or Captain Ramsay and his futile manoeuvrings. She wanted only to be back in the flat in Belgrave Square with Lucy to talk to and the nuns coming and going beneath them, or in Bloomsbury having Peter Wildgoose thank her for making him a cup of tea. The bombs could fall on Ashburton Grange, on Hermione and Tyler Kent and anyone else who happened to be passing, and she would not raise a hand to stop them.

It was about four o'clock and already threatening dusk. Tyler Kent's face loomed menacingly through the half-light. He was still getting over the misunderstanding about 'feudal.'

'Nobody's going to hurt you,' he said. 'We just need to know what you know. And all the things you've told Anthea Carey. It's the only way we can cover ourselves. As for anyone taking an interest in where you are, why, you're staying with old friends of your family while you recover from a bad attack of 'flu. As soon as the war's over, no one will care about presidential telegrams and membership books or even letters from von Ribbentrop, and Bannister will be delighted to let you go. There might be a little coolness next time you see him in London and quite how he'll explain things to your parents I don't know. That's something for Bannister.

'My line,' Tyler Kent said, in what was really quite a friendly way and looking so like Johnnie Town Mouse that it was as if he had a tail slung over his arm, 'would be the greater good needing a few personal sacrifices. That usually goes down well in dear old England. Not to mention,' he went on, suddenly sounding a great deal less friendly, 'one or two fundamentally misguided people being taught the error of their ways.'

The odd thing about Tyler Kent's visit to Ashburton Grange was that, for the first time, she was allowed out of her room to eat dinner with the Bannisters. Her first thought, when this idea was suggested to her, was that nothing short of main force could carry her anywhere near the Bannisters' dining room, but in the end curiosity got the better of her and she put on the dress she had worn on her first night, rapped half a dozen times on the locked door, and was eventually escorted downstairs by the glamorous yet sullen parlourmaid.

Even odder than being allowed to eat dinner with the Bannisters was the atmosphere that she found in the dining room, which was one of studious politeness and a determination to ignore the unpleasantnesses of the past few days. Mr Bannister hacked up a couple of capons with such bogus joviality that he might have been wearing a paper hat, Tyler Kent—very spruce again in a dinner jacket and a made-up tie—offered what were presumably Logan-derived remarks about the claret, and she could have screamed at the artificiality of it, the sense of unseen horrors gliding away into the darkness beyond the window.

Such entertainment as there was came from Hermione. Halfway through the capons, she said, 'Do you know, this afternoon I was listening to that new radio station?'

Mr Bannister looked at her warily. 'Which radio station was that?'

'The one Captain Ramsay mentioned in the House the other day. The New British Broadcasting Service, I think it must be called. When he asked the Minister if he would confer with the BBC to demolish its arguments objectively rather than just calling them German propaganda.'

'Hermione,' Mr Bannister said weakly.

'It was very good on the way that the Jewish financiers and the continental Freemasons are combining to enforce a credit monopoly.'

'*Hermione*,' Mr Bannister said, a little more loudly, 'will you kindly be silent?'

A minute or two into the dessert, without warning, during a discussion of the spring fishing prospects, Hermione threw her spoon and fork on the floor and ran out of the room.

'Did you ever take Hermione to that fellow in Harley Street?' Tyler Kent asked.

'Yes, I did,' Mr Bannister said, giving an agitated little snap of his hand, like a trap springing shut.

'And what did he say?'

'He said she was becoming very nervous and excitable.'

'Yes,' Tyler Kent said, 'I can see that.' He gave a little anxious grin, as if he were not quite certain of Mr Bannister or the company he was keeping, shot his cuffs forward over his wrists, glanced at Cynthia as if to say that he was still master of the situation, that the Bannisters and Hermione were, after all, merely pawns in the devious game of chess he had laid out before him, and went on with his dessert.

'Ramsay was wrong to mention that radio station in the House,' Mr Bannister said. 'Very wrong. He made it sound like an advertisement.'

'I thought everything Ramsay said in the House was an advertisement,' Tyler Kent said, not quite as suavely as before.

After that they went back to talking about the fishing prospects.

There was a brief moment as they sat taking their coffee in the drawing-room, in a kind of ethereal haze created by the Lalique lamps, when Cynthia thought that some kind of sanity had been restored to the situation, that when he got up to go Tyler Kent would be allowed to help her on with her coat, fetch her suitcase and escort her from the premises, while Mr Bannister offered his apologies for the inconvenience to which she had been put. Despite all the evidence to the contrary this feeling grew so strong in her that when, at half-past ten, Tyler Kent sprang to his feet and began thanking Mr and Mrs Bannister for the pleasant evening he had spent, she went and stood next to him as if to sustain the illusion that they were a hospitably entertained couple taking their leave.

'It was good to see you, Cynthia,' Tyler Kent said, buttoning on his gloves in the hallway. The heads of stuffed animals loomed above him in the flaring light. 'But you really have to be more helpful.'

For a second or two she wondered about making a scene, dashing off in the direction of the door and seeing if anyone would stop her, while telling Tyler Kent in a few well-chosen words what she thought of him. But a glance around the hallway told her that there was nothing that could be done, no object that could be usefully smashed, no insult that would have the faintest chance of hitting home, that Mr Bannister, if it came to that, would stop at absolutely nothing. A moment or two later she heard the sound of Tyler Kent's car skidding off across the gravel. After that the plain but kindly parlourmaid led her up to bed.

The routines persisted. Mr Bannister took to coming into her room just after breakfast. Sometimes he would talk nostalgically about his past dealings with her parents, the implication being that they would be thoroughly ashamed of her disloyalty if the facts were put before them. At other times he stood by the window and briskly cross-examined her.

'Did you ever meet any of Miss Carey's colleagues?'

'I met a man called Burdett. Norman Burdett.'

'And what did you say to him?'

'I didn't say anything to him. It was while we were having a drink at the Ritz.'

'I suppose that once you had walked away with the book, you were going to take it to Burdett.'

There were other occasions—faintly bewildering as they tended to follow on from the first and second kind—in which Mr Bannister abandoned nostalgia or briskness and began to lecture her in an almost fatherly manner about the complexities of the political situation.

'I suppose somebody has been filling your head with rubbish. "Democracy in peril" and that sort of thing. Isn't that right? But one has to try to see the situation from the German position. I daresay they shouldn't have gone into Czechoslovakia, but what has it got to do with us? Every country in Europe is crawling with minorities who think their interests are being neglected. If you asked an international commission to investigate the break-up of the Austro-Hungarian Empire they'd spend five years working out what the problems were, and another ten coming up with recommendations to solve them. By which time the problems would have moved on and become even less manageable. But it's no business of ours. We can't go around behaving as the Policeman of Europe. Those days are gone. Bad enough trying to manage the Empire. And that's another thing that any kind of prolonged European war is going to throw into jeopardy. In any case, no European war these days can be won without the Americans, and this time even the Americans aren't interested. You only have to talk to Kennedy to appreciate that. They don't forget what they went through in 1918.'

It occurred to Cynthia that when he pronounced these remarks, Mr Bannister was not really speaking to her but to some unseen audience high above his head, and that there was uneasiness in his voice which suggested that this invisible jury might have its doubts.

'Now, take Hitler. I'm not saying I like him. I think you'd have to be a German, or even a particular kind of German, to do that. But there's no doubting the man's ability. There are plenty of people who say we ought to have someone like him here. I wouldn't go as far as that. Demagoguery isn't part of the English tradition. If the Household Brigade started goose-stepping when it came round Hyde Park Corner, people would laugh. On the other hand . . .'

Cynthia had heard this kind of thing before, from one or two of the pink-faced subalterns who had taken her here and there in the pre-Henry days, and was not much impressed by it. Curiously, these public lectures—if that was what they were—coincided with a general air of slightly fraught activity at Ashburton Grange. Telephones rang at odd hours of the day. News bulletins crackled from the radio. There were times when Mr Bannister disappeared, or at any rate did not come to see her, for as much as forty-eight hours, other times when he stood nervously in the doorway as if he half-expected to be dragged off before he could impart whatever it was he had come to say.

Meanwhile, there was the plain but kindly parlourmaid, to cultivate. If not positively forthcoming, Gladys was at any rate prepared to answer questions, provided they were suitably innocuous.

'Do you know where Mr Bannister is today, Gladys?'

'I can't say I do, miss.'

'Has he gone to London, do you think?'

'Mr Bannister doesn't tell me what he does most of the time, miss, and I don't tell him what I do.'

All this was what Mrs Kirkpatrick, a martyr to irritations she was quite capable of fostering herself, would have called 'provoking.' But Cynthia had other lines of attack.

'How far is it to the village, Gladys? About three miles?'

'Two miles and a half I should say, miss.'

'Within walking distance, then?'

'I usually bicycles it, miss, unless I have Thomas to take me.'

Thomas, excluded from military service on account of his flat feet, was the under-gardener. Gladys's engagement to him was the great business of her life. But none of this was any help to Cynthia. After a bit she conceived another stratagem.

'What do you think of these shoes, Gladys? Are they ruined beyond repair? They were rather good when I got them.'

Gladys turned out to be interested in shoes. She fitted a hand inside the more battered of the two and held it up to her face.

'I don't think it's as bad as all that, miss. Look, the heels aren't hardly damaged at all. And you could get rid of the scuff-marks if you was to put something on it.'

The upshot of this was a smuggled pot of blacking. Some of this Cynthia rubbed carefully into the cracks of the court shoes, but the majority she spread, using her fingers as a pen, onto a rectangle of torn-up undersheet to form the words HELP ME, and hung in the window.

The girls in the boarding school novels Cynthia had read as a girl—Dimpsy and Maeve and Peggy—had spent much of their time escaping from things. No detention class was big enough to hold them. They were capable of abseiling out of upstairs windows on a rope of knotted sheets, of stopping nature rambles in their tracks with a feint into the bushes. But Dimpsy and Maeve and Peggy had not had Mr Bannister to deal with. He burst into the room just at the moment when she was taking down the banner, tore it out of her hand and ripped it in half.

'If you do this again,' he said, 'I'll put you in the cellar. You won't find any windows there.'

'I'll never forgive you for this,' she shouted at him. 'I don't care why you're doing it, but I shall never forgive you. And neither will Mummy and Daddy.'

'Believe me, Cynthia,' Mr Bannister said, 'that is the least of my worries. The very least.' He was looking extraordinarily red-faced and savage—like Henry, once, when she had seen him playing cricket.

'You're a traitor,' Cynthia said, 'that's what you are. A lousy traitor. And I hope they put you in Holloway with all the other ones.'

After that she screamed for quite a long time at the locked door, until she remembered that there was no point in screaming, and eventually subsided.

'You won't be seeing me tomorrow, miss,' said Gladys, who had been quietly sympathetic about the banner. 'Only I've got the day off to visit my aunt in Islington.'

'Gladys,' Cynthia said. 'If you're going to London, would you do something for me?'

'What's that, miss?' Gladys wondered nervously. She was very pale-faced and clearly not happy about the world she found herself in.

'Could you take a message to a friend of mine? She's called Anthea. She works in one of the Bloomsbury squares. It can't be all that far from where you're going to see your aunt.'

'I can't do that, miss,' Gladys whined. 'You know I can't.'

Outside the window there was a weak sun shining, and a faint vestige of spring. Mrs Kirkpatrick had always advocated a firm hand with the servant class.

'Gladys,' Cynthia said, hearing her voice crack as she spoke. 'If you do this for me I'll give you anything you want. Anything. I'll give you fifty pounds. A hundred pounds, even. I'll pay for your wedding. I'll buy you a dress from Hartnell. Just tell me what it is and I'll do it. Truly I will.'

There was an odd look on Gladys's face that Cynthia had never seen before: one of shrewd calculation. Catching her breath in gulps, clearly marvelling at her own effrontery, she said:

'I'll have your clothes, miss.'

'Which clothes? What do you mean?'

'Not all of them. I'll leave enough to keep you decent. And we can borrow some of Miss Hermione's. But I want the dress you had dinner in when you was here the first day, and that jumper you wore when you went out for a walk with the mistress in the afternoon. And two pairs of stockings. Then I might deliver a message to your friend in the Bloomsbury square, whatever her name is.'

While Cynthia wrote the note to Anthea and sealed it up in a half-torn envelope she found at the bottom of her suitcase, Gladys held the dress against her torso and silently appraised it.

'I'll look nice in this,' she said, taking the envelope and putting it in her pocket. 'Thomas, now, he'd like to see me in this.'

'Yes,' Cynthia said. She saw that her hand was shaking. 'I'm sure he would.'

Peter Wildgoose and Anthea were standing in what had been Desmond's office—emptier now, but still with a strew of unopened letters lying across the desk and little clumps of cigar butts disfiguring the carpet.

'And there's another thing about that wretched editorial of Des's,' Peter Wildgoose said. He had a book under his arm called *Divagations*. 'All the readers seem to think it's a kind of rallying call. Every contribution I've had in the past fortnight has shown pacifist tendencies. Even the poems.'

'Anth,' Lucy said, appearing suddenly in the doorway. 'There's a woman here wants to speak to you.'

'Not that girl from the advertising agent's?' Anthea said sharply. She was wearing what looked like workmen's overalls with splashes of paint over them and had had her hair cut even shorter than usual.

'I don't think so,' Lucy said. 'She looked more like a char-woman come for a job.'

'Well, you'd better ask her in,' Peter Wildgoose said courteously. 'She could start by clearing up Des's cigar-ends.'

CHAPTER 22

From a View to a Death

In Chester Square Peter Wildgoose sat writing letters. In the corner of the room a radio announcer was efficiently reciting the names of towns in north-eastern France, and the irrelevance of the task he was embarked on grew stronger by the moment. But he had decided to write letters this morning, and write them he would.

Dear Des, he began, still half-listening to the announcer's recitation ('Sedan . . . Dinant . . . Chanton-sur-Marne'),

> Thank you for yours, which in spite of everything amused me very much. I was wondering just the other day quite how long we had known each other, and decided that it must be all of twenty-five years. If you had half as good a recollection of all that has passed between us in that time as I do—and perhaps you have, and I am simply underestimating your powers of recall—you would realise that I can't possibly go back on what was said.

Don't you find these days that everyone always assumes that a quick handshake solves all and that any amount of moral evasion can be swept under the carpet if the people doing the sweeping believe that solidarity has the edge over whatever happens to be at stake? I certainly do.

But one has—I'm sure you will agree with me when you come to think about it—to be vigilant about these things. We live in a world of betrayals, and somehow the ones practised by people who know each other and don't have the excuse of international *realpolitik* to console themselves with are always the worst, don't you think?

Anyway, please excuse this lecture. I can't possibly throw the doors of *Duration* open to you again as if nothing had happened, and you know I can't. In any case, I gather you have another quarry in view . . .

Peter Wildgoose wondered whether this was too censorious, or too sarcastic, or even too subtle, and decided that, on the contrary, it was none of these things, and that Desmond deserved it, would understand it and perhaps even benefit from it. The announcer had got on to a statement that General Gamelin was supposed to be making on French radio, and there was nothing more to be done.

He sealed the letter up in its envelope and began on another one—more formal and much less ironic—to a friend in the Ministry of Supply.

She woke up one morning with a curious conviction that something had changed. At first it was difficult to establish where the roots of this transformation lay. The room was the same as ever. The rocking horse's ivory teeth were bared in contempt. There was a mouse scuttling across the carpet towards a hole in the wainscoting, but she was used to the mice.

After a second or two she realised that the change was to do with the house itself, that the radio downstairs was playing at what seemed a massively amplified volume and that there seemed to be footsteps running in all directions. Eventually one of the pairs of footsteps could be heard approaching along the corridor, the key creaked in the lock and Gladys, her face distended with emotion, more or less fell into the room.

'What on earth is the matter, Gladys?'

'It's the Germans, miss.'

So that was it. 'What have the Germans done?'

'They've come round the end of the Maginot Line, miss.'

'What? Invaded France?'

'That's what it said, miss.'

Cynthia found that she was interested in this information only insofar as it concerned her own immediate prospects.

'Do you know where Mr Bannister is, Gladys?'

'No, miss, I haven't seen him. It was the mistress that told me just now, after she switched on the radio.'

Somewhere in the depths of the house the telephone bell was ringing. There were more footsteps, at first above her head, then further away. A feeling of intense exhilaration at the thought of Mr Bannister, Captain Ramsay, and Tyler Kent being proved wrong was swiftly anaesthetised by deep unease.

She had to get away from this. If the Germans really were going to invade, Mr Bannister had even more reason for keeping her prisoner. Would Gladys stop her? She had obligations to Gladys, debts to be repaid.

Meanwhile, Gladys was calming down. The colour was returning to her face. With it came an awareness of her responsibilities.

'I'm sorry to rush in like that, miss. But I thought you'd want to know.'

'It's very kind of you, Gladys. Of course I should want to know.'

'I daresay Eunice will be along soon with your breakfast.'

There was something very heartening about this. Continents might be in flame and Stukas descending on the Ardennes, but Eunice would still be along with her breakfast. The light was falling through the curtains in yellowish daggers.

When Gladys had gone, she got out of bed and put on her clothes. The news had had a galvanising effect. Suddenly there was purpose in dressing herself in Hermione's cast-off jodhpurs and a jumper that smelled strongly of horse-liniment. As she got dressed she made plans: sharp, urgent plans. The contents of the room—the chair, the bedside table, the half-full water jug on its china plate—were her allies, each of them ripe to be chosen for the task she had in mind.

She had just finished dressing and was staring out of the window at the sodden grass when Eunice arrived in the room with the breakfast tray.

'Here's your things, miss.'

'Thank you very much, Eunice.'

Continents in flame; dive-bombers over the Ardennes; machine-guns strafing the sleepy French towns. It was all the same to Eunice. She had plucked her eyebrows again and painted them over in the shape of a couple of circumflexes. Nasty little bitch, Cynthia thought, rather surprising herself with the intensity of her dislike, nasty little Lisle-stocking-wearing servant-girl bitch.

If it had been Gladys, she knew she would not have been able to do what she now did, which was to seize the water jug by its throat, swing it round in an arc and deliver a brisk but decisive blow to the back of Eunice's head.

She had been prepared for the force of the blow, but not for the noise. Eunice screamed like a stuck pig, as her father would have said, and went down on her side. The breakfast tray clattered against the edge of the bed, sending a teaspoon leaping four feet in the air. The teapot broke in half. It was all so redolent of Hunca Munca and Tom Thumb, the two bad mice in the story book, that she almost laughed at the memory.

The key to the door was still in Eunice's hand, clenched so tightly that she had to twist up the fingers one by one. As she did this Eunice groaned slightly. The blood lay around her head now in a good-sized pool and her Lisle-stockinged flanks lay wantonly askew. The steam from the spilled teapot rose off the carpet. Cynthia found that she did not care in the least about Eunice. She took a last glance around the room and stepped out into the corridor.

There was no one about. Downstairs the radio was still blaring away. Somewhere a dog barked. She was surprised at how light-headed she felt. Perhaps it would have been a better idea to have eaten the breakfast before hitting Eunice on the head. She went quaking down the staircase with one hand on the rail, alert for trouble, but none came.

There were people in the house, but she could not see them. Several rooms away she could hear Mrs Bannister's voice raised in complaint.

Instead of making for the front door, which seemed too obvious a thing to do, she set off along the passage to the left, which led to the kitchen. The electric light had not been switched on and the photographs on the wall—photographs of old dead Bannisters in morning coats and picture hats—gleamed out of the murk. The noise of the radio, wherever it came from, was loud enough to pick out individual phrases.

At the entrance to the kitchen, in a little vestibule dominated by the portrait of some ancient Bannister dressed in the robes of a Cinque Port Warden, she came upon Hermione, still in her dressing gown, with a piece of toast in one hand and a strangely exalted glint in her eye.

'Have you heard the news?' Hermione said. The dense planes of her forehead made her look more than ever like a Cubist painting. 'Isn't it marvellous? Father says it's a terrible tragedy, but *I* don't think he does really believe that, do you?'

'I'm going now, Hermione,' Cynthia said firmly. 'And if you try to stop me I shall hit you as hard as I possibly can. Do you understand?'

Whether it was that Hermione remembered the scuffle in Bishop's Park or that she now occupied some spiritual plane where physical activity meant nothing to her, she meekly gave way. The kitchen was empty: no trouble there. It occurred to her that a really sharp operator—Anthea, say—would have made for Mr Bannister's study to see if she could find the book. But she knew that she was not up to this, that her own preservation was a matter of profound importance to her, that even what happened to the Bannisters did not matter as long as she survived.

Instead she went out of the back door, along the edge of the kitchen garden and a jungular conservatory stuffed full of moribund tomato-vines, through a low wicker gate in the red-stone wall, and out into the wider landscape beyond.

The obvious thing was to get away: but where exactly? It was a warmish day, but her shoes were already taking in water from the sodden grass. The land at the back of Ashburton Grange went incrementally uphill, reaching a peak about half a mile away in what looked like some clumps of beech trees. She decided to make for the trees as a preliminary to circling the house and, potentially, getting back to the Arundel road.

There was still no one about. In the distance, towards the beech trees, a few sheep grazed. The ground at the foot of the hill was more or less level and littered with tiny obstructions—packing cases, a miniature rail or two—all arranged in an irregular circle, like a dwarfs' gymkhana. Already exhausted by the effort of disabling Eunice, leaving the house, and dealing with Hermione, she sped past. Here there were other impediments: a bale of straw; a pile of flapping grey sacks; a hockey stick. The hockey stick troubled her, for it had *Henry Bannister* stencilled in ink on the handle.

She was seventy or eighty yards away from the kitchen garden now, but near enough to hear the sound that the fastening on the wicker gate made as it snapped open and Mr Bannister came rapidly out onto the grass.

It was a myth that fat men moved slowly. The evidence of a dozen dance floors and football matches played on bare earth under the Eastern sun confirmed this. Mr Bannister seemed to fairly motor on up the hill. The shotgun clasped to his chest she was prepared to regard as a piece of bravado. There was a pain in her side now, the side where her ribs had been stove in back in Ceylon, and the beech wood looked further away than it had two minutes before. Briefly, she wondered whether to throw herself upon Mr Bannister's mercy. But Anthea, she knew, would not have deigned to do this.

Red-faced, his eyebrows somehow furrier than usual, Mr Bannister was shouting something at her. One or two sheep looked interestedly on. If she could reach the wood she thought she would be safe. It would take more than Mr Bannister to catch her in there. Mr Bannister was shouting something else now: she could not make out the words. The ground, having risen sharply under her feet for a hundred yards, now levelled out sharply and the check to her momentum nearly tumbled her over. On the other hand, the beech wood was in sight: denser than she had imagined and a good quarter of a mile across, like one of the fairy-tale woods of childhood, whose bracken concealed imploring hands.

She was rushing on still, quite oblivious to where she put her feet: one of her shoes was twenty yards behind her on the hill. Mr Bannister was not moving quite so fast now, but shouting rather more.

On the whole, this was preferable. Someone else had emerged out of the wicker gate now, but they were too far away to make out. She had a vision of Mrs Bannister, her mad-terrier's face alive with anxiety, bicycling after them.

At the top of the hill the Bannisters' domain ended in a barbed-wire fence, measured out by stanchions five yards apart. There was a stile halfway along and she dashed towards it, her heart pounding so fast that it seemed the only part of her that really existed. There was a hollow beneath the stile full of deliquescing leaves, which disguised its full extent, and she misjudged her jump, fell awkwardly on one leg, felt her ankle turn, and then crawled away on her hands and knees, just as Mr Bannister reached the stile and reared up over its saddle.

Time, which had been passing very rapidly, suddenly seemed to slow to such an extent that she became aware of her surroundings again. A jay which had been surveying her from a fallen log took flight and went screaming away into the heavens. The blue sky overhead lurched as she twisted round to see what Mr Bannister was up to.

Henry's face was there somewhere in the grass, and the heaps of piled-up sticks in the forest's undergrowth and the evil-eyed monkey at the temple door. Later she could never remember exactly what had happened, and in what order, whether Mr Bannister had dropped the shotgun as he rose up over the stile or whether it had caught on the wire. All she knew was that one moment the furious, juddering outline of his face with its caterpillar eyebrows was looming over her and the next the gun was lying on the ground between them and they were both straining after it.

Her hatred of Mr Bannister, she realised, was terrifyingly intense. She could not bear to see him rolling around on the wet turf a yard or so away from her; she would do anything not to have him there. Her hand was on the gun's stock now, rough but consoling, and bringing back Henry again, blithe, red-faced Henry teaching her to shoot on the moor in Northumberland and telling her that it was a skill that would undoubtedly come in useful. Mr Bannister seemed to register what she was up to now and was making piteous little jabbering noises.

Of the shot, which sent every bird in the wood flying into the bright blue air in terror, she had no memory at all.

She lay on her back in the wet grass for what seemed like hours, staring up at the pale sky with the gun pressed against her thigh and no idea of what might have happened to her or to Mr Bannister. A little sighing noise not far away pulsed on for a bit and then disappeared. The water was soaking into the backs of Hermione's jodhpurs, and she remembered the blood streaming over her dress in the jungle thicket in Ceylon.

Another noise started up somewhere in the dense air above her head and she raised her shoulders an inch or two and stared anxiously towards it, but the figures making it shied away and seemed as frightened of her as she was of them, and so she lay back in the wet grass again, not anxious now but curiously detached and isolated, damp and disheartened, waiting for something to happen.

It had been a disappointing war so far at Lonsdale House. One or two of the girls had brothers serving with the BEF who sent occasional letters, and the local vicar had come to lecture them about a walking holiday he had once taken in the vicinity of the Maginot Line, but that was all. On the other hand, if war had been low on excitement, it offered substantial opportunities for malingering.

Just now the school seemed to spend most of its time digging for victory at a series of allotments that had been coaxed into being at the back of the lacrosse pitch. Supervision was not all it might have been. Keen girls tended to labour on strenuously. The more dégagée occupied themselves with long walks. It was in this spirit, emboldened by the news that had been conveyed to them over the breakfast table, well wrapped up against an uncertain spring, that Daphne and Marigold had set off in the direction of the Forty Acre Wood.

'I suppose it'll be a long war now.'

'I suppose it will.'

'Mummy says it will probably go on so long that by the time it's over there won't be anyone left for a girl to marry.'

'That was what happened to my aunt in the last war. Her young man got killed at Ypres. But Daddy said it was rather a relief, and she'd never wanted to get married in the first place.'

One or two lambs had begun moving tentatively around the fields through which they passed, and there was bright sunshine illumining the entrance to the wood. Neither of these attractions had any charms for Daphne and Marigold. They were essentially fireside girls.

'Isn't it frightfully cold?'

'Frightfully. . . . Do you think we ought to go back soon? We could call in at the sickbay and cheer up Mademoiselle.'

'Do you know, I think Mademoiselle is a fifth columnist? There's a look of absolute *scorn* on her face when Miss McGinley says the Victory Prayer. . . . What on earth was that noise?'

'The farmer shooting rabbits, I expect. Let's go round here.'

It was sodden underfoot and the shrivelled beech leaves stuck to the soles of their shoes. In the aftermath of the gunshot, the wood was unexpectedly silent. Then, turning a corner, on the margin of a spinney flanked by dense undergrowth, they came upon something quite unprecedented.

'Heavens! Isn't that somebody lying in the bracken?'

'I expect it's Miss Jeavons been out on the tiles.'

It was not Miss Jeavons, but a thin-faced and immensely pale girl only a few years older than themselves who had done something to her ankle and was on the verge of hysterics. The girls were used to hysterics. They had also been instructed in the rudiments of first aid.

They squatted on their heels and comforted her, and when she showed no interest in getting up or pulling herself together, promptly returned to the allotment to summon help, a mission which, as the headmistress later remarked, was highly creditable both to them and the school as a whole.

Johnson and Hegarty went south along the Brighton Road, through nondescript suburbs. The streets were remarkably free of traffic in the circumstances, but here and there gangs of Local Defence Volunteers lurked behind makeshift checkpoints. As none of these extended more than a few yards beyond the pavement, it was a comparatively simple task to drive round them.

'What are they waiting for, I wonder?' Hegarty said. 'Hitler's got his work cut out on the Marne. He can't possibly be expected to invade Croydon.'

'I don't think logistics mean very much at a time like this,' Johnson told him. 'It's symbolism that counts.'

'Symbolism,' Hegarty said bitterly. He had not quite decided if the morning's excursion appealed to him or not. 'That's one of the reasons I hate driving through Croydon. It always reminds me of one of the worst symbolic moments of my career.'

'What was that, then?' It was about half-past nine: with any luck they would reach Arundel by eleven.

'You won't believe me, but it was only two streets away from here that Mary Beaver decided to leave me at precisely the moment the poulterer delivered the dead duck we were going to eat for supper.'

Johnson had heard this before. It was a good story, but not really in keeping with the paraphernalia of the day: passing checkpoints, the angry faces of the Local Defence Volunteers—quite unappeased by the cheery salutes that Hegarty gave them out of the car's nearside window—and the memory of the early morning radio reports.

'Remind me,' Hegarty said, 'exactly what we are supposed to be accomplishing today?' He had clearly taken against the Arundel mission.

'I thought you saw Shillito's memorandum. It was certainly addressed to you.'

'If I read every piece of paper that arrives on my desk I don't suppose I should ever leave it. And Nancy Oglethorpe could go back to her husband every night unmolested. But you don't seriously expect Bannister to be there, do you? I expect he's in the north of Scotland or somewhere by now. Or with some Silk in Gray's Inn preparing his defence. The girl too, if it comes to that.'

'Shillito says the surveillance report reckons they're both still on the premises. Not to mention the membership book. But there's more than that. According to Anthea Carey the girl found a letter to Bannister from Ribbentrop.'

'I'll believe that exists when I see it. Really, though, I will. What's she like, this Miss Kirkpatrick?'

'I really have no idea,' Johnson said. 'But Anthea Carey absolutely told Shillito that if he didn't have this Miss Kirkpatrick released instanter it would go all the way to Downing Street. I believe she's the Prime Minister's second cousin or something.'

'So why on earth wasn't something done before?'

'Everyone seemed to think that you couldn't go marching into a gentleman's home and start asking questions about his house-guests. That was until this morning, of course.'

'If she's anything like Anthea Carey I shall look forward to making her acquaintance,' Hegarty said warmly. He had clearly forgotten about the dislocated finger he was supposed to have sustained in the incident in the lift.

At Hayward's Heath they turned right and headed for West Grinstead. Here the Local Defence Volunteers were less in evidence and the roads were full of slowly moving agricultural vehicles. Hegarty, who had been scowling to himself for nearly twenty minutes, said out of the blue:

'Do you know, speaking as the free citizen of a free country I strongly deprecate this war. Not in the way that Bannister and Ramsay do. Naturally one wants Hitler to be beaten. Who wouldn't? But sooner or later somebody will come along who'll realise that the only chance we have of winning will be to completely reorganise the way we go about doing things.'

'"Only socialist nations can fight effectively"? I've heard that said a few times.'

'All that, of course,' Hegarty said seriously. 'But then there's the Empire too. The dear old Empire. I can't see that lasting, even if they limit the war to Europe, which naturally they won't.'

'Aren't you in danger of mistaking effects for causes?'

'I suppose I am,' Hegarty said. 'It's the price of patriotism, I daresay. Are you sure we turn left here? I thought this was the way to Bognor Regis.'

It had gone eleven by the time they reached the approach way to Ashburton Grange. As they rounded the bend in the road and the high, machicolated turrets rose before them, Johnson had a presentiment of doom. He knew they would not find what they had come looking for. It was as simple as that. The bleak, sheep-ridden fields running away to right and left seemed to abet these inklings of disquiet. There was nothing for them here.

And so it nearly proved. They had given up hammering on the front door, and were about to smash in one of the vestibule windows, when it swung unexpectedly open and a plump, ungainly girl with an over-large head stood in the doorway regarding them slyly.

'I'm afraid the tradesmen's entrance is round the back,' she announced.

'We're not tradesmen,' Hegarty told her sharply. It did not seem necessary to say anything else. There were rooks taking off from the gravel drive, odd shafts of sunlight falling in the space between the car's wheels and the front of the house. They left the plump girl in the hallway and moved on into the main body of the house, where ancient Bannisters stared at them from their frames and in the middle distance someone was loudly crying.

The noise turned out to come from the kitchen. Here a white-faced and rather attractive girl with badly plucked eyebrows was leaning mournfully against the side of a table while a second girl with a figure exactly like a bolster dabbed at the back of her head with a towel. There was quite a lot of blood. It had gone over the attractive girl's dress, fallen on the table and run in streaks down the fat girl's forearms. Hegarty took in the situation instantly.

'Here,' he said courteously. 'That's not the way to do it. You'd better let me see. I've had medical training, you know.'

There was no gainsaying this authority. Meekly the fat girl surrendered her towel. The girl with the bloody head rolled her eyes and said, semi-hysterically:

'I'm going to have that Miss Kirkpatrick summonsed. You see if I don't.'

'You'd find it an awful lot more comfortable if you lay down somewhere,' Hegarty said. He was thoroughly in his element. When all this was over he would undoubtedly ask her for a date. The fat girl was lost in admiration. Johnson decided to investigate the drawing-room.

Here smoke was pouring from an over-stoked fire. Fragments of charred paper danced up above the flames into the chimney's interior. There were at least three box files noisily incinerating; typed memoranda; sheaves of envelopes; other things. Johnson wondered about trying to rescue some of them. The sound of crying had stopped. Eventually Hegarty came into the room.

'That was an unexpected bonus,' he said. 'Even if it was like a butcher's shop.' There were spots of blood on his fingers. His gaze fell on the fire.

'No sign of Bannister,' he explained. 'I expect all this is a case of *cherchez la femme.*'

It was not meant as a joke, but Johnson, hunkered down in front of the fireplace, his face scarlet from the heat of the Bannisters' incriminating bonfire, fire-iron poised above the cover of what looked like a scorched exercise book, began uncontrollably to laugh.

CHAPTER 23

Beverley Nichols's Diary IV

3 March 1940

When one thinks of the nervous strain to which one has been subjected over the past two weeks—and indeed over the six months that preceded them—it is a wonder one has the strength to write anything at all. On the other hand, there is one's duty to one's beliefs, not to mention that very considerable and exacting audience, posterity . . .

Naturally, my first thought when I heard of the *événements* on the French border—it is remarkable how the Gallic sense of irony extends even to war-reporting—was of profound regret: all our schemes in disarray; the wrong horse backed, &c.; not to mention an unutterable disgust at such bare-faced duplicity. To absolutely encourage the idea of a negotiated peace while secretly plotting to attack the Maginot Line! This kind of subterfuge, as I remarked to Victor, beggars belief.

Equally naturally, these sentiments immediately replaced by a great wave of patriotism (not that I have ever been motivated by anything other

362

than patriotism throughout this whole affair)—the country in danger, the duty of every true Briton, &c. In fact, so overwhelmed was I by these emotions that I very nearly rushed out to the recruiting office in the high street and offered myself for military service on the spot.

In the end, decided not to do this—it is something that Noël, in that devastating way of his, would call 'the path of least resistance'—and contented myself with writing a slashing article for Drawbell, saying that, with the government in chaos, Winston is clearly the man to lead us through these dark days.

In fact, I have a suspicion that Lord Halifax would make a far better Prime Minister—there is something rather ghastly and antediluvian about Winston—but this is clearly a moment at which one must temper one's opinions to the public mood. The public mood, needless to say, that of Albion Imperilled: all the Conservative MPs with the least connection with Ramsay falling over themselves to make patriotic speeches; the Labour pacifists silent to a man. A letter in *The Times* from some fatuous Quaker suggesting that what is needed is rational discussion and the mutual acceptance of opposed views, at which, I am afraid to say, I laughed out loud.

Meanwhile, there is the yet more alarming question—not to put too fine a point on it—of one's personal safety. Having heard nothing from anyone connected with the Faction for several days and, to be frank, rather dreading the return of Mr Hegarty, I decided to telephone Victor at the House.

He confirmed what I suspected: viz., Ramsay has been arrested, together with Kent from the American Embassy. Bannister, I discovered to my horror, is *dead*—although the news has not yet been released to the papers—either destroying himself or through some grotesque accident; no one seems quite to know. Also thought to have been playing some absolutely treasonable game of his own, letters from German ministries found at his house, &c. A dreadful story of a girl mixed up in the affair—apparently Kent's mistress and no better than she should be—being detained against her will at Bannister's house in Sussex.

All very shocking, and yet confirmed to me, on reflection, the instability of certain of the persons one has been dealing with. There is, for example, such a thing as prudence, which I do not believe that Ramsay ever possessed for a moment . . .

All this complicated, necessarily, by the fact that one has a social life and that it continues around one even though the Secret Services may be camped out in one's front garden. At Mary Ridgely Carter's the other night, for instance, I had to listen to an excruciating discussion of the 'traitors in our midst' and what ought to be done with them. Felt like saying that, judged by these stringent criteria, I was a traitor myself, but contented myself with remarking that personal motivation not always readily explicable, that it was sometimes possible to do one's best while appearing to do one's worst, &c.

Mary very fierce against 'collaborators' and 'fifth columnists' who should be 'shot on sight.' This made me wonder, with a sinking feeling, what might happen to Commandant Allen and the fanatical ladies, and, with even more of a sinking feeling, what might happen to myself. According to Victor, who I fancy knows a good deal more about all this than he lets on, the famous book has been destroyed, so that is a relief.

Even so, there is no knowing what Ramsay, or one of the others, may say. . . . Very nearly resolved to go to Scotland Yard and make a clean breast of it, but then told myself that this would be tantamount to walking into a lion's den and asking if anyone were hungry . . .

I continue to reassure myself that I acted for the best in the light of information available to me, and that is what I shall say, whether asked by personal friends or the gentlemen in Jermyn Street. And of course there is the fact that in this affair, as in any other, one can never choose one's associates.

Still, thinking that nothing could be lost, and that much might be gained, by a decisive gesture, I rang up Alan Clutton-Brock, who is in charge of the public relations department at Bomber Command, placed my cards squarely on the table and demanded: did he have a vacancy? It turns out that they need someone to tour aircraft factories in the north of England and write them up for official publications.

Hearing this, I immediately volunteered my services. It will mean a lot of tedious train journeys through some of the most dismal country in England and having to interview burly ladies with spanners, but at a time like this it is incumbent upon one to make sacrifices. Also it will be nice to see Gavin and Brian again, both of whom I gather are 'on the staff' . . .

6 March 1940

The Germans now at Reims.

Was sitting gloomily in the drawing room wondering whether, if people are tired of reading about one's gardens, it would be possible to write about one's cats, when Gaskin arrived in, or rather floated into, the room bringing an envelope on a silver tray. This, marked OHMS, but bearing a stamp rather than an official frank, and addressed in a hand I did not recognise, contained the following letter:

> *My Dear Nichols,*
>
> *And so our plans have gone awry, and we have all been grievously misled! I have, of course, spent countless years attempting to decipher the Teutonic mind, but confess myself baffled by its deceits. Naturally I am pained beyond measure—not only by the calamity into which we are now plunged, but by the abuse of our good faith. Needless to say, were it within my power to reward you for your Herculean efforts in the cause of peace I should do so.*
>
> *As it is not, I merely send my good wishes and heartfelt thanks.*
>
> *Yours sincerely*
Edward R.

Very nearly made a copy of this and sent it to Hardinge, but in the end allowed prudence to get the better of me. Instead put it in the japanned box along with the letters from Melba, King Constantine, Coolidge, and Lloyd George for my biographer to find and make of what he will.

To say that it is nice to find oneself so thoroughly vindicated and to receive the compliments of one's sovereign would be an understatement!

Later. Woke up at 6:30 A.M. in one of those dreadful hotels around the back of Paddington Station, with the noise of a pneumatic drill coming from beyond the window and the unmistakeable sounds of fornication echoing from the next room. *Y*, the cause of what Henry James would call this rash and insensate step, had already left. Very cross, on examining my wallet, to find that £10 had disappeared from it. When one thinks of all one has done for a youth who, if he had his just deserts, would be playing the accordion on a cruise liner, it is enough to make one's blood boil.

Slunk home through the wet streets to find a letter on RAF paper stating that Mr B. Nichols was requested to report for duty on the following Monday at an address in the Marylebone Road. Felt like informing them that Mr B. Nichols had been reporting for duty on an almost daily basis for the past six months. On the other hand, if the events of this time have taught one anything, it is that discretion is the better part of valour . . .

EPILOGUE

1941

Down in the Whitehall basements there was a dearth of natural light. This gave the people who tracked along their subterranean corridors a curiously blanched look, as if they were suffering from mortal illnesses. The few nautical men who passed this way seemed, if anything, even odder, their sun-wrecked skin turned unexpectedly swarthy by the combination of half-tones and shadow.

Sometimes, flitting along the passages from one cavernous room to another, Cynthia stopped at the noticeboards in the hope of diversion, but these, too, were drained of colour. Some of the notices were as much as a year old and referred to aspects of the war long vanished into history. Things were better in the large conference chamber in which she now sat, where a skylight sometimes let in sunshine from the street and there was actually a water-jug and some glasses, but even so the figures grouped around the elliptical table had an inhuman cast: effigies, perhaps, plundered from some long-sequestered vault, or a selection of Madame Tussaud's waxworks brought here for safe-keeping.

Apart from the table and the water jug, the room also contained a framed map of the Mediterranean on an easel, several packing cases, and some tins of corned beef. A fog of cigarette smoke hung permanently above the table and gathered in the cornices, and an asthmatic senior officer from one of the women's services who had once been invited there for a briefing had fallen into a dead faint within minutes.

It was about half-past eleven in the morning, and the figures around the table—a general, two lieutenant-colonels, three ministry officials, and a man with a cockney accent who represented one of the big grocery concerns—were discussing Near Eastern supply chains. They did this in a courteous but faintly exasperated way, as if they suspected that nothing they said would be of any value, while fearing that some higher authority might question the results of their deliberations at a moment's notice.

A month ago Cynthia would have transcribed each sentence that was spoken onto the shorthand pad on her lap. Now she was content to wait for an occasional resonant phrase. It was rare for anyone to ask her to read one of these utterances back, rarer still for any comment to be made about the minutes of the previous meeting circulated at the start of the one that followed.

Just now they were discussing whether it might be possible to procure certain items of tinned food in Cairo rather than shipping them over from Gibraltar. *Canned pilchards,* Cynthia wrote. *Desirability of continuous supply. General Chesterton questioned nutritional value.*

Of all the faces around the table, that of the cockney-accented grocer was the most animated. It was hard to tell if he was simply amused by the company on which he had stumbled or merely wanted the tasks set before them to be accomplished as efficiently as possible. He had a brisk exchange of views with one of the lieutenant-colonels, and Cynthia wrote: *canned pilchards a staple of the working-class diet.* This was the third committee Cynthia had worked for. The other two had been concerned with groundsheets and medical supplies and had, on balance, been more interesting.

At a quarter-past twelve there was a brief suspension of activities while the committee quietly reconstituted itself. The general and one of the lieutenant-colonels packed up their briefcases and left. On cue, other people emerged from the vestibule and began to occupy the vacated seats.

Cynthia took out a bar of chocolate that Lucy's squadron leader had given her, ate the topmost square and then returned it to her handbag, while one of the ministry officials stared at her enviously. Treats of this kind were becoming difficult to arrange. It was not until the newcomers had sat down, availed themselves of pens and pencils, and taken out their files that she realised that one of them was Peter Wildgoose.

Her first thought was that it was a pity that someone so immaculately dressed should be compelled to attend such a humdrum gathering. After this she contrived to examine his features, which were the same as she remembered them, if slightly thinner. She continued to take notes over the next half-hour without having any idea of what she had written down. Somewhere overhead an air-raid siren sounded and then fell silent.

If Peter Wildgoose had noticed her he did not betray the fact, but when at one o'clock they adjourned for lunch he came over to where she sat fastening up the straps of her handbag and said:

'This is an unexpected pleasure. I thought you were in the country somewhere.'

'I was,' she said. 'But it's terribly boring in Hampshire in the winter and the people I was staying with were going off to Wales to start a mushroom farm. . . . Peter, what on earth are you doing here?'

Peter Wildgoose laughed, so loudly that the cockney grocer turned and winked at him in a way that suggested only a sense of duty kept him from seizing his arm and launching into a comic song. 'Professional expertise,' he said. 'The products of the Wildgoose empire are in great demand just now. They need a ton of margarine a week in the Near East these days, and apparently I'm the only man who can supply it.'

The lieutenant-colonel was hovering a yard or two away, but Peter Wildgoose waved him off. 'You'll have to excuse me, Roddy,' he said, 'but I haven't seen this young lady in an age and I really must take her to lunch. That is, if there is anywhere round here where one can get any. I say,' he went on. 'I see an old friend of yours was making a nuisance of himself the other day.'

'Who was that?'

'Captain Ramsay. They put him in Brixton, of course, but that doesn't prevent him from tabling questions in the House. And apparently he tabled one yesterday wondering whether it mightn't be a good idea to reintroduce the Statute of Jewry.'

'I don't think I even remember what the Statute of Jewry is.'

'It was passed by Edward I in 1290. And then repealed sometime in Queen Victoria's reign. Among other provisions, it obliges any Jew over the age of seven to wear a yellow star on his hat.'

The corridor, with its flapping noticeboards, was mysteriously free of people. What looked like a line of stepping stones before them on the polished wood turned out to be a succession of dropped pieces of paper. Cynthia could not tell if Peter Wildgoose was genuinely pleased to see her or simply relieved to find an antidote to the overpowering gloom of the committee rooms. But for the moment she was merely content to bask in his presence.

'Do you know,' he said suddenly, 'when we were all in Bloomsbury together, I used to find the atmosphere horribly lax? Like a kind of permanent art school. Not that I ever attended an art school. But then, coming to Whitehall, one finds the protocols simply absurd. All those generals who insist on being called "sir" rather than "general" and all those earnest discussions about who the senior man present is.'

The mention of 'us' all being in Bloomsbury 'together' was painfully elegiac.

'What happened to everybody?' she asked. 'I mean, I know about Lucy.'

'Well now,' Peter Wildgoose said, 'I think they all keep afloat. The last I heard of Anthea she'd left the Secret Services and was going to marry an Air Vice-Marshal. A rather déclassé one, I grant you, with distinct literary leanings, but an Air Vice-Marshal all the same. No difficulty about the senior man present there, I should say.'

'And what about Des?'

'Des?' Peter Wildgoose laughed again, even more loudly than he had done in the committee room. 'I don't suppose you've heard about him. Des is in the RAF.'

She had a sudden vision of Desmond sitting in an armchair outside a Nissen hut, with a crowd of fighter pilots as they awaited the siren's call.

'What? Flying a plane?'

'The last I heard he'd just finished basic training in Blackpool and was about to be sent off somewhere like Newry to guard the Irish border. Which between you and me means stopping black-marketeers trying to smuggle petrol over it. No, Des volunteered for the infantry. Well, the RAF equivalent. He said that whatever happened to him it would be better than writing press releases at Bomber Command, which is where most of his friends ended up. Of course,' Peter Wildgoose said, with a rather startling gravity, 'it's all my fault.'

'Why is it your fault?'

'I could just have decided not to close the magazine. But you see I thought Des had behaved so desperately badly that he really ought to be taught a lesson. I'd spent my life avoiding having to teach Des a lesson, and I thought it would be a sign of moral weakness if I didn't go through with it. And then after I'd sacked him, I decided the magazine wasn't worth running anymore. So it was all my fault. On the other hand, I think Des would probably have volunteered for the RAF anyway. He said he did it out of sheer guilt.'

Somehow the subject of Desmond's guilt—and whatever it was that he felt guilty about—was too big to be gone into here on the grey steps of a Whitehall staircase. So she contented herself with asking, 'But what will he do in Newry? When he's not guarding the border, I mean?'

'Oh, Des has his resources,' Peter Wildgoose said. 'I expect he'll have them all subscribing to *New Writing* and getting up highbrow discussion groups.'

Coming out into the Westminster streets, they found that the early morning rain had disappeared and the sun was shining. This had the odd effect of magnifying everything, so that the gas masks hanging from the shoulders of the passers-by looked like enormous artificial proboscises in some avant-garde dramatic production. There were army lorries going by; WAAFs on bicycles; smoke rising desultorily over the South London sprawl.

'I don't really know anywhere round here,' Peter Wildgoose said apologetically. 'Perhaps we'd better find a Lyons. They say the raspberry jam in the doughnuts is made of turnips these days, but frankly the experience will do me good.'

They found a Lyons on the corner of Victoria Street, which was full of people from the abbey and girls who worked at the Army & Navy Stores. Outside there were boys from Westminster School lounging past, their caps set firmly on the backs of their heads. Cynthia gazed at them incuriously. This was another effect of the war, she thought: that you lost your interest in people; that the maintenance of the space around you—what you did for a living, your day-to-day acquaintance—was quite enough to be going on with.

Though he had ventured into the Lyons with the tentative air of a jungle explorer, hot in pursuit of some benighted Amazonian tribe but fearful of their turning nasty, Peter Wildgoose was wholly at ease amid this landscape of burnished chrome and black-clad waitresses, and ordered an anchovy paste sandwich with the most natural air in the world. But there was a quizzical look on his face, which suggested that he wanted information which Cynthia might not very easily yield up.

'How are your parents? Are they back in England now?'

How *were* her parents, Cynthia wondered. This was a difficult question to answer. Just at the moment they were staying in Southwold, where Mr Kirkpatrick was described as 'poorly,' another code word of Mrs Kirkpatrick's somewhere on the scale between being very mildly unwell and deliberately malingering.

'Yes. They came back at the end of last year. They said Portugal had been rather a mistake. They're staying with my aunt in Suffolk.'

'And what did they make of . . . ?' Even Peter Wildgoose could not find a form of words for the enormities of the previous spring. 'What did they make of it all?'

This, too, was not an easy question to answer. What had her parents made of it all? Certainly they had been acquainted with the essential facts. But the full extent of what had happened at Ashburton Grange had been difficult to convey to them. It had been even more difficult to work out exactly what they thought about it.

'They were very shocked. But Mummy said that Mr Bannister had always had a very volatile personality. I think they thought that after Henry died he'd become slightly unhinged.'

The tea in the cup an inch or two from her hand was a kind of ochre colour, but she was glad to be drinking it here in the chromium-furnished lotus-land of Peter Wildgoose's smile.

'What about you?' Peter Wildgoose said. 'What did you make of it all?'

The medium-term past had resolved itself in Cynthia's mind into a series of brightly coloured tableaux: Tyler Kent's flat in Bishop's Park, with Captain Ramsay's bald head bent over the desk; Sylvester Del Mar's chalk-white face as they carried him out of the Bloomsbury washroom; the water jug cracking against the parlourmaid's skull; Mr Bannister moving nimbly up the hill.

'I don't know. It was all rather terrifying. And yet somehow not, like a kind of play-acting, with saying things for effect. And then, when they were being deadly serious, not being able to take them seriously. Do you know what I mean?'

'Well, one or two people took it very seriously indeed. Your Mr Kent's in Wandsworth, just now. And there were half a dozen army officers got court-martialled.'

Cynthia thought about Tyler Kent, which was something she had not managed to do for a week or more. The memory of him, while still striking, was curiously diffuse. She could imagine the individual parts of him and the world in which he moved—the natty waistcoats and the bronze eagle—but the jigsaw they made up was shattered beyond repair. She said, 'What do you think will happen now? About the war, I mean?'

'It depends how Hitler does against the Russians. I should imagine it will go on for simply ages. What one wants, of course, is a long-term berth. How did you come to be taking the minutes for General Chesterton's committee?'

'It was Lucy's idea. She knew someone in the ministry. We're still sharing a flat,' Cynthia explained. 'Even though she's married. She says she can't stand married quarters, and then her husband's away so much.'

'Well, I have to go to the Middle East next month. All to do with the margarine. And other things. I'm allowed to take a secretary with me. Do you think you could bear to leave General Chesterton? It'll probably be either Cairo or Beirut. Too early to tell which, I'm afraid.'

Cynthia knew that back in the *Duration* days she would instantly have said yes to this. But the last eighteen months had taught her the value of circumspection. She said: 'That's terribly kind of you, Peter. I shall have to think it over and let you know.' All the same, she knew, knew as certainly as she had ever known anything, that she would go with him.

A bit later the waitress came with the bill and Peter Wildgoose paid it with a five-pound note, which caused rather a stir at the till. Afterwards they walked out into Victoria Street. Here the sunlight was still cascading across the pavement, but the Westminster schoolboys had all gone back to their desks.

High above them a line of birds went east in sharp, dramatic flight, and she stared at them, thinking of Cairo and Beirut, and destinies as yet unknown—minarets and muezzin bells, dust and olive groves, all the scattered paraphernalia of Araby—and then, by degrees, of the paintings of Claude Lorrain, in which she had always yearned to wander, passing mysteriously through their solitary glades and deep, romantic chasms, past their bevies of attendant nymphs and classical figures, both real and imagined, and on, to antique groves yet more sequestered, remote and silent in the Attic dawn, with no one to watch her but herself.

Author's Note

This is a novel. At the same time it contains at least half a dozen genuine historical personalities. Leaving aside King Edward VIII (1894–1973), later the Duke of Windsor, Captain Archibald Maule Ramsay (1894–1955), Conservative MP for Peebles and South Midlothian between 1931 and 1945, Tyler Kent (1911–88), a cipher clerk at the American Embassy, and Beverley Nichols (1898–1983), a prolific author, journalist and librettist, are all real people. Several other well-known figures of the period, from John Betjeman to the Sinhalese poet J. M. Tambimuttu, subsequently editor of *Editions Poetry London*, make fleeting appearances in the text. This raises an interesting procedural and, ultimately, moral question. Is it fair to put figures from history deviously on show in a work of fiction, set in an imaginary time, and attribute to them views which there is no way of knowing that they would have held?

The answer is that although the King, Ramsay, and Nichols are shown, directly and indirectly, as being part of a pacifist conspiracy to derail the war, none of them is, historically speaking, being traduced. Plenty of contemporary observers were worried by what they imagined to be the Duke of Windsor's pro-Nazi sympathies. During the period September

1939 to May 1940, prior to his internment in Brixton, Captain Ramsay was the guiding force of a clandestine organisation known as the 'Right Club,' dedicated to ending hostilities with Germany by way of a negotiated peace. The names of the club's members were recorded in a leather-bound volume, embossed with the letters 'PJ' (i.e., 'Perish Judah'), and its supporters included such veterans of the pre-war pro-Hitler groups as Admiral Barry Domvile and 'Commandant' Mary Allen. Tyler Kent, interned initially at Wandsworth, then at Camp Hill Prison on the Isle of Wright despite the fact of his US citizenship, did indeed abstract copies of presidential telegrams in the manner described here. Beverley Nichols, though not involved with the Right Club, was an ardent pre-war pacifist and a stalwart of Anglo-German fellowship societies. We do not know that they would have behaved in this way, had the political landscape of the period 1939–40 been a little different, but it seems entirely plausible that they might have done.

I should like to acknowledge the influence of Philip Ziegler, *King Edward VIII: The Official Biography* (1990), Richard Griffiths, *Patriotism Perverted: Captain Ramsay, the Right Club and Anti-semitism in England 1939–1940* (1998), and Bryan Connon, *Beverley Nichols: A Biography* (1991) which, additionally, contains many extracts from Nichols's diaries. For John Amery, who was executed for treason in 1946, see David Faber, *Speaking for England* (2005). 'Duration' was the name chosen by Evelyn Waugh for a periodical which he intended to found at the beginning of the war, only for the scheme to be abandoned when his friend Cyril Connolly got in first with *Horizon*. The latter's history, from which I have borrowed one or two details, is recorded in Michael Shelden, *Friends of Promise: Cyril Connolly and the World of Horizon* (1989) and Jeremy Lewis, *Cyril Connolly: A Biography* (1997).

My warmest thanks, as ever, to my editor, Juliet Brooke.

D.J.T.